MW00618171

VOODOU HOTEL

A Connor Jones West Novel
By
R J Linteau

VOODOU HOTEL
A Connor Jones West Novel
By
R J Linteau

Voodou Hotel is a work of fiction.
Any relationship to actual individuals, places, and circumstances, unless intentional, is purely coincidental. The words of actual historical figures are not quotes, but the product of the author's imagination.

First Printing: August 2021
ISBN Number: 1-7348403-2-2
All rights reserved. (92,390)
Copyright © 2021 by R. J. Linteau
Registration Number: TXu 2-231-865

THE NORMANDIE PRESS
Atlanta, Georgia

Also by the Author:

Novels:
The Architect
The Black Orchestra

Screenplays:
The White Rose
Second Trumpet

Short Stories:
Summer Kamp

Upcoming:
Motor City
A Novel

Cover photo: Grand Hotel Oloffson, Port-au-Prince, Haiti

Cover photography: Karl Grobl
Chicago, Illinois

Cover Design: Fedota Design Consultants
Atlanta, Georgia

Page Designs: Vèvè, the symbols of the Iwa
(Voodou Spirits)

Typeface: Georgia 11 Point & Algerian

Author e-mail: RJLinteau.author@gmail.com

This book is dedicated to my daughter,
Devin Michelle,
the better writer in the family.

thanks to my editor and wordsmith,
Kay Olsen
for her guidance, creative input, editing and her
attention to detail.
She is a much better writer than I.

Who will provide the grand design?
What is yours and what is mine?
Because there is no more new frontier
We have got to make it here.
We satisfy our endless needs, and
justify our bloody deeds
in the name of destiny,
and in the name of God.

They call it paradise,
I don't know why...
You call someplace paradise,
Kiss it Goodbye.

The Eagles
"The Last Resort"
Album: Hotel California
Written by Don Henley
Released: December 1976
Originally recorded in Miami, Florida

Enter the exotic land of Haiti at fabulous Port-au-Prince. High mountains, tropic forests, and the beat of native drums recalling ancient rites of Voodoo, are the background of this historic city where you will have ample time for sightseeing, shopping, and glimpsing colorful Haitian night life.

You'll enjoy the fascinating Iron Market with its strange oriental flavor and colorful native shops displaying drums and handicraft of sisal and mahogany, tinware, and unusual herbs. Cock-fights, a Haitian highlight, provide added excitement.

1954 Cruise Brochure by the Eastern Steamship Company, on the SS *Yarmouth Castle*, with sailings out of Miami to the Caribbean. Fares from as low as $175.00.

It is probably a safe bet that the tourism authorities of Haiti did not have much say when in November 1964, visitors were met with a terrible stench as they entered the arrivals hall at Port-au-Prince Airport. Strategically placed at the terminal exit, as a warning to all, tied to an armchair, sat the rotting corpse of a young man who dared to be part of an attempt to remove Haiti's incumbent president, Francois Duvalier.

**Roger Hanson
Opinion, STUFF
August 30, 2018**

PROLOGUE
APRIL 21, 1971

Presidential Palace
Port-Au-Prince, Haiti

The old man labored with each breath. Each gasp a wisp of his life, slowly slipping away. Never an imposing figure, but a small yet ruthless man; he lay still in the enormous bed, with a headboard made from a mapou tree. Hand-carved ornate fretwork surrounded prominent initials, "FD," around a filigree design typical of Haitian culture and craftsmanship. Only his head, oblong with a fading cap of all-white hair, and boney hands folded over his chest, were visible. He wore deep red pajamas, buttoned high at the neck. Gone were the thick glasses, the top hat, and the bow tie.

A coterie of family and staff looked down at the frail figure. Foremost among them stood his Mulatto wife, Simone, whom he married in 1939, and who bore him four children—Marie-Denis, Nicole, Simone, and the only boy, the youngest, Jean-Claude. The dim-witted boy, nicknamed "Baskethead" by the palace staff and courtiers, spoken only in whispers, looked out a window of the presidential bedroom, into an uncertain future. His father had anointed him the "Chosen One."

The chubby, 19-year-old boy wanted nothing to do with running a country. Let his sister Marie-Denise have the job. His indoctrination into the office by his father had begun at a young age. He witnessed the sadistic torture of opponents, watched the Tonton Macoute massacre entire families, and stared at the embalmed heads of opponents that his father kept in glass jars in his office. These memories became the stuff of nightmares and randomly flashed into his thoughts when awake.

But he would gladly take the monetary spoils of the dictatorship. The Duvalier's had skimmed millions from American foreign-aid. Multi-national foreign corporations established businesses in the country because of the cheap labor but paid nothing in the way of taxes for the good of the citizenry, only tithes to the family. And from the poor, the dictatorship took what little they had. After 14 years of rule by Francois Duvalier—President for Life, the Flag of Haiti, the Immaterial Being, and the reincarnation of Baron Samedi, the once beautiful nation of Haiti had become a nightmare. To his devoted followers he was affectionately known as "Papa Doc", one with Bondye and the Iwa, with Jesus Christ, and God himself.

Ministers and faithful government servants were also at the vigil, ready to take advantage of the new boy-man president the moment Duvalier passed into the afterworld. Luckner Cambronne, head of the Tonton Macoute, known as the Vampire of the Caribbean for selling blood and cadavers to the West for medical uses, saw himself as the power behind the new throne. Also at the death watch was General Claude Raymond, Papa Doc's godson, newly minted by Duvalier a day earlier as Army Chief of Staff to ensure a smooth transition of power to the clueless Jean-Claude. For him, the death of ailing Papa Doc was a long time in coming. It pleased him it was finally at hand.

Duvalier's dutiful wife, Simone, dabbed at forced tears as she waited by the deathbed. She knew full well that her husband's imminent death would yield her greater power and allow her to influence her son as only a mother could. As the fat, double-chinned little boy was not likely to marry soon, she would remain as First Lady of the Republic. Her reputation for arrogance, and jealously guarding her husband's affairs, would continue with her dolt of a son.

A Voodou priest, a Houngan, shook the asson rattle over the motionless president to ward off evil spirits. In his other hand, he held the clochette, the bell to be rung upon the death of the man in the bed.

Duvalier stirred and moaned. His arms slowly rose; his hands reached out to the Voodou spirit world and then dropped to the bed. His body began to arch in spasms and almost lifted from it. His head shook from side to side. A vision of Baron Samedi, Iwa of the Dead, formed in his mind; he heard a voice from beyond: "Vini avèk mwen."*

Dropping back into the bed, he uttered his last words, "Ou pa pral pran m 'Baron Samedi. Mwen imòtèl!" **

A last rush of air left the president's body. He lay still, and the head rolled to one side, his eyes lifeless. Francois Duvalier had transitioned from this life to another, his soul trapped for a year and a day in the water, or the trees, or in a cave, to call out to his followers in the deep of night. Afterward, his spirit would forever be a hushed whisper of fear in the winds of Haiti.

General Raymond turned and walked over to Jean-Claude, still staring out the window, the poverty of the city generously laid out in front of him. He was oblivious to what had just happened. Then the Houngan rang the bell three times.

Raymond placed his hand on the boy's ample shoulder. "The President is dead. Long live the President!"

The young president turned to Raymond. "After the funeral, I'd like to go somewhere. I need to get away. Reserve a suite of rooms in Miami Beach for a week. At the Versailles-sur-Mer; I understand it is the nicest hotel there." There was no emotion in his voice.

"But the government, President Jean-Claude..."

"You handle things with my mother. I don't really care about it."

❖

* "Come with me."
** "You will not take me, Baron Samedi. I am immortal!"

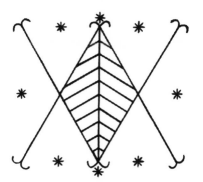

PART I
MARILYN
1975

CHAPTER ONE
AUGUST 5, 1975

St. Margaret's Home for Women
Eau Claire, Wisconsin

"There, there now, sweet lady, I think me should take the baby now. He needs to be checked by the doctor man, to make sure everything is all right if you knowing what I mean."

"He's perfect. I'm not letting him go. He is Connor's son. My son!" Marilyn glared at the small Black nun with the deep French Creole accent. She despised all the sisters at St. Margaret's but pitied Sister James more than anything. She was probably the only Black person within fifty miles of this home for unwed mothers.

"You've been through much. You need your rest. Maybe you'll see baby later, I do promise you. You can't want me being into big trouble now, do you, because I let you see the baby boy?"

"I don't care what happens to you. I have a right to keep my child. And I'm not giving him up for adoption. Do you understand?"

"Marilyn, lady, you must give me the baby child."

"No! You're not taking him!"

Sister James reached across the bed for the child, and Marilyn slapped her across the face. "Get away, you little witch! He's my baby!"

Sister James recoiled in pain and surprise. She wrung her small hands, rushed to the delivery room door, opened it, and looked down the hallway for help. The mother superior, Sister Blanche, was heading toward the room. This was not good; let it be anyone else but the mother superior.

"Is there a problem, Sister James?" She looked at Marilyn, holding the newborn, and gasped. "Why is she holding that child, Sister?" Her question was curt, angry.

Sobbing, the little nun spoke: "I told the lady that it be a beautiful baby, and then she made me give her the child to hold. Lord a mercy, I be so sorry." Sister James stepped back, head bowed, like a miscreant puppy.

The mother superior leaned over and whispered in a hiss, "Get me 15 CC's of Diazepam, quickly. We'll discuss your breach of protocol later, Sister James." She turned toward the bed where Marilyn was holding her son, glaring at the two nuns.

"There, there, my dear, you are exhausted from the labor..."

"You mean from the fucking pain you made me go through, the penance for my sin of fornication, don't you, you damned penguin? I can't wait to leave this place with Kevin."

Mother Superior gasped, her face a bright crimson, and then she regained her composure. "Who is Kevin?"

"My baby, you devil. You can call my parents. We're leaving tomorrow!"

Sister James returned with the syringe and handed it to her seething boss. She knew she would have to say novenas from now until eternity for her malfeasance. Her anger grew, not because of her mistake, but at Marilyn's demand, the slap across the face, and the trouble she had caused. Head bowed, she stepped back. Sister Blanche took the needle, and without cleaning Marilyn's arm with alcohol, jabbed it into her. She pushed the fluid in her arm as quickly as she could. Marilyn screamed.

"You bitch! What did you put into me? I hate yo....."

"Sleep tight, you mistress of the devil." As Sister Blanche pulled out the syringe, she twisted it around. Marilyn lapsed into unconsciousness. Mother Superior grabbed the baby from her arrogant ward's limp arms and handed him to Sister James.

"Get this child to the nursery. Do not let the mother ever see him again. This baby is adopted! Be in my office in an hour; I will deal with your stupidity!"

❖

The morning sun flooded the small dormitory room with light, intensified by the whitewashed walls. Sarah Jones emptied the drawers of the small dresser, placing the clothes into a suitcase. When finished, she turned her attention to the closet and the half dozen modest dresses and plain shifts. She squinted as she looked over at her daughter—sleeping beauty lying under the covers of the hard bed, a four-inch mattress with no box springs. Paul Jones stared out the shut window, smoking a cigarette, blowing smoke against the glass, as if it would magically disappear to the outside.

"My God, Paul, why must you smoke? Marilyn has been through so much. Can't she at least breathe clean air?"

"I just want to get her home, Okay? Get this whole sorry chapter behind us."

"Sister Blanche told me the baby is a boy."

"Boy, girl, who cares? It's the product of a rape. Let that nice couple from Minnesota have it."

"It's not an 'It,' Paul. He's your grandson!"

"Don't even say that; he's no kin to me!" Paul Jones' voice rose in anger. Over the last nine months, perpetual thoughts of his only daughter's ordeal had saddened and enraged him. Deep down, he hated himself for allowing Marilyn to live in the city, although he knew his wife was right. There was no way to shelter her from the big, bad world forever.

Marilyn stirred from the angry voices of her mother and father, struggling against the heavy sedation. When she opened her eyes, she didn't know where she was or what was happening. She leaned up on her elbows and focused on her parents. Events came back to her. "Where's my baby? Where's Kevin?"

Marilyn's mother was at the bed in an instant. "It's all right, honey. We can go home to Chicago. You had the baby; it's all over now."

Marilyn ran her hand through a tangle of hair. She rubbed her pounding head, an after-effect of the Diazepam. "Where's my baby?"

Paul Jones turned from the window. "It's, I mean, *he's* been adopted. They're a nice young couple from St. Paul."

23

"Marilyn, honey, we, you, gave the baby up for adoption. The agreement, the contract, stated that you would not be allowed to see the child. You have no rights once the baby is born."

"But I saw him. I delivered a month early because it's Connor's son. He belongs to Connor and me. I told them I wasn't giving Kevin up for adoption. Where is he?!"

Sarah looked at her husband. "Dear Lord, she's named the baby..."

Tears welled in Marilyn's eyes. "I want my son. I saw him; I held him. He's beautiful, and I know he is mine and Connor's. What did that awful nun do with my son?"

Paul Jones put his cigarette out against the window, let it drop to the floor, and stepped on it like he was crushing a bug. "Marilyn, that baby is the result of a rape. You're delusional. You have no rights to it anymore. The baby is gone! It's adopted! Now, we're going home. After a few months, you'll forget all this."

Marilyn threw back her head and let out a great moaning cry, and deep sobs of hurt and pain filled the room. Her mother tried to put her arms around her fragile body, but Marilyn pulled away.

"Leave me alone. Why did you send me to this place? I hate it! I hate both of you! If I had only seen Connor, been able to talk to him, we would have figured all this out. I would have never come here. Why didn't he come to my apartment or the house or try to find me?"

Sarah Jones looked at her husband and shook her head. "Let's go home, honey. Let's just go home."

Sister James kneeled at her cot but did not pray to the crucifix above it. Instead, she stared at a photo of the late Francois Duvalier, one she kept hidden in her dresser. "Mother Superior putting me on rations for a month, Baron Samedi! Can you believe? All because I let that woman sees the child. I wish I were in Haiti serving your son, President Jean-Claude, my dear Papa Doc, serving him and you, the Iwa of the dead."

24

The petite nun slowly rose and went to her closet. She took down a box from the upper shelf and opened it on the bed. There was cloth, wool stuffing, and lengths of different colored string as fine as hair, a pair of scissors, a bottle of ink, and a small paintbrush. Sister James went back to the bed and laid the items out. She began cutting the cloth in the shape of a dress.

"I be making this doll now, just like the other sisters taught me in the convent in New Orleans. It put on a powerful spell. When I done, Baron Samedi, he come for you, my sweet Miss Marilyn!"

CHAPTER TWO
SEPTEMBER 19, 1975

Key West, Florida

The window was open, but it didn't matter. The Key West evening was still a stifling eighty-six degrees at 11 P.M. The ceiling fan wobbled round and round, three blades instead of four—it did little more than move the hot air and cigarette smoke around the room. On the night table of the studio apartment, located a block off Caroline Street, rested a half-full glass of bourbon and an ashtray overflowing with Winston butts.

Connor West reached for the glass, found it, then almost dropped it. He gripped it and took a solid drink of the precious liquid. No need for ice; two empty trays sat on the Formica countertop in the kitchenette. Another deep swallow of the Jim Beam, then a long drag on the cigarette. He put the glass back on the table and dropped the butt in it. It drowned there, a merciful death. The last drink, the last smoke, and West dropped his head onto the pillow. Another day over and another night done. Just like yesterday and the day before. Tomorrow didn't have the prospect of being much different.

Over on Duval Street, the party was just beginning. The distant sound of a live rock-'n'-roll band attacked through the window. Connor closed his eyes, wanting sleep. The booze would help eventually, but before it did, he rolled over and looked at the nightstand. He made no effort to turn off the lamp, which illuminated the five-by-seven photo of him and Marilyn Jones on bicycles at a small bridge in Chicago's Lincoln Park. The image was fuzzy, but he forced his eyes to focus so he could stare at it and remember the best chapter of his life—two happy people in love. After a minute, he rolled over and closed his eyes, moist with tears. Then the sobs began. His arms wrapped around his aching ribcage to suppress the breaths coming in spasms until they subsided and sleep came.

❖

Rat Tomlinson knocked hard on the door of studio apartment 3C. He was in no mood. For the third time his first mate, his only mate, had not been at the dock at 6:00 A.M. And this was a critical charter. His father had arranged for two of his friends, both members of the New York Stock Exchange, to book a full-day fishing trip on *Daddy's Money*. He promised they would slay it on his son's boat. It was now 6:45 A.M. The two high rollers were expected at the dock by 7:30. Rat had requested they arrive at the marina by 7:00, but the men resisted, saying they were on vacation and wanted to party a little on famous Duval Street. Rat relented.

He pounded on the door. Much work needed to be done before they left the marina and motored the 20 miles to the "Trench," where the bottom of the Straits of Florida dropped to 21,000 feet. There in the deep, cold water were the trophy sailfish and the 30-pound and larger mahi-mahi. It would take them at least two-plus hours to get there. And it was going to be another hot September day.

"Goddammit, Sullivan, open the door."

"It's open. Enter at your own risk."

Rat tried the doorknob. It turned and opened. He should have figured his friend would have been too drunk to care about security, minimal as it was. There wasn't even a slide bolt. He looked around the single room that pretended to call itself an apartment. On the left, a kitchenette, just a six-foot counter with a small fridge, a small stove, and a small sink piled high with dirty dishes. On the right were a clothes closet and a door that led to the bathroom. In front of him was a disaster. The double bed was on the floor, rather the box spring was, and the bed, a tangle of sheets, held a motionless body. There was room for a small sitting area occupied by a chair with folded clean clothes and a couch with a pile of dirty clothes, books, magazines, shoes, baseball caps, and everything else a 26-year-old might need at a moment's notice. It was useless for its intended purpose—sitting.

"Geesus, Sullivan, this place looks worse every time I'm here. What a shithole!"

"Thanks for the compliment. It's going to be in *Architectural Record* next month. What time is it?"

"Time to fish and I'm tired of coming over here to get your drunk ass out of bed."

"I'm not drunk; maybe hung-over, but not drunk. Let's go. I'm ready." West slid over and rolled his feet off the bed and onto the floor. He slid into some Huarache sandals, pulled off the tee-shirt he had slept in, and put on a clean one. He had heard a new singer at Captain Tony's; a guy named Jimmy Buffett and liked the tee shirts he had for sale. This one boasted on the front: "Wastin' Away Again in Margaritaville." It seemed fitting enough.

"We got a couple of big shots from Wall Street my dad knows. We can't fuck this trip up, and we're already behind schedule. Seriously, Connor, you're pissing me off."

West knew that his best friend and boss was mad. Rarely did he call him by his actual first name. "Sorry, Rat, it won't happen again."

"You told me that last month, and the month before that, and here we are. Has it ever occurred to you I'm running a fucking business here?"

"You mean we're not yachting? Hey, I'm the one who smells like fish every night."

"There's always architecture, my friend; there's always architecture." Tomlinson held the door open, and as Connor passed his friend, he kissed his boss on the cheek.

"Hey, none of that! This is Key West, and people will talk."

It was 7:45 A.M., and it annoyed Tomlinson that his charter guests had not shown up, but he was also grateful. It allowed him and Connor time to buy a box of frozen squid; toss live bait into the well and check out the four main fishing rigs—

Penn reels on Shakespeare rods, all with 50-pound test line, except for the spinning reel with 20-pound test. West was piling ice over a copious amount of Miller High Life Beer and bottles of water in the chest that doubled as the mate's seat. The two guests could relax in the boat's cushioned fishing chairs. One thing was certain. Richard Auburn Tomlinson, "RAT" had spent a sizable part of his trust fund on the best. Built in 1973, 45-foot Hatteras Convertible fishing boat was built to catch big fish. It featured two fighting chairs, two outriggers, and a flying bridge. The cabin was comfortable, with polished teak and a comfy couch and side chair; next to it was a good-sized linear galley. In the bow was the main cabin, with a double bed where Rat slept, and another cabin with bunk beds with teak rails. Last, there was a small bath with a toilet and sink. Rat took showers on the foredeck with the freshwater hose connected to the boat's 160-gallon tank, and sometimes, with soap at one of his girlfriends' apartments.

Eight o'clock. From the flying bridge where Rat was double-checking the instruments, he looked back toward the main dock. Ambling along were two disheveled gentlemen. They wore tacky Hawaiian shirts and blue jean shorts that seemed all the worse for wear. One of them sported black socks and white tennis shoes. Thankfully, the other had on Topsiders. As he climbed down the narrow ladder, the captain waved at the men. Connor was at the gunwale to greet them.

"Welcome, guys. Ready to fish?" He glanced back at Rat, whose eyes were rolling.

"Got any Bloody Mary's?" The man's question sounded like a demand.

Connor looked up to Tomlinson. The answer was above his pay grade.

"Guys, please take your shoes off, ah... and the socks, and come on board. We're going fishing, not drinking. We have beer, and when were coming back to the dock, we can celebrate whatever you catch with an open bar. But it won't be open until four."

The two men climbed on board during the tutorial, or more accurately, the lecture, with help from West's brawny arms. They looked at each other and frowned.

"Damn, I sure could use a Bloody. I'm Stuart Coddington. Call me Stu. This is Roger Van Morton. Call him Roger."

"I'm Rich Tomlinson, but since you're friends of my father, I assume you already knew that." He pointed at Connor. "My first mate, Connor West. You can call me Rich or Rat, and he goes by Sullivan. Let's shove off. It's a long way out to the big fish. And I guess we can serve you up a couple of drinks. You guys look like you had a seriously good time on Duval Street last night."

"Fuck yeah, I think we hit every bar on the street." Stu was proud of the accomplishment.

"I'm not sure they award any medals for that effort," Connor muttered as he stepped off the boat and went forward to release the bowline, then trotted back and lifted the hook rope from the rear dock stanchion and jumped back on board.

Tomlinson was already up on the main bridge, starting the twin Detroit diesel engines. Each engine boasted 318 horsepower for a comfortable cruising speed of 12 knots. To get out to the deep trench in the Straits of Florida, he would work the engines hard at a speed of 15 knots.

West mixed a couple of Bloody Mary's with healthy pours of vodka, complete with celery and olives for the charter guests, then allowed himself a couple of shots to ease his own hangover. After that, there wasn't much to do during the two-hour trip except sit on the beer chest and re-live old memories. The roar of the two Detroit's made it impossible to have a pleasant conversation with the guests.

At first, working on Rat's fishing boat had been a necessary tonic for the disaster that was his life in Chicago. After he and Tomlinson graduated with master's degrees in architecture from Harvard, he moved to the Windy City because of a golden job offer. The position paid a handsome $25,000 a year from the prestigious firm of Nolan, Jefferson and Marlow.

The firm assigned Connor to help with the design of a massive building: a mixed-use complex, 75-stories tall along

Lakeshore Drive. He started dating Marilyn Jones, the executive secretary to one of the partners, Vance Jefferson. She was beautiful, smart, and fun. They hit it off immediately, and it wasn't long before they were in love. He asked Marilyn to marry him.

But boredom set in as he waited on his team's senior designer to develop a scheme for the project. For practice, he took it upon himself to design the building. After the senior designer's untimely death, the firm presented Connor's imaginative concept to the client, an unscrupulous developer. He chose it as the winning design. West was on top of the world.

Then things unraveled. Vance Jefferson gave another partner, the son of the founder, credit for Connor's effort who then bastardized his design to save money. West retaliated by doctoring up some shop drawings, a mistake fueled by anger that could have cost him his promising career.

Then Jefferson began putting his hands all over his girlfriend. Finally, the man raped her. West had not seen Marilyn since that awful night. And when he went to her home in Oak Park, her father refused to let him in. Despite his love for Marilyn, he was distraught and beaten down. The love for her became a gaping hole in his heart.

With a standing invitation from his friend and former schoolmate, who decided owning a fishing boat was preferable to an eight-to-five job in New York, at least for a few, fun years, Connor Jones West fled to Key West.

Now he realized that he was hiding from the world. He could not continue to live this way. Like his late father, Kevin West, he was an alcoholic or very close. And like his father, he was unfulfilled and angry at the world. Cutting bait, and catering to rich low-life's with lots of money... what a waste of a life. He was pissing away his God-given talent as an architect, the only thing that he ever really wanted to be.

The engines throttled down, and the boat responded quickly, slowing to seven knots. Connor snapped out of his sad reminiscences, got up, and looked at the bridge. Already hot, in the low 80s, the water was like glass. No flotsam in sight, and not even a breeze. Not the best indicators for catching fish.

"Get the lines out, Sullivan. Let's see what's down there."

"Anything on the sonar?"

"A small school of fish, nothing more. Let's go."

"Aye, aye, Captain..."

CHAPTER THREE

West pulled the box of frozen squid from the bait well and tied one onto each of three lines. He used his favorite lure for the 20 lb. test line, a six-inch affair in orange and blue with a shiny oval spinner, meant to look like a psychedelic squid. The bait attached, he hurried around the rear deck with an apologetic "Excuse me, gentlemen" as the guests seemed to do their best to get in his way. He attached the lines of two of the rods onto the outriggers with rubber bands and released them; they slowly leaned outward, away from the boat's hull on the port and starboard side. He set the two remaining rods into the rod holders on the back of the boat.

Rat decreased the speed further as West let out the lines to varying distances, 150 to 300 feet off the stern. He went back to the well, retrieved another box, and emptied its frozen contents into a chum bag, and dropped it over the side.

"We're all set, Rat. All lines are out. Stu and Roger, now the fun begins. Or we hope it begins."

"Roger, I'm going to kick your fat ass today. I've got a C-Note that says so." Stu swaggered toward the chair full of himself.

"Go right ahead. Oh, boy..." Roger headed for the side of the boat.

Connor looked up at Rat, and they shook their heads.

Daddy's Money trolled back and forth over the calm sea for what seemed like an eternity. Connor checked the baits several times, and though somewhat the worse for wear, it was mostly intact. Each time, he attached new squid and threw out a fresh chum bag. Rat even summoned up "Black

Water" by the Doobie Brothers and other 1970s hits that blared from the boat's Bose sound system. Nothing worked. Roger threw up twice over the gunwale, and Stu demanded cold beers all morning. Rat nodded down to Sullivan, who accommodated the wealthy guest. They were paying $500 for the day's adventure, after all.

"Pull the lines in, Sully. I've got a new location to try out."

I think that would be a good plan, thought West, and in a matter of minutes, Rat had the boat moving from its trolling speed of five knots to an all-out fifteen knots. But he was heading west, in a new direction. Connor climbed up to the bridge.

"Sir, First Mate West would like to know why you are heading west, sir?"

"It's like this, Sullivan. Last night while you were drowning your sorrows in your apartment, I was at the Green Parrot having a beer. I sat next to another fishing boat captain, new in town. He just moved his boat back here from the Dominican Republic, but he's originally from Haiti. Two years ago, he fished these Straits. I liked him; I enjoyed his accent, and he recalled great stories about Haiti in the early fifties, before that guy Duvalier took over and turned the country into a shithole. I bought him a drink, and he bought me a drink. His name is Armand Jolicoeur. He told me that everyone moves up the trench toward Miami but that the secret is to go west where it all begins. The fish are feeding there in the shallower water before going deep. It's like they're taking on fuel for a long journey."

"I see. Sounds like a good plan. If you don't get these boys some fish, they'll mutiny."

"Don't I know it, and so will my dad. He'll make me come back to New York City and get a real job. When I slow down, get the lines ready. Shit, you already know that..." Tomlinson chuckled and gently slapped West on the face.

"Yes, I do. Hey, later, can we talk?" West hoped his friend and boss didn't have a date that evening.

"I can hear Captain Tony's calling." It was their favorite watering hole. "Get down there; we should be at the spot in ten minutes."

"Aye, aye, Captain!" Sullivan smiled and climbed down from the flying bridge.

Connor finished tying new squid and a new jig in varying shades of luminescent green with gold spinners as the boat slowed to five knots.

Roger headed for the rail again; this time, it was the dry heaves. Stu crushed another empty can of Miller High Life and threw it into a pail. "I hope we fucking find fish here."

"Stu, they call it fishing, not 'catching.' While I get the lines out, perhaps you can get your friend a ginger ale from the cooler. It will settle his stomach; he might be busy in a few minutes. I'll put on the Eagles' newest album. There's a song on it I think is appropriate, 'Take it to the Limit'."

West put out the four bait offerings and Tomlinson slowed to four knots. Connor got himself a bottle of cold water and watched the lines through polarized aviators from the gunwale. The boat had trolled about five minutes when one line snapped free from the outrigger and ran out at a furious pace. Connor raced to the reel, set the drag on the Penn, raised the rod, and jerked upward to set the hook. At that moment, he saw the sail jump out of the water. "It's a sailfish, Rat! He's on! Guys, who's first?"

Stu jumped up from the cooler, where he was getting another High Life, and headed for the fighting chair. "I'll do it!" He climbed into the chair, and Connor slid the rig into the gimbal between Stu's legs and carefully handed him the rod, the sailfish taking the line out at will.

"I probably should have asked this earlier, Stu, but is this your first time deep-sea fishing?"

"No. Well, yes. I guess so."

"No problem. Just hold on and keep the line taut. The fish is strong. He'll take out a lot of line but prepare for when that bad boy slows or stops. Then you pull the rod back and reel in on the way down. Just repeat that again and again. Pump and reel. Pump and reel, as Hemingway described it. You'll be busy for a good while, that's for sure."

Connor was about to exercise standard protocol of bringing the other three lines in to avoid the rigs tangling when the Garcia Mitchell spinning rod went taut, bending to almost 180 degrees. "Shit, another fish!" Leaving Stu to fight the sail, he went over to the spinning rig, pulled it up from the outside rod holder, and gave it a hard yank. Then he flipped the bail loose and let the line go limp. Immediately it went taut again, the line uncoiling fast from the reel. It was the light 20 lb. test, and he feared that the drag was too tight. Connor opened it up to ensure the line would not snap, and then closed the bail again. With the artificial lure, he was confident that they had hooked a mahi-mahi, a huge one.

"Roger, you're up. Get in the chair." Roger was still admiring the water around the perimeter of the boat. He straightened up and walked uneasily to the other fighting chair. He was ashen white and not looking forward to fishing. Connor handed him the fishing rod and said: "Hold on!" The fishing line kept exiting the reel as if they had harpooned Moby Dick.

Rat had put the boat in neutral. West looked up to the flying bridge. "Boss, we might need a hand here."

"I'll be down in a minute. Get the other lines in."

"I'm trying, but I've got a couple of rookies to deal with." The comment earned a scowl from Stu, but he said nothing; he was holding on tight while the fish took out more line. Roger came to life as the adrenaline pumped and color returned to his cheeks. A smile appeared on his face, and Connor could tell by the way he handled the equipment that this was not his first fishing trip. He was a better fisherman than a bar-hopper.

As Connor pulled in the third line off the outrigger and reeled it in, the last line went taut, the reel hissing as line raced off the spool. "Holy shit, Rat, another fish! Do I cut it loose?"

"Hell no! It's yours. I'm coming down to help!" Rat scrambled down the ladder, swung around, and landed on the deck.

"Is everybody having fun? Who wants a cold beer?"

Forty-five minutes later, it was all over. Stu's sailfish was 80 pounds, a real trophy fish. Roger's mahi-mahi was a huge bull at 45 pounds, and Connor had tagged and then released a 60-

pound sail. The guests, exhausted were still hungry for more action. Connor switched bait and went back to the original lure he had first thrown in the water. They quickly hooked two more mahi-mahi that both weighed in the mid-thirties.

Arms and legs now spent, Connor made Rum-Runners and *Daddy's Money* headed for port. Five pennant flags announced their catch. They slowly motored past Mallory Square for everyone to see that this was a fishing boat to be reckoned with. Stuart Coddington and Roger van Morton sang the praises of their young fishing crew, and each gave Connor $100, and Rat received $700 for the charter, a nice $200 tip. Rat would be the beneficiary of a great report to his dad, which allowed him to continue his pursuit of sunshine, fishing and women. Connor West, however, had other plans fully formed in his mind during the two-hour trip back to the marina.

CHAPTER FOUR

"You can't quit me. We're having too much fun. And look, you just made $200 today, plus what I pay you. Okay, I'm sorry I got pissed at you this morning." Rat Tomlinson stared at his friend of many years while taking a drink of his Red Stripe. He hated to admit it, but he would be lonely in Key West without his best friend and first mate. He didn't want to hire some old, smelly, bar-fly sailor to help him.

"Rat, I can't do this any longer. I'm pissing away my talent and my life cutting bait. And I've got to find Marilyn. She may not want to see me, but she'll have to tell me that to my face. I love her; I've loved her from the minute I laid eyes on her. I should have pushed her old man aside, told him to go fuck off, and walked into their house. But I turned and left, just like I did with my old man, on the building design I did, on the firm I worked with..."

"Connor, that firm screwed you up and down."

"Jefferson did, little Francis too, but not Bob Marlow. When you're a grown-up, you don't doctor up some stair shop drawings to get even and leave town. You stay and fight for what is yours. Thanks for letting me work and hang with you. It was a respite I needed to work stuff out, but it's time for me to go. But I do have a favor to ask."

"Sullivan, anything. What is it?"

"I can't go back like this—a long-haired hippy who drinks too much. I need to dry out and get in shape. I need a coach because I can't do it on my own. At least, I'm pretty sure I can't."

"Happy to help. I have an idea, but it doesn't involve sitting here at Captain Tony's and drinking."

"Yeah, what's your idea?" Connor was curious.

"We'll go yachting. The off-season has started, and I don't have any bookings for the next two weeks."

"Sounds like too much fun. But how's that going to get me sober and in shape?"

Connor labored, swimming off the starboard bow, trying to keep up with *Daddy's Money* as it moved at a barely noticeable two knots.

"Come on, Sullivan, keep your head down and dig those hands deep!" Rat was smiling as he looked down at his friend in the water, trying to keep up with the slow-moving boat. He took a sip of his Coke and laughed. "West swims with the fishes!"

Connor could hear the remonstrations of his so-called coach. *Screw you, Rat, and the boat you sailed in on,* he thought, his biceps burning along with his hamstrings. But, for the first time in a year, his head was clear, and his body felt stronger, and he had gotten a haircut. Amazing what a week off the sauce will do.

They docked at a marina in Islamorada to purchase additional food supplies. Sullivan was an excellent cook, and when they didn't eat fresh fish, they had shrimp or steaks. There was iced tea, Cokes, and Sprite, but not a drop of booze—not even beer. It had to be tough on his friend, and West was grateful for Rat's abstinence, all to help him get sober and in shape for the trip to Chicago. Only one more week.

The thousand meters swim accomplished, a tired West climbed back on board and toweled off. He looked down at the dumbbells on the deck.

"Seriously, man?"

"Let's go. Ten arm curls, five reps."

"I hate you, Rat, I really do." Connor reached down for the weights and slowly began his curls. However, he only yearned for a cold Sprite.

CHAPTER FIVE

Bob Marlow flipped through the sheets of preliminary drawings of Nolan & Marlow Architects' latest project. He took a drink of his cold coffee, too lazy to make a new pot, and shook his head. *This design sucks,* he thought. *Any architectural critic would think the firm's main office was somewhere in the USSR,* he mused silently, a sarcastic smile breaking across his face. He checked the initials in the box in the lower right-hand corner. Drawn by: DC. Where was Taubert, his chief designer, to review this piece of mediocrity? Marlow got up from his stool and left his large cubicle. Even though he was a senior partner, he had refused the trappings of a fancy office with a lakefront view. He loved being where the action was: the acrid smell of the ammonia-produced prints, the aroma of lead filings and India ink, and the unique scent of Design-Art markers.

"Caudy, did Taubert review your design for the Gibraltar Building in Oakbrook?"

Dan Caudy looked up from his onion skin sketch, a Marlboro hanging from his lips. "No, he was too busy with that big hotel on Michigan Avenue."

"Why didn't you bring it to me?"

"We were on a deadline, and I had to get the preliminaries to them. Sorry." Caudy turned back to his sketches for a new restaurant in Chicago World Tower. He didn't want Marlow to notice his glassy eyes, a by-product of a doobie he had just smoked across the street in Grant Park.

"Thanks. Do me a favor. Take another look at the Gibraltar Insurance project. Try to make it look, well, more American."

"American? Okay, you got it, boss."

Marlow went back to his office, looked down into the empty coffee cup, and then at the wall clock: 4:30 P.M., the witching hour. His shoulders were tight. He had been sober almost a year. The last drink, or lots of drinks, had been on Saturday, November 23, 1974. Today was October 6, 1975.

I guess I'll get out of here and head to my AA meeting, he thought.

The commuter train exited the tunnel and slowly rose from its underground home onto the grand, old steel structure, dating back to 1892, known as the "L" for elevated. Marlow loved this part of the trip. From the darkness to the light, from dank, concrete walls to white buildings, crowds of people, civilization. The car swayed back and forth, not uncomfortably, but enough to let you know you were on a proper train.

He thought about the day. Another boring, pedestrian design created by the architectural department that he had been part of for twenty years. During that time, great buildings were designed by the late Francis Nolan, Sr., then Leo Skoroshod, and even by Gerhard Dietrich, his Miesian leanings notwithstanding. Now, he felt the firm had lost its edge. Taubert and Caudy were good, sometimes better than good. But not good enough. Not if Nolan & Marlow and Associates was to compete with the big New York firms and the many young upstarts in Chicago like Harry Weese and Bertrand Goldberg. The firm needed fresh blood—just like it had in 1973 when it hired Connor Jones West. West, who was fishing down in Key West, wasting his life away. Fifty thousand dollars a year and head of design had not swayed him. *What would get his interest?*

Marlow smiled. Tomorrow he would travel to Oak Park. It was time to find Marilyn Jones. Only she could bring Connor back to Chicago. The "L" toddled on to Lincoln Park.

CHAPTER SIX

At 10:30 A.M., Bob Marlow walked up the steps to the uniquely American colonial home. White clapboard siding, six double-hung windows across the second-story façade, two pairs on the first, flanking a handsomely painted door with sidelights, and framed by two Doric columns. A sunroom and porch book-ended the house. The narrow drive headed back to a modest one-car garage. Marlow thought for a moment about how his partner's rape of Marilyn Jones must have shattered this family's tranquil suburban life. Their only daughter traumatized forever, estranged from the young man she loved and giving birth to a baby that she didn't want.

He rang the doorbell. Since it was Wednesday, he was sure that Marilyn's father would be at work. He only had to get by her mother, and he didn't think that would be an issue. He had sent them a check for $50,000, even though no amount of money could atone for Vance Jefferson's criminal behavior. Someone had cashed the check. He felt guilty that he had not come earlier to see Marilyn. But her parents had always hung up, and no one returned the many phone messages. He rang the doorbell again, and when the door opened, it was Marilyn. No longer a young lady but a grown woman, her hair a mess, not wearing any makeup, in an old Chicago Cubs jersey and cut-off shorts. She looked tired but beautiful. In her hand was a half-full glass of wine.

"Marilyn..."

"Mr. Marlow, Bob, what are you doing here?"

"I, I came to see you. To see how you're doing."

"I'm getting along, all things considered."

"Good. I'm sorry, may I come in?"

"Of course, please. But the house is a mess." She ran her hand through her hair, somehow trying to make it neater.

Marlow peered at the living room on one side of the large foyer, and the dining room on the other. It was all neat as a pin. Marilyn led him through the living room filled with traditional, comfortable furniture, past a brick fireplace, with family photos on the mantle, and into the brightly lit sunroom. She motioned Marlow to a floral pattern Chesapeake armchair and went over to a table full of decanters, bottles of liquor, and crystal glasses. As he sat down, he watched Marilyn re-fill her already half-full wineglass.

"It's good to see you, Marilyn."

"Yeah, well..."

"Pardon my saying so, but isn't it a little early for wine?"

"You would know all about that, wouldn't you?"

"I'm sorry, I had no right. And you're correct. I've been sober almost a year now."

"I'll drink to that." Marilyn sat down on a love seat, taking a sip.

"Marilyn, what Vance did to you was despicable. I feel complicit. You weren't the first one; I should have warned you. Connor told me he had been making advances, and I told Jefferson to leave you alone. Obviously, it didn't do any good."

"Look, I took some bad advice from Jane, my roommate. He wanted to wine and dine me, and she told me to go along, but I should have told him no. But I didn't want to lose my job, or Connor to lose his."

"Don't blame yourself. The man is a pig. I hope the money helped. I tried to call; I left messages."

"I'm sorry. My father wanted me to have nothing to do with the firm, you, and especially Connor. But he accepted the check. Thank you so much. I'm using the money until I get another job."

"I'm sorry you had to go through nine months carrying his child. Knowing it was the..."

"Yeah, his child. Well, he's in a good home now. In Minnesota."

"A boy? It must have been hard."

"You have no idea. If you must know, the baby is Connor's son, not Vance's. But I had signed the adoption documents. I had to give him up. So, really, why did you come here?"

"My God, Marilyn, I'm so sorry. How can you be sure?"

"When I went into labor, I thought it was a month too soon. I counted back the months. We conceived the baby in early November, not December when Vance raped me."

"Then you need to tell him. Connor misses you."

"He misses me? He sure has a funny way of showing it. He never even came to see me after what had happened. That bastard! I guess he didn't want a slut for a girlfriend."

"That's not true. He told me he went to your apartment that night. Jane had given you a sedative, and you were sleeping. Your father accused him of ra... of what happened to you, and Connor left in a rage to find Jefferson. The next day he about killed him in at the office—he beat Vance bloody. Then he told me he came here, but your father wouldn't let him in. He's just sick about it."

"Really? Oh my God. Where is he?"

"He's in Key West, working with his friend, Rat, on his fishing boat."

"Oh, yes, the postcard. When he was down in the dumps, he said how much he envied Rich Tomlinson. I always told him it was his destiny to be a brilliant architect, not a playboy like Rat."

"I offered him a job to come back to Chicago and head up the design department, with a big raise. But he's drinking. A lot. He refused the offer. All the booze has clouded his vision. What happened with the firm, with you, messed him up pretty bad. What he needs is you."

"I think of him every day. But it just seems that so much has happened. Goddamn my father. He hates Connor because of his long hair and because he loves me. No one is ever good enough. My father didn't even tell me about Connor coming to the house. Or any of it. And I called Connor a bastard. It's my father who's the real bastard."

"I'm sorry. Marilyn, I think you are the tonic Connor needs. You're the one that can pull him back from his drinking and his depression. He needs to be an architect, designing buildings. It's what he is. Not a mate on a fishing boat. Go to Key West. I'll even pay for the ticket."

"My father still hates him."

"What does your father have to do with it? Isn't it about how you feel? Go see him and bring him back to Chicago."

"Oh, I see. Now I understand. That's why you came here. You need Connor to come back and save the firm."

"Okay, I'll admit, I have an ulterior motive. I need a designer, a very talented designer. We're turning out boxes of mediocrity at Nolan & Marlow. With what I'll pay him, you two can get married and have a wonderful life." Marlow was pushing hard.

"Fair enough, I guess. Can I think about it and call you tomorrow?"

"Certainly. I'd better go." Marlow got up and stood there looking at Marilyn. "Marilyn, I'm so sorry..."

"It's alright, Mr. Marlow. At least now I know where Connor is and that he tried to find me."

"Look, I know I'm no role model when it comes to drinking, but I think you'd be better off putting on some running shoes and going for a two-mile jog. It's just a suggestion."

"Thanks. You are probably right about the jogging. I'll call you tomorrow. But I think I might take you up on your offer. Oh, and Bob, you are a role model. You are to Connor."

CHAPTER SEVEN

Simone Duvalier paced around her late husband's desk, now the one she occupied as first lady and prime minister. Luckner Cambronne, head of the Tonton Macoute, was late.
The "Vampire of the Caribbean" exerted total control over the 25,000-man army of thugs, terrorists, and murderers.

Created in 1959 by her husband and called the Volunteers of the National Security, the local populace soon adopted the Haitian Creole term after the mythological bogeyman, Tonton Macoute, or Uncle Gunnysack. Legend had it that Uncle Gunnysack kidnapped and punished small children by snaring them in a sack and then carrying them off to be eaten for breakfast. This paralleled closely the reality of individuals and entire families disappearing, never to be seen again. Rumors that the Tonton Macoute possessed great Voodou powers, many of them being priests or Houngan, were rampant. Their uniforms of straw hats, dark sunglasses, and blue denim shirts, usually without sleeves, inspired fear. Their weapon of choice was the machete, backed up by semi-automatic guns.

The door to the office opened. A guard spoke.
"Madame, Minister Cambronne is here to see you."
"See him in." Duvalier sat down at the desk.
A tall, scrawny man entered the ridiculously large office. His hair was thinning, and his eyes pierced right through you. He was a captain of the VNS and dressed the part.
"You're late, Luckner. I have a busy schedule." Simone was more daunting and scarier than Papa Doc, who always spoke softly. His actions spoke for him. Simone believed both worked hand in hand.

"My apologies, I was waiting for some information on another plot against the government."

"Tell me."

"A family near Kenscoff has been holding meetings at night. They talk about the government, your government, and how nothing has changed since your husband passed. They want to organize demonstrations in the city at the Jean-Jacques Dessalines Monument."

"How do you know this?"

"I imbedded one of my people in the group. They plan to demand new elections, freedom of speech and assembly and..."

"And what?"

"And an end to the Tonton Macoute."

"Deal with this family right away. Dismissed."

"As you wish, Madame. As you command."

Mindy and Johnny Boberg cuddled and cooed during the entire flight from Miami to Port-au-Prince. It had been the same on the Eastern Airlines non-stop from Cleveland to Miami. The stewardess gave them free champagne and even made an announcement about their recent nuptials the day before, Saturday, over the PA. The passengers applauded. Now they were on their way to their "Dream" honeymoon in Haiti. The travel agent in Bay Village had assured them that under the new administration, Haiti was a tropical paradise. They would be secluded in their own suite at La Reserve, Kenscoff's most exclusive resort. Little did Mindy and Johnny know that the travel agent garnered a free cruise with each booking at the two-star property.

The heat and humidity hit them like a blast furnace as they climbed down the steps from the plane. Duvalier Airport had no air-conditioning, and after waiting 45 minutes for their bags, they queued in a line for a cab for another fifteen minutes.

"La Reserve Hotel, please."

"Oui, monsieur, oui. Êtes-vous Américain?"

Johnny looked at his new bride. "Yes, we are, I think."

"Très bien, j'aime l'Amérique! Je m'appelle Pierre."
Johnny said nothing more.

The cab moved out into the midday traffic of Port-au-Prince, past shanties and slums, smoky fires, women with baskets on their heads, people holding chickens by the necks, others hawking cheap souvenirs. Pierre maneuvered through the narrow streets, his hand fixed to the horn. Mindy kept the window rolled down in the non-air conditioned interior, dust and heat flowing in freely. Street people stuck their hand into the cab's open window and pleaded "Blan, lajan tanpri," begging for money. The two huddled together in the center of the old Toyota cab.

Mindy exhaled. "I didn't expect this. This is awful."

Johnny squeezed her hand. "I'm sure once we get to the resort, everything will be fine."

Finally, the crowds and buildings thinned out, the road rose and the surrounding countryside pretty and peaceful, lined with palm trees, tropical plants and bougainvillea.

As they made their way up the hilly road, a small village appeared up ahead. Pierre slowed the car. Several tap-taps, or brightly colored pickup trucks, a favorite of the Tonton Macoute, parked by the roadside. A crowd had gathered. Pierre tried to move through but had to stop in front of the commotion. Five men with straw hats and dark glasses dragged a family of seven from the house, screaming and crying. The men placed the family in a semi-circle around an older man, perhaps the head of the family. They bound him with a rope around the back of his arms. The five thugs in sleeveless shirts wielded machetes.

Pierre spoke in broken English. "No look, Madame, no look. Is bad." He looked in his rear-view mirror to see if he could back up, but the crowd had blocked him.

Mindy grabbed her husband's hand. "What's going on?" Her voice trembled.

The leader of the Tonton Macoute placed a small tire around the neck of the man in the center. They poured gasoline into the well of the tire. Members of the family screamed. "Non, non, tanpri gen pitye!" please have mercy.

The Macoute pulled out a pack of matches, lit one and threw in it into the tire. Flames erupted, and the man screamed, moving from side to side. The lighted gasoline splashed on his head, igniting it. He had become a human torch. The Macoute laughed. They herded the sobbing family members into several tap-taps, and drove them off, never be seen again.

Mindy Boberg watched it all. "I want to go home to Cleveland, now!"

CHAPTER EIGHT

Marilyn sat in the waiting area at Gate 6 at O'Hare Airport. Her American Airlines flight to Miami boarded in fifteen minutes. Bob Marlow had purchased a first-class seat for her. She was only ten the last time she had flown, on a trip to Disneyland. Her parents were not big on taking vacations or traveling; a big outing was to see relations in Wisconsin. Marilyn clutched her purse and fidgeted in the uncomfortable seat, looking around at the throngs of people. Maybe this was a bad idea.

The first order of business was to find Connor. Bob told her to go to the city marina and look for a fishing boat named *Daddy's Money*. Despite what Marlow told her, questions lingered. She was anxious; butterflies danced in her stomach.

"Your attention, please. American flight 3507 non-stop to Miami, Florida, is ready for departure. First-class passengers may now begin boarding, rows one through six."

Marilyn looked at her watch: 10:05 A.M. She stood up and looked down the long concourse. *This was a bad idea,* she thought. *Connor, his baby, my baby, the whole sorry business. I should get a job in Oakbrook and meet another man.*

She headed out of the waiting area and walked toward the overhead sign: "Ground Transportation and Baggage Claim." She stopped and looked back at the passenger's boarding flight 3507. *Be brave, Marilyn, don't give up yet. Find Connor and find out.*

Marilyn Jones walked back to the gate and joined the small queue, waiting to go to Miami.

50

❖

Sullivan and Rat were sitting at a two-top at the Conch Flyer restaurant off of Key West International Airport's small concourse. By 1975, the word "International" was completely inaccurate, a holdover from the pre-Castro days when there were several flights a day from Havana. Now, all the flights, eight of them, came from Miami or Tampa. The airport was now just the lonely last stop at the end of America. The worn and tired bar-restaurant illustrated the history of the place on its walls: huge Pan-American Clippers and shiny DC-3's; a photo of Juan Trippe stepping from one of his planes back from its inaugural voyage to South America. A framed photo of the very first Pan-Am ticket office down on Caroline Street.

Connor was finishing his second cup of coffee; Rat was having another of the establishment's good Bloody Mary's.

"I guess you're glad to get rid of me," Connor said, eyeing the vodka drink with a small degree of envy.

"Not at all. I'm just celebrating that you're sober and, on your way to see your true love. All I meet in this town are skags and divorcees."

"It's your irresistible charm, Rat."

"No, it's my boat and my money."

"I'll tell you one thing. Love isn't easy. We were too busy at Harvard to have a social life, and then when we find someone, we're unprepared for how to deal with them. Marilyn will probably have another boyfriend. She should, the way I just up and left."

"Don't beat yourself up. A lot of shit went down. Consider this time in the Conch Republic as an opportunity to heal. You had to become a drunk, see the bottom, and finally realize what is important in life. Then I single-handedly got you sober and in shape."

"You did indeed, and I owe you big for that."

"Glad I could help. I am enjoying this Bloody, however. There were many times on our two-week cruise I yearned for an adult beverage."

"Anyway, thanks, Richard Tomlinson."

51

"Sullivan, I have an idea. No, an epiphany. Why don't you and Marilyn come back here to Key West? I'm sure you could make a nice living designing fancy homes and maybe even a hotel or two. This town is going to be booming in a couple of years. Hell, my dad can give you a loan, and I'll be your business partner."

"What about the fishing boat?"

"I'll hire a captain and mate to run it and take a third of the profits. I'll also buy a restaurant and become a conglomerate." Rat laughed and finished his drink.

Connor smiled. "We better get going. The plane leaves at 2:00 for Miami."

"Yes, and the gate is only 150 feet away. You still have fifteen minutes."

"Let's just get to the waiting area. I don't want to miss the flight."

"Fat chance of that, but if you insist."

"I don't mind telling you I'm a little nervous."

"About a plane ride?"

"No, about seeing Marilyn."

The two comrades ambled down to Gate 2, the farther of the two gates at the decrepit airport.

"There, now you have ten minutes before you board. So, I think I'll say goodbye. The passengers from your flight are arriving. I'm gonna walk down to baggage claim and see if any hot tourists are getting off."

"You do that, you might get lucky... you usually are."

The two friends hugged, shook hands, and Tomlinson headed for baggage claim, only two hundred feet down the single-level facility. He stopped, turned, and saw Connor sitting with his head in his hands, looking like a scared little boy.

CHAPTER NINE

Connor looked at his watch. It was almost two o'clock, and no announcement. He seconded guessed himself and the trip. There was no doubt it would end in disaster. He got up to leave. Maybe he could still catch up with Tomlinson. The PA clicked on.

"American Eagle flight 182 is ready for boarding. We hope you enjoyed your time in Key West. Come back and see us soon. Again, American Eagle 182 is boarding at Gate 2. Thanks, and have a great day."

Connor sighed, picked up his backpack, and got in line. At least he would visit Bob Marlow and have dinner with him. When he was about to exit the terminal into the bright Key West afternoon, he thought he heard his name called. The shout became clearer as he walked toward the twin-engine aircraft parked on the tarmac. He turned.

"Connor, Sullivan, stop!"

Rat was walking fast toward him, pushing bystanders aside. Following behind, and clinging to his hand, was Marilyn Jones. As soon as she saw Connor, she stopped and beamed a fantastic smile. Connor, still in the boarding line, stopped and looked at Marilyn in confusion and amazement. Marilyn continued to stare at him, frozen in her tracks. Tomlinson led her out onto the tarmac to Connor.

"Hey buddy, the plane's boarding," the passenger behind him said with a tinge of annoyance.

"Sorry." Connor moved sideways out of the line, never taking his eyes off Marilyn, and mouthed the word "sorry" again. Again. And again.

"I believe you two know each other," Rat said, grinning between the two former lovers and looking like a referee at a football coin toss.

Slowly, the same word formed on her lips. "Sorry. Sorry, sorry, oh, Connor, I'm so sorry." She rushed to him and wrapped her arms around his strong, broad shoulders. She kissed his lips, his face, and his forehead. She mussed his hair, grabbed his hands, clutched his face, and kissed him again and again. Tears of happiness streamed down her cheeks.

"You guys need to get a room. Perhaps I should go fetch your luggage, Miss Jones, if you tell me what it looks like?" Rat was standing at attention like a dutiful bellboy.

"Brown suitcase, with my initials, MEJ." Marilyn never took her eyes off Connor and went back to kissing him.

Connor held Marilyn away momentarily from their embrace and looked into her eyes. "What are you doing here? I was about to board a plane to come and see you. But you're here..."

"Bob Marlow told me you were in Key West. Oh, Connor, I believed such terrible things about you. Bob told me what happened. I'm so sorry."

"No, no, no. You have nothing to be sorry for. It was entirely my fault. I should have confronted Vance and gotten you out of that place. When I came to see you at your home, I should have pushed your father aside and gone to you. But I gave up. He said you were leaving town."

Rat quickly returned with Marilyn's suitcase. "Perhaps we can take this happy reunion somewhere other than this dump airport. Anyone need a lift?"

Connor's visage went from one of ecstasy to horror. "Can I talk to you a minute, Rat?" He grabbed his friend's arm and pulled him to one side. "I can't take Marilyn to my place. It's a disaster!" he whispered.

"Yes, it is. And you wouldn't want to stay on the boat sleeping in bunk beds. May I suggest the Casa Marina Resort?"

"I can't afford that place. It's the nicest hotel in Key West." Connor's face was flush with panic.

"Relax, I know the night manager. I'll get you a good deal. And why don't you take your lady to A & B Lobster

House tonight? My treat. Consider it a gift from me for your indentured servitude on my boat."

"You're the best, man; you're the best!"

"That's correct. I might even go to your place and tidy it up a bit. But I'll need a few days."

"Rich Tomlinson, I owe you."

❖

Connor and Marilyn sat at a table for two, alongside a picture window facing the marina. Candlelight flickered from a small ship's lantern on the table and danced on the white tablecloth. The running lights of the yachts and sailboats splashed across the dark water of the Old Town Marina. Overhead lights illuminated the toys of the rich, docked in Key West for some R&R, while their masters drank and caroused at Sloppy Joe's, Rick's, and the Pier House. Guests enjoyed meals at the Commodore next door, or, like Connor and Marilyn, at Alonzo & Berlin's, with no thought about the price.

A party of twelve was consuming bottle after bottle of Dom Pérignon to accompany their surf & turf. Fortunately, the noisy party was on the other side of the restaurant, and their carousing did not interrupt a conversation that had been waiting for eleven months. "I'm sorry" gave way to "I missed you so much" to "I love you." Tears of happiness ran down their cheeks, and they tightly held hands. The fine meal was secondary.

But during the hours of conversation, not every fact surfaced. While Marilyn had told Connor that she had become pregnant, she held a deep secret in her heart—the baby was Connor's child. As she picked at her chocolate cake, she couldn't bring herself to tell Connor that he had a son. Such knowledge might be more than he could handle.

"I'm full. That was a lot of food." Connor drank the last of his iced tea.

"Yes, it was. It was wonderful. Connor..."

"Listen, Marilyn, I know I've said I'm sorry a lot tonight, but I'm just so sad that you had to endure nine months carrying Vance's child. It tears me up inside."

"Connor... I have something..."

"Yes?"

"Oh, never mind. Can we go back to the Casa Marina now? That room is so beautiful. You shouldn't have spent so much money. We could have stayed in your apartment."

"I don't think that would have been a very good option. Maybe the day after tomorrow. Sure, let's get outta here. Let me get the check."

It had been so long. Marilyn was nervous, even scared. The last time she had been intimate with someone, it was a criminal act, a violation of her body. In their nakedness, kissing Connor, she felt her body tense up. Marilyn tried to tell herself that it was Connor beside her, not that pig, Jefferson. She looked at his face, his trim, muscular body, his manhood, but nothing helped. In the recesses of her thoughts, she dreaded what was about to come, even if it was with Connor West.

He sensed her reluctance. "It's been a long day and, I don't mind telling you, an unexpected one. Let's just hold onto each other and get some sleep. We have plenty of time."

"Thank you. I don't know what's wrong..."

"Shush now, don't worry about it."

Connor and Marilyn slept in each other's arms until 2 A.M. when Connor woke.

"Is something wrong?"

"No. Just too much iced tea. I'll be back in a minute."

In the bathroom, Connor stared into the mirror and then hung his head, letting out a deep sigh. Had the rape scarred her forever? Would she never be comfortable with a man, never intimate? He returned to the bed, slid in under the sheets, and slowly moved toward her lithe body. She assented. Connor brought her in tight against him, and her legs wrapped around him like ivy, her soft, warm body molding with his. She was now willing, no longer so tense; she reached for him, kissing him deeply. She let out a deep sigh of happy surrender. He reached down and touched her between her legs. A small gasp erupted, then a slight cry of desire and pleasure, so long withheld. She kissed him hard and reached for his hand, guiding it into her.

"Tell me if you want me to stop."

"No. Don't stop. Don't stop." She reached for his hard cock. "I want you. I want you inside me."

Marilyn stood on the suite's balcony at the Casa Marina looking out at the blue-green water of the Florida Straits. Palm trees swayed slightly in the cool October breeze. Connor came up behind her with a mug of coffee, kissed her gently on the neck.

"Room service just brought breakfast. Hungry?"

"Famished. It's been two days."

"Really? I hadn't noticed."

"So, now what? This suite is costing you a lot of money. Let me help."

"No way. You're my guest here in paradise."

"It is that; it's so beautiful here."

Connor and Marilyn sat in silence at the table on the balcony. They'd devoured every morsel of their breakfast.

"You must have been hungry; you barely said anything while we ate. Tell you what: let's stay one more night, enjoy the pool today, and have lunch down by the beach. Tonight, I'll take you to Louie's Backyard for dinner—its right down the street, and tomorrow, you'll get to see my luxurious bachelor pad."

Marilyn managed a weak smile. "Connor, I have to tell you something."

"What?"

"You have a son."

"What? What do you mean, 'You have a son?'"

"The baby I carried wasn't Vance's, he's yours. I saw him. He looks just like you."

"Oh my God... how can you be sure?"

"I'm sure. I'm Kevin's mother. I know he is our child."

"Kevin? Who's Kevin?"

"I named our son Kevin, after your father."

"You named the baby after my father? My father?"

"Yes, I hope you don't mind..."

"No, I guess not... after my father. Well, good. Yes, that was nice of you. Very nice."

"And his middle name is Robert, after Bob Marlow."

"I have a son. Kevin Robert West. Why didn't you tell me earlier?"

"It's not that simple."

"Where is he? Are your parents taking care of him?"

"A young couple from St. Paul, Minnesota has adopted him. That's all I know. I signed the papers; there was nothing I could do. I always assumed it was Vance's child so I didn't hesitate to agree to whatever they wanted me to. But I went into labor after only eight months and when I saw the baby, I knew he was ours."

"Surely, we can get the baby back. You made a mistake. You want the baby, don't you?"

"Oh, yes. I'm still heartbroken. They said there was nothing that could be done."

"We'll go to Chicago. I'll hire a lawyer. Kevin will be ours; I promise. I want us to be a family."

"My arms ache for him, Connor. I grieve for him, but now that you're here with me, I believe together, we can find him and bring little Kevin home."

"I wonder if Bob Marlow still has a job open."

"He does. Bob paid for my ticket. He told me to come to Key West and bring you back, Mr. Chief Designer of Nolan & Marlow."

"I see. You two have been in cahoots." Connor smiled.

"Maybe a little. But I would have come anyway, even if he didn't buy my ticket."

"Marilyn, a long time ago, I asked you to marry me. Remember? Is the answer still yes?"

"How could I forget? Yes, it's yes. It will always be yes. I love you so much."

CHAPTER TEN

"When is Marilyn coming back from your sister's? It's been a week. And I thought she disliked Clara. Why in God's name would she want to visit that old spinster?" Paul Jones puffed on his pipe. Sarah Jones forbade him to smoke cigarettes in the house. At least he smoked a pipe infrequently, and the sweet smell of pipe tobacco wasn't so noxious.

"Ahh...she just wanted to get away for a while. She was sick of being trapped in this house."

"Marilyn was free to go anywhere she wanted, except Chicago."

"You mean anywhere in Oak Park. She did that the first two weeks."

"But your sister Clara? She's a terrible cook to boot."

"All right, Paul, if you must know. I lied to you. Marilyn went to Key West."

"Key West? What are you talking about?"

"She went to find Connor."

"Connor! That rapist! How could you!?"

"Connor never raped Marilyn. Vance Jefferson did. Connor and Marilyn are in love. And after the lies you told her, I'm proud that she went to find him. She went there to find out if he still loves her, and tell him he has a son."

"You don't know if that boy is the father."

"Marilyn does. The baby was full term. There is no way Jefferson fathered it. The baby would have been a month premature. Anyway, a woman just knows."

"How could you let her see him? She needs to get on with her life and meet someone new!"

"Paul, I'll never understand your self-righteousness. Connor *is* Marilyn's life. He's handsome, talented, and has a master's degree from Harvard. If I recall, you graduated from Mundelein Community College."

"I won't have her marrying him! They fornicated."

"So what? She loves him, can't you understand that?"

"Truthfully, I can't."

❖

Marilyn and Connor walked down Whitehead Street toward the non-descript, red brick WPA building called the Monroe County Courthouse. Rich Tomlinson, and his current girlfriend, Cassidy, ambled behind.

"You're sure you're okay with coming here to get married?" Connor worried about Marilyn. He knew most women wanted a big wedding and reception.

"It will probably upset my mother. She always wanted a Catholic wedding for me. But now I don't care, just so we're married." Marilyn looked at her soon-to-be spouse. He looked anxious.

"Aren't you nervous?" Connor hoped she shared the same butterflies he had.

"Oh, no! I'm excited." Marilyn smiled and kissed Connor on the cheek.

"I confess, I guess I'm a little nervous. I've never married anyone before."

"You knucklehead. Neither have I!"

"Are you sure you don't want a church wedding? There's a Catholic church on Truman Avenue. I even went there a couple of times."

"After St. Margaret's and those hateful nuns, I'm not very happy with the Catholic Church. It may preach love, but it was in short supply there."

Marilyn squeezed Connor's hand. She was wearing a new off-white dress and cream-colored pumps that she had bought at J. C. Penney. The sweetheart neckline showed off her Key West tan, accentuated by a string of pearls. She was a stunning bride, even though her ensemble had cost only $65.00.

On the same outing, Connor purchased a dark blue linen sport coat. Under it was a new white shirt, sans tie;

khaki slacks finished the outfit. With his 6'-2" frame, tanned face, dark brown eyes, and freshly cut dark brown hair, he looked the perfect groom. He was Hollywood handsome, as handsome as James Dean and Cary Grant rolled into one.

The two turned off the sidewalk and up the courthouse steps, the best man and maid-of-honor following them. Inside the large marble lobby, a directory with missing letters showed that the county clerk's office was on the second floor. They proceeded up a wide set of old wooden steps into their life together, into their future.

❖

"Well, how does it feel to be Marilyn Jones Jones West?" Connor smiled broadly.

"That's a mouthful. How about I just call myself Marilyn West?"

"I like it. Short and sweet." Connor kissed his wife.

Rich shook his head. "Listen, you two lovebirds, how about we go to Pepe's for a celebratory lunch? My treat."

"Rich, I was wrong about you. I took you for a playboy. But you're such a good friend to Connor." Marilyn leaned over and kissed Tomlinson on the cheek.

"I am that. And, if you must know, I am also a playboy."

Cassidy jabbed Tomlinson in the ribs, and the wedding party walked out the door into the bright Key West afternoon.

❖

Sister James admired the handmade doll, turning it around in her tiny hands. It had taken two months of her minimal free time to complete it, yellow string for hair, a face painted with ink, and a mouth sewn shut so that Marilyn Jones could never tell Bondye, the good God, what had happened to her. On the chest of the doll, Sister had sewn a small red heart.

Her small room was dark except for the light of six votive candles she had stolen from the chapel's nave, which contained rack after rack of them. Light a candle, pray hard, and all your wishes will come true. She placed the white candles in a semi-circle on her desk, like an altar. In the center was her treasured photo of Papa Doc Duvalier, wearing dark glasses and a top hat. There were wide, black circles under his eyes from charcoal of the sacred mapou tree, ordered destroyed by the Catholic Church in the 1940s, because superstition tied the trees to the Haitian religion of Voodou. The doll lay on the table in front of her.

"Baron Samedi, I pray to you, Iwa of the Dead, spirit saint of Guédé, bring damnation to this woman who has caused me great troubles."

Sister James reached inside her black tunic and pulled out a large silver pin. "Fanm femèl chen, soufri menm jan mwen te soufri."* She took the tiny dagger and slowly inserted it into the doll's head.

The four friends were enjoying lunch on the patio of Pepe's. Cassidy inquired, "Are you sure you don't want to stay in Key West? You guys seem to love it here."

"No. We're going back to Chicago. Marilyn has it on good authority that I can get my old job back."

Marilyn interrupted. "No, your *new* job. You'll be head of design."

Cassidy sipped on her Bloody Mary. "Impressive Connor. I'm dating a pirate..."

This time Rich jabbed Cassidy in the ribs. "Arrrrgggghhh!"

The foursome laughed and toasted. Connor finished his virgin Bloody.

"We also have to attend to some unfinished business. Marilyn's going back Thursday, and after I pack, I'll be on the road by Sunday."

"We'll miss you guys," Rich said with a sigh.

"We miss you al..." Marilyn put her hand to her head and moaned.

"What's wrong, babe?"

"I don't know. Suddenly I have the worst headache." Her other hand went to her head. She cried out. "Connor..."

* *"Bitch woman, suffer as I have suffered."*

CHAPTER ELEVEN

Marilyn and Connor sat in Key West's small concourse, the walls adorned with dated travel posters to the Caribbean and South America. He held her hand.

"When you get back to Chicago, I want you to go to a doctor about those headaches." Connor looked at her, concern on his face.

"I'm sure it's nothing to worry about, just the stress of everything."

"Listen to me. Go see a doctor."

"I have a lot to do when I get back to Chicago. I need to see Bob Marlow and tell him you're coming back to work. I have to look for an apartment. I'll use the money Bob gave my family for a deposit. The furniture I own is in my parent's basement; I can get a moving service. Should I get a one-bedroom or two?"

"Marilyn, let me call Bob. I want to discuss a few things with him. And I'll be there in four days. We'll have plenty of time to find an apartment, and with my money, okay? The only thing you have to do is see a doctor about the migraines. Oh, and mention to your parents that we're married. Make peace with them; I don't want a father-in-law who hates me." Connor squeezed his bride's hand tightly.

"He doesn't hate you. He's just protective."

"Yeah, right."

"Knucklehead."

"Your attention, please. American Eagle Flight 1028 to Miami departing at 12:45 is now ready for boarding at Gate 2. We hope you had a great time in Key West. Come back and see us. Again, American Eagle 1028 is boarding at Gate 2. Thanks, and have a great day."

"I'd better go. The plane's leaving." Marilyn stood up and took a deep breath. "I'm already missing you."

"It's only four days. I'll see you in four days. And I miss you too, already." Connor brought Marilyn to him and kissed her deeply. She let it linger, then pulled away.

"I don't want to miss the plane."

Connor held on, kissing her again, and again, parting only to say, "It's not leaving without you."

Marilyn separated, smiling, gently stroking Connor's face, then squeezing it. "I thought you said it was only four days, you knucklehead."

"Okay, get going. I love you!"

"And I love you." Marilyn picked up her suitcase and purse and headed for the line to board the plane. And in an instant, she was out the door, onto the tarmac.

Connor sighed, turned, and headed for the parking lot. He had a lot of packing to do.

❖

The DC-3's cabin was hot. It was like an oven; the late October day hotter than normal. The stewardess had served mimosas to everyone, all 12 off-season passengers. Marilyn had two, leaving her slightly high, but it didn't ease the nervousness that she felt.

Why hasn't the plane departed? What are all those men doing around the engine? Their heads are shaking; they're wiping their hands with rags, putting tools down, looking disgusted. One of them is on a walkie-talkie.

The comely young flight attendant went into the cockpit, talked to the captain, and turned to the passengers. She lifted the microphone off the holder on the bulkhead. There was no need. If she spoke in a loud voice everyone on board could hear her. The microphone crackled.

"Ladies and gentlemen, I have just spoken with the captain. As those of you on the right side can see, there is a problem with the prop, and the ground crew does not have the part to fix it. I am sorry, but we cancelled the flight. You may de-

plane and see the gate agents inside for re-booking onto another flight. American Eagle Airlines apologizes for any inconvenience. Have a nice day."

Oh God, Marilyn thought, *maybe I should call Connor. No. Maybe I'll see what they can do inside first.* She followed the passengers off the disabled aircraft.

❖

After going to the restroom, Marilyn got in line and realized she was the last person in it. Everyone else had probably booked all the remaining seats on the next flight before she could reach the agent. She looked around for a pay phone to call Connor. Another evening with him would be wonderful.

The queue moved slowly. Finally, there was only one passenger in front of her. After harsh words with the agent, he turned from the counter, unsatisfied and angry.

"I don't suppose there are any more seats on the next flight to Miami." Marilyn hoped the answer would be no so she could see Connor again.

The flustered gate agent looked at Marilyn and smiled. "I'm sorry, it's fully booked."

A smile came across Marilyn's face. "I understand. Thanks."

"You know what; let me check if Air Sunshine has any seats to Tampa. It's the next plane coming in." She punched the keys on her computer, waited, and punched more keys. "Well, look at that. There's been a cancellation. I should give the seat to the passenger in front of you, but he was a real jerk. Do you want it?"

"Air Sunshine?" Marilyn really wanted to spend another night with Connor.

"It's a small airline that flies between here and Tampa. There are two flights a day. It's due to arrive in thirty minutes."

"Tampa? But I need to get back to Chicago."

"I think they have connecting flights from Tampa. Let me check." More typing, more pauses, more typing. "Oh, yes, there is a six o'clock Eastern Airlines flight to Chicago. I can book you on it. You'll have plenty of time to make your connection through to Chicago. You'll be home tonight!"

"I guess that would be wonderful. How do I pay you?"

"Let me see about the difference in fare." Pause, typing on the computer. "Oh, it will be only $23.50. And you'll be first-class on the Chicago flight. A check will be fine."

"Thank you so much. Oh, how many engines does the Sunshine plane have?"

"Four. It only holds fourteen people, but it's perfectly safe. It comes in here twice a day, no problems."

"Okay, thank you." Marilyn pulled out her checkbook, disappointed as her thoughts returned to Connor. *It's alright, Marilyn. You'll see him in four days.*

Sister James knelt at the small alter, fondling the doll she had made. The votive candles flickered, dying. She had pulled out the needle from the head and held it in her hand. "Sister Blanche be sending me to a worse place than this. A place called South Dakota, to work in an orphanage. I don't want to be tending to no chilrin. I likes the little babies. This be all your fault, Marilyn bitch woman. Your fault, and that baby boy you gave away."

The tiny nun's body shook as she began to mouth Voodou chants, calling on the Ghede, the family of death; to Simbi, the Iwa of magic; and Baron Samedi, the Iwa of the dead.

"Bawon Samedi pote mizè ak gwo pwoblèm pou fanm sa a ki pèdi m."* Sister James took the silver needle and jabbed it into the red fabric heart of the doll.

* "Baron Samedi, bring misery and great troubles to this woman who has ruined me."

CHAPTER TWELVE

Air Sunshine Flight 242 came in hard, bouncing twice on Key West's short runway. Then the captain hit the brakes and the plane skidded. It was 3:39 P.M., nine minutes late. It would have to de-plane the 14 passengers, the aircraft's maximum, their luggage, re-fuel, and board another full complement of ticket-paying customers to Tampa in less than a half-hour. Raindrops covered the windshield of the cockpit.

First officer, Matt England, looked at Captain Steve Conroy, smirking. "We need to work on your landings."

"I was in a rush to get here."

"And we're going to hit weather going back. Did you hear that weather advisory from Miami Traffic Control? The National Weather Service issued a WW Sigmet for all South Florida. Thunderstorms are popping up all over. It must be the unusually warm October weather."

"I was too busy landing the Heron," referring to the four-engine deHavilland plane he had piloted for three years.

"The trip back won't be fun."

"Yeah, the wind is already picking up; the crosswinds were a bitch. I need a smoke and a leak; you button up here and I'll take care of the passengers and the door."

"Roger that, Steve. Hey, Captain, no drinking today, okay?"

"Got it, Mother."

Conroy used his arms to lift his bulky frame out of the cockpit's seat, one that was too small for his generous girth. His weight, and drinking on the job, was the reason he no longer flew with Pan-American. He waddled back through the small cabin, nodded and smiled at the passengers, some still clinging to the arms of their seats, their faces as white as Key West sand. He twisted the arm of the main door at the back of the plane, opened it, and pushed. It fell forward and three steps appeared. The ground crew was already there with a step stool for the final descent. He turned back to the cabin. "Welcome to Key West. I hope you all enjoyed your flight on Air Sunshine. And I'm sorry about that landing. You can de-plane now."

The passengers stood up quickly, more than happy to get off. Conroy overheard one of them say, "Next time, I'm on American Eagle!"

Marilyn stood as soon as she heard the boarding announcement. An attendant opened the terminal door to the tarmac. Marilyn craned her head to see a steady rain coming down outside. Her heart sank. The plane she was about to board was much smaller than the American Eagle DC-3. Yes, it had four props, but it was half the size of the aircraft that she had just been in for over an hour. She took a deep breath. *You can do this girl.*

Assisted by the ground crew holding umbrellas, Marilyn and 12 other passengers crossed the tarmac and climbed up the four steps and into the Heron's small fuselage. She found her seat, 3D, and sat down, and wondered if they would serve mimosas.

❖

The Conch Flyer Restaurant and Bar was busy for a Thursday afternoon, full of passengers because the airline cancelled their flight, or impatient to board a plane that would get them to their eventual destination. Drinking seemed an excellent option to pass the time.

Having relieved himself, Captain Conroy walked into the bar area, wiping his forehead with a handkerchief, and sat down at one of two empty stools. The bartender ambled over, shaking his head slightly.

"Captain Steve, good to see you again. Can I get you a tonic and lime? Bad weather coming in."

"Jesus, is everyone my mother today? Bobby, double bourbon, rocks, please. And if it makes you happy, I'll just have one."

"Really?"

"Yes, really. As you said, we're gonna have some rain on the way back to Tampa."

❖

Matt England finished the pre-flight check, then looked out and saw his captain jogging to the plane smoking a cigarette. His large belly jiggled up and down with each small step. *Steve-o, you're gonna die soon if you don't start taking care of yourself,* he thought.

Conroy entered the cockpit and squeezed his corpulent body into the captain's seat, breathing heavily. "Is everything done on the pre-flight, brother Matt?"

The faint aroma of cheap booze filled the cockpit. England shook his head and frowned.

"Yes, and I just got the paperwork. Some jerk-wad passenger was late. He was on Duval and lost track of time. It's already 4:15. Let's get the hell out of here before the weather gets any worse, okay? I really don't want to spend the night sleeping in the airport." The first officer looked out the window. The rising wind inverted the gate agent's umbrella.

"I know. Cheap bastards that run this airline won't even pay for hotel rooms. The rain's picking up too. Let's get the hell out of Dodge."

The radio came to life. "Air Sunshine 242, will you be ready to go at the end?"

"Ready as we'll ever be," England responded while Conroy stuck a piece of chewing gum in his mouth, checking the instruments. The fuel gauge now read full. *Damn, they didn't need to top off the fuel. We don't want the extra weight taking off on this short-dick runway.* He kept the thought to himself, not wanting to alarm his rookie co-pilot.

"Sunshine 242, taxi into position and hold, runway 09," the tower instructed.

"No shit! Can we get off this stinking piece of coral and get back to civilization?" Conroy's temper was rising, fueled by the drinks. He had inhaled another double bourbon and earned a scowl from Bobby the bartender.

"I'm looking at the radar. Lots of thunder cells are starting to pop up as close as 20 miles to the north and east. Right in our flight path."

"Well, I guess we'll have to go around those bad boys. First, I have to make a hard left and avoid the prohibited airspace above the Naval Air Station, three miles east of here."

The flat voice of the control tower came back on. "242 to Tampa, you're cleared for takeoff. Have a safe trip."

"Tower, final wind check, please."

"Roger that. Winds 140 degrees at 15 knots, gusts to 25."

"Just great. Well, Matt, let's dance with the devil and see if we win."

"I don't like the sound of that at all," Matt stared at the radar screen. Storm cells were popping up like popcorn kernels in a hot skillet.

Conroy advanced the throttles to full takeoff power; the plane shook. He kept that posture for 30 seconds, released the brakes and the aircraft jolted forward, rapidly gaining speed.

In seat 3D, Marilyn gripped the armrests with all her strength and said a silent prayer, thinking of Connor. She wished they had made Key West their home so she would be safely on the ground with him. Her seatmate was reading an industry periodical, oblivious to her fear or the rapid liftoff.

The plane rose quickly. Marilyn glimpsed Smather's Beach and the Straits of Florida out her window until the plane's steep bank revealed only dark grey, ugly clouds. As it gained altitude, the deHavilland began to shake and bounce up and down. Marilyn took a deep breath, grabbed the armrests and said a Hail Mary.

The plane continued to climb as it banked steeply toward the northeast. Once it broke 3,000 feet it leveled off, and Captain Conroy gained some speed with a nice tailwind. The shaking and bouncing stopped.

"See, my boy, piece of cake." Steve smiled at his first officer.

"You amaze me, Conroy. And after six shots!"

"Tsk, tsk, it was only four. But don't tell anyone."

"I should, but I won't. Just get us to Tampa."

"Any clear airspace?"

"Looks good for now. Most of the bad shit is east of us. I think we won this dance."

"Good. Take the controls then. I'm going to close my eyes and relax a minute."

Marilyn looked out the tiny window to a deep blue sky. She let out a deep breath. The take-off and turbulence were like nothing she had ever experienced. *Relax, you'll be in Tampa soon and then first class to Chicago.* While she was anxious to tell her parents of her new surname, she was also excited. Marilyn knew her mother would be happy, even though there wasn't a big wedding. Perhaps they could plan a celebratory party for later. She relaxed as she thought about a tent in her parent's backyard, and friends wishing her and Connor good luck for their future.

"Ah, Captain, you awake?"

"Hell yes, just relaxing. You're a great co-pilot, England."

"Thanks for the compliment, but we're heading into a brand-new cell. It just popped up and it looks like a scalloped edge hook on the radar. Never seen that shape before."

Conroy shook his head from his half-slumber. "Shit, that's the worst."

"There's no way around it. Should I make an announcement?"

"Yeah, I guess. I need to figure out a plan." Looking out the windshield, he could see the wide, swirling thunderhead rapidly forming ahead. It looked like some sort of funnel, air rushing up, and in a flash, air rushing down at cosmic speeds. There was no time to bank to the left or right.

"Ladies and gentlemen, this is your first officer. Remain in your seats with your seat belts securely fastened.

We are expecting turbulence. It shouldn't last too long. Thank you."

Marilyn's daydream of a lawn party ended. She looked out the window. Blue had turned to a deepening gray. Her seat mate seemed unfazed.

In the cockpit, Conroy didn't want to admit it, but the four bourbons were kicking in, and the new situation was making him light-headed. He could almost feel his blood pressure rising. "Raise Miami Center. We need permission to get out of this mess and alter the flight plan."

"Roger that." England tried to make contact without any success. The turbulent weather throughout South Florida was creating a plethora of radio traffic trying to communicate with Miami ATC. Pilots asked for re-routes to find clearer skies; the small deHavilland from tiny Key West airport was ignored. Matt repeated his call sign and a request for re-routing again and again. Finally, he momentarily heard a reply but then the radio static distorted any message Flight 242 might have received.

Mother Nature's fury engulfed the little plane. The aircraft shook, bounced, and groaned, and with each jolting movement the passenger's screams. Outside, St. Elmo's fire danced like the Northern Lights on the wings and off the edges of the propellers. Mesmerized by the weather's un-natural performance, England took his eyes off the instruments. The vertical speed indicator increased to over 3,000 FPM, and the airspeed indicator decreased rapidly toward stall speed. Flight 242 was tossed around like the whip ride at a carnival. An updraft increased the plane's vertical climb. Matt came back to reality and looked at the instruments.

"Fuck! The vertical speed is over 3,000!"

Conroy was sweating. "This is getting bad. Forget raising Miami. I'm going to use my captain's authority to get us out of this mess!" As the words left his mouth, a bolt of lightning seared across the windshield, temporarily blinding both men.

The screams from the back increased. Marilyn cried and grabbed the hand of the passenger next to her. The man put down his magazine and tried to speak calmly. "It's all right, Miss; I've been on this flight many times. The pilots are very experienced." The man tightened his seatbelt and held Marilyn's hand in a firm grip.

The plane continued its steep ascent, powered by the dangerous updraft. Matt looked at the instruments; they were now over 12,000 feet in altitude. Any second, it could envelop them in a vicious downdraft.

"Captain, lower the nose." England looked over at Conroy. His sweating face was bright red, eyes bulged; he grabbed his chest then tried to loosen his tie, and small groans emanated from his mouth. He jolted forward, then back, and let out a painful cry. He slumped over onto the controls, motionless.

"Sweet Jesus! Fuck me!" The first officer trembled. *Remember your training, England. Aviate. Navigate. Communicate. You can do this.* He looked out. Ice formed on the windshield. The stall speed indicators went off. Then downdraft winds hit the plane and with the ice over the aircraft, forced the plane downward.

Aviate. The nose is too low, speed building. Nothing I can do now except wait until we get to a lower altitude and get rid of the fucking ice. England held tight, pulling the yoke back, trying to pull the plane back to level. The maneuver wasn't working, but he couldn't force the yoke and risk the wings shearing off.

Navigate. I'm only 14 miles out of Key West. Try a rudder turn towards the south. Maybe get some airflow over the wings, stop the dive and live. But nothing helped. Another warning beeper sounded. The number four engine quit, the plane's descent increased.

Communicate. Matt keyed his mike: "Mayday, mayday, mayday. Squawking 7700. Do you read?"

The speaker miraculously came alive. "Read you, 242. State your emergency and intentions," the voice without emotion.

"Miami, I'm trying to turn back to Key West. Clear all runways at Naval Air Key West. Alert Crash, Fire and Rescue."

"Roger, 242."

England continued his effort to raise the nose of the aircraft and stop the downward spiral. It was futile. The plane passed through 5,000 feet and now had the aerodynamic qualities of a beveled brick. Occasionally, the storm buffeted the small aircraft upward and Matt attempted to take advantage of it. But as quickly as he did, the wind shifted again and the plane's trajectory headed back toward earth.

As he passed through 2,000 feet, the rookie first officer pulled back with all his strength on the yoke. He was pulling against a dead engine, the ice, and most of all, gravity. Slowly, the craft eased out of the dive. At 1,000 feet he could see large pieces of ice fly off the fuselage. He was now gaining some control of the recalcitrant Heron as it leveled off at 1,500 feet. He thought of Steve's words, "Let's dance with the devil." Matt had, and he might just win. Under the unforgiving weather that was above him, it was smooth sailing. Now, First Officer Matt England only had to return to Key West.

CHAPTER THIRTEEN

Rat banged on the door.

"It's open for Christ's sake." Connor's voice responded in annoyance.

Rat entered to see an apartment that looked like a bomb had hit it. Connor was in the kitchen, just inside the door, packing dishes into a cardboard box.

"What are you doing here? Gonna help me pack?"

"You're on your own, buddy. I cleaned up this pigsty a week ago."

"So, to what do I owe the pleasure?" Connor being curious.

"I just got a call from the Coast Guard. They think a plane might have gone down in the flats north of Johnston Key. Reports are unconfirmed but they're mobilizing the Auxiliary, anyway."

Connor dropped the plate in his hand, and it fell to the floor, breaking. "Oh shit, I just put Marilyn on a plane. But that was hours ago."

"It's almost 6 P.M. What time was her flight?"

"12:45."

"Relax. It can't be the plane she was on. Plus, Miami-bound planes always fly south of the Keys, not north."

Connor let out a sigh of relief. "Let's go. I can use a break. But my God, a plane may have crashed."

"I'm sure it's just a false alarm."

Steve England had barely relaxed when an ominous cracking sound came from below his seat, directly behind him, on the right side of the plane. It quickly grew loud and threatening;

tearing metal, a screeching, moaning sound of finality. Though not sure, he judged that it was the right wing spar tearing and separating from the wing. The appendage of the plane flapped violently up and down, the result of the tremendous aerodynamic stresses the small plane had endured. Like a barn door in a tornado, the wing swung wildly and any attempt at control the aircraft was futile. Air Sunshine flight 242 quickly lost altitude and was now only 200 feet above the blue water of Johnstown Basin.

Relaxed for only a brief moment, Marilyn now squeezed the hand of her seatmate, crying, trying to catch a breath that wouldn't come. Her body shook, and the only thing she could hear was the sound of terror that filled the cabin.

As the plane hit the water, her last thought was of two people in love, on a small bridge in Lincoln Park, seated on bicycles, on a warm spring day. The two people were beaming at each other, smiling.

Daddy's Money motored through the shallow waters above one of Johnston Key's smaller outcroppings, tiny islands of coral or mangrove trees in the vast outer reaches of the Gulf of Mexico. The dying flames from the wreckage were about a half-mile away and night was falling. Rat could see the running lights of other civilian boats, the largest a Coast Guard cutter. Overhead, a helicopter approached from the Stock Island Naval Air Station. There was no straight water route to the wreck unless Rat wanted to run aground. "We're only six feet to the bottom. I don't want to get stuck. I need to go north to deeper water. Then maybe I can turn the boat south toward the wreckage."

"You didn't tell me that being first mate included fishing dead bodies from crashed planes."

"The only other time the Coast Guard called me was when a boat full of weekend partiers capsized. No one was dead, but they were all pretty drunk."

Rat turned *Daddy's Money* north and increased the speed to seven knots, then ten when the depth showed eighteen feet. In a few minutes, they were just north of the downed plane. He turned the wheel right and headed south, flipping on the two floodlights mounted above the flying bridge. The depth decreased until it was at four feet.

"I can't go in anymore. It's getting too shallow."

"Rat, there's debris up ahead. Come on."

Rat throttled down to the minimum, and the boat inched toward the smoldering wreckage of the downed plane. Other boats were trying to get in close to the wreckage, but were having the same problem with the shallow, rough water. After five minutes, the two comrades-in-arms could make out the tail of the small four-engine craft, a deHavilland Heron. Metal parts, propellers, seat cushions and baggage floated in the surrounding water. They could see the tail of the plane and its logo, a partial bright red sun.

"That's an Air Sunshine plane. It flies back and forth to Tampa. I took it once to see my aunt who retired in St. Pete. Marilyn wouldn't have been on it."

"Thank God! I didn't want her to fly back; she could have gone with me, but she insisted. Bob Marlow had already paid for her flight and she wanted to tell her parents about us. She wasn't looking forward to that. Hey, go left. There's some luggage ahead."

Rat motored slowly. The depth gauge was at three feet. "I'm gonna to run aground, Connor, if I go much further."

Connor retrieved the hook used to grab big fish by the gills and pull them on board. "A little more! There's a suitcase here on the starboard side." He reached out with the hook, trying to grab the handle of the suitcase. Missed. Another try, another miss, but he hit the bag, and it floated closer to the fishing boat. Another try and the hook caught the handle. Slowly, he pulled the case to the boat, and he lifted it onto the deck.

"Sullivan, I don't want to run aground for a suitcase. We're looking for bodies, remember."

Connor gave no response. Finally, "Rat, get down here!"

"What?" Tomlinson put the engine in neutral and climbed down onto the rear deck. "What?"

All Connor West could do was point. On the brown suitcase were the initials MEJ.

CHAPTER FOURTEEN

After they found Marilyn's suitcase, and shortly after, three bodies, one of whom was the love of his life, Connor and Rat returned to West's apartment at 2 A.M. Connor assured Rat he was all right. It was a lie.

Rat looked throughout the small apartment, and satisfied there was no liquor on the premises, told Connor to go to bed. His friend had promised that he was not about to go back to that dark, unstable place again, even if his wife's tragic death was the best excuse to drink. Yes, he had wanted to go over to Captain Tony's, find a dimly lit corner of the bar, and ordered double bourbon's until the bartender threw him out for being shit-faced drunk.

After a fitful sleep, and a nightmare where his wife had died in a plane crash, he woke sweating, shook his head, and thought it was all just a bad dream. He breathed a sigh of relief. Then the reality of Marilyn's death crashed into his memory, and he sobbed as he looked at the photo by the bed.

Unsure of what to do in his grief, Connor got dressed, went outside, and aimlessly rode his bicycle up and down the empty streets of the town, then to the breakwater at Fort Zachary State Park, to sit and ponder the events of the last 24 hours. Connor had looked at this last piece of land hundreds of times as *Daddy's Money* motored out into the Straits of Florida. He sat on one of the large boulders, a stone barrier that jutted out into the ocean and stared at the wild surf. It was the end of America. The waves crashed against the rocks of the jetty, a sad metaphor for his life. Like everything he'd ever had or wanted... all dashed against the rocks.

He was beyond grief, beyond tears. When he moved to Key West, losing Marilyn and his job threw him into a deep depression, but at least he knew she was still alive. The unspoken thoughts of seeing her again were small shreds of hope that got him through the day. Without that hope, this sorrow would be with him forever. He could still see her face, feel her hands caressing his cheeks after deep kisses, reminding him of his own words, "Only four days, knucklehead." Connor looked at the rough surf. *I could jump in. Let my body crash against the rocks. It would all be over, the pain, the loss, this crushing weight I feel in my chest and the sadness in my heart. All over.*

Shaking his head, he dismissed those dark thoughts. Connor began to let all the memories of his life fly across his mind. Growing up in a tenement apartment; his unhappy, drunken father; his troubled childhood; his enduring, wonderful mother; high school and wrestling; discovering architecture and going to Harvard; a dream job in Chicago; his design bastardized by Nolan; Jefferson's rape of Marilyn; and finally, his escape to Key West. The images were like a puzzle of reality and dreams, some fitting together, others outside the neat border, not knowing where they belonged. A few pieces, like Marilyn, were lost, never to be found.

The sun rose, and while it took second place to the much-touted Key West sunsets, this one was unique. Connor watched it, and it brought some comfort; some things were still beautiful, hope was out there somewhere, and he wanted to believe that his young life was still full of possibilities. The overwhelming grief however, precluded any more positive thoughts.

Earlier, at the apartment, Tomlinson had suggested that Connor might stay in Key West, work with him, and let the world go by here in paradise. But that was not what Marilyn wanted him to do. She was proud that he would be head of design at Nolan & Marlow. She didn't fall in love with a first mate on a fishing boat, but with a talented architect. His mother had toiled as a maid to send him to school to become one. And it was all he ever wanted to do. He thought of Chicago World Tower constructed as he had designed it, not bastardized by Francis Nolan, Jr. It would be a part of the skyline of Chicago for 100 years. And he, Connor Jones West, was its creator.

He tried desperately to overcome the dark, sad thoughts that kept creeping back into his consciousness. He sat, staring out to sea. The morning passed; it was almost noon. As the sunlight illuminated the water, turning it crystal blue, his thoughts came into focus. Life was fragile, precious: not to be taken for granted, not to be lived in compromise. So far, he had lived life on those terms, without concession. There were mistakes, but those came with the path he had chosen. Now it was time to double-down. He would never give in, he would live life as he wanted, or not at all.

Connor got up and headed for the shore and his bicycle. It was time to finish packing and drive to Chicago. He would claim his new job, visit Marilyn's parents, and find his son, Kevin Robert West. First, however, he needed to go to New York.

The sadness would last forever, but he knew he had to move on.

PART II

JEAN-CLAUDE & MANNY

CHAPTER FIFTEEN
OCTOBER 30, 1975

Port-au-Prince, Haiti

President for Life, his Excellency Jean-Claude Duvalier, lay on the king-size bed, a silk dressing gown covering his large girth. He stared at the television, a 35-inch Magnavox color, one of the few on the island of Hispaniola, and probably the only one in all of Haiti. Next to him on the bed was a half-naked mulatto girl and a plate of fritay that he washed down with a 24-ounce bottle of Prestige Lager Beer. The 7:00 P.M. news was about to begin. He was interested to hear what the government-run channel, one of two in Haiti, would say today to glorify his administration.

Welcome to Haiti Now, your local and international news at 7 P.M. All glory and honor to our President Jean-Claude Duvalier. Tonight, we have breaking news from Florida. A small passenger plane carrying two crew and fourteen passengers has crashed in the Florida Keys. At present, it appears that there are no survivors. Though it is the off-season, the small plane was full, indicative of the growth of tourism in the Florida Keys and the island of Key West, in particular, the last and most boisterous island in the Florida chain. We will provide updates as they are available.

Now to local news. Our first lady issued a new decree today...

The chubby 24-year-old virtual monarch finished his fried chicken wing, dropped it on one of many pornographic magazines spread about the bed. He held out his hand. The concubine lying beside him leaned over and licked his greasy fingers, slowly, erotically, displaying her firm caramel-colored breasts.

Duvalier pulled his hand away. "Get my clothes. I need to see my mother."

"Do you want to have sex first, my President?"

"No, get my clothes, now!"

"As you wish, your Excellency..."

The president walked slowly from one wing of the Presidential Palace to the other, trying to summon the courage to confront his mother, First Lady of Haiti, Simone Duvalier. It was courage he had tried to muster in the last year as he grew bored with living *The Lifestyles of the Rich and Famous*. His favorite playgrounds were the French Riviera and Monaco. Duvalier particularly enjoyed the Casino de Monte-Carlo, where he happily gambled away thousands. His luck at the Baccarat table was always slim to none.

Portofino was a close second, where he kept a small 70-foot yacht and young women who were happy to sleep with a head of state, albeit a poor one such as Haiti. Jean-Claude's preference was for young virgins and piña coladas with extra coconut cream.

However, nothing could match Miami Beach for quick getaways or two-week parties. The Versailles-sur-Mer had been party central ever since that week in 1971, immediately following his father's death. The boy-king lost his virginity, enjoyed the best marijuana in South Beach, and snorted cocaine through hundred-dollar bills he had recently inherited from his dead paterfamilias. More recently, Jean-Claude rented the entire top floor of the aging hotel—all thirty rooms—for his entourage. The presidential suite was his alone, except for the four or five "special assistants" who tended to his every whim and sexual appetite.

There was no end to the money and the parties, but after four years President Jean-Claude Duvalier wanted more. He knew they considered him a joke, a rich playboy that no one took seriously. The only way to gain respect was power. Power over institutions, power over the land, and ultimately, power over people. He had witnessed this as a boy at his father's side. Slowly, the nightmares had subsided, and the daily memories of the torture and mayhem became a surreal past. Fear and only fear would make the people obey. But his father had taken it too far.

By 1960, the American and Canadian dollars and English pounds, the Brazilian reals and the Argentinean pesos were no longer coming into the country. Tourists stayed away, terrified of Papa Doc Duvalier, his Voodou and his secret police, the Tonton Macoute. They were no longer interested in visiting this piece of paradise turned police-state in the Caribbean.

The never-ending money from the tobacco administration monopoly was about to dry up: monocropping, arcane agricultural practices, and continuous soil erosion had exhausted the land. The multi-national corporations were resisting more payoffs to an overtly corrupt regime. Many countries had cut off foreign aid, although Nixon had re-instituted a paltry amount in 1971. Other sources of income needed to be found. It was not a pretty picture in 1975 for the young president. Since the United States occupation ended in 1934, the oldest independent country in the Caribbean had suffered through nine coup d'états, followed by the 14-year reign of terror by his father.

Baby Doc had seen the tourist money that dripped all over Miami Beach, creating a boom in hotel occupancy. It fueled lavish spending at nightclubs, call girls, and booze and drugs. He saw the incredible wealth of the rich flaunted in foreign lands. Now this. The Florida Keys were becoming a tourist trap. Time for his mother, and her coterie of advisors, 'The Dinosaurs,' to go. It was time for Jean-Claude Duvalier to exercise the power that was rightfully his as the president of Haiti. He would bring prosperity back to his tiny island nation. The tourists and their money would return. Perhaps he would proclaim himself king or emperor. Baby Doc quickened his pace toward his mother's regal office.

CHAPTER SIXTEEN

"Mother, we must talk."

"What is it, my sweet plum?"

"Do not call me that. I'm not a fucking plum! I am the President of Haiti." Jean-Claude Duvalier tried to be assertive.

"Indeed, you are. My apology. Do you need more money? What is this month's party? Or is it time to go to the French Riviera again?"

"No more parties, no more trips. I run this country from now on; I am 24, and believe I can, no, I will, handle all affairs of state." The boy-man's voice was cracking.

"Really? And what makes you think you can do that?" Simone Duvalier expressed a realistic skepticism.

"You and your cronies are bankrupting this country." It wasn't the answer to his mother's question, but a statement he had rehearsed.

"You needn't have any concern about having enough money for your lifestyle. I have it all under control. There is plenty. You look tired. You should go to Florida."

"I'm not going to Florida. I am going to run this country, but not into the ground as father did."

"He did nothing of the sort. He brought about the People's Revolution. His people loved him!"

"If they didn't, he'd have them killed!"

Madame Duvalier rose from behind her imposing desk and walked toward her son, angry. "How dare you disrespect his memory with your slanderous talk?"

"I'm going to get rid of Cambronne and Raymond. Their time is past."

"You'll do no such thing! They are necessary to me. Plus, it would be a dangerous move. They are powerful men."

"No one is more powerful than the President-for-Life."
Jean-Claude was sweating. The meeting was not going as he
hoped. He could not whisk away the last four years of
inattentiveness with a few vacuous words to his domineering
mother.

Simone reached out and touched her son's hand.
"What is this about, my precious son? You cannot be serious
about running the country. Nothing has prepared you for it."

"My father prepared me all too well."

"Tell me what troubles you, and then you can go back
to your magazines and your pretty girls."

"No one comes to our country. I have seen how the
wealthy spend their money in Miami and Monte Carlo. We
have beaches, sunshine, blue water, but no one comes. I
remember as a boy seeing the cruise ships in port and all the
visitors who came down the gangplank. Then father came to
power. It ended. Now we only have the Tonton Macoute."

"The Tonton Macoute keeps us in power."

"There is nothing but fear; the vacationers won't come.
They are terrified of this island! I will take over control of the
Macoute. I will rein them in!"

"I'm not sure anyone can control them. They have
become a force unto themselves."

"We'll see. I learned much at my father's side."

"And what about me? Am I still the first lady?"

"Move out of the palace and stay at your villa in
Pétion-Ville. I will call you if I need you."

"You contemptuous child; after all I have done for you!
I will not go easily, my son, and you will need me soon
enough. You must be smart and wily to govern this country,
and you are neither."

Simone walked slowly to her son and stopped to
curtsy. "My President." Her tone contained a hint of
contempt. "By the way, how will you bring the tourists back?
Tourists hate to see poverty, and we have much of that."

"Do not worry about Haiti any longer. I am in charge.
Good day, Mother. Oh, and you are no longer first lady or
prime minister."

"Then I think I'll go to Paris for a month. But don't call
me. Be smart and wily on your own, you ungrateful plum."

CHAPTER SEVENTEEN

Menachem "Manny" Lazarus sat at the lobby bar in his favorite hotel, the Versailles-sur-Mer. He had designed it in 1955; it was a success from the day it opened. Unlike Mies Van der Rohe's motto: "Less is more," Manny's was "More is never enough!" He believed that if you created a grand, outrageous Hollywood stage set, the public would play their part. And for years they did, dressed to the nines, entering the hotel as if they were attending a movie premiere. The hotel hosted genuine celebrities too, including Frank Sinatra, Elvis Presley, Judy Garland, Danny Kaye, Bob Hope, and Lucille Ball. In Miami, it was the place to be.

The immense bar complemented the abundant 17,000 square foot hotel lobby, with its staircase to nowhere, huge, scalloped marble columns, and black onyx bow ties embedded in the sparkling terrazzo floors. The tired, worn-out blue and pink Naugahyde seating with chrome arms showed decades of wear. Gold drapes, torn and faded, flanked the floor to ceiling windows. On the other side of the glass, gardens that once mimicked the ones at the Palace of Versailles needed attention.

The bar was a grandiose ellipse, seating 50 patrons and manned by four of Miami's best mixologists, including Ramon, who had escaped Castro's revolution in Cuba in 1960. Now, he alone held court at the counter, doing his best to attend to both sides of it. Above the bar, mirroring its shape, was an imposing oval crystal chandelier, glittering with every movement by the prisms shaped like small fish. White lighting in the ceiling intermingled with red, blue, and green spots that once undulated in time to the background music, now silent because of the broken sound system.

The back bar was a full height, a back-lit onyx marvel, reaching up to the ceiling and illuminating every variety and brand of liquor available. At each end were enormous six-foot-high lava lamps, the guests mesmerized by the slow movement of the viscous fluid inside. Only one was operational.

Manny sipped his dirty martini and stirred it with a plastic sword holding the large olives. Now in the twilight of his career, he took pleasure in this daily ritual, his eyesight failing, not noticing the toll that time had taken on his architectural triumph. He gazed at the array of bottles on the bar through Coke-bottle eyeglasses. A gnarled hand held a Cuban cigar, as arthritis had invaded every joint in his 5'-6" frail body.

The hotel was like an aging silent film star, covered in too much rouge that could not hide the years of wear. The guest rooms were last renovated in 1965; occupancy was in the low forty percent range. Little did Manny know that the famous Versailles would declare bankruptcy by 1977. Now, it was just Manny and Ramon at 5:30 P.M on this Friday afternoon, plus a retired couple from New Jersey on the opposite side. Every day, Manny, cane in hand, crossed Collins Avenue from the sixth-floor offices of Lazarus and Berger. His partner, Bernie, had died two years previously from cancer. From his office, Manny could look out at his crowning achievement, the Versailles-sur-Mer. It was all the inspiration he needed in a career that spanned thirty years. He had left his mark on Miami Beach, so much so that his style became known as "Miami Modern."

"Where are all the fucking customers, Ramon?"

"No conventions this week, Mister Lazarus. Maybe a few people come down later, about six, seven."

"Damn bar used to be jammed every Friday. You and three other guys were busy as whores on a Saturday night."

"Just yours truly now. So, Mr. L. how's the business? Designing any new hotels?"

"It's for shit, Ramon. No one wants glamour anymore. They want modern. They want concrete. Everything looks like a fucking prison. And they criticize me. They tell the world my work is gaudy kitsch! Who the fuck is Paul Rudolph anyway, mister big shot Yale architect with all his hammered concrete? I came from Russia, and all them new designs look like Stalin designed them. Well, fuck 'em!"

"Sorry to hear, Mr. L. I don't know why they say that. Look at this bar! It's a creation from God himself, and you designed it."

"Even that bitch from the New York Times, Huxtable, puts down my work. Says it reminds her of a bad gilded eggplant."

"Seriously?" Ramon said, cleaning wine glasses.

"I don't think I can go on much longer. Fucking AIA, they think I'm incompetent. Do you know they say my designs are vulgar and cheap? Hell, I've designed most of the hotels on this street. The Tortuga, the Bal Harbour, the Eden Beach, and don't forget the Sun Coast. And the tourists come in droves, don't they?"

"Not so much here anymore. I'm a little worried about my job. Another?"

"Sure, what the hell, it's Friday. Don't you worry, Ramon, they'll be back. This is the place. Always has been, always will be. What other hotel has a pool shaped like a dolphin?"

"I hope you're right, Mr. L., but I got a family to feed. I got an offer from that new hotel in South Beach, the El Dorado."

"Don't you leave me! You make the best dirty martinis. Listen, I'll talk to Stu Levine, he's the owner; we go way back."

"Mr. Lazarus, he sold the place back in 1970. It's owned by some big corporation now, the Global Hotel Group."

"Goddamn, I'm getting too old for this business!"

An elderly lady walked toward the bar. She had a pencil in her hair and did not look like a bar patron. It was Esther, Manny's secretary.

"Menachem, Menachem," she called out. The portly secretary gasped, out of breath from crossing the street and walking across the lobby.

"Jesus H. Christ, Esther, can I not have a cocktail in peace? It's Friday friggin' afternoon!' Lazarus gulped of his martini, preparing to leave the bar.

"Mr. L, there are four big Negro men at the office. They asked to see you. I told them you were busy. They said they'd wait. They're kind of scary, with their dark suits and sunglasses. I think you had better come."

"Did they say who they're with? Damn, Ramon and I are having a conversation here."

"The president of Haiti."

CHAPTER EIGHTEEN

"Bob Marlow."

The senior partner of Nolan & Marlow answered the phone expecting a returned call from an acoustical ceiling supplier he had contacted earlier in the afternoon.

"Bob, this is Connor West..."

"Connor! How the hell are you? And where are you?"

"Well, I'm in Valdosta right now at a Howard Johnson's Motor Lodge. Been driving all day and had to stop. It's raining cats and dogs outside."

"Valdosta? Where the hell is that and what are you doing there?"

"Georgia. I'm on my way back to Chicago as soon as I see my mom in New York."

"Back to Chicago... that's great. Did you see Marilyn?"

"Yes, I did. She said you two talked. You sent her to Key West to get me to come back. I guess your scheming worked. Do you still have a job for me?"

"You bet I do. Head of design, young man. Is Marilyn with you?

"Bob, she's dead."

There was no sound on the other side of the line.

"Bob?"

"Connor, the connection might not be too good. Did you say she's dead?"

"I did, sir, I did. She was on the plane that crashed off the Keys three days ago. We were just married."

Marlow held the phone away from him. His mind was swirling; he struggled to catch a breath. "Oh God, Connor, I'm so sorry."

"Thank you," was the only response Connor could muster.

"Did you say you had married?"

"Yes, a few days earlier. She was flying back to Chicago to tell her parents. Her original flight had mechanical problems, so she got on a small plane bound for Tampa with a connection to Chicago. The aircraft got caught in a terrible storm. Her body is being sent back to Illinois tomorrow. They had to do an au... autopsy." Connor's voice broke as tears ran down his face.

"Oh, God, it's my fault. I sent her to get you."

"Bob, it's not your fault. Thanks to you, we re-connected. The last three weeks have been the happiest of my life. I guess you know I have a son."

"Connor, I do. I still feel this was my fault. I'm so sorry."

"I wish she had driven back with me. But she was eager to let her parents know. Don't beat yourself up. I have wonderful memories. I keep telling myself she'll be in Chicago when I get there."

"Oh, Connor."

"She was proud I was coming back to work for you. An architect is all I ever wanted to be, and she knew that."

"Connor, take whatever time you need. God, Marilyn is de... gone. Oh, Jesus!"

"Bob, I have one question for you. When I come back, how's Francis, Jr. going to take my return? We didn't leave on good terms. I'm the one that stuffed the drawing of his shitty design in his mouth. He hates my guts."

"Let me handle him. He takes care of the business side and marketing, not the design side of things. You'll hardly see each other."

"Okay, fair enough. But talk to him. I don't want this to be a surprise. So what if I report for duty in a week, say November 17?"

"Sure, that will be fine. But, Connor, if you need more time..."

"I need to get back in the game. Find me a nice project to take my mind off of everything."

"Okay. The seventeenth. I'll have an office ready for you with a view of the lake."

"If it's all the same, I'd like to be in the big room, near you and close to Taubert and Caudy. Otherwise I'll spend all day looking out the window thinking about Marilyn."

"Right. You got it. How can I help? Maybe help you find an apartment?"

"Yeah, that would be great; thank you. Any high-rise with a view of Lincoln Park."

"They just finished a new building a block from me. It looks pretty nice from the outside. I'll check it out. Studio or one-bedroom?"

"I'm head of design; make it a one-bedroom with a den." Connor's tears had ceased and he nodded, focusing on his new future.

Bob Marlow hung up the phone. He stared out to the drafting hall, trying to process all the information Connor had conveyed. Sorrow gave way to guilt. First, he had not done enough to warn Marilyn about Vance Jefferson. Then he should have acted much more forcefully to keep him away from her. As a result, Jefferson raped her. Then he schemed to get Connor West back to Chicago by sending Marilyn to bring him back. And, as a result, she had died.

"My God, what have I done?" He got up, reached for his coat and left the office. The tightness in his neck was like the old days when booze solved any problem. Tonight he needed his AA meeting more than ever.

Connor was lucky. There was a parking space along West 26 Street, a short distance from his mother's apartment. He walked the block to the 21–story mid-rise, part of the six-building Chelsea-Elliot Homes development. He'd lived there until he ventured off to Harvard in 1971. Connor turned on the sidewalk that led to the public housing project. It was much nicer than he remembered.

In his youth, he hated being poor, despised his abusive and alcoholic father, and considered the building a tenement.

But it was not. They had moved into the building shortly after completion in 1964. Connor had gone to school with a black eye and other bruises. The night before he tried unsuccessfully to protect his mother from his father's drunken rage. There were inquiries from his high school guidance counselor, a Catholic brother. Connor broke down and told about being beaten by his father. With the brother's help and influence they moved to the new apartment. Then Connor joined the wrestling team.

In the eleven years since Connor had moved into the projects, the trees had grown and matured, and the small park in front of the building looked well-maintained. He had not called his mother; he wanted his visit to be a surprise. He entered the compact lobby, devoid of any furniture, and buzzed unit 1507. It was just after 5:00 P.M.; Connor hoped his mother would be at home, done with a day of cleaning some wealthy person's condominium uptown.

"Hello, who is it?"

"Mom, it's me, Connor."

"Connor?"

"Yes, Connor, your son."

The door buzzed. He was halfway to the elevator when the buzzing stopped. He smiled, hoping his mother would be happy and surprised to see him. She was, and more.

After Connor had related what happened in Key West, his tears and hard breaths of anguish stopped. He looked about the apartment where he and his mom had been safe. It was a small place, homey and tidy, and full of his mother's treasured porcelain figurines. Delicate cloth doilies covered the arms of chairs, tabletops, and even as a placemat for the television's rabbit ears. A crucifix hung above the entry door.

The aroma of the place was cedar and mothballs. It used to be his home; now it was his mother's, and she was at peace there. It was her refuge from the big city. The rooms were misty green, except the kitchen, white walls with white metal cabinets, and a white sink with a drainage board. It

97

amazed him at what wonderful dinners she made in such a small space.

"Connor, my son, I know how much you are hurting now. I'm so saddened that I'll never meet your Marilyn; she sounds wonderful. Wonderful in every way."

"Mom, how did you make it through all those years of hurt? I'm not sure how I'll be able to go on."

"You are young and strong and have no choice. Life goes on, and it is just beginning."

"Mom, I'm twenty-six..."

"A man, I know, but an entire life of adventure and success awaits you."

"I'm not sure I can."

"I have something to tell you I never told you before. You know your father was over fifty when you were born. I never thought I could have children; I was already forty-five, so you were a miracle. We didn't expect you, but you were the joy of my life. Especially since your father was, well, you know. What I never told you was that I married once before."

"You were married before Dad?"

"Yes, to the most wonderful, handsome, funny Irishman ever. I was only sixteen, a child, really. My husband, his name was Patrick Dewey, joined the army like most everyone to go fight in the Great War. We had three months together before he shipped out on the *Mauretania* to go to France. He was killed in the Argonne Forest. The love of my life, and I had such a short time to love him. Devastated, I never thought I would marry again. But ten years later, I was so lonely; worried I'd grow old without a husband I met your Dad at a church dance. He was a proud man, full of himself. He drank, but everyone did despite prohibition. We married. Soon after the stock market crashed, and well you know the rest."

"Mom, why didn't you tell me?"

"Our generation keeps a lot of things to ourselves, hidden deep in our heart, especially the things that cause sadness. And I hurt for ten years. Patrick was everything in my life and I lost him after just three months. But it was the most wonderful time of my life. I survived, and so will you."

"I don't know what to say..."

98

"You'll find someone else, someday. But make sure she is as fine as Marilyn. Don't settle, like I did."

"Mom, now it's my turn to tell you a secret. You have a grandson."

CHAPTER NINETEEN

"I'm Manny Lazarus. What can I do for you?"

"Mr. Lazarus. I am Dominique St. Jacques, Assistant Interior Minister of the government of Haiti. His excellency, President-for-Life, the esteemed Jean-Claude Duvalier sends his compliments and would like to meet with you."

"Meet with me? Why the hell does he want to meet with me?"

"He holds your talents, your architecture in the highest regard. You are familiar with the Duvalier family, are you not?"

"Goddamn, who isn't? But I think you got the wrong guy. I don't do business with dict... with a foreign country. I'm strictly an American architect."

"I assure you; you will want to make an exception in this case. A private plane is waiting at Opa-locka Airport. His excellency is expecting you."

"What? I ain't goin' nowhere today. Plus, it's sundown. It's the Sabbath."

"That didn't seem to concern you when you were at the Lobby Bar of the Versailles." The burly assistant minister towered over the diminutive Jew, the hint of a scowl developing on the Black man's face. He opened his coat, revealing the handle of a large revolver. "Monsieur Lazarus it would not be prudent to turn down this invitation. The president of Haiti is summoning you to Port-au-Prince."

"I'm not going anywhere tonight. Maybe tomorrow, understand Saint whoever you are?"

"Saint Jacques. If you insist, sir. We will take you to your residence in Miami Lakes, and we will depart in the morning. Consider this a holiday in beautiful Haiti."

"How the hell do you know where I live?"

"We know all about you."

"Excuse me?"

"Will nine o'clock be suitable?"

"Ah, sure, nine is fine."

"Pack a suitcase. Light clothing. It can be quite warm in Haiti, even in November. We will drive you home. One of our people will stay outside your house tonight, purely for your own protection."

Manny looked at his concerned secretary. "I hope I'll see you Monday, Esther."

The Lockheed Jet-Star did a wide arc above Francois Duvalier Airport. The small, well-appointed jet with the Haitian coat of arms on its tail—a palm tree, six flags, six rifles with bayonets and two cannon, in bright red, blue and green with the motto *L'Union Fait La Force*, "Union Makes Strength" bespoke a larger, wealthier nation.

The view below startled Manny Lazarus. There were few tall buildings. The city looked like a great slum, wooden and cardboard huts everywhere, smoke from scattered wood cooking fires rising. He saw the imposing presidential palace, brilliantly white in the morning light. It was the exception.

What the hell have I gotten myself into? Manny thought, as he stared out the window at what looked like a third world afterthought. Across the small aisle, the hulk of the Assistant Interior Minister sat stoically, Ray-Ban sunglasses covering his eyes for the entire trip. In the front row, two of the other "emissaries" spoke a strange form of French; the last man sat in the back, an Uzi sub-machine gun upon his lap.

The landing was smooth. Once they completed a short taxi to an area away from the main terminal, Manny followed St. Jacques through the cabin door and headed down the small set of stairs. The sun blinded his deteriorating eyes. As he focused them as best he could, he made out a stretch Lincoln Town Car on the tarmac. It displayed flags of Haiti and the USA above the front headlights. He took solace that it was a big American car with a beautiful American flag. He walked past the four large Haitians, still wearing their Ray-Bans and stepped into the limousine, the door held open by another large man.

The drive to the Presidential Palace was a brief fifteen minutes during which Lazarus' questions to his host went unanswered except for the response, "You will know shortly, Mr. Lazarus."

❖

The Grand Foyer of the Presidential Palace did not particularly impress Manny Lazarus. Designed in 1912, the neo-classical building was the second-place winner in a competition for a new national palace. The foyer's design resonated with that also-ran history. The palace was begun in 1915, after the occupying American army suppressed yet another revolt whereupon the president of Haiti was assassinated. The grand edifice was completed in 1920, the construction supervised by U.S. Naval engineers.

Manny thought the space too large and poorly proportioned, though the dome was imposing. Flanking the foyer were two grand staircases, the scale not unlike his singular grand staircase to nowhere at the Versailles-sur-Mer. Between the stairs was a large and imposing portrait of Toussaint Louverture, Haiti's revolutionary leader who led the slave revolt for Haitian independence against France.

"If you will follow me, Monsieur Lazarus, the president is expecting us." St. Jacques led the way up the grand staircase; Manny winded by the time they reached the second floor. "Do you need a moment, monsieur?"

"No, I'm fine, lead the way." Manny wiped his forehead and looked down the long hallway. Interspersed between potted palm trees were soldiers in blue uniforms. They were milling about, smoking, and laughing. Once they noticed the retinue led by the assistant minister they quickly stood at attention and received his disapproving stare. At the end of the gallery was a pair of carved mahogany doors. St. Jacques opened one.

"Please, monsieur..."

Jean-Claude Duvalier looked up from papers on his desk when the door opened and stood up.

"Your Excellency, may I present Mr. Lazarus from Miami."

Duvalier got up from behind his desk and moved toward a model of an island, set up in a vacant area of the imposing forty-foot square president's office. "Mr. Lazarus, thank you for coming."

"I'm not sure I had a choice in the matter."

"It is my singular pleasure to meet such a great architect."

"Thank you. And it's nice to meet you too, Mr. President. Why am I here?"

St. Jacques outstretched his hand toward the model, and Lazarus followed. He walked up to the round president and shook his hand. It was like shaking a dead fish.

"May I get you some refreshment?"

"Water would be nice, thank you."

Duvalier nodded to an aide, who left the room.

"I'd like to discuss a business proposition with you. I admire your work greatly. I have stayed at the Versailles-sur-Mer many times. You are a genius of architecture."

Flattered by the additional compliment, Lazarus smiled.

"I'm hardly that but thank you."

"Is this your first time in my country, Mr. Lazarus?"

"Ah, yes, it is."

"Why have you not visited before?"

"Just never had the time, I guess. Too busy, and most of my work is in Miami."

"We have beautiful weather, beaches, mountains..."

"I'm kind of a workaholic, Mr. President."

"Let's be frank, Mr. Lazarus."

"Manny, please."

"Thank you, Manny, the reason you did not come is because of what you read in the American papers about the state of my country, about my father, and perhaps even me."

"Yeah, I know, but the papers, they exaggerate."

"In our case, I'm not so sure. But I want to change whatever perceptions they may have. Before my father came to power, tourists flocked here. I want that to be the case again. This model in front of you is a small island off the coast of Haiti. It is called the Île-à-Vache. The pirate Henry Morgan used the island as a base for his pirating operations. It has beautiful white sand beaches, flat land for an airport runway, reasonably close to Port-Au-Prince by boat, and of course, that pirate history. Tourists love pirates, yes?"

Lazarus nodded. Now he understood. "I suppose so. They like fantasy. I've always said that there is more to a hotel than just a bed."

"Indeed, but that is certainly a pre-requisite to everything else."

Manny tried to size up the boy-president. If this meeting headed where he believed it would, the president of Haiti was in way over his head, building a hotel on a deserted island. He walked around the model. The island was small, eight miles long by two miles wide. There appeared to be two small towns. The northwestern end of the island possessed a lovely sand beach. "And you want to do what on this island? Build a hotel?"

"No. I intend to build the finest resort in the Caribbean. At least three hotels initially totaling 1,000 rooms in several properties, a world-class casino, a convention center, several 3 star Michelin restaurants, and perhaps even a few swimming pools shaped like dolphins."

Manny whistled. "As we Jews like to say, you got chutzpah, Mr. President!"

"After the bad press of the last thirteen years, we cannot do anything less."

"Pardon my saying so, but the press ain't been too kind to you either, the last four years."

"I was not in charge."

"That's not what I read. You're president for life."

"I was, as you Americans like to say it, 'sowing my wild oats.' My mother ran the country and followed my father's policies. I am going to change that. Even now we are discussing substantial loans from your government. My ambassador tells me that Mr. Ford intends to grant them."

"Mr. President, where do I fit into all this, although I think I know the answer?"

"I would like you to design *Paradi sou Latè.*"

"Care to translate?"

"*Paradise on Earth,* my friend."

"I'm not your friend, sir, no disrespect. And I grew up in Russia. Frankly, I don't do business with dictators."

"Monsieur Lazarus, I would like to be your friend. You have my deep respect for your talent, though your fellow countrymen in the profession do not share that. Please explain the word 'kitsch' to me. And, I am not a dictator. My people duly elected me in the last election. Overwhelmingly, I might add."

"Yeah, I read about that, too. You got 99% of the vote."

"A landslide. So what? Let's cut to the chase, shall we? I would like you to design my resort—all of it. You will have full design control, no committees to deal with for approval. If I approve, it is done. Name your fee."

Manny's head was spinning at the offer. "Name my fee?"

"With one condition."

"Oh, the one small condition. And that would be?"

"It must be unique, grand, and a little outrageous. Maybe we could include an aquarium that people can walk through? And since you did the staircase to nowhere and the dolphin pool, amaze me with something else. I want the world to notice so it must be, as you say, over-the-top."

"Name my fee?"

"Yes, but within reason. I do have to answer to the legislature."

"I'm sure. The budget?"

"None, but there are expectations. If this resort does not resurrect Haiti as a vacation destination, it will most displease me. And it will displease others as well."

"And... you'll stiff me on my last payment."

"You will be stiff I can assure you, one way or the other."

"I want twelve percent of the cost."

"Monsieur, your typical fee is what, seven, eight percent."

"Maybe in Miami. Here, on this island, it's gonna be twelve."

"I'll pay you ten percent to be my architect. Of everything."

"Well, Mr. President, then I guess I am your new friend. I believe we have a deal."

CHAPTER TWENTY

Bob Marlow perused a set of drawings in his office, flipping back and forth through the same sheets. He was procrastinating. He didn't look forward to telling Francis Nolan, Jr., now calling himself "Danny," about his new hire.

His partner despised Connor West, not only because he had once stuffed a ball of bumwad, or tracing paper, into his mouth, but because Connor was so talented. He had designed Chicago World Tower over a weekend. Francis had spent three weeks designing a piece of mediocrity. Then the client picked Connor's design. Of course, it was over budget. Elliptical walls, outside elevators, and a rotating restaurant at the top. A world-class design. And the developer had Francis despoil it to save a few bucks.

In Nolan's hands, it became another piece of pedestrian architecture. Thank God, the new developer had torn down the project and started over with Connor's original design. The resentment lingered. But if Nolan & Marlow were going to compete with the new hotshots in Chicago, they needed a singularly gifted architect. And his name was Connor Jones West.

"Hey Danny, got a minute?"

"What's up, Marlow?"

"Got a new guy coming on board. Going to head up design for the firm."

"Really. What about Taubert and Caudy?"

"Good. Not great. We need better."

"I'm all ears."

"Connor's coming back." Marlow looked at Nolan for a reaction; he got one.

"West? Connor West is coming back?" Danny Nolan dropped the papers he was re-arranging and began to pay attention.

"We need his talent."

"The fuck we do! Last I heard he was fishing in Key West."

"If your girlfr...sorry, if Vance raped your friend, what would you do?"

"No, not West. Anybody but him!"

"Danny, you've got to get past your differences with Connor."

"He doesn't deserve the position. He takes a nine-month vacation, and decides he wants to get a real job again." Daniel Nolan's face flushed with rising anger.

"You'll have no interaction with him. You're not in the design department now. Just bring us some new commissions, and we'll take care of the rest." Marlow knew this would be a tough sell, but didn't think it would be this tough.

"You don't get it, do you?" Nolan stared hard at Marlow.

"Yeah, I get it. He humiliated you, stuffing that bumwad in your mouth. Get over it."

"That's not it. His presence here would remind me every day of what a piss-poor designer I am!"

"Was. Your father forced you to become an architect. It wasn't your fault. You're a business guy and you're doing a great job at that"

Nolan turned and looked out the window to Lake Michigan and sighed. "Why wasn't I consulted? We are partners after all."

"You're right. I'm sorry about that. I found Marilyn Jones at her home in Oak Park, convinced to go and find Connor and get him to come back, which she did. She died in that plane crash in the Keys."

"Jesus, Bob. I didn't know."

"So, cut Connor some slack, okay? It's a done deal."

"Alright, I'll try to find him some new projects to design so he can amaze us with his great talent." The sarcasm hung in the air.

"Thanks, Danny." Marlow turned and left the large office, not sure if Nolan had bought into the new head of design. As he returned to the large drafting room, he spotted Taubert and Caudy. He hadn't broken the news to his two designers about West's return. Marlow shook his head.

CHAPTER TWENTY-ONE

Connor West fidgeted in a pew next to Sarah and Paul Jones inside the majestic English Gothic edifice that was St. Edmund's Catholic Church in Oak Park, Illinois. In the center aisle in front of the main altar of white marble, flanked by priceless stained-glass windows handmade in Munich, was the polished walnut casket that held the remains of Marilyn Jones West. Connor gazed around the sanctuary appreciating the workmanship, if not the out-of-place 18th Century European architecture in the heartland of America. But, despite trying to think about craftsmanship and design, he always returned his gaze to the casket of the love of his life, his spouse, his everything, Marilyn. He looked again and again at his watch. The Mass of the Resurrection was to start in ten minutes, an eternity.

The day had not started well, not any better than his visit to Oak Park several days earlier. Then, Paul Jones was cordial but cool. He didn't know how to respond when Connor had told them he and Marilyn had married. Sarah seemed to accept it and felt more empathy for Connor because of it. Paul, however, spoke as if he was holding back rage, a desire to blame Connor for his only daughter's death. Connor tried to explain that it was her decision. Marilyn wanted to return as quickly as possible to tell them the news. The words had little effect.

That morning at the house in Oak Park, before they left for the church, Paul Jones asked Connor if he expected to get Marilyn's life insurance proceeds. Sarah rebuked him, saying it was neither the time nor the place for such a discussion. Connor said he didn't care about any money. He only wanted to know how he could find their son, Kevin. Paul Jones told him to forget about the child, but when he was out of the room, Sarah Jones gave Connor a note, with the address of St. Margaret's Home for Women in Eau Claire, Wisconsin. Connor and Sarah talked in hushed voices, Connor wanting to know if Sarah had the name and address of the couple in St. Paul that had adopted his son. She did not.

The organ played the *Ave Maria*. From the rear of the church, the pastor, Father Kelly, walked slowly toward the casket, covered with a large spray of white roses. Two altar servers followed him, one carrying a bowl of holy water and an aspergillum. He took the implement and circled the casket, sprinkling the blessed water.

Later, at the cemetery, as they lowered Marilyn into the ground, Connor walked off to a nearby tree. Knees crumpling, he broke down wailing, deep cries emanating from his shattered body. Paul Jones got up and walked over to him.

"Act like a man, son. Show some spine."

"Go to hell." Connor turned and walked toward the limousine.

The wake was painful. The white colonial house in Oak Park filled with well-wishers, none of whom Connor knew. Each stranger who came up to him and said "I'm so sorry for your loss," seemed to make the loss worse.

At times he heard laughter. There was a dining room table full of sandwiches, potato salad, ice tea, pies, cookies, and cakes. It sounded and looked like a garden party.

Connor went into the sunroom and stared at the bar. If only he could choose anything from that counter to take the pain away. As he wandered back to the living room, he noticed photos on the mantle of Marilyn, from childhood to just last year, before the rape. His heart was pierced by each image. Connor felt sick and dashed to the bathroom, shut the door. Turning on the faucet, he threw water on his face, and the nausea subsided. As he exited, Paul Jones was in the hallway. They passed each other, no words spoken.

There were more comforting wishes from the guests, but they did little to ease the pain or sorrow. It all reminded him of his father's funeral, his mother not knowing what to say to the many well-wishers who were distant friends of his unhappy drunk of a father.

Connor went out to the small backyard for some fresh air and sun. Sarah Jones was there. She walked up to him, put her arms around him and hugged him. "I'm so sorry about the graveside. Paul hasn't been himself since the... you know."

"He blamed me for the rape, and now he blames me for her death. Doesn't he see how much I hurt as well?"

"He doesn't want to share the hurt with anyone. I'm afraid it will be a cancer that will destroy us."

"Mrs. Jones, I've got to go. Thank you for everything. I'll be in touch."

Sarah kissed Connor on the cheek, and he turned toward the front door.

Gladys, a next-door neighbor was at Sarah's side. "He's such a handsome young man. And already so successful. It's all such a tragedy." She hoped the words would comfort her friend.

"You have no idea, my dear. You have no idea."

Two months later Sarah Jones, against every instinct of her lifelong Catholic faith, filed for divorce from Paul Jones.

Connor drove back to the lake and parked in the multi-level garage of Bob Marlow's apartment building. He was sleeping on the couch until he could find an apartment. It was nearly 5 P.M. and the darkness enveloped the city.

"Fuck it!" Connor changed into jeans and a sweatshirt, put on sneakers and a winter jacket borrowed from his host, and left. The walk to the lake was maybe ten minutes, fifteen adding the detour to North Avenue Liquors. A brown paper bag in hand, cradling a fifth of Jim Beam, he made his way to the North Avenue Beach and found an empty park bench. He had no company; it was late November and cold. A slight wind brushed his face and he wished he had brought his Cubs baseball cap. Connor set the bag down and stared out into the blackness. The lights of one of several water intake stations and that of a freighter far out in Lake Michigan were the only interruptions to the dark night.

Connor remembered his mother's words: "You are young and strong and have no choice. Life goes on, and it is just beginning." At that moment, he didn't think that was possible. The day had been one of remembrance, heartache, and conflict. There were too many emotions for any sane person to deal with in the time frame that is a single day.

More lights appeared on the horizon—another freighter bound for Cleveland, Detroit or Montreal. Each light a small flicker of hope in the night's darkness. West reached for the brown bag, lifted out its contents and stared at it. He cried, soft tears, what few tears remained. Opening the bottle, he sniffed the contents, lifted it high, and then brought it to his lips.

"One night Marilyn, okay, just this one night. A toast to us." Connor took a drink, and then another, set the bottle down, and finally took one more. He looked out at the lake. The ships had disappeared. Only the light of the intake shed shone. Then it too disappeared, perhaps hidden by a cloud.

CHAPTER TWENTY-TWO

Rat Tomlinson inflated the rubber dingy that he kept on board *Daddy's Money*, a requirement of the Coast Guard. He pulled out a small outboard motor from the engine area, pushed the boat over the side and guided it back to the stern. He balanced the five-HP motor on the gun-whale and climbed into the small craft. Five minutes later he was motoring out of the marina, into the open water, and toward Cow Key Channel. On A1A, once you crossed the small bridge over the channel, you were officially in Key West, the last coral reef in the Keys. It was the end of the Americas. For many, it was just the end.

The dingy made its way toward House Boat Row, a group of thirty or so floating "residences" permanently moored in the channel that widened considerably at the actual spit of land called Cow Key. About half were docked alongside busy Roosevelt Avenue. Though it was almost nine o'clock, Rat knew his way in the dark, motoring slowly and sipping on a Red Stripe. The lights of the channel markers, green and red, aided him in his short journey, one he had made innumerable times since arriving in Key West. He had invited Connor West to join him on more than one occasion, but Connor demurred, saying he preferred to keep what little money he had in a bank, not on a card table.

Every Wednesday night there was a high stakes poker game on board *The Pirate of Penzance,* one of the few boats not accessible by a gangplank to the breakwater and land. The floating, immobile vessel painted green and deep blue blended in with the surrounding water, long and one-story, featuring black shutters. Its owner was Mike "Seadog" Fineran, a former Navy Seal at the Naval Air Station. All the best poker players in town attended, Seadog being an excellent host. He could afford to be. For 2% of the high stakes winnings at two tables he provided cold beer, hot wings, and the best booze. More than that, he provided discretion. For a few of the patrons who arrived by cab, there was a rowboat at the ready, powered by Fineran's mountainous biceps.

Tomlinson choked the small motor, and it went dead. He glided the craft to the rear of the houseboat where there was a large deck, complete with hammock, outdoor grille, and a table for four. Gingerly walking to the front of the dingy, he grabbed the railing, tied up and was quickly inside the main lounge of the comfortable floating abode. The walls were cheap mahogany paneling, festooned with nautical memorabilia, small colorful buoys, and framed illustrations of WWII planes and battleships. There were mermaid lamps on tables and wall lanterns that looked like channel lights. The place looked like Long John Silver was the interior decorator, but somehow it all worked and felt like the exclusive men's retreat that it was. In the center were two poker tables modeled after the one Navy carpenter's had built in 1947 for Harry S. Truman. The top was green felt and around the perimeter were wells for drinks, poker chips, and brass ashtrays for cigars.

"Rat, good to see ya. How's the charter business?"

"Slow, Councilman, slow."

"Aye, it's November. Maybe your luck will change tonight and get you enough cash to get through the winter doldrums."

Rat nodded, looking toward the open bar. "I hope so. I can't keep losing money like I have the last four weeks." The number returned to his memory, despite efforts to forget. Exactly $31,750.00. At that rate, Richard Tomlinson would exhaust his trust fund in weeks. "I think I'll get a drink. Councilman?"

"Richie, please call me Pat. I'm fine; I just poured me another Jameson."

The young charter captain reached for a bottle of rum, poured three fingers, added ice, and checked the bulge in his front pocket. There was $10,000, all Benjamin's. Withdrawing that amount earlier in the day left him with a balance of $597.34, barely enough to buy fuel and groceries, much less pay the monthly dock-slip fees. He took a deep breath. *This better be the night, Tomlinson,* he thought.

❖

"Two pair." Rat looked up from his cards, trying to detect emotion from Cicero Jackson, a large bald-headed Black fellow across from him, tat sleeves on both arms, one with the initials USMC, and a single gold hoop earring. It was rumored that he owned several of the most prosperous bars on Duval Street and a whorehouse on Petronia.

Rat and Cicero were the only ones left holding cards, the other four players folded. Rat had asked for two cards, hoping for a full house, but only drew a second seven. Still, it was a solid hand. In the center of the table was three thousand of his needed cash, the pot totaling over five grand. He stared at Cicero thinking, *"Jesus, aren't there any normal-looking people on this island?"*

"Full house, my brother, full house." Cicero smiled, showing off a solid gold front tooth.

"Shit." Tomlinson downed his third rum, looked down between his knees, and counted his remaining cash under the table. The thick wad had grown desperately thin. Six hundred left.

Seadog came over to the table. "How are we doing, gentlemen? Captain Tomlinson, I see your luck still hasn't turned."

"Unfortunately not."

"The house will spot you one last round if you don't have enough betting cash to get you through a good hand. But you need to borrow it upfront, not after you've drawn the cards."

Rat looked at his watch. 2:17 A.M. "Sure, why not. One last hand..."

"How much?"

"Two thousand."

"I'll get it out of the safe. Pat, I think it's your turn to deal. And Rat, the vig is ten percent per week."

"Understood." Rat got up and headed to the bar. His head was numb, and he wanted a beer. One thing about

116

poker, you didn't have to be very sober to play. Either lady luck gave you the cards, or she didn't. You just had to remain stoic. He reached for a beer in the cooler and felt a presence standing next to him. Beer in hand, Rat righted himself and turned. It was a new player, one he had noticed earlier who was at the other table. He looked Latin, with a hard brown face, scar on the chin and slicked-back hair. He wore a guayabera shirt, several buttons undone. Around his neck was a silver chain from which hung a doubloon, a black tuna design the center.

"Tough night, huh?"

"You can say that. It'll turn on this next hand. I know it."

"The man, Seadog, says you're good at cards. Just a rough patch. I'm Carlos, by the way."

"Rich. Rich Tomlinson, but everyone calls me Rat."

"Let me know if you ever need help, Rat."

"What kind of help?" Rich looked at Carlos, sizing him up. The vibe wasn't good.

"Financial. What other kind is there?"

"Thanks, I'm fine."

"Trust fund kid, huh?"

Rich stared at Carlos without emotion and went back to the poker table; Pat was dealing the cards.

Rat's head was pounding as he guided the small dingy back to the marina at 3:30. His pockets were empty, and he owed the house two thousand dollars. Two thousand two hundred dollars by next Wednesday, to be exact. He thought the last hand was golden—a flush, all spades. He bet everything. Only a grizzled fishing boat captain known as Captain Jack stayed in the game. His face faintly showed disappointment when Rat called, the pot at $5,200. Rat smiled as he laid out his hand, but as Jack placed down four-of-a-kind, all three's, Rat's face turned ashen. *Beat by a bunch of fucking threes!* he thought.

A distance behind him, a small skiff followed. He wasn't worried about being robbed; he had nothing. But he was wary and throttled the small engine for all it could muster. He wanted his bed on *Daddy's Money*. Tomorrow he'd call his father.

❖

The small skiff negotiated Cow Channel, one running light on the bow.

"He's ripe for pickin', I think." Carlos took a drag on his Salem and exhaled a billow of smoke.

"Don't be so sure. Kid's got money, but I figured you needed to get to know him. Never can tell."

"Sooner or later, he'll be in deep shit when daddy cuts him off. Then we'll become best friends."

"I tell you what. He musta got some kinda trust fund. Had a brand-new Hatteras 45 Convertible when he got here in '73 from Miami. I think he's from Boston or New York. Good kid really. Just in over his head." Cicero took a swig from a quart of milk and steered the boat past the City Marina, headed for Old Town.

"That boat's what we need. Coast Guard will never suspect its running product."

"Do me a favor?" Cicero's voice was earnest.

"Sure." Carlos threw his cigarette into the black water.

"Don't hurt the kid."

"No intention, but you never know."

CHAPTER TWENTY-THREE

Manny Lazarus sat at his drafting table perusing the most recent issue of *Architectural Record*. A steaming cup of hot coffee in a monogrammed mug from the gift shop at the Versailles-sur-Mer occupied his free hand. He couldn't believe his good fortune. One day, his firm is on the ropes, with no new commissions in months. No one wanted "glitter" architecture as Ada Louise Huxtable, the design critic of the New York Times, had recently described his last project. The Tropicana, one of his best efforts, was rising in nearby Fort Lauderdale. He had finished drawing that project a year ago.

Since then, his only work had been a couple of fast-food restaurants for a new company, Roy Rogers's Roast Beef that was trying to compete with McDonald's. Good luck with that. All he had to do was put their pre-determined building design on a vacant lot. He thought the interiors were boring, but they told him it was the approved corporate look. Manny thought he could improve on the staid interiors by mimicking Roy's brightly colored, rhinestone tasseled shirts. Corporate wasn't interested.

But at that moment he couldn't believe his good fortune. He had just landed the biggest commission of his life. A $150 million dollar resort, if not more. A ten percent fee— $15,000,000! With that kind of jack, he could design and build a retirement mansion in Boca. So what if the client was a banana republic dictator, son of one of the most ruthless tyrants ever to rule in the Americas? His father had been a virtuoso violinist who hated the Czar. Still, he would play for Nicholas II at the Winter Palace if there were a couple of rubles to be made.

But there was a problem. Manny looked around the small drafting room. Lenny Berger, son of his late partner, was trying to get thirty parking spaces to fit on a small lot in Aventura around a Roy Rogers—more spaces than they would ever need. Seated in a small cubicle in the corner of the room, Sid Swearoff was writing specifications. He was good at it, having done nothing else for thirty years, and Manny rented out his services. How was he going to handle a job this large with a green kid and an old spec. writer? And then there was the contract.

"Esther, get me Stu Cohen on the phone..."

There was no response from the small lobby where Esther held court. She was the receptionist, secretary, business manager, and gal Friday, and had worked for Manny going on twenty years. Manny got up and walked to the open door that led to the tired reception space, adorned with fading renderings of his greatest accomplishments and a couple of sparkly lime green Naugahyde chairs he had owned since the Versailles opened. They were samples provided by the salesman who let Manny keep them after securing an order for 100 of the tasteful seats for the casual restaurant at the hotel.

Manny walked into the door jamb. "Dammit, who moved the door?"

Esther looked up. "Good God, Mr. L. that doorway has been there forever. I told you to have your eyesight checked. Last week you walked into my desk."

Manny wouldn't admit it, but his eyes were losing their battle with cataracts. The world was closing in on him, slowly, inexorably, and without remorse. How was he going to design Baby Doc's great resort half-blind?

"Get me Stu Cohen, Esther. And don't worry about my eyesight. It's fine."

"Menachem, this new project is too much for you. It'll give you ulcers. And your blood pressure's already high. Ruth told me all about it. 150 over 103. Did you take your pill today?"

"Yes I took the Goddamn pill. You let me worry about the new project." He turned, stopped, took a step to the left, centering himself in the doorway, and went back to the drafting table.

Esther was right. He had no business undertaking such a large commission. Maybe back in the fifties when the office hummed with thirty draftsmen, a couple of hot interior designers who he messed around with on the side, and of course, Sid the spec. writer, who even had an assistant. There was a model shop, and a full-time artist on staff to churn out renderings of his eccentric, over-the-top building designs. It wasn't bad architecture; the buildings were simply ahead of their time.

"Stu's on line one," Esther called out. She didn't like to use the intercom on the phone.

Of course he is. There's no one else on the phone, Manny thought, as he picked up the receiver to speak with his old friend and counselor of seventeen years.

"Stu, how they hangin'?"

"Manny, I'm fine. Haven't heard from you since Castro became a communist."

"Has it been that long?"

"I think so. You keep using the same contract over and over again; the one I did for you in 1959. That's a lot of Wite-out."

"Nah, your lyin'. I needed you two years ago for the Tropicana contract. Some big hotel group was behind it. I couldn't understand their fucking legalese."

"How's Ruth? Esther sounded perky..."

"She's fine. Got the Hadassah and her bridge club." Manny, slightly irritated, was ready to get down to business, and Stu accommodated.

"So, to what do I owe the pleasure, my friend?"

"Ever heard of the Duvalier's?"

"The Duvalier's, as in the Haiti Duvalier's?"

"Yeah, them." Manny could tell his lawyer's interest was piqued by the sound of his voice.

"Manny, you think I live under a fuckin' rock? Of course, I know them. Why?" Scenarios raced across Cohen's quick mind. *Why's my friend asking about the Duvalier's?*

"Stu, I got some news. You won't believe it. Jean-Claude, you know, Baby Doc, just hired Lazarus and Berger to

121

design a world-class resort on an island off Hispaniola. It's a giant commission."

"No shit! And how you gonna do that? Like the other Lazarus, resurrect Bernie Berger from the dead?"

"Not funny Stu, God rest Bernie's soul. I'll figure out a way. But I need you to draw up the contract. Iron clad. I don't want to get schtuped by this tin-horn dictator."

"He'll probably kill you before he screws you. What's the fee?"

"Ten percent of the cost of the project. I figure with the hotels, casino, conference center, amenities, we're looking at one-hundred-fifty mil."

"Fuck, Manny. That's fifteen million dollars!"

"Geez, you're a Goddamn accountant now!" Manny knew that Stu's accurate math would end up as a big invoice for a simple contract. If Stu knew one thing, it was how to draw up "screw you" contracts. He could probably do it in an hour and charge Lazarus fifty K for the effort.

"I'll get right on it. One thing. Did you meet his excellency?"

"I did. They flew me down in their jet. Met him at the palace. He said he admired my work. End of story. No conditions except one or two."

"Oh, and what is that?"

"He wants an aquarium, and a pool shaped like a fish. And..."

"And what?" Stu said as he wrote on his legal pad: *Fee $60 large!*

"He wants it to be gaudy, over-the-top."

"Mazal tov, my friend! At that, you have no equal. We'll talk." Stu Cohen hung up the phone. He'd grab an early lunch at Joe's Stone Crab, have a couple of Old Fashions, and get back to begin work on the iron-clad covenant for the architect to the stars, Manny Lazarus.

Manny smiled as he looked at the dead receiver. *Son-of-a-bitch can't wait to bill me! Fifty grand, so what? I'm rich.* He flipped through the *Architectural Record*, a monthly publication of what's-what in the profession, full of color photos of the latest ground-breaking projects. As he turned the pages, his thoughts returned to the problem of producing construction documents that would encompass hundreds, if not thousands, of sheets of drawings. As the pages dimmed around the edges of the periodical, he thought of the grandiose project that had to be designed with his failing eyesight, and the arthritis that burned his hands with small bolts of lightening in his fingers. The pages turned. Then Manny stopped. He took a deep breath.

"Shit!" He stared at the color illustration covering almost the entire page, and the headline above it:

Chicago World Tower Resumes Construction

Manny consumed the article, looked at the rendering again, took a deep breath, and re-read the story.

"Esther, get me the number of Nolan & Marlow Architects, in Chicago."

CHAPTER TWENTY-FOUR

Connor and Bob Marlow stood on the balcony of the model unit of Lincoln Towers on North Clark Street. The building was brand new, and on this Friday afternoon the Sales Center was busy, as agents signed up tenants for the desirable new high-rise whose front yard was Lincoln Park with Lake Michigan beyond.

"A guy could get used to this," West said, impressed by the uninterrupted expanse of land and water in front of him. The day was typical for Chicago in the fall, chilly with a hearty breeze coming in from the lake. He zippered up his new Eddie Bauer jacket and pulled the collar up. "I guess my blood is a little thin after a year in a tropical climate."

"Then you better get inside and get signed up. These apartments are going like hotcakes." Marlow didn't mind the cold or the wind. He had spent his life in Chicago, except for the five months of rehab at the New Day Clinic in Boca Raton a year earlier. The following week, on Sunday, would be his one-year anniversary of sobriety; he never thought he would make it this long and took pride in the accomplishment. Only nine more days. He was planning on spending the day with his two boys and taking them to a Bears game at Soldier Field, followed by dinner somewhere on Rush Street. The boys were getting older and wanted to see what Chicago nightlife was like.

"Yeah, I suppose, but I'm a little nervous. This is way better than my dump in Key West, but a lot more money. Imagine $550 a month for a one-bedroom apartment."

"One bedroom and a den on the fifteenth floor, Sport. And a balcony like this. I think you deserve it." Marlow hoped Connor would take the apartment, if for no other reason than to ease his conscience over the death of Marilyn. And he wanted to see Connor happy, as he was before... everything.

Earlier in the day, over lunch at P.J. Clarke's, Marlow was pleased to see Connor's reaction to the latest issue of *Architectural Record*, which featured Chicago World Tower in its original manifestation. It was a full-page spread, and in the lower left-hand corner, it duly noted Connor Jones West as the project's principal designer. Seeing the article gave the young head of design such great satisfaction that Bob thought he detected a tear or two well up in his eyes.

"Get the apartment, Connor. Make this a red-letter day for you. There are so few of those in life."

Connor stared out at the lake, saying nothing, finally his gaze turning right toward Sandburg Village. He bowed his head and his eyes closed. "If it's all the same to you, Bob, I think I need a change of scenery. Too many memories around here. Maybe I'll look for an apartment tomorrow on the Southside by the Museum of Science and Industry."

"Hyde Park is nice, but kind of quiet for a single guy. There's no Rush Street." Marlow thought the popular North side destination with its singles bars and nightclubs would be more to the young man's taste.

"I'm not supposed to drink anymore, remember? Why tempt myself?"

"That's right. I told you the new job came with that condition. Good for you. How many days is it?" Marlow had not asked Connor about his bouts with the bottle but imagined they had not developed to the level of the battles he had fought.

"Let's see, fifty-four before last night."

"Oh, the funeral. Tough, huh?"

"Beyond tough. Excruciatingly painful."

"I guess you deserve a pass on that one. But don't make it a habit. Anyway, congratulations are in order. Almost two months."

"It hasn't been as bad as I thought it would be."

Marlow thought about Hyde Park. "You know Steel Simpson developed an apartment tower down there," referring to the dirtbag developer who had hired the firm to design Chicago World Tower. He was in prison now, serving a hard seven-to-ten for manslaughter. The site of the building contained a homeless encampment. Simpson had his errand boy driver, Lothar Jensen set it on fire one night. Two of the residents died, burned to death. It took two years of dogged police work by the Arson Unit to nail Simpson for the malfeasance.

"Really?"

"I heard it didn't do very well. Ahead of its time. Check it out. I think it's on South Shore Drive."

"Great. I will." Connor was eager for Saturday to come; he wanted to get settled in Chicago for the second time and make a fresh start. "I gotta go, Bob. I think I'll check out some furniture stores; I don't want to sleep on the floor in my new digs."

"I'll see you back at the apartment at, what, five, six? We'll grab some dinner. My treat. For the article in *Record*."

Will Taubert stood at the door of Francis Nolan's office. He knocked gently.

"Taubert, what's up?" Francis, aka Danny Nolan, looked up from the accounts payable report, delivered every Monday morning by Norman Weese, the firm's bookkeeper. Despite his rosy reports to Bob Marlow, who disliked the business side of the architectural profession, the firm was in trouble. Deep trouble. Francis had secured a lot of commissions but at low-ball fees. A firm the size of Nolan & Marlow paid top-dollar rent for three full floors of the Santa Fe Building on Michigan Avenue. They maintained a structural, mechanical and an electrical department, as well as an interior design group; it went through money like shit through a goose. The overhead was killing the operation. Every week more and more of the bills moved into the ninety-day column. Pleas to Asa Morton, the firm's banker at First National Bank, went unanswered. Though the firm had a two-million-dollar line of credit, Morton rebuffed pleas from Danny to give him more than half that. The firm's financials were a mess.

"To be frank, I'm pissed. Connor West is back, which is fine, but Marlow made him head of design. I thought I was head of design. What the fuck's going on, pardon my French?"

"Taubert, I had nothing to do with that. I was against it. But Marlow told me it was a done deal, and truthfully, it's his call. As far as I'm concerned, you're still the head of design and always will be."

"It's not fair. He takes a one-year sabbatical on a fishing boat because his ego is bruised, while I'm here busting my ass, and he comes back with a big promotion."

"I feel your pain, Will. I told Bob I was against it. He thinks we need to up our game. Our game is just fine. We just need bigger fees."

"So, that's it. I just have to suck it up?"

"Let me pull in a few more jobs. Then I'll propose two separate design groups, one under West, one under you. In due time, I know you'll outshine him."

"Thanks, Dan. I guess that's something."

"Will, you're my guy. I got your back." Nolan picked up the phone; the discussion was over. Taubert turned and headed for the drafting room. He needed to welcome Connor back. Marlow told him to accept the new arrangement. He wasn't sure he could.

"Norman, this is Danny. Do you have any connections with banks other than First National?"

When Connor walked into the large hall, full of drawing tables, drafting lamps and parallel bars, the fifty employees there rose and applauded. Most had heard about Marilyn Jones' tragic death, and that alone garnered the showing of support. But most realized that things were about to change for the better. The level of design and creativity would go up a notch, maybe several notches. Bob Marlow watched from his office and realized he had made the right decision. He looked toward Taubert's workspace. He was sitting at his desk, flipping through a magazine.

CHAPTER TWENTY-FIVE

The black Lincoln Town Car followed by several black Mercury Marquis' turned down a narrow street off Rue Paul Morale to a well-maintained, nondescript, gray-white building. Several steps led up to a brown steel door under a small canopy. Above the door on an ornate plaque were the words:

HEMO-CARIBBEAN, LTD.

President Jean-Claude Duvalier exited the Lincoln, the door held open by one of his bodyguards. He took a deep breath. He did not look forward to the visit for several reasons. Duvalier buttoned his jacket, somewhat tight for his large girth, and walked up the steps, followed by Dominique St. Jacques, his assistant interior minister. He stopped. Another bodyguard hurried to the entry and opened the door. The odor of formaldehyde and death hit the president-for-life immediately. Duvalier reached in his pocket for a handkerchief and covered his nose and mouth and entered, his retinue following behind. The group walked right past a startled comely mulatto receptionist, through a pair of fiberglass doors with round windows.

The next room was a long, large rectangular space, brightly lit, with three rows of overhead fluorescent lights, whitewashed walls, and a black linoleum floor. Along one wall were over twenty stainless steel gurneys, a lifeless body on each one, with tubes inserted into the subclavian and femoral arteries, and the aorta. Red fluid flowed slowly but continuously through the tubing. The black or brown skin of all the bodies save two Caucasians looked starched and whitish. The corpses were political prisoners, many arrested on trumped-up charges, tried by a kangaroo court and sentenced to death, all for a singular purpose—keeping Hemo-Caribbean in business.

The multiple tubes in each body joined at a single intersection into one larger tube and emptied into a large plastic bottle on the floor that held up to ten pints of life-giving blood. Every table had a corpse. At some, lab assistants lifted the cadavers into body bags and then wheeled them to a large refrigerator in the next room. Now they were ready for shipment to medical schools throughout the Caribbean, and even to the United States. They sold the blood everywhere, no questions asked. Several years later, the AIDS epidemic would become front-page news; blood from Haiti was a principal source of the epidemic.

"Where's Cambronne?" The president demanded.

A mulatto, hunched-back attendant in a dirty lab coat turned his head upwards toward Duvalier. "I'll fetch him, Excellency."

"Be quick. I don't want to spend anymore time here than is necessary."

"Yes, yes." The little man, hump protruding from his left shoulder, scampered off to a room marked "Private." Momentarily a tall, thin Black man with a boney face and hands exited the office dressed in a surgical gown and hurried toward the waiting retinue.

"Mr. President, what an honor! But you should have called. I would have prepared a meal."

"Not necessary or desired, Cambronne." Duvalier's voice was hard.

"I know, let me do better than that." Luckner Cambronne whispered to the little man, who once again walked as fast as his small legs would take him to another room off the main production area.

Three Tonton Macoute came out, machete's in hand, dragging three screaming men, hands tied behind their backs. Cambronne nodded. Forced to kneel, they were decapitated, then the heads held high, displayed in the grip of each assassin. A pool of blood formed around each of the lifeless bodies.

"Get them up now," Cambronne said. "That blood is valuable."

Duvalier, nauseated at the sight, sick memories returning in a flood, turned to his assistant interior minister. "And we wonder why we have no tourists."

"Monsieur President, perhaps these heads might adorn your office. They were your enemies. Let me embalm them for you." The 'Vampire of the Caribbean' hoped the offering would please his boss.

"Cambronne, it is because of you and your Tonton Macoute that no one comes to Haiti."

"I only do what is necessary to protect you from those that wish you harm, Excellency."

"You do what you do to make money off dead bodies. Many of them are innocent people. And you steal from the treasury. My treasury!"

"My President, that is not true!"

Duvalier nodded to one of his bodyguards. A Glock semi-automatic pistol appeared. Three shots went off in rapid succession and Cambronne dropped to the floor. The hunchback gasped and dropped to his knees above the body of his employer. Another two shots rang out. The little disfigured body fell on top of Cambronne. Two other bodyguards dispatched the three executioners in short order with Uzis.

"Koulye a, ou ka pase letènite ak Baron Samedi ak Ogou jan mwen a an chaj."* Duvalier looked at his minister, who had gained a new respect and now fear of his leader.

"St. Jacques, you are now in charge of the Tonton. Make them somewhat respectable."

"Respectable, Excellency. How?"

"Get them some uniforms or something."

"And what about Cambronne and his friends?" St. Jacques nodded toward the five bodies.

"Strip them. Take their blood and sell it. Then shut this place down." Duvalier turned and left the room, his bodyguards in tow. As he left the chamber of blood through the front office another shot rang out.

In his limousine, Duvalier turned to St. Jacques.

"Bring me Cambronne's head in a jar of embalming fluid. I think I need some new décor for my office."

* "Now you can spend eternity with Baron Samedi and Ogou, as I am in charge."

CHAPTER TWENTY-SIX

"How was the apartment hunt?" Bob Marlow handed Connor a cup of coffee in the old Chicago Cubs mug Connor had kept in Marlow's office for their morning ritual. There was always a fresh pot of Joe in his office, and it was exceedingly better than the vending machine's product.

"I checked out Simpson's project. He named it 2120 Hyde Park. That's the address on South Shore Drive. It was really nice. And..." West hesitated on purpose.

"And what?" Marlow was very curious.

"I got a two-bedroom, two-bath apartment with balcony, on the 16th floor, facing the lake for $450.00 a month, electricity included."

"Good for you. And welcome home!"

"I asked who owned the building and they said a guy named Patel. I thought Simpson owned it?"

"Did. Lost everything when he went to prison. How's the leasing?"

"About 75%. And, yes, it is a lot of little old ladies. I met one already in the lobby; she invited me to tea." Connor grinned, pushing his hair back.

"You'll get lots of invites, I'm sure."

"They might adopt me. But I'm excited about the place. I bought a bunch of new furniture at a store near the University. It's pretty contemporary stuff. Being delivered Wednesday, so I might need to leave early."

"The director of design doesn't have to check in with me. You're your own man."

Connor looked at Marlow, the grin disappeared. "Taubert's pissed. I'm not sure you should have made me..."

"Stop! He'll get over it. His ego is hurt, that's all. If you let him do his thing and make a few suggestions, tactfully, he'll come around." Marlow spoke the words, but only half-believed them.

"Easier said than done, but I'll try."

"What about Caudy?"

"He's cool. We were good friends already, and he's happy to see me back. Asked if he could be my wingman. I told him absolutely, so I think everything is good there."

"New office okay?"

"Great, but I just wanted to be in the open area, with everyone else. I didn't need an office." Connor looked out toward his fifteen-by-fifteen corner space. The windows peered down into the narrow abyss that was Jackson Boulevard. Once a year, during the Summer Solstice the sun reached into his work home.

"Rank has its privileges. Head of design comes with an office." Marlow looked at Connor for a reaction and got none.

"Then why didn't Taubert have an office?"

"He was only de facto head of design; never officially offered the job."

"Another reason he hates me."

"Connor, in this world, not everyone is going to like you. You're more talented than most people, Taubert included, and some will resent you. Even try to bring you down. Don't let them." Marlow finished his coffee and hoped the morning conversation was done.

"Thanks for the pep talk, boss. So, what's my first assignment?"

"Caudy's been struggling with the office building design for Gibraltar Insurance in Oakbrook. I told him to try to make it more 'American.' See if you can help."

"American? What the hell is that supposed to mean?"

"That's why you're here, Sullivan," referring to West's nickname after America's first great architect. "Now if you'll excuse me, I have some CDs to review."

"I'm gone. Later. Oh, and by the way, I signed a two-year lease. Was that smart?"

"I'm sure the little old ladies wish it was four; I do."

CHAPTER TWENTY-SEVEN

Daniel Nolan gazed out the floor to ceiling windows of his Lakepoint Tower condominium at the twinkling high-rise residential buildings lining Lakeshore Drive. Endless ribbons of cars illuminated the night with a thousand headlamps. It was a magical view. Only a privileged few could afford to live in Chicago's most exclusive lakefront residence. He took a sip of his red wine. It was a rare French Bordeaux, vintage 1962.

His new lover, Stefan, worked in the electrical engineering department of Nolan & Marlow and was in the kitchen preparing dinner. Stefan Pazin emigrated from Yugoslavia in 1974, although escaped might be the more accurate term. He was several inches taller than Danny, boasting dark black hair and deep brown eyes, and with rich, brown Mediterranean skin. The moment Nolan had spied him talking to one of the firm's mechanical engineers, he had to have him. And he did. Steffan shared the aerie with Danny for a paltry, all-inclusive contribution of $150 a month.

"I have a surprise for you, Steffy." Danny inhaled the aromas of the dinner his lover prepared. Steffan was an excellent cook, as Danny's expanding waistline testified.

"What? You must tell."

"After dinner. Be patient, love. What are you making tonight? It smells wonderful."

"Prawns with penne pasta and vegetables in cream sauce. Is specialty in Croatia."

"You're the best cook, Stef," Nolan said, thinking back to his former boyfriend, Riccardo. With him, it was always boring tamales and refried beans.

"I must know secret. I am impatient person." Stefan hoped that his relationship with Daniel Nolan, who he didn't find very attractive with his small physique, growing paunch, freckles, and red hair, would gain him a permanent green card. Then it would be "Arrivederci, stronza," to his American boyfriend.

"Well, okay." Danny returned to the kitchen and re-filled his glass, giving Stefan a peck on the cheek. "You're so demanding, but that's what I love about you. How would you like to go with me to the AIA Regional Convention in New Orleans next week?"

"New Orleans, as in jazz, Bourbon Street? I hear about, never been." Stefan stirred the dinner in the skillet, a smile on his face.

"Jazz, Bourbon Street, beignets, Voodou, Hurricane drinks, the works, my love. I'll book us in a little hotel I've heard about that caters to our special desires."

"What is Voodou and Hurricane?"

"Oh, Voodou is a superstitious Negro religion. It started in Africa, and it's practiced by Creoles in New Orleans. And a Hurricane is a drink."

"I thought Hurricane was bad storm. I do not have money for such a trip."

"Stefan, it's my treat. I get to write it off as a company expense." Nolan stroked Stefan's cheek.

"You very nice to me. Later tonight, I return favor." Pazin put down his large spoon and kissed Danny hard on the lips.

"I can't wait." Danny took another sip of the expensive vintage.

CHAPTER TWENTY-EIGHT

"Mr. Nolan, a Mr. Lazarus is on the phone. He says he needs to talk to the head of marketing."

"Lazarus? Take a message; I'm busy." The head of business development for Nolan & Marlow rubbed his temples and stared at the Alka-Seltzer as it dissolved in a glass; it seemed to take forever. The night before with Stefan had been a crazy orgy fueled by Sazeracs made to toast their upcoming trip.

The phone buzzed again. "What, Amanda?" Nolan curtly responded to his secretary, head pounding.

"Mr. Lazarus insists he needs to talk to someone. He says it is very important."

"Who's he with?"

"Lazarus and Hamburger, or something like that. No, it's Lazarus and Berger. That's right. He said he's calling from Miami."

The fog of the morning lifted slowly. Nolan was not ignorant to happenings in the world of architecture, and the who's-who in the profession. The name was vaguely familiar.

"Okay, I'll take it." He punched line three and lifted the receiver. "Daniel Nolan."

"Good morning, Mr. Nolan. This is Manny Lazarus. Perhaps you've heard of me? Are you in charge of new jobs?" Lazarus felt that all of humanity should know about him and his work.

"Yes, Mr. Lazarus, I'm in charge of business development if that's what you mean. Your name rings a bell. My apologies. Are you an architect?"

"Jesus H. Christ, Mr. Nolan. Ever heard of the Versailles-sur-Mer, or the SunCoast Hotel? How 'bout the Tropicana in Lauderdale?"

Bells and whistles went off in Danny's brain. Of course—Manny Lazarus, the crown prince of over-the-top architecture, the modern-day purveyor of glitz and shtick. "Mr. Lazarus, please forgive me. Yes, of course! Your reputation precedes you. A... a... marvelous body of work, and a lifetime of it, I must say. Sorry, I had a long night; dinner with a potential client. Not operating on all cylinders yet. How can I be of service?"

"Now, that's better, Mr. Nolan. Everybody knows Lazarus and Berger. I don't want to waste your time, and you sound hung-over, but I'm no one to judge."

Nolan didn't care for the personal observation from this man he had never met but tried to be tactful. "Just need a cup of coffee, Mr. Lazarus. Again, how can I be of help?"

"I wanna hire Nolan & Marlow to help me on a big project I just got. Interested?" Manny threw the offer out there like hundred-dollar bills to a South Beach hooker.

Amanda walked into the office and placed a steaming hot cup of coffee on the desk. Nolan gave her a thumb up. "Mr. Lazarus..."

"Please, call me Manny."

"Okay, Manny. Nolan & Marlow does not normally take, how may I put this, second chair on a project. Most firms are happy to be associated with *us*. We are one of the country's pre-eminent firms."

"That's why I phoned you. Can I call you Daniel?"

"Danny is fine."

"Danny, listen, if you're talking about top billing up on the movie marquee, my name's first, you get that? But the project is huge, and I could use a little help on it."

Not placated by the comment, Nolan was still curious. "What sort of project is it... Manny?"

"The biggest resort in the Caribbean. It's called..." Manny looked at the notes he had written a piece of paper in a meeting with Dominique St. Jacques. "Here it is. Paradi-sou-Latè. Paradise on Earth, Danny. Paradise on Earth. The client wants 1,000 or more hotel rooms in a couple of separate buildings, a casino, convention center, the whole works. Lots of swimming pools, maybe a couple designed like dolphins, which, by the way, is my specialty. It's a big project. I need help. Whadda ya say?"

"Manny, you've piqued my interest certainly. Who is the client and where is it going to be located?" Nolan was scribbling the rudimentary program down on yellow legal paper. His headache dissipated with the possibility of salvation from the firm's economic troubles.

"Sorry, Danny, can't say. Won't say. You could tell me 'No thanks,' and call the client yourself and screw me out of the work. I didn't just fall off the beet truck, you know."

"I would never do such a thing. How is this project to be financed?"

"Fuck, Nolan, I don't know. The government of the country where it's going to be built is 100% behind it. Look, you interested or not?"

"Sorry, Manny. We're just very careful here at Nolan & Marlow these days. We had issues recently with a client on a very large project."

"If you mean that project that was in the *Record* this month, Chicago World Tower, that's why I called you. We get together on this deal, I want that Connor Jones West as the designer helping me. No one else; it's a deal-breaker."

Nolan's headache returned with a vengeance. *That damn West; why is he so special?* "Mr. Lazarus, I'm sorry, but I'm afraid we can't be of assistance to you on this project. Mr. West is busy with many other projects, and, as I said, we don't take second billing."

"Your loss, Danny, your loss." The phone went dead.

Nolan stared out the window at the lake, drinking his coffee. With the firm's financial troubles, he would soon be staring at a parking lot in Schaumberg from a Class C office building. *Damn, what did I just turn down? And all because he wants West!*

The phone buzzed again. "What now, Amanda?"

"Norman Weese on two. Want it?"

Nolan punched the button. He was hoping Norman had some good news. "Talk to me, Norm."

"Boss, I talked to two banks. One was Banker's Trust. Your dad did some business with them in the sixties. They said they could do a hundred thousand, but only because of your late father. The other was Oak Park National Bank. I got a friend there, a senior VP. They'd be willing to do a buck fifty but said our financials suck and we need to get our act together. Marvin, the SVP, said he was doing it as a favor to me."

"What's our 90-day AR?"

"Over six hundred large," Norman spoke without emotion, but he was angry. In twenty years with the firm, things had never been this bad. Francis Nolan, Jr. was a good marketer, but a lousy negotiator.

"Goddamn, two hundred and fifty thousand is a drop in the bucket, with six out there." Nolan took another drink of his coffee.

"With the 30, 60, and 90 days combined, we owe one point two million, Danny. And remember, that 250 is a loan with interest. We gotta pay it back."

"Don't you think I know that?" Nolan slammed the phone down and slumped in his ergonomic chair. Maybe he'd go to New Orleans and never return. Open a restaurant with Stefan and fuck architecture. And that sleazy architect, Lazarus, wanted Connor West on his project. Nolan sat up in his chair, a broad smile forming on his face. *Lazarus wants Connor West on his project. He wants West and West alone.* Danny picked up the phone and buzzed his secretary.

"Yes, Danny?"

"Get that asshole Lazarus back on the phone now."

"The man from Miami?"

"Yes, Goddammit! Him!"

CHAPTER TWENTY-NINE

"This is Manny." Esther had not told Lazarus who was calling.

"Mr. Lazarus, Manny, Daniel Nolan. I'm sorry but we did not get off to a very good start." Nolan was ready to eat crow.

"Or to an end, either. Have you reconsidered?" Manny was pleased that Nolan had called back; he might yet secure their hotshot designer.

"Perhaps I was hasty. As I told you earlier, yesterday was a long day."

"So, you're hung-over. Hey, I get it. Been there, done that. So whaddya say, we gonna team up on this project, or what?"

"What do you think the project's cost will be?" Nolan knew it would be significant and that the dollar benchmark would determine his negotiating posture.

"Hard to say. Maybe $150 million. Maybe more. And I forgot to mention the four Michelin-grade restaurants, a marina that needs to be built, an airport and the terminal for it. Did I talk about the golf course with clubhouse, worker housing, maintenance buildings..."

"Manny, you definitely have my interest. What help do you need?"

"I'm gonna need your man West to help with the design. Truthfully, my eyesight's not too good anymore. Maybe an assistant to help him. Gotta be here in Miami though. Your firm can produce the construction documents in Chicago. I got a great specifications writer and ten to twelve draftsmen that can handle some of the work here. You have structural, mechanical, and electrical in-house; that's a plus. No need for me to go outside."

Nolan smiled at the demand for Connor West's presence in Miami. "What kind of fee are you getting from your client?"

"That's not important." Manny wasn't about to let Nolan know he had garnered a whopping ten percent fee. "What's important is what I'll pay you to help. How's three percent sound?"

"Manny, it sounds pitifully low. We'll need five." Nolan took out his calculator. He couldn't even punch in $150,000,000. He typed $15,000,000, multiplied by .05 and saw $750,000. He mentally added a zero and shook his head. $7,500,000! Nolan knew he had to have this deal.

"Okay, I must be crazy to tell you this, but I'm getting a standard six percent fee. I'm splitting it with you."

"We're going to be doing the lion's share of the work, including design. Four and a half percent."

Manny smiled. "Four percent."

Nolan was silent. He scribbled the numbers down. At four percent, he could still make $6,000,000. More with all the other projects. "Alright then, four percent. How soon can we get together?"

"Right away. Come to Miami. I'll have my lawyer work on the contract tomorrow." Manny was grinning from ear to ear. He would still make six percent and hardly have to lift a finger. This deserved a couple of dirty martinis at the Versailles bar.

Nolan paused. "If it's all the same to you, we have an in-house attorney. He's done these kinds of arrangements before. I'd like him to prepare it for your review." Dennis O'Flaherty was not Nolan & Marlow's in-house attorney. He was a one-man show with an office on the ninth floor of the Railway Exchange Building, the behemoth terra cotta edifice where N&M resided. Most of his work was collecting money for architects from errant clients who thought nothing of letting their architect twist in the wind for 90-days plus.

Manny frowned and then realized that having Nolan prepare the contract would save him a bill of at least fifty from Stu Cohen. "Fine, but I'm gonna go over it page by page to make sure you don't slip anything by me. You gonna come to Miami so we can discuss?"

"Manny, I have a better idea. I'm going to be in New Orleans next week for the AIA regional meeting. Why don't we meet there?"

"Suits me. But I want nothing to do with those AIA schmucks. They've always criticized my work."

"I assure you we are big admirers of your unique style. And I promise the contract will be entirely equitable." Nolan, pleased with his recent negotiation, was eager to flatter his potential partner.

Lazarus had fond thoughts of the Big Easy. He liked Bourbon Street and Jazz. "When I stay in the Big Easy, it's the Roosevelt. I'll buy you a couple of Sazeracs. They were invented at the bar there."

Nolan's head hurt at the thought. "Sounds great. I'll have my secretary, Amanda call you later this week with our arrangements."

"Terrific. Oh, and Danny, tell your lawyer Mr.... ?"

"O'Flaherty. Dennis O'Flaherty."

"Tell O'Flattering to remember that Lazarus and Berger get top billing." He thought, *Of course, an Irish lawyer! Micks and Jews together. That's a formula for a fight!* Manny looked at his watch. 11:00 A.M. Lunchtime was around the corner.

The throbbing in Nolan's head increased. "Fine, Manny, just fine."

CHAPTER THIRTY

Rich Tomlinson picked up the receiver and dialed the number from the ship-to-shore phone on *Daddy's Money*. He was not looking forward to the call, but it was necessary. He was broke.

"Charles Tomlinson." The number was a direct line to his father's office, allowing Rat to bypass several secretaries. The brokerage firm of James, Merrill, and Tomlinson was one of New York's prestige investment firms and catered to the rich and ultra-rich. Buy-in for their services was an initial investment north of a million dollars.

"Good morning, Father. It's Richard. How are you?"

"Richard. Long time. How's the charter business?"

"Slow, sir. Very slow."

Charles Tomlinson winced and instinctively understood the purpose of the call. He had not become a partner at thirty-three for nothing. He was against giving his spoiled son any of his trust fund upon graduation from Harvard, but his wife Candee, short for Candace, doted on her only son and thought a year or two experiencing life in the "real" world was a good idea. There was plenty of time for a career in New York City in architecture, a romantic profession in her mind. Charles thought it a frivolous pursuit. At least at Yale, Rich studied architectural engineering, even working construction during summer vacations. Then his son decided he wanted to design buildings, not build them. He might as well have become a painter or an actor. He should have secured an MBA.

"Don't tell me, let me guess. You need money." The senior Tomlinson's voice was frosty.

"Father, there's not going to be any charters until late February. It's the off-season."

"What did you do with the last twenty-five I sent?"

"The number one engine burned up after the propeller got caught in a massive weed bog. It over-heated before I knew it. That cost $17,000. The dock slip fees have increased, and fuel too. Everything costs more down here." The tale was a mixture of truth and lies, but Rat didn't care. He detested his cold and distant father, and no longer had his mother to fight his battles. She had died a year ago of lung cancer from a three-pack a day habit smoking Pall-Malls.

"Richard, let's see if I have it here. Yes, so far, you've divested yourself of $243,800 of your inheritance. At this rate, you'll be penniless by the time you're thirty."

"Father, it takes time to build a business down here. There's lots of competition. But I promise you that *Daddy's Money* is getting a solid reputation in town. Just ask your friends, Coddington and Van Morton."

Daddy's Money, how apt, thought the senior Tomlinson. "All right, how much do you need to get you to charter on-season? And I'm doing this only because your mother would have insisted, God rest her soul."

The young fishing boat captain sucked in his breath, deciding to swing for the fences. "At least twenty, Father."

"When do you intend to return to the real world and start making an honest living, son?" The voice had gone from frosty to North Pole cold.

"This is an honest living, Charles." Rat knew his father disliked his son calling him by his first name.

"Richard, it's not too late for you to sell the boat and come to work for the firm. It's time, don't you think?"

The thought of working as an apprentice stockbroker made Rat nauseous. Sitting with a hundred other City College grads playing dial-a-dick all day, hoping to bag the elephant was not his idea of a life. "You told me the trust fund was my money..."

"Fine. I'll wire it to the Keys Bank later today. But that's it, understood."

"Understood, and thank you, Father."

"Goodbye son." The phone line went dead.

Rat sighed. He had sucked up to his old man but had solved his immediate problem—paying Seadog twenty-two hundred.

The rest would be a nice stake for Wednesday night's game. He knew his luck was going to change. It had to.

CHAPTER THIRTY-ONE

The estate in Pétion-Ville, high above the chaos, squalor, and confusion of Port-au-Prince, had been a sanctuary for Simone Duvalier. The stately pink-stucco mansion on three acres of manicured grounds, full of swaying palms, hibiscus, and oleander, was a piece of paradise, albeit one surrounded by an eight-foot-high stone wall topped with barbed wire. Now it was a prison to the former first lady of Haiti.

Dressed in a white linen dress with matching pearls, Simone strolled through the grounds of the estate with General Claude Raymond, defense and interior minister, and right hand to Jean-Claude Duvalier. The general looked at the widow of his late godfather, Papa Doc Duvalier. His brow wrinkled. Upon her exile to this velvet prison, he promised to keep her informed of her son's growing power. He had bad news to deliver.

"Madame, I must report that Jean-Claude executed Luckner Cambronne and several others at Hemo-Caribbean two days ago."

Duvalier stopped walking and took a sip of Haitian coffee from a fine china cup. A saucer occupied her other hand. She looked at Raymond. "Why?"

"He wants to rein in the Tonton-Macoute. They're bad for tourism. He cut off the head of the snake."

"The Tonton are an independent and ruthless lot. He cannot put that genie back into the bottle. You know that; I know that." She delicately placed the cup back onto the saucer.

"He told St. Jacques to get them uniforms and reinstitute their name to the Volunteers for National Security."

"Uniforms. Seriously? Tell me more about this St. Jacques."

"The assistant interior minister; he is loyal, but he is an opportunist. He sees that by fully supporting the president's plan to build a resort on Île-à-Vache, he will gain favor." Raymond looked at his companion and tried to detect some emotion in the first lady's demeanor. There was none.

"Oh yes, Paradi-sou-Latè. Paradise on Earth. It's almost comical. And how much will this boondoggle cost the national treasury?"

"You mean how much will it cost you and me?"

"I have no idea what you are talking about."

"The money will come out of our *retirement account* if you get my drift."

Madame let the comment go unanswered. "Tell me, do you fear my son?"

"All that I can say is that after Cambronne, my guard is up. Tomorrow, I am scheduled to tour Île-à-Vache with his Excellency. I'll try to take his temperature then."

"Who will design this paradise? And, more to the point, who will build it?"

"He has hired an architect from Miami. As for the labor, our own Madame. We have many unemployed, do we not?" Raymond followed the first lady up several steps to the veranda of the mansion, the meeting nearing its end.

"You mean conscription, forced labor, don't you?" Duvalier set her coffee cup down on a rattan table, turned, and kissed Raymond softly on both cheeks. "For now, we bide our time, love. Let's see what my precious son does. And I want to know all about your visit to that pretty little island." Raymond bowed, and then kissed his lover on the lips, turned, and departed.

On a rise above the mansion in Pétion-Ville, with a clear view to the grounds of the property, a Tonton Macoute adjusted his binoculars. He could see the pair clearly, now that they had reached the open space of the veranda. The mother of his boss had kissed the minister of defense. He, in turn returned her kiss. He got up, smiling, scurrying down the hill to the dirt road where a tap-tap was waiting. He hoped the information meant a promotion.

CHAPTER THIRTY-TWO

Suite 1512 of the Versailles-sur-Mer had been rented by one company, the Bureau of Caribbean Tourism, for a year. It featured a large living/dining room, a small kitchen and bar, and three bedrooms. The generous, though worn, suite looked out to the Atlantic Ocean, beyond a full-length balcony.

Carlos Delgado ran his fingers through his thick, pomaded hair, then rubbed the scar on his chin. He knocked on the door, answered promptly by a thickly muscled bodyguard. Recognizing the visitor, the door opened, and Delgado entered. His boss sat on a white sofa, beer in hand. Bobby Flatshorn, the titular head of the Black Tuna Gang, watched a soccer match broadcast from Mexico. It was a day late in airing; the picture faded in and out. He looked up at his visitor.

"Carlos, my man in the Keys. Pour yourself a drink, sit down and talk to me." Carlos did as instructed. No matter what Flatshorn told you, you did it—no questions asked. Flatshorn was wearing a snug-fitting black tee-shirt that accentuated his biceps, along with black Armani jeans. His hair was curly, eyes dark brown. He reminded people of the singer, Tom Jones. Hung from a gold chain around his next was an ancient Spanish doubloon engraved with a black tuna.

The Black Tuna Gang was the unofficial name of a coterie of drug smugglers, given to the group of Americans, Cuban nationals, and Bahamians by the DEA. Each member wore the doubloon to identify themselves as part of one of the largest drug operations in the United States. They were sophisticated, clever, and elusive. Over the previous sixteen months, they had smuggled over 10,000 pounds of marijuana into the country. Demand was growing, not only for "Mary-Jane" but for the new drug of choice amongst the glitterati of

Miami and South Beach, to points north as far as Myrtle Beach, and south to Key West: cocaine.

Bobby Flatshorn had a problem though. He needed more fast boats or ones that the DEA would not stop and scrutinize. Like fishing boats. Carlos was the gang's recruiter in the Florida Keys, a virtual gold mine of pleasure craft. And it also had its share of people down on their luck: seniors who had pissed away their life savings or scalawags, pirates and gamblers. Rich Tomlinson and his "Jones" for poker was the perfect target.

"Boss, I got a big fish on the line."

"Do tell." Flatshorn picked up his Dos Equis from the coffee table and took a long pull.

"A friend in town…"

Flatshorn interrupted. "You mean Key West?"

"Yeah boss, sorry. That guy named Cicero owed you a favor for that Dry Tortugas thing."

"I remember. What about him?"

"He owns a couple of bars there. He's in on a high stakes poker game every Wednesday. I asked if he knew of any marks. Told me about this kid, a young fishing boat captain with a sweet new Hatteras 45. He likes the cards but is gettin' in way over his head. Had to borrow from the house last week."

"Were you there?"

"Yeah, Cicero got me an invite, but I was at the other table. Shit, the mayor, a councilman, and even a county commissioner plays there."

"I bet you fit right in."

"I caught a glance or two, but Cicero vouched for me. Seadog, the host, invited me back this week. I'm gonna make sure I'm at this kid Rat's, table."

"Seadog, Rat?" Flatshorn loved the colorful names of South Floridians, and they got more colorful the closer you got to Key West.

"His name is Rich, very apt, but he said to call him Rat. Cicero says he comes with a silver spoon in his mouth. We got a bet to see how soon it comes out. I bet it's this week when I'm across from him."

"You're pretty good at cheating at poker." Flatshorn smiled, got up, and went to the bar. "That calls for a bourbon."

CHAPTER THIRTY-THREE

Connor, Caudy, and a few other young apprentice architects stood around a high top at the Berghof on Friday night. Each had a stein of the Chicago establishment's signature German beer. In the center of the table were pretzels and hard-boiled eggs. Bob Marlow was not present. He had decided that the place was off-limits to his fragile drinking system. Connor had one beer and then switched to tonic and lime. Caudy told a dirty joke, and Connor laughed. Then he stopped; he realized how good normal felt again.

He couldn't believe how quickly the week had flown by. It was good to be back in the real world. Everyone had welcomed his presence. He and Caudy had worked together to improve the proportions and symmetry of the Oak Brook office building for Gibraltar Insurance. He got up to speed on other projects, the designs too far along to change, but each one adequate for their intended purpose. He made minor changes to the interior organization of spaces, always as suggestions, not as demands.

Then there was Taubert, wrestling with the grand lobby of the Marriott on Michigan Avenue. During lunch, Connor went over to his workspace and looked at the design. He thought of improvements to the dynamics of the space, but he did nothing. There would be time.

A figure came around the old wooden revolving door into the restaurant with its red-checked tablecloths. It was Will Taubert. He walked up to the group and faced Connor.

"Good to have you back, boss." He reached out and grabbed Connor's hand, and shook it.

"Call me Sullivan, okay?"

"Okay. Hey, I'd like you to look at the lobby for the Marriott. I think it could be better, but I can't figure out how. Monday?"

"Sure, first thing Monday. Let me buy you a beer."

❖

On Saturday morning, Connor got up early, 7 A.M. After a breakfast of cereal and bacon, he made a couple of sandwiches and departed for the parking garage. The trip to Eau Claire, Wisconsin, would take all of five hours. He planned on seeing the Mother Superior after lunch when visiting hours began. Sarah Jones had told him that her name was Sister Mary Blanche and she was as tough as nails. That was not good news. Connor still had an innate fear of the species from his Catholic grammar school days.

Surely, the rigid nun would listen to reason when she found out he was the father of Kevin Jones. Final didn't mean final when a living parent wanted custody.

Since Sarah Jones didn't possess the most important piece of information he needed—the name and address of the couple that had adopted his son—he would have to secure it from the nun. Connor determined he would not leave St. Margaret's Home for Women without it.

As he drove north toward Milwaukee on the cold and cloudy Saturday, the reality of what he was doing hit him. If he could locate the child, and if the new parents were agreeable to giving Kevin back, a heartbreaking proposition for them, how would he then care for the child? Single, surely working ten to twelve hours a day, living in an apartment full of elderly people who would not take kindly to the early morning cries of a child. And he knew nothing about caring for a newborn, a four-month-old.

Connor, you're out of your mind. This is a fool's errand. Turn around and go home. There will be time for children in the future. But he kept driving. If he couldn't have Kevin as his own, he needed at least to see his son.

❖

153

Sister Mary Blanche was every bit the rigid old nun he anticipated. Her demeanor was as starched as the tight coif and bandeau around her head and face. The office of the mother superior was ascetic, the walls all white and the only adornment a crucifix and a poor copy of a Renaissance painting of Christ suffering on the cross. In a small alcove off the main office was a file room, metal drawers four high. Connor noticed they were arranged alphabetically.

The nun reached under her tunic and retrieved a hanky and lightly blew her nose. She was biding her time, knowing this meeting would not be to the visitor's liking.

"Mr. West, how do we know you were married to Marilyn Jones at the time of the child's birth?"

"I wasn't. I mean we weren't. We were married in October. I have the marriage certificate here." Connor tentatively handed the document from Monroe County, Florida, to the nun. She perused it, shaking her head.

"This is a civil document. Where is the certificate from your local parish?"

"We weren't married in a church. After her time here, she didn't want to."

"I see. Well, she was quite obstreperous. Our information is that the infant was the product of a rape. Did you rape your wife and then marry her when you found out she was pregnant?"

"No."

"Well, that would have been the honorable thing to do, Mr. West."

"I never raped Marilyn. She was raped, yes, by her boss. Marilyn was his secretary."

"I'm confused."

"The child is ours. We conceived him before she was raped."

"You conceived a child out of wedlock. Ideal, and a small mortal sin." The sarcastic remark stung Connor.

"Listen, Sister, we were in love. Get it? I am the father of Kevin Robert West and I need to know where he is. He is my child. He is my, what is it that you say, my seed. He is my issue."

"Then where is your new wife, Mr. West? Why isn't she here?"

"She's dead. She died in a plane crash. The one that happened recently in the Florida Keys."

Sister Blanche's face turned ashen, shock written across it. "I see. My condolences; I will pray for her soul tonight." The nun omitted the modifier she was thinking of: blackened.

"Sister Blanche, now that you know all the circumstances, tell me where to find my son. The adoptive parents are in St. Paul, I know that. Give me their name and address."

"I'm afraid that is out of the question, Mr. West. Once an infant is placed from St. Margaret's the adoption is final and all the papers sealed. The birth parents relinquish all their rights."

Connor's Irish temper was rising. "I never relinquished my rights! I didn't know she was pregnant with my child."

"You young people do not seem to have a proper appreciation of God's laws, which if you had followed them, you and your late wife would have been walking step by step alongside our Savior. Now if you'll excuse me, I have to greet some new charges. These girls have also strayed from the path of righteousness. Good day, Mr. West."

Connor glared at the rigid messenger of God, further argument futile. He turned and left.

After a fitful night of sleep, Connor got out of his overly soft Holiday Inn bed and dressed. It was 4:30 A.M. The night before, after a cheeseburger dinner at What-A-Burger, he had gone to a hardware store and bought a good-sized flashlight, batteries, and a pair of rubber gloves. He remembered the brothers at Regis High School telling the students of getting up at the crack of dawn to say their morning prayers, the Matins. Surely the nuns did the same.

The night was without stars or moonlight as a cold, light rain fell. He raised the collar of his coat and put on a wool knit cap. He decided against shoe polish to blacken his face; that would be a little over the top. All he wanted was an address from the file drawer marked "J/K."

The drive from downtown Eau Claire to St. Margaret's took ten minutes. When he reached the imposing gate, he doused the headlights and slowly made his way down the long, straight gravel drive. He parked alongside the cars of visitors who had stayed the night with their pregnant daughters, getting them prepared for their six-to-seven-month ordeal at the hands of these loving daughters of God.

Connor was correct. He looked at his watch. It was 5:15 A.M. A door opened from the convent, and with his eyes adjusted to the dark, he made out the shadows of the sisters, dressed in their black tunics, proceeding toward the chapel. Bits of white gave away their movements. He looked toward the main administration building and got out of his car. A door to the building opened. He crouched down. He hadn't expected it to be occupied. Then saw two figures leave. It was the Mother Superior and another nun. Once the two sisters were closer to the chapel, he made his way behind the parked cars toward a stand of trees. He meandered through them and then dashed across a manicured lawn to the door of the main building.

Inside, the lights were on in the stairwell and hallway. Two stepping the stairs, he was quickly on the second floor and entered the main office. He turned on his flashlight, went through the reception area into Sister Blanche's private office, and quickly to the alcove. He didn't know how long Matins lasted, but his covert task wouldn't take long.

He opened a drawer marked "J/K" and he flipped through the files until he came to one marked Jones. Rather, nine manila files marked Jones. Damn! Why couldn't her name be unusual; Polish or Russian? Beads of sweat formed on his forehead. His heart was pounding. He decided that a career as a spy was not in his future. Connor tried to slow down and flipped through the files. Emily Jones, Jeanie Jones, Mary Beth Jones, Rebecca Jones. Shit! Where was Marilyn Jones? Veronica Jones, Yasmin Jones. Connor's heart sank. No more Jones. He wiped the sweat now pouring down his face. He took a deep breath.

He went past a thick divider tab marked "K." He had no idea there were so many women in the Midwest who gave their babies up for adoption. Then he saw it. The first file was "Jones, Marilyn." Sister Blanche had probably pulled the file to review after Connor left and then misfiled it. He set the file on top of the cabinet and quickly turned page after page. He assumed the information he wanted would be at the back of the file, but he wanted to be thorough. Through the thin window glass, he faintly heard the chanting of the nuns. At the back of the folder, he found it, a sheet titled "Adoptive Parents." He pulled a pen and notepad from his pocket and began writing: James and Norah Collins Patterson, 271 North Elm Drive, St. Paul, Minnesota.

Connor returned the file to where he found it, under the "K's" and turned off the flashlight. Quickly, he was out of the office, down the stairs, and out the door. He looked toward the chapel—the nuns were walking out. He had to cross the open lawn over one hundred feet wide. *Damn! I'm screwed,* he thought.

He went back inside and looked for someplace to hide. The staircase wasn't enclosed. It was open underneath the steel steps. Connor dropped his head and went in, then got on his knees and slid into angled space between the stairs and the terrazzo floor. He wedged himself into the crevice, sure no one would notice his body, with its jeans and brown coat in the dark space. The door opened.

"The young man insisted he was Marilyn Jones' husband, that she had died in a plane crash. He demanded the name of the child's new parents. It's enough to make you laugh!" Sister Blanche raised her tunic enough to not trip on the stairs.

"He's probably some child trafficker. We can't be too careful, Mother Superior. The world is full of the devil's minions." The assistant blessed herself, following her superior up the stairs.

When the footsteps faded, Connor got up and ran to the car. He was confident that no one had seen him. He started the old Pontiac Tempest, slowly headed to the gravel drive and the long ride back to Chicago.

CHAPTER THIRTY-FOUR

With a nod to superstition, Rat rode his bicycle to Roosevelt Avenue rather than travel by his inflatable dingy. Seadog met him by the breakwater and Tomlinson got into the small rowboat.

"Young Captain Tomlinson, on a bicycle, I see. How are we tonight?"

"Just fine, Seadog. Tonight, my luck changes, so I thought I'd ride over on land. Oh, I have something for you." Rat reached in his pocket and pulled out an envelope. "Two thousand and the interest. We square?"

Seadog took the envelope and put it inside his tight-fitting shirt, straining against his sailor's physique. At 40 he was in magnificent shape, having kept up his daily workout regimen from his Navy Seal days. It was rumored that he mined harbors in North Vietnam. The eye patch over his right eye was a souvenir from the Viet Cong.

Geez, everyone looks like a pirate down here, Rat thought.

"As square as square can be, son."

The two rowed in silence, finally broken by a question from Rat. "Seadog, who's Carlos?"

"Friend of Cicero. He vouched for him, and I Okayed it. From Miami, and Cicero said he was working for him. The councilman wasn't too happy with me; only wants locals in the game. Locals like you. You have a lot of friends here in Key West, even for a rich kid from New York."

"That's good to know. I consider this town my home now. Not sure I'd ever be happy in New York."

"You work hard. Run a good, professional charter."

"Yeah, thanks, but I wish I still had my first mate, Connor West."

"I'll check out a few of the guys at NAS. Someone might be interested."

"Appreciate that. Is this Carlos going to be at my table tonight?"

"Most likely. Be wary of him kid, be wary."

"Thanks for the advice, Seadog."

"How much you got to bet tonight, Rat?"

"Fifteen. I'm pissing away my inheritance."

"I have a rule. I always leave five in my pocket. Never borrow from the house if you can help it. It signals to the other players that you're desperate and desperate makes for stupid bets."

"I'll remember that, sir."

The rowboat reached the *Pirate of Penzance*. Rat got out and Seadog headed back to pick up a couple of other gamblers. Inside the lounge, he greeted the mayor; Pat, the councilman; Commissioner Eddie Ortega; and Cicero. Then he turned and headed for the bar. The brown-skinned man with a scar and slicked back hair stood there, pouring a double tequila.

"Carlos, right?"

"Rat, nice to see you. Ready to play cards?"

"It's Wednesday, right?"

❖

Rat did well at the first hands, winning four, losing two, and folding twice. His best set of cards was a flush, queen high. He was up four thousand dollars. Carlos had won a hand, sporting two pair.

Delgado had been studying Tomlinson's demeanor, looking for a blink of the eye or a tightening of his facial muscles, something that might give his position away. He looked down at his opponents' hands. Tomlinson's pinky finger was twitching, and the boy didn't realize it. A solid hand of cards made the finger move up and down, tapping the felt while he held the cards. Carlos noticed the twitch. On the last hand, the one Rat won with the flush, he noticed that same nervous reaction. On losing hands, or when he folded, the pinky was still.

He had his opening, and now it was his turn to deal. Though not a professional shark, Carlos worked the Bahamas casinos and found side games where he dealt the cards every fifth or sixth time. He was a pro at riffle stacking the deck, the overhand shuffle, the end jog, the up jog, and then the break of the deck. He always got high- value cards after he dealt the first four out. He repeated this on the second offering. He was patient; it would be a long evening.

He dealt the cards after multiple shuffling of the deck. The other players imbibed their drinks, not paying attention to his sleight of hand. Carlos dealt the cards, five to each player. When done, two kings were in his possession. Rat had two nines. The first round of wagering began after the minimum $100 ante and minimal betting. Tomlinson asked for three cards and garnered another nine. His finger twitched. Pat, the councilman, asked for two cards, took them and slipped a look. Without realizing it, a thin smile broke across his face. Carlos took three cards and added another king. The other players folded, not happy with the cards dealt.

Pat bet three hundred, followed by Carlos, who matched the bet and added only two hundred more. He did not want to spook Rat into folding. Rat equaled the five hundred and added two more chips. Pat matched the bet plus one, and Carlos did the same. Another round of betting, each one raising the pot one hundred. The pot now held $4,000. Rat decided it was time to call. He laid out his three nines, the pinky twitching. Pat showed his cards, two pair but queen high. No good. Carlos laid his cards out. Three of a kind, king high. The pot was his, and Rat lost all the money that he had previously won.

The evening continued, and Carlos played his mark slowly and carefully. He let Tomlinson win enough to keep the adrenaline flowing, but made sure he lost on the bigger pots, the ones where the pinky's thumping gave away his hand of cards.

"A straight, ace high." Rat beamed, sure that he was going to win the sizable pot of $5,600. Carlos laid down four of a kind, jacks high. He had dealt himself three jacks to begin and Lady Luck did the rest.

Rat's smile disappeared, and he felt sick. He knew he was down to $300. He had lost $14,700 in two-and-a-half hours. The young captain got up and headed to the bar for rum, but not before he asked Seadog to accompany him. "Seadog, is the bank open?"

"Boyo, have you been through your stake already?"

"Sadly, yes."

"Did you keep five back for that rainy day? If so, have your drink and go outside. I'll be out shortly to get you to shore." Fineran shook his head, feeling sorry for the young player. At his age, he was lucky to have fifty bucks in his pocket, never mind thousands of dollars to piss away on a card game.

"The five is gone, too. The last hand I knew I had won with a straight. Then Carlos throws down four of a kind. Shit? Something's not right."

"Richard, I told you to be wary. I've watched him deal; he shuffles a lot, but that's it. I think it's just luck. Anyway, the bank is closed, son. It's for your own good."

"But..."

"Go home, and I'll see if I can drum up a few charters for you. Got some Seals coming in next week for R&R."

"Thanks." Rat took his drink and walked outside. Carlos noticed, called a pee break and after using the head, went out the door leading to the rear deck. Rat was staring out into the dark, not knowing where he was going to get money for his docking fees or even for a loaf of bread.

"Lady Luck is a cruel mistress." Carlos reached into his breast pocket for his pack of Salem menthol's, shook one out, and lit it. He was ready to set the hook.

"Not for you she isn't. She's giving you blow jobs." Rat looked down at the waves slapping against the side of the houseboat.

"Hey, no worries. I told you if you ever need a little help... I'm enjoying the game tonight. I'm happy to give you a chance to make back your losses. What am I gonna do with that much money, anyway?"

"How much?"

"Five? That enough?"

"Make it ten. The interest?"

161

"Please, I'm offended. You lose it, we'll discuss a fair return on my investment. Let's go back inside and play some cards. It's supposed to be fun."

Rat nodded. "Fun, indeed."

By 3 A.M. Rat owed Carlos Delgado $15,350. The fun was over.

❖

"Well, you got yourself in a pickle, lad, a real pickle." Seadog lifted the oars, set them back into the water, and stroked through, the skiff gliding in the water toward Roosevelt Avenue.

"Tell me about it."

"What about daddy's money?"

"My boat?"

"No, your father. He controls the trust fund, right?"

Rat looked up, surprised. "How do you know about that?"

"Son, I don't think you have a printing press. You came down here two years ago in a $75,000 fishing boat."

"That well has run dry, Seadog. He gave me twenty last week. After I paid you back and overdue bills, and fueled the boat up, I'm dry."

"How much is the vig on Carlos' loan?"

"He said he'd catch up with me and we'd work out an equitable arrangement."

"Something's up. That's not good. And I ban you two from the game."

"Why?"

"I don't like him, and I'm going to protect you from yourself. I'd take that full tank of gas and leave town for a bit. Stay clear of Delgado. I'll deal with him."

"How?"

"Don't worry. Just get out of town."

Seadog had decided to ask the other players to contribute to Rat's trust fund by kicking in a thousand each. All the players liked the boy, silver spoon or not. They'd help out. He'd offer the $10,000 to Delgado and tell him to head back to Miami, no questions asked. Hopefully, he'd get the drift that he was no longer welcome in the Conch Republic.

CHAPTER THIRTY-FIVE

After Connor returned from Wisconsin, he arranged his new furniture and unpacked the boxes he had brought from Florida. By six he was hungry and ordered a pizza. Though the night was cold, the clouds earlier in the day had moved through. He pulled a folding chair onto the balcony and ate a slice, washed down with an iced tea. He was once again a "cliff dweller" as the young professionals who lived in high-rise luxury along the lake were called.

The trip home yielded no insights into how he was going to let the Patterson's know about the existence of their adopted son's father. He would figure that out in due course. For the moment it was enough to know that he had located Kevin. Connor felt settled into his new home with a view toward Soldier Field, ablaze with lights as the late afternoon game against the Bears moved into the fourth quarter. He made a mental note to pay attention to the local teams, the Bears, and despite of his new address on the Southside, the Chicago Cubs. Beyond the stadium were the buildings arrayed along Lakeshore Drive. It was a million- dollar view, but only cost him $450 a month.

Monday morning Connor boarded the downtown express bus one block from his new home on South Shore Drive for the brief twenty- minute trip.

"Next stop, Art Institute."

The driver's announcement ended Connor's random thoughts, and he got off for the one block walk to the Santa Fe Building. His second week was about to begin, and he anticipated it with relish. It was good to be back in the game.

"Good morning, Faye. How are you doing today?" Connor's mood was chipper and upbeat.

"Fine Mr. West, Connor. Just fine. Oh, Mr. Nolan left word that he would like to see you and Mr. Marlow in his office at nine."

"Really? Alright, tell him I'll see him then." West proceeded to the drafting hall and his new office, wondering what the meeting could be about. He had avoided Danny Nolan the past week, and thankfully, Nolan returned the favor.

❖

"Good morning, Bob, Connor. Have a seat." Danny Nolan went over to a new leather couch he had just purchased. Across from it were two Mies Barcelona chairs. He had retained the gray polished granite desk with polished stainless-steel workhorses that belonged to J. Vance Jefferson, the office's previous occupant. Connor found the chairs exceedingly uncomfortable, but sat in one, wanting to face Nolan. He was grateful that the young partner had gotten rid of the couch where his late wife had been raped, but bad memories still hung in the air like a thick fog. West hoped the meeting would be short. He looked around the re-decorated space. Not a drafting table in sight.

Bob Marlow sat in the other Mies chair, sipping a cup of coffee, curious about the meet. "What's up, Daniel?"

Nolan offered a weak smile. "Before we get started, I want to say welcome back, Connor, and congratulations on the promotion. Much deserved, and much needed here at N&M."

Connor looked at Bob but said nothing. Marlow's eyes were as wide as saucers. He took another drink from his mug.

"I know that you and I have had our differences in the past, but I want you to know I bear no ill will, no grudges. You were young and impulsive, and I can understand the pride you took in your design for Chicago World Tower. And look, now it's being built as you designed it. So, let's move forward to new challenges, to new projects."

Connor nodded and shot another glance at Marlow, who looked like a weight had been lifted off his shoulders.

Nolan saw that he had captured the interest of his guests and continued. "I'm in serious negotiations for us to accept the assignment as associated architect for a massive resort project in the Caribbean. It will have three hotels totaling a thousand rooms, a casino, a conference center..."

"Hold on Danny." Marlow interrupted, "Did you say associated architect? We're only doing the construction documents?"

Nolan wanted the details to come later in the discussion when he was confident the two were fully onboard. Now, forced to disclose the details of the agreement, he worried the terms would be a deal-breaker for Marlow and West.

"No, that's just billing on the credits. We're going to do over 70% of the work, and he wants Connor as lead designer. In fact, he insisted on it."

"Who's *he?*" Connor inquired in a flat voice.

"Manny Lazarus. Lazarus and Berger in Miami. His firm has designed most of the hotels in Miami Beach. They're world-renowned."

"Yeah, but I'm not sure it's for great architecture," Marlow commented.

"I saw some of their stuff when I took a few trips to Miami from Key West. It's pretty interesting, maybe a bit too much. But it works in a Miami sort of way." Connor contemplated what kind of relationship he'd have with this crazy architect.

"Great. You know Miami! You'll be going back to paradise. And no snowy, cold Chicago winters." Nolan was putting a spin on the sales pitch.

"What are you talking about? I just moved here. I'm not going anywhere. I just rented an apartment on the South Side. And as you acknowledged, I'm head of design. That means Chicago." Connor's voice rose with each syllable.

"That's right, Danny. What kind of deal did you make?"

"Lazarus insists that Connor and another associate of the firm work in Miami. He wants Connor as the lead designer."

"Then he can forget it. Connor's not leaving the mothership. He stays here."

"Marlow, Bob, we're going to make over six million dollars in fees on this job and we need the money." Nolan's voice was anxious. Connor said nothing; he knew Marlow had his back.

"We don't need second billing and to lose our new head of design that much. We're collecting plenty of fees. Now, just find us some work in the Midwest."

Nolan took a deep breath. "Bob, we're broke. Our 90-day accounts payable are over, way over, six hundred thousand dollars. We need this project and the money. We're getting a four percent fee, for God's sake."

Connor stared at Marlow. *How could the firm I just re-joined be broke? They're paying me $50,000 a year!* Marlow's face told the story—one of disbelief. "The fuck, Francis, how can we be broke? We have plenty of work."

"Secured, I'm afraid, at very low fees. It's a tough market out there, Bob. We need this job. And if Connor is truly a part of this firm, he'll take one for the team and go to Miami for a year, or two, and work with Manny Lazarus. If Connor won't go, Lazarus said the arrangement is off."

Connor's rage erupted. "Take one for the team? That's bullshit! As soon as you knew I was coming back, you couldn't wait to get rid of me. You son of a bitch! I should have known."

"Connor, that's not how it went down. I got the call from Lazarus last week and he saw the article in the *Record* and your attribution for the design. He recognized your talent and wants only you. His eyesight is failing, and he needs a first-class designer for this project. This is an incredible, once-in-a-lifetime opportunity! It will put you on the map, and N&M as well."

"Daniel, a long time ago your father told Jefferson that we're already on the fucking 'map.' I've always remembered that. So, who's the client, and where is it, this world-class resort?"

"I don't know. I'm meeting Lazarus in New Orleans later this week to discuss the contract that Dennis O'Flaherty is drafting. I'll get more details then."

"You don't know who the fucking client is, or where the project's located? Francis, you're a partner, for Christ's sake. You can't take a flyer on this deal. Didn't Chicago World Tower and Steel Simpson teach you that?" Marlow glared at Nolan.

Connor interjected. "And there is no fucking way I'm going to Miami. I just got settled in Chicago. I've got a team of designers happy to be working with me. This is the big get even, admit it; Francis."

"It's Danny now, not Francis! Listen to me, West, the firm needs this work. As I told you a long time ago, you work for this firm. We own your ass! If that means living in Miami for a year, then so be it!"

"He's not an indentured servant, Nolan. You can't order him around like a trained chimpanzee. I brought him back to improve our work across the board, not just on one project. Tell this guy Lazarus that he can have Caudy, and Connor will oversee the work from here." Marlow was fighting for his boy, but all he could think about was how the firm, his firm, could be so deeply in debt.

"Bob, this one project will get us back where we need to be financially. Lazarus insists on Connor. Once we're back on a solid footing, he won't go anywhere, I promise." Nolan was desperate.

"I'm going to check with Norman Weese. Find out how bad it is. In the meantime, go to New Orleans, meet with this guy and try to get him to see reason for stealing our top designer. And ask for a million-dollar retainer. Tell O'Flaherty to put two signatures on our side of the contract, one of which will be mine. We're done; let's go, Connor."

❖

"I see. Thanks, Norman." Marlow hung up the phone and looked plaintively at Connor.

"No, Bob, no! Don't make me go to Miami."

"Connor, if you don't go, you'll be out of a job in six months. We all will be. First National won't give us anymore credit. We owe over two million dollars. Rent a nice apartment there. The firm will pay for it. You can come back on Fridays for the weekends."

"Fuck, I knew it!" Connor shook his head.

"Danny's right about one thing. You won't have to deal with winter in Chicago." Marlow offered a wan smile.

"Well, at least there's that. I better start packing." Connor left Marlow's office, his life once again turned upside down.

CHAPTER THIRTY-SIX

Rat peddled his bicycle hard toward the marina. He owed some grease ball gangster over fifteen large with no means to pay it back in the next ten years. He would take Seadog's advice. Head to sea and let the storm blow over. His mind raced. He'd use his father's credit card to take on provisions in Key Largo. A full tank of fuel would get the Hatteras 45 easily to Bimini, far away from Key West. After lying low, head for the BVI's, maybe set up shop there for a while doing charters. Change the name on the boat, grow a beard. Tomlinson's heart raced. It was 4 A.M. He'd be out of the marina by five. *Adios, motherfucker*, he thought.

"So, you set the hook. You gonna reel him in tonight?" Cicero asked out of curiosity and concern for Rat. He liked the kid in spite of betraying him to Carlos. However, his score with the Black Tuna Gang was settled. The messed-up delivery of marijuana in the Dry Tortugas, costing Robert Flatshorn over $20,000, forgiven. Cicero decided that drug running was not for him; he'd stick with his bars and prostitution. He steered the boat toward the Old Town Marina.

"You bet I am. Hey, I told you to head for the City Marina. Rat gets schooled tonight, and you gonna help."

"Man, I thought I be through with you. Now what?"

"Two against one. Better odds. You get inside the fishing boat. I'll greet Rat on the dock. No funny business that way." Carlos puffed on his Salem and reached into a small cargo hold for his .38. Finding it, he located Cicero's .22 and tossed it to him. Cicero put it in his pocket, shaking his head.

"I tole you not to hurt that boy. Take his boat, run your damn product and leave me out of it."

"You're along for the ride at least until we get to Tavernier. We'll take on extra fuel for the trip."

"Trip? I ain't going on no trip. I'm done with your sorry ass in Tavernier."

"Cicero, you hurt my feelings. I thought we were friends. Don't you want to go to Haiti? Port-au-Prince?"

"Shit no! Haiti, that's a long-ass way. I'll catch a shuttle bus from Tavernier back to Key West. Don't worry about me."

"I wasn't."

Rat rode across the wooden boards of the marina, making considerable noise. But he didn't care. He was anxious to disappear. As he slowed down, his heart sank. Carlos was sitting on a bench across from *Daddy's Money*. Thoughts of overpowering the man raced through his head, clouded by too much rum. *Throw him in the water, loose the lines and gun the engines. If he tries to get on board, jab him with the fishhook.*

"Good morning, Rich. I thought I'd stop by and discuss re-payment options with you. Is this a convenient time?"

Tomlinson stopped, got off the bicycle, and set it down onto the aft deck of his boat. "Carlos. I'll call my dad. You'll have your money with what, 10% interest by the weekend. Deal?"

"Rat, I told you, what am I going to do with all that money? I have a better idea." Carlos reached into his shirt pocket for the Salem's.

"Yeah, what's that?"

"A trip. A pleasure cruise, really." Delgado lit the smoke, took a deep inhale, and blew the smoke out in Rat's direction.

"You going to commandeer my boat?" Fear rose in the young captain.

"One and done. One trip and maybe we're square. Very fair terms, I might add."

"Where?"

Carlos pulled out his .38. "Just get in the boat!"

"Tell me where we're going, then I'll get in." Rat tried not to show how scared he was.

"You best do what he says, boy." Cicero appeared from inside the craft, holding his .22 caliber pistol.

Rat looked back to Cicero and realized he was outnumbered. He made a move to run, but Carlos grabbed him and threw him onto the rear deck, falling hard. Carlos jumped on board and pointed the gun at Tomlinson.

"Start the fucking engines!" In an instant, he had turned from friend to enemy.

Rat got up, climbed onto the bridge and opened up the twin diesels. He realized he was shaking. Cicero jumped onto the gunwales and loosed the ropes. In a moment, they were heading out into the channel. "Watch him. I've gotta go take a leak." Carlos disappeared into the boat.

"Sorry, Rat, I had no choice."

"Yes, you did. Where are we going?'

"Tavernier, then Port-au-Prince.'

"Haiti?"

'That where it be, son. You be a drug runner now."

"Holy shit!"

"Do as he say, you be okay. He needs you to pilot the boat; like he tole you, one run and you done."

"Yeah, right..."

Cicero climbed down from the bridge and sat in one of the fishing chairs.

On the bridge, Rat dialed the harbor master's number. It rang until the answering machine went on. He placed the receiver on the console. Then he used the end of his knife to tap out dots and dashes.

```
-.. -- --..--  /  -  /  .-  /  ....-  /  .  /  .-.  /  -.  /  ..
/  .  /  .-.  --..--  /  ...
```

It was Morse code for DM, Tavernier, and S. Rat hung up the phone, interrupted by Carlos who climbed up the ladder to the bridge.

"Head for Tavernier, and don't be stupid."

"Aye, aye, Delgado."

"Now you're getting the drift of things. Smart kid."

Daddy's Money made its way into the open water to the Gulf of Mexico.

PART III

RAT, CONNOR & ARMAND

CHAPTER THIRTY-SEVEN
DECEMBER 1, 1975

Île-à-Vache, Haiti

The presidential yacht motored slowly toward the lush green island. Cows grazed on green rolling hills, and palm trees swayed in the cool breeze. Flowering plants of all types bloomed in abundance. Off to the right, the land was more rugged, and small cliffs jutted out into crystal-clear, light-blue water. They passed snow-white sand beaches that went as far as the eye could see. Jean-Claude Duvalier looked through binoculars to a pristine tropical paradise, framed by deep azure sky with a few interloping white clouds.

"All my life, I have never seen this island. It is everything you said it is and more, Interior Minister." The president lowered the spyglass and glanced at his newly promoted deputy, Dominique St. Jacques. His chief of staff, Claude Raymond, stood on the other side, listening attentively to every word.

"The Island of Cows, sir. The Spanish brought them here in the 1500s and left them when they went on to find Aztec gold in Mexico. The cows thrived as they had no natural predators. When the pirates, Henry Morgan and Francis Ollannis, landed in the 1600s, they found the island a perfect hideout, full of an abundance of fruits, fish, and cows. They barbequed the meat and called it 'boucan.' From there the term buccaneer was born."

"You have done your homework, St. Jacques. That is why I am putting you in charge of this project." Duvalier looked at Raymond for a reaction, but he was looking down at the teak deck.

"If I may, Excellency, one more interesting fact."

"Yes, tell me. I want to know all about this paradise on earth."

"The Americans tried to settle this island in 1863. President Lincoln made an agreement with our president, Fabre Gaffard, to bring freed slaves here. It was a trial program, as Lincoln was searching for ways to deal with the millions of former slaves after the Civil War. An American entrepreneur, Mr. Kock, persuaded Lincoln to permit him to bring almost 500 'contraband' slaves here from Fort Monroe. He owned a cotton plantation but was against slavery."

"Interesting. Go on."

"They arrived having contracted smallpox on the long trip, and they had few provisions. Mr. Kock set himself up as governor of the island, even issued money, and treated all the freed Blacks as indentured servants paying them sixteen cents a day to toil in cotton fields. The land was hard to till. Kock thought the native Haitians were lazy because they wouldn't work for the low wages. Eventually, the new settlers rebelled and a ship was sent to return them to the United States. A few stayed, and their descendants live here today."

"Perhaps we should include a history museum as part of our plans," Duvalier said.

"I think a water park would be a better idea, sir."

"Yes, you are probably right. The American tourists do not like to be reminded of their country's cruelty to the Black race. What they do not realize is that we, Black people, have been an independent country since 1804, long before slavery ended in America. A water park, yes, I like it."

The launch approached a rickety pier in a small natural harbor. Wooden buildings, huts, lean-to's, and the small spire of a church were visible. The yacht slowly came abreast of the dock, a few people standing at the ready to tie the lines fore and aft. They had never seen such a magnificent vessel.

The entourage of seventeen people slowly walked across a gangplank onto the old wooden dock in the small town of Madame Bernard. Two presidential bodyguards carrying semi-automatic rifles went ahead of President for Life Jean-Claude Duvalier. His white short-sleeved tropical shirt quickly showed signs of the day's heat. An aide opened an umbrella to shade him from the sun, but he waved it away.

The mayor of the town approached hesitantly. No one from the mainland had ever visited his small island. In many ways that was a good thing. Political upheavals and the Tonton Macoute were non-existent to the 12,000 or so residents of this small spit of land, barely twenty square miles in size. The old man wore a straw hat, ragged shirt, worn, three-quarter length pants, and walked in bare feet.

"Hello. Are you the President of Haiti? I was told you would be visiting." The old man stood upright and did not bow.

"Yes, I am. I am Jean-Claude Duvalier. And you?"

"Charles Picot. I am a fisherman. Welcome to Île-à-Vache. Why have you come here?"

"To improve your life, Monsieur Picot, to improve your life." Duvalier smiled broadly and held out his hand.

"If it's all the same, monsieur, my life is fine."

"Excellency, we will have to lay a cable to the island from the mainland for electricity. Then power will need to be distributed throughout, and telephone lines installed. A sewer plant must be built. Concrete docks are to be constructed for freighters bringing in supplies, and the harbor has to be dredged, and many wells dug for water. There are no roads, as you witnessed; we cannot transport tourists around on wagons pulled by mules. And then we have to build an airport. Property has to be expropriated, and people displaced. Certainly, we will build resident and worker housing, and..."

"Yes, yes, St. Jacques. I understand. It is all possible. It can and will be accomplished." Duvalier sat at a table at a local restaurant, a community dining hall, drinking lemonade and wiping his brow, his shirt drenched in sweat.

Raymond sat across from him. "Mr. President, this project, all these projects, will bankrupt the treasury! We cannot afford it."

"That didn't seem to bother you and my mother these last four years." Jean-Claude's eyes narrowed as he looked at his late father's godson.

"You have been the beneficiary of all that as well," the general said timidly.

"Tell me, Raymond, how much have you and my mother deposited in foreign banks, in the Cayman's, for your retirement?"

"My President, I do not know what you are talking about." Raymond was nervous. He did not expect the conversation to take this turn.

Duvalier nodded. Several bodyguards walked up behind the army chief-of-staff.

"General Raymond, I should throw you to the sharks that swim around these waters, but as you have been my protector since I became president, I have a new job for you. You will be my ambassador to Spain. It is a one-way ticket and a one-way passport. My mother will be in France, in Paris, should you care to make love to her there."

"My president, you cannot do this. I have been loyal to you."

"Pack your bags. I am sure you will be a fine ambassador, Claude." Duvalier looked at his bodyguards. "Get him out of my sight."

CHAPTER THIRTY-EIGHT

New Orleans, Louisiana

Manny Lazarus sat in a booth at Brennan's, sipping on a Gin Gimlet, waiting for the man who was going to help him retire with a fortune. The maitre d' came up and stopped at the table. Behind him was a short red-headed man, nattily dressed in a linen hounds-tooth sport coat, rep tie over a spread collar and a foursquare in the coat pocket. Manny had on an open-neck blue button-down shirt and an old blue blazer.

"Manny Lazarus, I believe. I'm Daniel Nolan." Nolan held out his hand.

"Sit, please." Manny squeezed Nolan's tightly. He was taught to give a strong handshake.

Nolan sat and appraised his future partner. He was pretty much what he had expected. Diminutive little Jewish fellow, coke-bottle glasses, gnarled hands, thinning, dyed hair. But, having read copiously about the body of work accomplished by this man for over forty years, he knew he sat across from a legend. A strange and unique legend, an outrageous legend, a man who had flipped off the architectural elite of the profession with a big fuck you. One thing was for sure, the man had done it his way.

"Order a drink. This is a business meeting." This was how Manny did business. Alcohol was a great leveler.

"Ah, sure."

The waiter appeared.

"I'll have a Sazerac. On the rocks."

"There you go. So, when did you get into town, Danny?"

"Yesterday, late. The convention started this morning. Pretty boring stuff."

"I've never been. Not a joiner, anyway. Maybe that's why the AIA don't like me, or my architecture."

"I'm sure it has nothing to do with that. They like to think of themselves as the watchdog for the profession, trying to keep everything within certain aesthetic boundaries."

"Like the Academies did in France in the seventeenth century. Well, I was never one to follow the playbook."

Nolan's Sazerac arrived and the legend architect offered a toast. "To artistic freedom."

"To our working together." Danny thought about the proposed contract in his pocket. He hoped the sentiment would come to pass.

After a lunch of a dozen oysters, Eggs Hussarde, and a couple of French 75's, Nolan reached into his coat and pulled out the draft of the contract. The alcohol loosened up his mood and his negotiating posture.

"Manny, I think you'll find this agreement acceptable. A couple of things. Connor West stays in Chicago, and we send one of our best designers down to Miami to assist."

Lazarus finished his second 75 and looked for a waiter to order another. "No good. Deal-breaker. What else?"

"We want a retainer of one million dollars." Danny stared at his lunch partner for a reaction. There was a brief scowl, then nothing.

"I hadn't thought about what kind of retainer to charge the client. That's a lot of moola, but then it is a big project. And I know they got the money. They better. Okay, I'll ask for two million, but I need West in Miami for six months minimum."

Nolan hoped that Lazarus would not budge on the Connor move. He smiled and was not about to fight it; he wanted the talented designer out of his sight. "Deal."

"Deal." Manny held out his hand, and the two shook hands. "Let's have another round of drinks. Fuck your AIA convention."

"Yeah, I think I will. Now tell me where this project is, and the client?" Nolan was curious but was already disbursing the million-dollar retainer to pay bills.

181

"I'll tell West when he shows up."

❖

After he bid goodbye to his new business partner, Danny's head was spinning. The thought of sitting through meetings on the new AIA contract language was out of the question. He walked back to the Hôtel de Beaux Hommes, where he and Stefan were staying. Nolan hoped he would find him waiting. He was in luck.

Stefan was watching a soap opera. "Thank God you come back to me. I am bored to tears watching *As the World Turns.*"

"Come on; let me show you the French Quarter."

"You are drunk, I think?"

"Maybe. Let's get you there too." Nolan smiled.

After hitting every other bar on Bourbon Street, the inebriated couple strayed off the beaten path. The two walked up Iberville, past Basin and stopped at Maras Street.

"Look, Stefan, a Voodou store. Let's go in."

A sign hung perpendicular to the front door:

MARIE LAVAL VOODOU
POTIONS ◊ ELIXIRS ◊ DOLLS ◊ CHARMS

"Yes, I remember. Superstitious religion for Black people."

A bell rang when they entered and a Black woman, wearing traditional African garb, came out from behind a curtain from the back room. She was a large woman with strong green eyes and deep red, polished fingernails. She wore a bright Kente Akoma patterned dress, topped by a matching Modu hat.

"Good afternoon, gentlemen. How may I help you?"

Danny looked around the store. There were rows and rows of bottles full of white and brown powders and candles with images of Jesus of the Sacred Heart, the Blessed Mother, and saints, all of whom were brown- skinned. In another area was a display case full of charms, talismans and amulets known in the Voodou religion as 'Gris-Gris.' There was Five Finger Grass, Dragon Blood Sticks, and Dixie Love Perfume. Along a top row from the front of the store to the back was an array of dolls—Voodou dolls, some simple, others ornate, made of bright multi-colored cloth.

"Oh my, I had no idea. This is all so interesting. Tell us about Voodou."

"Certainly. First, do not believe what you read in the papers or see in the movies. We are a religion of love. We brought it with us from Africa when we came as slaves. Oppressed and grief-stricken, Voodou gave us comfort. We developed potions and charms to ward off bad people, to cure sickness, and sometimes to bring troubles to others. For instance, Ouanga is a charm used to poison an enemy."

"Tell us about the dolls up there." Nolan pointed to the top shelf.

"Oh, yes, the dolls. Very popular. They have many uses. We use them to help heal others, to communicate with the dead and..."

"And?" This new, odd religion mesmerized Nolan.

"Some say, if you believe strong enough, you can bring harm to your enemies by sticking a silver pin in the doll. Look, I have several here." She opened a case and brought out three shiny silver pins for Nolan to examine.

"I want the doll up there," Danny said, pointing to what seemed to be a male doll with long, brown hair. "And this pin."

Stefan was looking at the Gris-Gris. "What is Dixie Love Perfume, please?"

"My dear, it is used to encourage romance."

"I buy."

Later, back at their hotel suite, Danny placed his new purchase on the mantle above the fireplace, the silver pin beside it. "Stefan, this is my little Connor doll."

"Come here. I splash Dixie Love Perfume on you."

"It smells marvelous."

CHAPTER THIRTY-NINE

Rat kept *Daddy's Money* within sight of the land, hoping to be seen by a Coast Guard cutter. If he spotted one, he would lay on the ship's horn until the maritime police realized something was amiss. Then he would jump off the boat, a flare gun in his hand, ready to fire it off.

Carlos insisted they look legitimate, so Rat threw out two lines with artificial lures. For a few brief minutes, fishing took Rat's mind off his predicament.

They had been lucky, hooking a couple of good-sized mahi-mahi. Cicero sat in the chair and reeled them in, and enjoyed himself. The tasty fish would provide fresh food for the long trip to Haiti. But food wasn't the problem.

The fuel tank held 550 gallons. From charts, Rat had calculated the distance from Tavernier to Haiti at 598 nautical miles. Presuming that Carlos would be in a hurry, Rat did calculations based on a cruising speed of 15 knots, a little under the maximum of 20 knots. Even at fifteen, the twin 318-HP diesel engines drank gas like a camel at a desert well. Topped off, and assuming fairly smooth seas, which were highly unlikely, they were good for just about 490 nautical miles: and a long day and a half trip. They would need more fuel. Rat assumed that the stop in Tavernier was not about cocktails and dinner. He took some comfort that Cicero was aboard; though he wasn't completely sure he could trust the man, either.

It was late in the afternoon, close to dusk as they approached the retiree's paradise of Tavernier, Florida, midway between Key Largo and Plantation Key. Just off the shoreline was a speck of land, Tavernier Key. Carlos came up to the bridge.

"Motor in closer to that little island and signal it with your running lights. One long, two short, one long, off and on. My people are there, and they'll know it's us."

"Well need more fuel to get to Haiti."

"They'll have fuel for us and provisions for our trip."

"The tanks are down a quarter. I need to top them off at the marina."

"Then after you signal my guys, head for the harbor. You got a credit card?"

"Your trip, your dime. My plastic's maxed out and I'm broke, thanks to you."

"I'll take care of it. But you run off, I've got your boat and you still owe me fifteen large. My organization will hunt you down like a dog; we've got a long reach in these parts. Be smart. Do this run and maybe we'll be square."

Rat said nothing. Cicero heard the conversation and came up to the bridge. "Rat, you got any booze on this boat?"

"In the cabinet to the right of the sink in the galley. Everything your heart desires. Carlos, for you, it's $25 a drink. By the time we get to Port-au-Prince, you'll owe me."

"We got a fucking comedian, Cicero. Stay with him. I'll go help myself."

While Carlos fixed a cocktail, Rat looked at the imposing black man with the sleeves and the USMC tattoo. "Cicero, you gotta help me! I can't go to Haiti with this asshole." He spoke in a hushed, urgent tone of voice.

"I'm sorry I got you into this mess, but if I help you, they come after me, too. I fucked up a shipment of MJ, and I owe them. And I sure as shit is getting off at that dock. I'm done with these motherfuckers."

"Cicero, they're gonna kill me once the trip is done, I know that."

"I don't think so. They drug runners, but not murderers. Tell you what. I'll stash my piece under the mattress of the upper bunk before I get off. You got a long trip to Port-au-Prince. Take advantage of it. I'll see you back at the poker table in Key West."

"Thanks, that helps. I'm scared."

"You be fine. Start thinking like a pirate."

Carlos came back up to the bridge, a rum and coke in hand. "See, Rat, it's a pleasure cruise. Let's get some gas."

Daddy's Money motored toward the Tavernier marina, and Rat hoped Cicero was as good as his word.

CHAPTER FORTY

Carlos paid cash, $135, to top off *Daddy's Money*, and went to a payphone to call Flatshorn and get final instructions for his first trip to Haiti. Rat walked around the small grocery/convenience store that was a part of the marina, picking up as many odd items as he could find.

Cicero Jackson asked the clerk if there were any nearby motels and was told to check out the Manatee Inn about a half-mile down the road. He bought a six-pack of Schlitz Malt and argued when the grizzled old man behind the counter asked for an ID. He said his goodbyes to Rat, who stepped up to the counter dropping a variety of items from Johnson's Baby Shampoo, SPAM, Little Debbie Snack Cakes, Slim Jims, a quart of Havoline Motor Oil, a 16oz. Tab and one roll of toilet paper. He tried to pay with a credit card that was maxed out, predictably got denied, and paid with cash. He always kept $100 on the boat for emergencies. This qualified as one.

"Hurry up, kid. We gotta go."

The toilet paper's for you, Carlos, you ass-wipe, Rat thought.

Daddy's Money motored out of the marina to the rendezvous spot off Tavernier Key. Within five minutes a Grady White motored out and pulled alongside. There were two surly looking men on board with 25 five-gallon gas cans, plus several cardboard boxes with food, beer, and ice.

One man jumped on and they quickly unloaded the gas and provisions. Rat looked at all the cans. His boat would become a floating inferno should even a small fire start. And there was the weight. He did a quick calculation in his head.

"Carlos, I know we need the fuel, but we just added 1,000 pounds to this vessel. That's like five other guys, besides you and me. It's gonna slow us down."

"You, me, and Trevor. He's coming with us."

Rat's demeanor deflated like a pool raft. He was still outnumbered, and Trevor didn't look like the kind of person you messed with. He was black, not as in Negro, but his skin was as black as night. His eyes were bloodshot, dark and menacing, and he sported an Afro, an Afro comb permanently lodged in it. On his belt was a large Bowie knife in a leather sheaf.

"You want to get to Haiti or not? This gasoline should get us the Port-au-Prince with a little to spare."

"With the added weight I'll be lucky to get 15 knots out of the boat. That's a 40-hour trip. I'll need a break."

"Trevor is from the Bahamas. He can steer a boat. The supplies are on board. Let's get going. Motor out a few miles and drop anchor. At first light we're off to paradise."

Paradise my ass, Rat thought, but he did as instructed.

By late afternoon Friday, *Daddy's Money* was cruising ten miles off the east coast of Cuba, well away from Cuban gunboats that assumed international waters started wherever they wanted. The day had been clear, the waters somewhat calm for the end of the Straits of Florida, as they entered the far western reaches of the Atlantic Ocean. Earlier in the day, off the Keys, they saw a few other fishing boats, but there had been nothing since noon, not even a cruise ship. No one traveled to Havana anymore.

Rat looked to the south. Great billows of gray and charcoal clouds were forming and fast. He cut the speed to ten knots, trying to determine the direction of the storm. It was enough to rouse Carlos from his game of gin rummy with Trevor. He climbed up to the bridge.

"Why'd you cut the engines?" Carlos said, assuming some sinister plot was afoot.

"Look..."

"Shit."

"Piss and shit. I'm trying to determine the direction of it, maybe buy us some time." Rat had never been in a big storm out of sight of land. He had never ventured further than 25 miles off of Key West. Though he was only ten miles from land, it belonged to the Communists, so heading west was not an option.

"You've been through storms before, right?" Carlos was concerned.

"Not like this, Carlos. I'm fucking twenty-six years old. I only got my captain's license two years ago. I do pleasure cruises, remember?"

"Which way is it headed?"

Rat looked at the radar. He looked at the storm. There were now more black clouds than gray ones. They blotted out the bright sun that had been present all day. He took another look at the radar. "Not good. It's moving east, but north too, towards us. And it's big and getting bigger. Come on, let's get inside. I'll pilot the boat from there. Secure everything. I don't need any gas cans flying through the windows."

Carlos nodded, looked up at the ominous clouds and a gray, hazy mist at the horizon. The water was already getting rougher.

Rat shut the door to the main cabin and locked it. Trevor and Carlos were moving the gas cans down to the lower deck where the two cabins were, stuffing them in tight with pillows and then covering them with mattresses. Carlos came back up to the main cabin. Rat saw that several of the cabinets were open, particularly the one containing the liquor.

"Close those doors and lock them. And there are plates and stuff in the sink. Stow it! It'll be flying around in a minute." He looked out and turned on the windshield wipers as a light rain started, and it was increasing. The boat was now pounding against four-foot swells, and Rat increased speed up to fifteen knots. If they had to go through the storm, he wanted it to be quick.

The rain came sideways, the wind had picked up, and the waves were now at least six feet high. Rat's heart pounded. Between the two drug runners, the storm, and a visit to a land ruled by a ruthless dictator, he was certain he would be dead in short order. Suddenly, a job at a drafting table or calling wealthy widows in New York with stock tips seemed like a good idea.

Carlos was at his side, grabbing the side rail by the console. "Rat, you did this on purpose!"

"Right, I invent the weather! Get in the stairwell and hold on with both hands! It's the safest place. Trevor too."

Daddy's Money pounded into the increasing waves, now at nine feet. The boat rode up and down the swells like a rollercoaster. The waves hit it from side to side, Rat, furiously turning the steering wheel to right the boat, listing at times twenty to thirty degrees. The wind increased and the windshield wipers were useless. The Hatteras was a solid vessel and fought back as it rolled in the angry swells of great water. Rat throttled up the engines. More power meant more control.

There was a sudden calm. Then the wind screamed through the glass windows. The boat turned violently and seemed to rise out of the sea. Rat had no idea what was happening. He turned to starboard and headed right into a twelve-foot wave. The boat quickly jerked upward, then hard right. Rat rose off the floor, lost his footing, and hit the bulkhead hard. There was a flash of light then darkness. Tomlinson fell to the floor unconscious, blood flowing from his forehead.

❖

Rat blinked, two shadowy forms above him. He realized he was flat on his back, but the deck was still. His focus improved. Trevor and Carlos stood over him, and Carlos pressed something cold against his forehead.

"What the hell happened?"

"I don't know but you got us through that storm. Cut your head pretty good though. I found the first aid kit below. I put iodine on the cut. Here, hold this compress against it. Good job, kid; you'll make a drug runner yet." Carlos smiled.

Rat sat up, looked out the windows of the cabin. No rain, a few puffy clouds. "Help me up. Need to check things out. I think we got sucked up into a waterspout."

Trevor's strong arms lifted Rat; his head was spinning. He steadied himself; eyes focused he took a deep breath. Rat went to the console and checked the gauges. "Damn, the number two engine is down."

CHAPTER FORTY-ONE

The phone line hissed and crackled. Then it was free of static.

"Hello."

"General Raymond, this is Black Tuna." Robert Flatshorn's voice was without emotion. He was about to begin a new enterprise—dealing with the Haitian government to buy cocaine. His first boat was already on the way to Haiti to pick up as much of it as $500,000 would buy, about 4,000 kilos. If this first run succeeded, the Black Tuna gang would send as many boats as it could secure, legally or illegally, to the distant island to pick up tons of the white gold. Demand was skyrocketing in South Florida and up the east coast.

"I've been expecting your call. Have you wired the funds to Port-au-Prince State Bank?"

"As soon as we confirm a few things."

"Such as?"

"How can I be sure, there will be product waiting for my people at...?" Flatshorn looked down at a piece of paper, notes written down during an earlier negotiating session at the Versailles-sur-Mer with Dominique St. Jacques. "Here it is. Petit-Goave."

"I am a man of my word. Petit-Goave is a safe place; it is a small fishing village west of Port-au-Prince. My people will motor out one mile in a launch and signal your boat. What type of boat is it? A speed boat?"

"No. it's a Hatteras."

"Sorry, I am not familiar."

"A sport fishing boat. It has a flying bridge and outriggers. The name is *Daddy's Money*. It's better suited to this run. A speed boat with four outboard motors would scream out drug runner, not to mention that it wouldn't be able to carry enough fuel for the long trip."

"I understand. We will have your cargo, but I must have confirmation of the funds being wired." Raymond was an old hand at selling drugs to pirates and scoundrels.

"And if I wire the funds, and there are no drugs?" Flatshorn was skeptical. He knew all about the corrupt regime of this third-world country.

"Monsieur, we are about to embark on a mutually beneficial enterprise. One that will benefit us both. What you are buying from us for five hundred thousand has a street value of several million in Miami. I assure you; this is the beginning of a beautiful friendship."

Flatshorn looked up and nodded to one of his associates standing by another telephone in suite 1512. "General, the funds are being wired now. Expect them in an hour."

"When will your boat arrive?"

"Tonight, if all goes well. Tomorrow at the latest."

❖

Rat climbed out of the engine room, wiping his dirty hands with a rag. Sweat was pouring down his face and the bandage around his head was soaked as blood seeped through.

Carlos looked at the captain. "You can you fix it, right?"

"No, the bearings are shot. Probably overheated when I was unconscious. I pushed the engines at full throttle to get through the storm, but after running hard for a day, it was too much. The number one engine is fine. It will just take longer to get to Haiti."

"We need to be there tonight, Rat!"

"Carlos, after that storm, you're lucky to get there at all. It's a miracle we survived that vortex. We can run at ten knots on number one. I have to compensate for the boat veering to starboard the entire time. Now if you'll excuse me, I need to change this bandage."

"How much longer?" Carlos added impatiently.

"Overnight. We'll be there in the morning. Why don't you get down to the galley and make some dinner? You do know how to cook, don't you? And Trevor, take the wheel and hold it to port."

❖

"Marius, this is General Raymond."

The manager of the Port-au-Prince State Bank sat up erect in his chair; this was an important call. "Monsieur, le General, it is always good to hear your voice. How may I be of assistance?" Though it was Saturday afternoon, he had received word earlier to be at the bank and make sure that the phone lines were open and operational.

"You should be receiving a wire deposit of $500,000 from a bank in the Bahamas momentarily." Raymond looked at his watch. 5:15 P.M. The flight to Madrid, the one Duvalier had ordered him to be on, would leave at 6:30.

"Let me check Mon General, it will only be a moment." The banker to Duvalier's corrupt regime got out of his chair and went to the Teletype machine. He was trustworthy and well aware of the millions that the dictator and his family, as well as members of the government, had stolen from the treasury. His involvement had made him rich. The Teletype ticked furiously. Indeed, the half-million dollars had come through, now officially and safely deposited in his small institution. His share to park it there until further instructions would be five percent. He ambled back to his desk, wiping his brow in the warm, unairconditioned bank.

"It is here, monsieur. Safe and sound."

"Good. Now transfer all the money, after taking your stipend, to this bank in Madrid." Raymond's voice gave no hint as to the reason.

"Madrid, Spain, General?"

"Yes."

Marius wrote down the bank, account number, and routing instructions. He knew not to ask questions. "I will do it immediately, sir."

"Thank you. Goodbye, Marius. You have been a faithful servant of the Republic." Raymond hung up the phone, a smile on his face. Screw the fat little president and his new favorite lapdog, St. Jacques. The $475,000 would be nice walking-around cash in Spain. Add that to the millions he had deposited in Swiss banks, and he would live like a king. He had already bought a 20-room villa along the coast, near Barcelona. Life was good. As for the regime, a prime source of drug money would dry up in the double-cross he had just pulled on St. Jacques and Robert Flatshorn.

"Good luck building Paradi sou Latè now, you fat shit!"

Raymond picked up the phone again and began dialing a number. The caller answered immediately. Raymond spoke.

"Listen carefully. A private fishing boat will be arriving tonight, looking to pick up a shipment. Do not give it to them. They are frauds. Detain them."

Raymond listened to the response. "Why, because they are drug runners!" He listened again.

"Whatever you need to do. Arrest them. Kill them if necessary."

More silence. "I was told tonight, but they are coming from the United States. It could be in the morning for all I know. Destroy the boat and as for those on board, if you don't kill them, take them to Fort Dimanche. Understood?"

Silence. "Good!"

One more call was placed to the judge and head jailer at Fort Dimanche, Arijhon Perrault. When finished, he got up.

General, soon to be Ambassador Raymond, looked around his regal office one last time and looked up at his lieutenant. "It's time to go to Spain."

CHAPTER FORTY-TWO

Connor walked into the lobby of the Versailles-sur-Mer and toward the check-in desk. He booked the hotel specifically because Manny Lazarus had designed it. He recalled the great sweeping façade and the horizontal lines flowing to the beachfront on a trip to Miami with Rat. It was as if the hotel were paying homage to its raison d'être, the Atlantic Ocean.

He carried a large suitcase, purchased for his new commute to south Florida, and a hang-up bag. As he walked through the immense lobby, he gained respect for the man he would be working with during the weeks to come. Yes, the property was a little tired, but through the age and the wear, he could see that the architecture fit perfectly into Miami's personality. Big, brash, sunny, and unapologetic.

Connor thought back to earlier in the week. Perhaps he had been too arrogant with his new title, too brash and cocky, returning to Francis Nolan's office after the meeting with Bob Marlow. He accused him once more of sabotaging his career with this forced assignment in Miami. They argued again, without reason or compromise. Connor knew that Nolan hated him and would never accept his talent. He thought Nolan was simply the incompetent son of the founder of the firm. Before he left, he noticed a small doll on the credenza on Nolan's desk. It looked like a Voodou doll. A silver pin was beside it. Curious.

After a shower, Connor returned to the lobby and went to the bar, smiling at the oversized lava lamps that flanked it. *Crazy,* he thought. *Crazy good!*

"Welcome, may I get you a cocktail?" Ramon tossed a paper napkin in the air, and it landed right in front of Connor.

"How about a tonic and lime?" Connor longingly peered at the rows of liquor, wishing he could partake of a tonic drink that included gin.

"Right away."

❖

After a dinner of surf and turf at the hotel steakhouse, Connor decided to walk along the beach.

The night was windy, and the waves came in hard onto the white sand. He wondered how he would be able to help the master of Miami architecture in designing an oceanfront hotel. He wished his mentor, Jerzy Stanizski, the head of structural engineering at Nolan & Marlow, was walking with him. He missed their strolls along Lake Michigan, discussing design and structure. His lecture about sailboat masts being the perfect structure was the inspiration for Chicago World Tower with its references to an old Great Lakes barkentine.

He walked closer to the edge of the water. The waves were mesmerizing. Great volumes of water, curling up just before the shore and then the circular shape, several suspended sprays out front, were crashing onto the beach. Again and again. Some of the curls were solid, some hollow. He remembered watching a surfing competition on TV, and the competitors dropping down into the curl, into the tunnel of water. Others rode on the crest of the wave. Smiling, Connor had an idea, perhaps the concept for this hotel on the ocean. He looked around. Maybe Miami wasn't such a bad place to be for a while. He'd work non-stop beginning on Monday and by Friday, he and Caudy, who arrived the next day, Sunday, would have this new Caribbean resort designed. He hoped Manny Lazarus would help in that effort. The two might learn from each other.

Then on Friday, he'd head to Key West to visit his best friend, Rat.

CHAPTER FORTY-THREE

Rat was up at 4:30 A.M., unable to sleep. After a search, he found Cicero's .22 caliber pistol. The storm and the waves had re-located it to the far corner under the upper bunk mattress. Now he had a gun; he just didn't know quite what to do with it. He tucked it inside his pants, a loose-fitting shirt covering it.

He returned on deck and then to the bridge. The night sky was clear, and the boat was motoring nicely at eight knots. Trevor had done a good job keeping *Daddy's Money* on course. With luck, they would be at their destination by early morning, nine at the latest.

Though interaction with this new member of the crew had been infrequent, Trevor did not seem like a bad sort. Before Rat gave over the wheel to the imposing Black man at 11 P.M., they had a short conversation. Trevor Rollet grew up in Freeport, quit school after the eighth grade, and worked in construction on new hotels during the tourist boom, rising to superintendent. Tiring of the long hours he became a longshoreman, unloading freighters in the Free Trade Zone on Grand Bahama Island. There he caught a whiff of the drug smuggling that was going on, with ships arriving daily from Columbia and Mexico. It was not long after that the Black Tuna Gang recruited him. He was wearing the same talisman around his neck as Carlos, a doubloon with a jumping, black fish in the center.

"Mon, you do good job getting us through that storm. I respect you."

"Thanks, I was lucky. Now my head hurts. Though that may have been all the rum I drank after dinner."

"Oh, yes, the rum. Always good for what ails the mon."

"Can I ask you a question?"

"If you cross my palm with a century note." Trevor let out a laugh.

"Yeah, remember I'm broke. That's why I'm on this trip. Look, is Carlos going to kill me after we get the drugs? I mean you seem to handle a boat pretty well. Why does he need me?"

"He was told by the boss man to recruit you. You young, smart, and own the boat. You better off alive than dead. And you can make much money in this business. Go tell you ol' man to fuck off."

"I think he already told me to do that. Want some coffee? I'm going to grab a cup."

"No, I think I'll get some shuteye before we get to Haiti."

❖

Rat guided *Daddy's Money* past a large island, a rock outcropping named Île de la Gonâve, which would have been a perfect place for Duvalier's paradise on earth were it not so barren. Past it, he could make out the city of Port-au-Prince, with its few mid-rise buildings and smoke rising from the fires in the slums. He could see the shoreline all the way west.

"Head due south. Petit-Goave should be straight ahead."

"You got it. So, what's the plan, Carlos?"

"We should see a boat. They'll be flying a Jolly Roger."

"How appropriate."

"We'll follow it into the town and dock there. I'll have someone go into Port-au-Prince to get new ball bearings and there should be a local mechanic around that works on boats. Hopefully, he can get the engine fixed by nightfall. We'll refuel and after dark we'll head a little way down to a mango reef. Our cargo will be waiting, plus new gas cans."

"It's certainly a well-oiled operation."

"Get us to Key Largo, and there might be a bonus in it for you. It's better money than running fishing trips. Think about it."

"Let's just get the shit you're picking up and leave this paradise."

"Look, there's the boat. Signal them, same as before. One long, two short, one long."

Rat did as instructed. He watched as the hand-built wooden launch with a single high-horsepower motor picked up speed. It was heading right for them. Inside the longboat were six large men, wearing sunglasses and sleeveless tee shirts.

"Quite the welcoming party, Carlos."

"That's not right. They don't look like our people. Gas it and turn around! Head toward Port-au-Prince."

"What do you mean 'not our people'? Easier said than done. We got one engine, remember?"

Rat turned the wheel hard left, throttling the single engine, but the turn slowed the vessel. The welcoming party was gaining fast. The slim-hulled launch with a 100-HP motor was too much for the wounded fishing trawler. In a flash, the Tonton Macoute were alongside and jumping onto *Daddy's Money*, machetes flailing and semi-automatic weapons brandished. Carlos reached under his shirt, pulled out his .38, and fired. One of the boarding party fell onto the deck. Rat froze, the gun still tucked in his pants. Trevor was below, wakened from the gunshot and the noise of boots on the deck. Rat looked at Carlos, then to the walkway outside the main cabin.

"Carlos, behind you!"

Carlos turned and aimed at another Macoute. But before he could fire a shot, the machete came down. His arm fell onto the deck as he screamed. The assailant jumped down onto the rear deck, grabbed Carlos by the other arm, and threw him overboard. In less than a minute a trail of blood was all over the blue water. A dorsal fin appeared. Then another. Then two more. Carlos came up for air, thrashing with his one arm, screaming. Then the bull sharks were upon him, and the screams were like nothing Rat had ever heard or could imagine. As Trevor hurried onto the deck, another Tonton Macoute aimed at him with his Uzi. Rat yelled, "We surrender!" He raised his arms, and Trevor did the same. Searched, they found the .22 pistol on Rat and removed Trevor's Bowie knife. Their hands tied with rough hemp rope, the Tonton Macoute un-ceremoniously threw the two into the skiff.

Two Tonton stayed on board long enough to empty the remaining gas cans all over the deck and below, leaving a full one opened. One grabbed a fishing rod, wrapped a towel around it, soaked it in gasoline, and lit it. Then, just after he jumped back onto the longboat, he threw the rod like a javelin into the stairwell. A roar of flames erupted, and *Daddy's Money* was consumed in fire.

With tears in his eyes, Rat watched his beloved vessel incinerate.

After a huge explosion, the flying bridge disappeared and the hull split into two pieces. The fishing boat slipped under the water, black plumes of smoke rising in the air accompanied by the evil hissing sound of fire meeting water, the white steam a sad by-product of the destruction.

Trevor, voice trembling asked, "Who are you? What did we do?"

"You are drug runners, and you are under arrest. We are the Volunteers for National Security."

"Where are you taking us?"

"To Fort Dimanche and justice."

CHAPTER FORTY-FOUR

Connor got up early Monday morning. He wanted to be at the office of Lazarus & Berger to work on his design concept. Dan Caudy met him in the lobby of the Versailles-sur-Mer and they went to the casual restaurant for breakfast. Connor smiled at the sparkly, lime green Naugahyde chairs, the material dulled from years of wear, the upholstery braid frayed and broken.

Caudy looked around the room, one side a curving façade of floor-to-ceiling windows looking out to the massive dolphin-shaped pool. A fountain with three jumping dolphins in the center was inactive. Around the pool, a maintenance man was doing his best to contain the abundance of overgrown shrubbery.

"This must have been the place to get a tan back in the day. Kind of sad to see it now." Caudy looked for a waiter to get a glass of OJ. He had a cocktail of vitamins he liked to take every day. Connor wanted coffee and thought about his mornings with Bob Marlow drinking from his Cubs mug. He knew he would miss their morning chats, wondering what the great Manny Lazarus would be like.

While he already missed the bustle of Chicago and the quiet energy of the drafting hall, he looked forward to solving the great puzzle, the design of an entire resort on a small island. He wondered where it would be located. He looked outside. The day was sunny, the skies a deep blue, and that bolstered his mood.

"How's your wife taking it, you being gone for a while?"

"I'm the breadwinner, so we do what we gotta do. I'm glad I have you here; at least I know somebody. Anyway, I'll go home every Friday after lunch and come back Monday first thing."

After an expensive breakfast of over-cooked eggs and over-crisp bacon, the two designers headed to their temporary office home. Connor had the address and was prepared to take a cab, and then realized the office was across the street from the hotel. Both he and Caudy carried tackle boxes containing 30- and 45-degree triangles, scaled architectural and engineering rulers, mechanical pencils, a lead sharpener, felt-tip markers, and various templates—the tools of the architect. Everything would be drawn on massive drafting tables with parallel bars in pencil or ink, by hand.

"Menachem, there are two gentlemen in the lobby from Chicago." Esther loved to call her boss by his proper name. It was either that or Mr. L, never Manny, which she considered coarse. In a bow toward proper office protocol, she called on the intercom.

Manny jumped up from his desk and hurried to the lobby. He wanted to meet the great Connor West, the designer of Chicago World Tower, and his assistant. He was careful to avoid the door jamb. Through the opening, he stopped in his tracks. Two kids were in front of him. One tall, 6'2" with long brown hair, deep brown eyes, and a tan. He was movie-star good-looking. The other, about 5'7" with combed-over red hair, looked older, perhaps because of the handlebar mustache. The shorter man smiled, and Connor held out his hand.

"Connor West, Mr. Lazarus. And this is Dan Caudy. Reporting for duty."

"What's this, a bait and switch? Where's the big-shot designer that did that big building in Chicago? You're barely old enough to shave. You're a coupla kids!"

Caudy used his thumb to point to Connor. "That's him. He designed it. I helped. Dan Caudy, Mr. Lazarus; it's a pleasure to meet you."

Connor and Caudy looked at the elderly architect. Thick black-framed glasses with big round lenses hung from his neck with a brightly colored strap. He put them on his nose with gnarled, veiny hands, took a step closer, and looked up at Connor. "You're still a kid. Geesus!"

"Nice to meet you too, sir. Can we get to work? I understand we have a lot to do." Connor wanted to move ahead; he was getting annoyed that the old architect questioned his talent simply because he was young. He studied the little man. Lazarus was wearing a paisley shirt with a brightly patterned tie. His hair was reddish-brown, a bad dye job that Ruth did on Sunday, insisting that her husband look younger for his visitors from Chicago. The effort failed. The outrageous shirt complemented the equally appalling mismatched baggy brown slacks and scuffed, lace-up black shoes. *This is the master of Miami modern architecture?* Connor thought. He shook his head just slightly.

"Mr. Lazarus, I'm... we're excited about working on this project. I already have some ideas. Just show us where our drafting tables are."

"Please, call me Manny. Come on."

The three went into the back room with about thirty-five drafting tables, all empty except for Lenny, working on another Roy Rogers site plan, this one for Hollywood, near the dog track.

"Where is everyone? Where's your staff Manny?" Connor wasn't sure what to think of the empty room.

"Well, that's Lenny over there, and then there's Sid. He writes specs. He usually comes in late. We get the designs done, I'll fill this room up faster than a cheap gambling cruise to Nassau. Look, settle in, then I think we should have a meet. Give you the program the client gave me and let me put down a few ground rules."

"Ground rules?"

After a lengthy three-hour meeting, the team had divided up assignments, the only ground rules being that Manny got to design the casino hotel of 500-rooms and had final design approval over the other hotels. Connor would design the 250-room resort hotel, a low-rise structure hugging the white sand beach of Abaka Bay, and Caudy, the 150-unit singles-only bungalow property on a remote blue water lagoon. A fourth hotel, added later, would be a high-end affair containing 175-rooms adjacent to the convention center.

"Who's going to do the master plan?" Connor inquired."

"I guess we do. The client is relying on me for everything."

"My degree is in planning, not architecture," Caudy interjected. "When I graduated, I couldn't find a job, so I went to work as a draftsman at NJ&M. Maybe I can tackle it?"

"Wonderful. Have at it, Dan. Now, let's go have lunch. I'm buying." Manny seemed to warm to his new reinforcements."

"Manny, can I ask a question?"

"Sure, West, sure."

"Who's the client, and where is this island?" Connor looked serious; he expected an answer.

"Over lunch. I'll tell ya all about it. Solid gold client, solid gold! Hey, Esther, make us a res!"

CHAPTER FORTY-FIVE

The tap-tap was waiting at the dock. Rat and Trevor were dragged out of the launch, and wooden broomsticks slid between their back and arms, their eyes covered with dirty rags. The Tonton Macoute seemed to take pleasure in hitting them for no reason. Rat was so scared that he pissed himself. Trevor leaned over to whisper advice. He could sense his partner's mood.

"Don't show your fear, mon. They see it, they get off on it. Then they hit you more. The boss man straightens this all out. Carlos, rest his soul, told me the deal was solid with the government."

"The government's selling us the drugs? The government, who just arrested us?"

"They be thugs, not government. I think."

"You think?"

A Macoute slammed Rat on the side of the head with the handle of his machete. Rat moaned and fell backward. The guard held the machete up, ready to slice off Rat's ear. "Fèmen bouch ou, estipid!"

After a short drive they could sense activity, the smell of fires and food, sweat, and humanity. The tap-tap slowed, its horn honked frequently, and they heard commands issued by the Tonton driving the old vehicle, then speeding up as if given the right-of-way, yelling and laughing. Trevor leaned close to Rat, shoulder to shoulder, as if his bodily contact would provide a little comfort. The only time the frightened scion of a wealthy New England family was scared was during hell week for his fraternity at Yale. There was no comparison.

The truck slowed, stopped, the tailgate opened.

"Deyo!"

The Tonton lifted them from their sitting position and removed the blindfolds. They were on a small side street in La Saline. A crude, long stone wall topped with barbed wire ran parallel to the pickup. The butt of a rifle told them what to do, and they jumped down from the bed of the pickup. The tight bindings and pole trussed behind his back caused Rat to fall onto the gravel street, scraping his face and his wounded forehead. Pain streamed through his body. A soldier grabbed him and stood him upright. He trembled in terror.

"Holy fuck, Trevor, where are we?"

"Some sort of jail I be thinking."

Rat looked at his new friend. He could see that Trevor was scared as well.

A gate opened, and they stumbled inside. A long hallway reeked of excrement and urine. A continuous row of steel doors only four feet apart lined the corridor. It was quiet, except for the occasional cough, a cry, or a plea for mercy.

At the end of the corridor, there was another door, this one ornate, carved wood. A guard opened it and the retinue of Rat, Trevor, and five Tonton Macoute, nonchalant in their dirty work, laughing and talking, went into a large space resembling a lobby. On one wall was a large photo of Jean-Claude Duvalier. Across from it was a pair of carved hardwood doors, like the one they had just passed through. Above the doors was a plaque:

TRIBUNAL POPULAIRE DE LA RÉPUBLIQUE

The guards dragged the two men through the door into a well-appointed courtroom. Seats for spectators, a wooden railing, and in front of it two tables, each with four chairs, awaited the prisoners. Behind the ornate wood dais stood flags of Haiti flanking a portrait of Papa Doc Duvalier. There was a large leather chair for a judge. They dragged the two to the front. A rear door opened. An officer dressed in the formal uniform of the Volunteers for National Security entered, and then a diminutive man in black robes with a white rectangular bib and black skull cap followed. He climbed up to the dais and stood by the chair that was too large for his small frame.

"All rise for his Excellency, Justice Arijhon Perrault."

The "Executioner of Fort Dimanche" sat down, his small, evil eyes looking down on the two prisoners. He knew who they were. General Raymond had called him before he left for Spain. A wedding gift of $10,000 to the judge's unwed and pregnant daughter was all that was necessary to secure his assistance.

"What are the charges?" The judge spoke in Haitian Creole. Rat did not understand a word.

"Smuggling drugs into the Republic."

"How do you know this to be true?" Perrault's voice was high-pitched and annoying.

"Your honor, we found many kilos of marijuana and heroin onboard their boat." The leader of the Tonton Macoute spoke with a straight face.

The little judge looked at Rat and Trevor and screamed, "Ki jan ou gen odas profane peyi sa a pi ak salte nan dwòg! Ou degoute m! Kisa ou di nan defans ou?"*

Rat looked at Trevor in confusion; the Tonton Macoute behind them said, "You speak now" in broken English.

Trevor spoke in perfect Haitian Creole as Rat held back tears. "Pa koupab onè ou. Nou te yon bato plezi ki t ap vin jwi Ayiti."**

Rat looked at Trevor in amazement. "You speak whatever it is they're speaking? What did you say?"

"Yes. My parents were from Haiti. I told them we are not guilty of drug smuggling."

The judge screamed, "Se tout manti! Kenbe yo isit la nan Fort Dimanche jiskaske yo fikse yon dat esè."***

The judge pounded down his gavel and the two indicted felons were yanked out of the courtroom.

"Where are they taking us?" Rat looked at Trevor, terrified.

"To jail, until a court date is set.'

"When will that be?"

"Not soon."

After walking down several corridors, all filled with the foul odor of human waste, sweat, and death, they arrived at two unlocked doors. The guards pulled the wooden rods away, cut the bindings, and threw each of them in a cell that resembled a tall box. There was clean straw on the floor, and after a month of catching their piss and shit, they would get new straw. A rusted steel wall separated them, covered with dried vomit, feces, and blood.

"You okay, Rat?"

"What do you think? This is a fucking box, not a jail cell."

"Indeed. I know this place. My father spoke of it with sadness. It is the notorious prison, Fort Dimanche. Fortunately, my parents escaped the reign of terror of Papa Doc. I was born in the Bahamas, but I understand and speak some Haitian Creole. My parents spoke it when I was a child."

"Do we get a lawyer?"

"I don't know; I doubt it. We must be strong."

Rat slumped down on his pile of straw and looked around the box that was his cell. He began to sob. Trevor heard him through the steel wall.

"Be strong, my brother, be strong."

* "How dare you desecrate this pure country with the filth of drugs! You disgust me. What do you say in your defense?"

** "Not guilty, your honor. We were on a pleasure boat coming to enjoy Haiti."

*** "It is all lies! Hold them here at Fort Dimanche until a trial date is set."

CHAPTER FORTY-SIX

The lunch was enlightening. Connor and Caudy were now in the direct employ of the Caribbean's most notorious dictator. Though he was more knowledgeable about the father, Francois Duvalier, who ruled Haiti from the time Connor was eight until he had attended Harvard, the news was still unsettling. It was hard to not see a newspaper story about the corrupt regime, the poverty, the Tonton Macoute, the torture, and the random murder of its citizens.

"Boys, I promise you..."

"Manny, we're not boys." Connor quickly realized that Manny respected people who didn't take any crap.

"Sorry, you guys are just so young. I wish I was twenty again."

"Twenty-six."

"Fine. Whatever. Look, President Jean-Claude, you know they call him Baby Doc, is nothing like his old man. He wants to bring tourism back to his land. I did a little checking. He's made reforms. Reigned in this Tonton Macoute. Even got President Ford giving 'em more aid, millions of dollars. This project can turn around all the bad press they been getting."

"Where is Île-à-Vache, anyway?'

"Right off the southwest coast. Duvalier says it's a paradise. The pirates used it. Ever hear of Henry Morgan?

"Captain Morgan, the rum guy?"

"Yes, him. Captain Henry Morgan lived there when he wasn't looting or pillaging and burying treasure."

"Manny, this is as bad as getting in bed with some sleazy developer, and I know all about that. My people won't like it. I'm going to have to call Nolan."

"When you do, tell him the check for a million dollars is on its way."

"Connor, lovely to hear from you. How's Miami Beach and our new partner?"

Connor could hear the disingenuous tone through the phone. "Manny's fine; sends his regards. Said to tell you the blood money is on its way."

"The blood money? Whatever do you mean?"

"Your fucking retainer of a million dollars."

"And why is it blood money?"

"Because the client is President-for-Life Baby Doc Duvalier. The project is in Haiti!"

Nolan took a breath. *Not Haiti. St. Lucia maybe, or Trinidad, maybe Grenada, even Jamaica. But Haiti? Bob Marlow won't like it one bit. This isn't good.*

"I'm sure Mr. Lazarus has guarantees of payment from the government. Why don't you just worry about designing the hotels and let me worry about the business end of things."

"Francis, it's not just the money, it's the principal. It's a corrupt government that murders people."

"Connor, they, like any government, deserve the benefit of the doubt. I'll speak to Mr. Lazarus. Make sure everything is on the up and up."

"Nolan, what the fuck is that supposed to mean?"

"West, stay there and design. Do your job and stay out of mine!" Nolan hung up the phone. He looked down at the contract prepared by Dennis O'Flaherty. Turning to the back page, he saw that there were lines for two signatures, his and Bob Marlow's. He took out his Mont Blanc pen and signed it. Then he rendered a fair forgery of Bob Marlow's.

"Amanda, come in here. I have something to mail." Nolan spoke into the intercom, and she was at his desk a minute later. Nolan had the strange-looking doll that he had brought back for New Orleans and a silver pin in his hand.

"Mail this contract airmail to Manny Lazarus. Make sure it goes out in today's mail."

As she took the contract, she watched Nolan stick the pin into the head of the doll, smiling.

❖

Connor and Caudy worked until eight every night, sometimes nine. When finished, they found several good restaurants up and down Collins Avenue, so they could avoid the over-priced fare at the Versailles eateries. One day they quit early and went apartment hunting, finding a decent place with two bedrooms overlooking the Intracoastal Waterway in Miami Shores. All that mattered was that it had a large balcony with a good view of the water. It was a sublet, and fortunately came fully furnished.

Caudy was eager to start on the master plan for the development but could do little until he saw the island. Connor was also ready to kick the dirt and get a feel for the customs and indigenous architecture of Île-à-Vache, whatever that might be. They decided to travel there the following week, and Manny approved the visit. He would arrange for a government official to meet them at Duvalier Airport and thought the honored guest treatment would change Connor's mind about the regime.

In the meantime, Caudy looked into the logistics of construction on a remote island in the Caribbean. Manny was a great help, as he had once designed a resort hotel on Eleuthera. Everything had to be brought in by ship to Freeport, off-loaded on barges, and towed to the site, to a temporary dock. A concrete batch plant would be constructed to provide concrete for the project. In addition, a crude block factory was setup on-site. Worker housing had to be provided for the workers and laborers. Kitchens and dining halls would be constructed, as well as recreational facilities, including a soccer field and basketball courts. Skilled trades rented houses nearby or rented apartments in Freeport. It was an enormous undertaking.

Connor showed Lazarus his concept of circular bearing walls poured in concrete that mimicked the shape of waves crashing onto the shore. He loved it. Between these four-story-high walls would be the generous hotel suites: 17 feet wide by 30 feet long, a luxurious 510 square feet. In addition, a five-foot-wide balcony ran the full length of the room. Between each round bearing wall, two suites would be accommodated. The floors would be 36-foot-long pre-cast concrete decking, four-feet wide and one-foot thick. The manufacturer of the precast planks ensured their delivery to Fort Lauderdale by truck and then shipped to Haiti. The only problem with the design was the building's bearing walls four stories, 45-feet-high. If the walls were two-feet to three-feet thick to carry the weight of the floors, massive shoring and forms would have to be constructed to contain the wet concrete, which, with every foot poured, became an incredible weight, pushing against the sides of these temporary walls. Connor knew he needed Jerzy Stanizski to weigh in. He had solved the difficult problem of building over an underground stream at Chicago World Tower. This issue would be a walk in the park for him.

❖

It was late Thursday, a long week, exacerbated by splitting headaches that had tormented Connor for four days. They were absent when he got up every morning, but developed around lunchtime, and by nightfall, his head pounded. No amount of aspirin would help.

As he worked on layouts for the rooms of his waterside resort and held his head in one hand, he decided to see a doctor for the migraines. Caudy ambled up to his drafting table.

"You okay?"

"The headaches."

"Yeah. So, let's call it a day. I'm heading home tomorrow and you're gonna go see Rat in Key West."

"Sounds like a plan. Let me hit the john and throw some cold water on my face. Maybe that will help."

"Maybe a bar would help."

"Okay, why not? Let's go to the lobby bar across the street. I love the huge lava lamps."

"And I love Ramon's mojitos. We need to tell him goodbye, too. Next week we're in our new apartment."

The two young architects cleaned their drafting boards and said goodbye to Manny Lazarus, whom they had come to like and enjoyed working with. He was a straight shooter, no bullshit kind of guy. Though aged, with bad eyes and arthritic hands, his concepts were as fresh and daring as anything produced by the architectural elite up north. He seemed to possess that childlike love of design, the adventure of discovering something new and fresh, and particularly outrageous. Though not wanting to admit it, both were becoming disciples of the mantra "More is never enough!"

"Hey Ramon, how they hanging?" Caudy seemed to be in a particularly ebullient mood, perhaps because he was enjoying the great challenge of planning the massive Paradi sou Latè, and also because he was heading home to Chicago to see his wife, whom he missed terribly.

"The two amigos. Good to see you on a Thursday." He flipped two napkins, landing precisely in front of Caudy and West.

"You know what I want. A Ramon special mojito."

"And Mr. Connor, a tonic?"

"Fuck it, Ramon, make it a gin and tonic. With Gordon's Gin, please."

"You got it!"

Two hours later, Connor and Dan stumbled out of the Versailles in search of a neighborhood steakhouse. Connor loved that he was drunk. And the headache had disappeared.

CHAPTER FORTY-SEVEN

Connor slept in on Friday morning, or as best he could, as the bright Miami sun skirted around the curtains of his hotel room and washed the turquoise walls in streaks of white light. There was no reason to head to Key West early as Rat would probably be out on a charter, not to return to the marina until three or four.

When he got up at 10:00 A.M. his head felt as large as a casaba melon and ached like it had most days when he was drinking. He had forgotten how unpleasant and unforgiving hangovers were during his sixty days of sobriety. The only thing to do was power through it. He showered, dressed, and went downstairs to the Blue Pelican Restaurant. Regardless of the cost and lack of cooking prowess he needed OJ, coffee, and breakfast.

Three aspirins and $13.50 later, West crossed Collins Avenue to the parking garage that was part of Lazarus & Berger's office building and found his car. He was looking forward to the ride across the Keys with its almost continuous views of the Gulf and the Straits of Florida, culminating in the famous 7-Mile Bridge. He hoped the weekend traffic of pickup trucks pulling boats, and RVs would not be too bad.

By noon he was on fabled US-1 heading southwest to the town he had come to love. Just south of Key Largo he pulled off the road at Tarpon Liquors. *Fuck it! It's the weekend,* he thought. The brief head-pounding reprieve after breakfast had returned. He bought a Styrofoam cooler, a bag of ice and a six-pack of Miller High Life. Back on the two-lane road, he popped a top and wished that his 4-door Pontiac Tempest was a convertible.

By 3:30 P.M., he had arrived at the city marina. As he drove over the bridge beside the slips, he looked for *Daddy's*

Money. The berth he knew so well was empty. He parked the car; at 4:30, there was still no sign of Rat or his pricey fishing boat. West considered the possibility that Tomlinson had put it in dry-dock. It was December, a good time to perform maintenance and clean the hull of the boat. If Rat was anywhere on the island at 5:00 P.M., it would be the Green Parrot. He started the car and headed toward Mile Marker 1, the end of the fabled road, as the signpost was right outside the bar. He would be there in less than fifteen minutes.

❖

The bar was busy. It was happy hour and Friday. The place seemed to be always dimly lit, deep roof overhangs preventing both the daylight and tropical breezes from entering. Today, several large ceiling fans and the cool December day made it comfortable. Connor found a place at the rectangular bar. A female bartender was busy. He tried to get her attention as he looked around the large room for Rat. This was getting annoying. Where the hell was his friend?

"Hey, miss, can I get a drink?"

The young brunette with a short brown pageboy glanced at him with deep blue eyes. She was wearing a white tank top and short shorts, both articles of clothing accentuating her tan and a perfect 5'8" body. The top flattered her breasts, and the shorts her strong and shapely runner's legs.

"Miss? Nobody says 'miss.' Babe, darlin', even bitch maybe, but not 'miss.'"

"Sorry, okay, ah honey, I'd like a ginger ale." Connor smiled, noticing a tattoo of a mermaid on the back of the pretty barmaid's neck. Interesting, even a little sexy.

"Honey? Seriously. What's your name, Cowboy?"

"Connor. Maybe if I knew yours, I wouldn't use such bad nouns. You new here?"

"Started two weeks ago. What's a regular at the Green Parrot doing ordering a ginger ale? You fighting a battle with the bottle, Connor?"

"I fought it and lost. Didn't do so well last night either. You haven't told me your name, honey?"

"Stop with the honey. I'm Annie."

"From here."

"Lauderdale. Business was slow. I'm giving the Conch Republic a whirl."

"Annie what?"

"Annie Gallagher. I'll be right back, got a real customer." She gave Connor a wink and a smile. The hairs rose on the back of his neck. Despite his lame drink, she was back quickly.

"Now that you know all about me, what's your last name?"

"West. Connor West. I used to live here."

"Used to? And I was just getting to like you."

"I'm in Miami right now. How about getting me a refill? But add some bourbon to it." Connor knew it was only a matter of time, and he would need a quick tongue to keep up with Annie Gallagher.

"Now you're talkin', Cowboy!" Annie went to the back bar and pulled down a bottle of Jim Beam. She handed him a generous pour, straight up.

"You could be trouble for me." Connor looked lovingly at the drink and sipped it.

"And vice versa. How come I haven't seen you here before today?"

"It's a long story. You wouldn't happen to know a young guy named Rat, would you?"

"Rat? Nice name. Friend?"

"Best friend. Rich Tomlinson. Owns a fishing boat, *Daddy's Money*. He likes this place"

"As I said, I'm new. Young guy. Hmmm. Don't go away."

"No chance." As Annie turned, Connor took note of her perfect ass.

Annie went around to the other side of the bar. In a moment, a light-skinned black man with a bottle of Red Stripe was standing in front of Connor. His hair was salt and pepper, long and pulled back into a ponytail. He was in his early fifty's, medium build, with muscular arms. His eyes were brown and welcoming, not sinister. He smiled and held out his hand.

217

"Armand Jolicoeur. Are you Connor?"

"I am. Connor West. How did you know?"

"Lucky guess. You are looking for Rich? I know him well. Where is he?"

"I was hoping to find him here. I haven't heard from him, and his boat isn't at the marina. Thought it might be in dry-dock." Connor started to worry.

"This is a concern. I have not seen him since a week ago last Wednesday. He told me he was going to his poker game. He plays too much and too badly, I fear. And his boat was not in dry-dock when I last saw it. I have a boat too, at the marina."

Annie had returned, looked at the two, and Armand nodded. She prepared two more drinks, mouthing to the older man, "He's cute."

"Rat invited me to those games. I never had the money or the desire. Pretty high stakes from what he told me."

"It is not like Richard. I know he was in trouble financially..."

"Rat in trouble financially? He's got a huge trust fund."

"Yes, but controlled by his father. His father funded some more but he told me he had to win at the game that night. We need to find him. He is a good man, and we have become good friends. Let's go talk to the harbormaster, Tom, at the marina."

"Now?"

"Yes, now. I sense some evil. Papa Legba has told me so in my dreams."

"Papa Legba?"

"In Voodou, he is the guardian of the crossroads of life. I worry Rat has made a wrong turn."

"That's right. Rat told me you are from Haiti."

"Was. It is a bad place now. Let us go. I will buy your drink."

"No, let me, please." Connor turned to the bar and waved at Annie.

"Sorry, I gotta go, Annie Gallagher. Will twenty cover it?"

"Yeah, and more." Annie took the Jackson and pulled out her pen. She wrote down her phone number and handed the bill back to Connor. "You owe me, Cowboy, so you'd better come back."

Connor smiled. He knew he would.

CHAPTER FORTY-EIGHT

They took Connor's car for the short ride back to the marina. Tom, the harbormaster was about to close up after a long day. Armand greeted him with a handshake and a hug. Connor added a strong hello as he knew Tom well.

"Tom, what do you know about *Daddy's Money*? It hasn't been here in almost two weeks."

"I've been wondering myself. Rent is due on the dock slip. Gone since, let's see, it's on my calendar. Here it is, a week ago yesterday."

"Did he leave a message on your phone? Every boat needs to report to you when they leave the marina, in case they don't come back. Coast Guard regs." Connor remembered that from his time on the boat, often calling in the day's itinerary for Rat.

"Come to think about it, there was a bunch of static that morning. I couldn't make it out."

"Do you still have the recording?" Armand was curious.

"Yeah, I keep all messages for two weeks. Come inside and I'll play it back."

Tom scratched his head and pressed the rewind button on the recording machine. The three listened to the noise. "See, there's no message, just static."

"Rewind it and play it again," Connor insisted.

As they listened again, Armand grabbed a pen and began writing down letters. "It's Morse code, Tom, you should know that, my friend." He kept writing letters down, deciphering the series of dashes and dots. "Replay it one more time, I've almost got it."

After the third time, he looked at the letters. "D, M, that's *Daddy's Money*. Then T-A-V-E-R-N-I-E-R. The boat was going to Tavernier. Then only an 'S'."

Connor stared at the single letter. "Maybe he was starting to tap out SOS and had to quit. Damn, what kind of trouble did he get into?"

"We'll take my boat to Tavernier in the morning, Connor. You can sleep on it tonight. It's down in slip 15. It's the *Joli's Revenge*."

"The *Joli's Revenge's* your boat? It's a nice vessel, and it's damn big."

"I needed big to get here from the Dominican Republic. Let us have some dinner, Mr. Connor, then turn in and get an early start."

It was only 8 P.M. and Connor was already thinking about returning to the Green Parrott and getting better acquainted with Annie. But he didn't want to be rude, and Armand was as concerned about Tomlinson as he was.

"Sounds good. Let me get my bag out of the car. I'll see you at the boat."

The 58-foot Bertram Yacht was more a pleasure boat than a sport fisherman, though it did have a fighting chair on the small rear deck area. The thirteen additional feet in length allowed for a spacious, even luxurious interior. Armand showed Connor to his cabin with two twin beds and an adjacent bath.

At a small seafood restaurant adjacent to the marina, Connor got to know Armand Jolicoeur.

"The *Joli's Revenge* was my father's boat. When he died in 1972, it became mine. We escaped on it from Haiti in 1971 and went to the Dominican Republic. My father was a prominent lawyer, as was my mother. By Haitian standards, we were quite well off. We lived in a large house in Kenscoff with servants. We are mulattos, light-skinned blacks. During Papa Doc's reign, he targeted us. He wanted the native Haitians in control, though we were the educated minority. When Baby Doc assumed power in 1971 upon the death of his father, my mother began to speak out. She was a judge and had reached the point where she would no longer tolerate the corrupt Duvalier's. The father ruined the country, forcing the

221

brain-trust to flee to the United States, France, or for us, the Dominican Republic, where there was stability."

"Did your father speak out, too?"

"No, he kept his head down as you might say, but he hated the Duvalier's as much as my mother."

"What happened?"

"She was speaking at a rally in Port-au-Prince in a large plaza. My father and I were listening to the speeches. Suddenly, military trucks and tap-taps converged. The Tonton Macoute overwhelmed the area. We barely escaped through a small alley. Later that night, we returned. My mother and eight others were hanging from the trees in the plaza, their mouths sewn shut."

"Oh, God. Baby Doc did that?" Connor lost his appetite for the fried grouper in front of him.

"We got back to our house in Kenscoff, got a few treasured belongings and clothes, and managed to get to our boat. It was near midnight, the Macoute were everywhere, rounding up people, shooting them and burning houses. It was hell. Fortunately, they weren't looking at the small marina west of the city."

"I'm so sorry." Thoughts of Manny's client, his client, filled Connor's mind.

"A year later, without my mother, my father died of a broken heart. His spirit wanders in the Dominican Republic, but it is not his home. His home is Haiti."

Early Saturday, Armand Jolicoeur throttled up the twin Caterpillar diesels that powered *Joli's Revenge*, and he and Connor headed for Tavernier on the inland side up through Florida Bay. He motored under US-1 and made his way to the Tavernier Marina. They tied up alongside the dock, the boat's size overwhelming most of the smaller craft.

A grizzled old man stood behind the counter of the Mini-Mart. Connor remembered he carried a photo in his wallet of him and Rat in front of *Daddy's Money*, taken after a successful fishing trip. Ten fish spread out on the dock in front of them, including a large sailfish, and they were both smiling.

"Excuse me. Maybe you can help me. Do you recognize this man and the boat?" Connor doing his best Joe Friday imitation.

A quick uninterested look and the reply, "Nah, never saw him."

Armand stepped up to the counter and grabbed the man's dirty shirt. "Look again, monsieur. It is important!"

The old man shot up straight and looked at the photo again. "Oh yeah, I remember. Came in last week after dark. Bought a bunch of weird shit and tried to pay for it with a maxed-out credit card. Then he gave me cash."

"Did he buy fuel, monsieur?" Jolicoeur let go of the man's shirt and patted out the wrinkles.

"No, another guy. A Spic. Slicked back hair, necklace around his neck. He paid with cash, $135. I remember that."

"Glad your memory's returning," Connor said sarcastically. "Anything else?"

"There was a third guy. Big Black man. Tats all over his arms, gold earring and gold tooth."

"Did he buy anything?"

"A six-pack and got pissed when I asked for ID. Boss says I gotta ID everybody. I don't think he was getting back on that fishing boat."

"Why, my friend?"

"He asked about motels nearby. I told him to go a half-mile down the road to the Manatee Inn. He walked out and headed in that direction."

"Mind if we keep the boat here for an hour?" Armand slipped the clerk a twenty.

"Not at all. Glad I could help."

"Yeah, right..."

In fifteen minutes, Armand and Connor were in the small lobby of the Manatee Inn. Faded posters of Key Largo yellowed on the walls. There was an old Naugahyde sofa against full height picture windows that angled out from the floor to the ceiling. A bunch of old Life Magazines rested on a pink Formica coffee table. 1955 had returned.

"Check-in isn't until three, gents. And I don't rent to queers." The middle-aged woman looked hard at the unusual pairing, conjuring up what the relationship was like and who played the bitch.

"We're not checking in, thank you, madame. May we look at your guest register from a week ago? We're trying to locate a friend who was passing through."

"Oh, I see, you guys are cops. Got badges?"

"Yes, this is my badge." Armand took out a .40 caliber Smith & Wesson and laid it on the counter. Connor's eyes widened, and he took a step back. His new friend meant business.

"Let me get it for you." The woman reached below the counter, a brought up the guest book. Her hands were shaking.

"Thank you so much." Armand flipped the pages back to Thursday. He didn't recognize any of the names. A quick perusal by Connor had the same result.

"He is a large Black man, tattoos on both arms, a gold earring, a gold tooth. He checked in last Thursday night after dark."

"Oh yeah, I remember him. Scared the living shit out of me, but when he opened up he seemed nice enough. There's his signature there, C. Jackson." Her shaking finger pointed at the name on the register.

"How did he pay?"

"In cash. Oh, and he asked if there was a shuttle to Key West in the morning. Told him it came by at 9:00 A.M. I assume he got on it, but I was off the clock by then."

"Thank you, madame, you have been most helpful. And sorry about the gun. Perhaps this will assuage matters." Jolicoeur took out a twenty and placed it in a Jerry's Kids donation jar on the counter. "Good day."

❖

"We need to get back to Key West and find this Mr. Jackson." Armand headed for *Joli's Revenge*, Connor following behind.

"Got any ideas?"
"Yes, now I think I know of this man."

CHAPTER FORTY-NINE

Rat was quite sure he was going mad. He had been in his cell, his box, for four days. In one corner was a pail, now practically overflowing with his feces and urine. During the day, even though it was December, the temperature reached the high eighties in the cramped space, which smelled worse every day. The wound on his forehead was so sore he could not touch it and he thought he was getting a fever.

Only Trevor's encouragement from the next cell kept him going. Every morning he led a drill of calisthenics-squats, jumping jacks, stretches, and quasi-pushups. The cell was so tight that he couldn't fully stretch out. Though not religious, Trevor insisted they pray together. Rat repeated Catholic prayers before they ate. Once a day, a combination of black beans and yellow rice with a few pieces of tough meat passed through a 4" by 12" opening in the old wood door. Though it tasted stale and maggots crawled through the food, he devoured it.

When the guard came, Rat demanded to see the American ambassador. The plea, translated by Trevor, met with a laugh.

Rat heard footsteps of more than one guard. His sense of hearing had become more acute as he tried to suppress sight and smell. The steps stopped at his cell, and the key went into the lock. The door opened and Rat looked up at two burly guards in sleeveless tee shirts and wearing aviator sunglasses. They dragged him out of the cell.

"Leve! li lè pou rekreyasyon ak douch."

With a free hand, Rat banged on the metal wall. "Trevor, what did he say?"

Before Trevor could answer, his cell door flew open, and he was in the corridor, his stiff legs shaking. "Rich, we are going outside for exercise and a bath."

Rat looked at Trevor as the two inmates were led down the hall. He had grown a short beard and his Afro matted. He thought he saw lice crawling around in it, making a nest.

"Trevor, you look like shit," Rat smiled.

"And you, my friend, look little better. That wound on your forehead is infected, I think. You need to go to the infirmary if this place has one."

"Mesye, zanmi mwen bezwen yon doktè. Blesi nan tèt li enfekte."* Trevor nodded toward Rat's head wound.

The guard grunted, then grabbed Rat by the cheeks, looking at the head wound. He scowled.

The short walk down the corridor ended, prisoners now in front and behind Rat and Trevor. They came to a door that the guard opened. The morning light blinded the pair. As soon as they were outside, a torrent of water from a fire hose hit them. Trevor grabbed Rat.

"Drink the water. Drink as much as you can. And strip if you want to clean your body and then try to wash your clothes." Rat did as his friend instructed. As he ran his hands through his hair, he saw little pink mites come off in his hand. He felt sick. Then the hose hit his wound and a bolt of pain coursed through his body. He fell to the ground, unconscious, into the newly created mud in the outdoor courtyard.

Two guards came over to him with a stretcher. They lifted him and, on their direction, the water hit Rat again to wash him off. They put his body on the canvas stretcher and left, Trevor calling out: "Be strong, mon. Be very strong."

When Tomlinson awoke, he was in a large dormitory, cots lining both sides. The walls were gray-white, and dried blood splattered portions of the walls. A few fans moved the hot air around. It smelled of rubbing alcohol, iodine, and disease.

An older man in a dirty white medical jacket loomed over him. "Hold still." The doctor placed a towel over Rat's eyes, nose, and mouth. Rat knew they were going to suffocate him. There was no reason to keep sick prisoners alive. He flayed his arms and tried to free himself.

227

"I say hold still! Do you not understand English, Blanc?"

Rat realized the man was speaking English. He felt a liquid pour over his head. Then there was nothing but burning pain. He cried out. The doctor dabbed the wound and poured on more liquid. More pain, though not as intense as before. He felt the doctor grab his forearm and the sting of a needle.

"There, I have cleaned your wound and given you a shot of penicillin. You will stay here for two days, then you will be well enough to go back."

"I can't go back. I'll go mad."

"Tell me, why are you here? You are a Blanc and an American, I think. Did you murder a prostitute?"

"No! I came here on my boat. Your people think I smuggled drugs. We had no drugs. I need to see the American ambassador. Help me, for the love of God."

The doctor proceeded to wrap a clean white bandage around Rat's head. As he did, he spoke. "I can do nothing for you. I am a prisoner as well from the Dominican Republic. I do this work to get better treatment and food."

"What we're you guilty of?"

"Nothing. Everyone here is innocent."

"Can you give me something for the pain? My head is on fire."

"Tomorrow, yes, if you still have pain. You have a fever. The shot today will help that. I will add another day here in the hospital. If you see someone die, grab his food and eat it. Learn to survive. Now you must rest."

Rat looked around the dormitory. Compared to his cell, it was a palace. He wished he could stay there for at least a week.

* "Mister, my friend needs a doctor. His head wound is infected."

Dominique St. Jacques dialed the number of the Port-au-Prince State Bank in his spacious new office. He was enjoying the promotion to interior minister and was only beginning to comprehend the great power he possessed. He was in charge of the greatest development ever attempted by the government since the construction of Duvalierville, a postmodern utopian city begun by Papa Doc. The result, however, was less than stellar. It had become one of Port-au-Prince's largest slums. St. Jacques determined that Paradi sou Latè would be different.

The deal with the Black Tuna Gang alone would bring in millions of dollars of drug money, with Haiti providing home-grown marijuana and as a transshipment point for cocaine and heroin from Columbia and Honduras. New economic aid was being offered by the United States, France, and the Bahamas. A new baseball factory had opened outside the capital and the payoff from the Rawlings Corporation would be millions a year.

"State Bank."

"Let me speak to Marius; this is the interior minister."

"Right way, excellency." St. Jacques waited, fiddling with a pencil.

"Monsieur St. Jacques, an honor; to what do I owe the pleasure?"

"Marius, good day. I was checking the accounts. I do not see the funds from our friends in Miami on the ledger. I believe it was to be initially $500,000."

"From Mr. Flatshorn? Excellency, General Raymond handled that transaction personally a week ago, last Saturday."

"Raymond? He is in exile in Spain. He had no authority. Where is the money?"

The bank officer opened his shirt collar and wiped his brow. "Sir, the money is in a Spanish Bank per his instructions. No one told me he was no longer in charge. I have dealt with him on many governmental and personal financial matters."

"In Spain? Call that bank and get the money back."

"I will do my best, monsieur."

St. Jacques slammed down the phone as his secretary buzzed on the intercom. "Minister, a Mr. Flatshorn from Miami wishes to speak with you."

The interior minister paused. He did not want to take the call but decided if he didn't things would be worse for it. "Mr. Flatshorn, how are you?"

"St. Jacques, where's Raymond, and where's my fishing boat with 4,000 kilos of product? It should have been here Tuesday. It's fucking Thursday."

"My friend..."

"Don't give me that 'my friend' shit. I've been calling General Raymond's office for two days. There is no answer. What the fuck's going on?"

"General Raymond has been re-assigned as Ambassador to Spain." St. Jacques wanted to say as little as possible.

"I talked with him on Saturday, confirmed our deal, and wired the money. The bank sent verification. You have my money, but I have nothing to show for it."

"Perhaps the boat got caught in a storm..."

"St. Jacques, the weather is clear all the way to Florida. I haven't heard from *Daddy's Money* since last Saturday evening. They expected to arrive at Petit-Goave Sunday morning. And Raymond never said anything about Spain. This is total bullshit!"

"My apologies. I meant to tell you and arrange for all business between us to go through me. An oversight on my part. As to the boat, let me make some inquiries." St. Jacques began to re-think his new responsibilities. An 'assistant' minister didn't do much but got paid handsomely.

"Inquire fast, St. Jacques. And until I see my fishing boat and my product, our entire deal is off. I should have known better than to do business with the Duvalier's. They're as corrupt as they come!" Flatshorn put down the receiver, got up, and went to the bar for a double bourbon. Not having 4,000 kilos of cocaine would wreak havoc on his suppliers and customers. He'd lose a lot of business; maybe even his life.

CHAPTER FIFTY

By nightfall, Connor and Armand had returned to the city marina and tied up *Joli's Revenge*. The trip back had been informative for Connor. Armand told him many disquieting stories of Haiti and its slow ruin under the rule of the Duvalier's. What Manny had told him about the regime turning a new leaf now seemed like so much bullshit, but there was a glimmer of hope. Armand reminded Connor that he had left the country in 1971 and that perhaps now, in 1975, things might indeed be different. The development of a great resort on Île-à-Vache was certainly a step in the right direction.

"I am the eternal optimist, Connor. And I do not think Baby Doc is the same as his father. From what I found out, when the Tonton Macoute murdered my mother and had their night of terror, he was playing on the French Rivera. I keep up now with the events in Haiti from friends. They tell me he had the head of the Tonton killed. That is a positive sign."

"I wish the project was in the Bahamas. What you have told me gives me heartburn. I am going there this Wednesday to see the island. Do you want to come? I may need a bodyguard."

"I dare not return under the circumstances. But with your position as designer on this project, they will lay out the red carpet for you. You will be under the government's protection."

The boat safely secured, the two sleuths got into Connor's car and drove to Old Town. They parked in the alley behind the Curry Mansion on Caroline Street, home of Key West's first millionaire, and walked to the Bull Bar at the corner of Duval and Caroline. Its large open-air seating along Duval Street made it popular with locals for people-watching. After a quick inquiry by Armand at the back bar, he motioned Connor to follow him up the stairs to the Whistle Bar, again open to Duval as well, and as suitable for viewing the tourists, lovers, hustlers, and colorful creatures that strolled Duval at night looking for a good time.

"Is Mr. Jackson here?" Armand looked to the back where the office was located, and then off to the stairs that led to the third floor. It featured the only clothing optional bar in the city, The Garden of Eden. Rat had taken Connor there once. West vowed never to return, as the only naked people were old men.

"He's in the office. Let me get him. Anything to drink?"

"Two Red Stripes, please." Armand looked at Connor with hope. "I think this is our man. I know him only by reputation. He owns this place and a couple of others. Plus, I heard he handles some women in town. An unsavory type. Be on your guard."

Cicero Jackson came out of the backroom wearing a holster with a Colt M1-911 handgun. He was a massive man, sporting a gold earring, biceps bulging through his dark brown long sleeve shirt, cuffs rolled up.

"Who wants to see me?"

"Mr. Jackson, I do not believe we have had the pleasure. I am Armand Jolicoeur. I run a fishing charter. This is Connor West who used to work for Rich Tomlinson on *Daddy's Money*. We are trying to locate our friend. Perhaps you can help?"

"I know nothing about him."

"Perhaps you are familiar with the Manatee Inn in Tavernier, and buying a six-pack at the marina there after you came off that boat?"

Jackson stopped, grabbed a glass mug and poured a draft beer, not saying anything. Filled, he took a gulp. "You're not with the Black Tuna Gang, or you'd have the medallion. How do you know this?"

"Gang? No, we aren't with any gang; we are merely trying to find Rat. I fear he has run into trouble."

"You got that right, but I had nothing to do with it. Well, almost nothing. Rat owed over fifteen large to a guy named Carlos, who belonged to that bunch of drug runners. Lost it in a poker game. I was along for the ride until Tavernier. I got off *Daddy's Money;* I didn't want to go to Haiti."

Armand's eyes widened. "Haiti?"

"Yeah, Port-au-Prince. They were picking up a load of blow, that's all I know. I had settled... affairs with the gang and headed back here. That drug business ain't for me."

Connor took a drink of his Jamaican beer. "Do you know Rat?"

"Yeah, I'm a regular at the card game. He's a good kid. Listen, I'm sorry I got him into trouble with those assholes, but I had a debt to repay and I repaid it. I've felt real bad about it ever since they took his boat... "

"The Black Tuna Gang took his boat?"

"He didn't exactly volunteer to go on the trip. Carlos commandeered the boat. It was payback for the gambling debt."

Connor looked at Armand with alarm and turned to Cicero. "Thanks for the info."

"Beers are on me. And if you need help to find Rat, let me know. Like I said, he's a good guy."

❖

"What are we gonna do?" Connor finished his beer as he and Armand sat along the rail, looking down on Duval.

Armand looked at his new friend. "I'm afraid nothing for now. Wait a few days. Maybe he will have repaid his debt with a successful run and come back all the wiser. Maybe he'll decide he likes the money and keep running drugs for the adventure and the adrenaline rush. It is quite common."

"Rat, a drug runner? It's not possible. If he's in Haiti, maybe I can find him when I go there this week."

"And where will you look? At the American country club? Perhaps the U.S. Embassy? Hopefully, if all went well, he's likely back in Tavernier or Miami."

"What if he got caught? He'd be in jail or prison. I could ask around." Connor displayed his youthful naiveté.

"My young friend, I would not wish that situation on anyone. I know all about Fort Dimanche. It is a grist mill of death. A sign above the main entrance reads 'Tout moun ki antre nan pòt sa yo abandone espwa ou nan Bondye.'"

"Care to translate?"

"'All who enter through these doors abandon your hope in God.' You had better pray he is a good drug runner. And I'm sure your hosts will not let you see anything as unpleasant as Fort Dimanche."

Connor looked down on the busy street full of young couples. He lifted his beer and realized it was empty. The Green Parrot was only six blocks away.

"Well, we won't find Rat tonight, that's for sure. At least we know something."

"Will you be going back to Miami in the morning? You are welcome to stay on the boat tonight."

"Even if it's late?"

"Certainly. Go see Annie. I think she likes you."

Connor didn't know what to say. He shook Armand's hand and then decided a hug was in order. "Thank you, my new Haitian friend. Rat was right. You are good people."

"When you have seen all the evil I have, good is an easy choice. Regards to Annie."

CHAPTER FIFTY-ONE

The sign above the bar said: **No Sniveling**. Connor sat patiently for Annie to make the rounds to where he was sitting, directly under the placard. "Hey miss, I've been waiting a long time here. What does it take to get a drink in this joint?"

"What does the sign say, Cowboy? And you owe me twenty bucks."

"Got it right here."

Annie reached out, stroked his hand and took the bill, and smiled. It was close to real sex. "Whadda ya have, sailor?"

"How about one of those Jim Beam's with a splash of ginger ale?"

"Now that's my kind of patron."

"What time do you get off work?"

"You cut right to the chase, don't you? 2 A.M."

"Nooooo. Really?"

"Read the sign above you, Connor."

"I'm not sniveling; I'm depressed."

"I'm messin' with you. Fortunately for you, I came in at two today. So, I'm leaving at ten. Where are you taking me?"

"To paradise."

"You get that pickup line out of a self-help book?" Annie handed Connor his drink and leaned over the bar, kissing him on the forehead, smiling a killer smile. The faux sex was getting better.

❖

After a late dinner at Schooner Wharf, an open-air restaurant-bar off the Old Town marina, which featured local singers who didn't make too much of a ruckus, Connor and Annie had reached the awkward moment—the next move in the budding relationship. She found out all about him and loved the complexity that was his life.

When he reached the part about Marilyn's untimely death and he choked up, she took his hand and squeezed, saying, "It had to be tough. Did you cry at the funeral?" He responded he had, and she said, "Good, now it's time to move on." Connor looked at her and thought that Annie Gallagher was the tonic, the medicine that he needed to ease his sorrow. But moving on was easier said than done.

"I better go. It's late and I don't want to wake Armand." He looked at the check and put twenty-five dollars on the table.

"I've got a better idea. You are a gentleman, aren't you?"

"In every respect. I even went to Harvard."

"That's what I'm afraid of. Come on, I live a couple of blocks from here."

They reached the coach house on William Street above a slightly tilted two-car garage behind a large old Conch house built in the early 1900s. A set of outside steps led to the doorway, and Annie took out her keys.

"You can sleep on the couch, Cowboy."

"My intention all along, miss."

A hand mussing his hair interrupted his sleep at 3 A.M. Then a kiss on his neck and a hand reached for his. Annie tugged. He got up and did as instructed, the hand pulling him toward the bedroom. And paradise.

Annie nuzzled against Connor, but he didn't respond. She got up on her elbow to see his face. A waning full moon provided a soft pallor of light. Tears ran down his face.

He got up and went back to the front room where his clothes were. Annie followed.

"I'm not ready, Annie. I'm sorry."

"You know where to find me, Cowboy, anytime."

236

"Thanks, miss." He kissed her lightly on the lips and walked out into the moonlit night and the drive to Miami.

CHAPTER FIFTY-TWO

Connor arrived at work early on Monday, his head full of design ideas for his hotel; concerns about working for a ruthless and corrupt client; fears about what had happened to his friend Rat; and mostly, thoughts about Annie. He wasn't sure he had done the right thing, leaving her in the middle of the night for a memory. He had carried a piece of Marilyn in his heart for almost a year while he worked on Rat's fishing boat. An aching heart, and all for nothing. Then brief happiness and it ended again. How much longer was he going to let her memory keep him from living life?

"Good morning, Esther, is Manny in yet?"

"No, hon, but there's a package for you that arrived express mail late Friday. From Chicago."

"Thanks." Connor looked at the return address. It was from Jerzy. He hoped it was the structural design of his great circular bearing walls for his beachfront hotel. He took the package, dropped it on his desk and headed for the break room where hot coffee waited. Unlike Chicago, good coffee was a requirement in South Florida with its large and diverse Cuban and Central American population. He had usurped a Miami Dolphins mug, winners of back-to-back Super Bowls in 1972 and 1973. They fell short in 1974 but were a force to be reckoned with in the NFL. No one had complained about it missing, so it was Connor's by default.

As he sipped his coffee and opened the envelope, his mood was melancholic. He couldn't stop thinking about Annie. Had he lost her for good? Probably. And then there was his friend Rich Tomlinson. Headed to Haiti to run drugs. He looked around the drafting room. Its large windows flooded the space with uplifting morning light. Connor sighed and opened up the structural drawings.

Nothing I can do about Rat or Annie now. But I'll talk to Manny about Haiti when he comes in, he thought. On the first page of schematic structural drawings, in elegant scribbling, was a handwritten note from Jerzy.

> *Dear Mr. Big Shot Designer,*
> *Have you ever heard of columns and beams?*
> *No, you have to have walls. Worse, round walls!*
> *But I figure out, even though I have no soil*
> *report. Maybe you can secure for me so your*
> *big design won't fall down?*
> *Can I come to Miami? It is cold as Poland here*
> *in Chicago!*
> *Regards,*
>
> *Jerzy*

Connor laughed and took another sip of coffee. He heard sounds in the reception room. He could tell it was Manny from the distinctive voice. He was quickly in the room. Behind him were three other people, and Manny was directing them to vacant drafting tables. Reinforcements had arrived. They appeared to be familiar with their surroundings, and after a few words of instruction Manny went off towards his corner workspace. He did not have a separate office; he liked to be in the center of the action. Connor was at his space in a flash.

"Morning, Manny. Got a minute?"

"For my whiz kid designer, of course. Hey, you get lucky down in Key West? I've been there a buncha times—always a lot of hot twat. Geez, what I'd give to be young again!"

"I had a nice time, Manny. But I also found out a lot about the Duvalier's. Are you sure you want to be in bed with them?"

"Oy vey, not this again? Connor, it's a done deal. We're committed. I pull the plug, they'll probably kill me."

"My point, Manny. These are bad people."

"I just sent your buddy Nolan a big check and just deposited mine. It's too late. Look, here are your tickets to Port-au-Prince for Wednesday. First-class on Pan-Am, compliments of those bad guys. A guy named St. Jacques and his people will meet you at the airport. Until you see that island, meet Baby Doc, do me a favor, and hold off any judgment."

"Fair enough..." Connor didn't want to fight a battle he knew he'd lose. He had noticed the checks late Thursday on Lazarus' desk. A million dollars each.

"I seen that package from Chicago. Good news?"

"Yeah, Jerzy designed the wall. But we need soil reports."

"Shit, yeah. Forgot about that. I'll call Lerner and Stein. Harry Stein's done all my dirt work for years."

"You do any work with any, well, Christians?"

"You mean Goyim? Sure...you, Caudy, and Nolan. But here in Miami? They don't call it little Tel Aviv for nuttin'. Now, let's go look at the Pollack's design. Oh and let me introduce you to Maury, Levi, and Arnold. I brought them back out of retirement so to speak."

Connor rolled his eyes. "The pleasure will be all mine."

"I like it. The walls taper from the base which is three-feet, six-inches to the top, which is one-foot thick. And we can use that pre-cast plank. Good. I see he has six-inch insets for the decking cast into the walls. We'll need to set up a batch plant for sure. We're gonna need a mother-fucking lot of concrete."

Manny did a quick calculation. "That's over 175 cubic yards of mud per wall, not including what Jerzy's showing here as drilled piers or caissons. Then there's the shit-load of reinforcing for such a tall wall. And the formwork will be quite something. It's gonna need to be a couple a pours. Maybe here in Miami or New York, they could do one wall 45 feet high, but not down in the boonies."

"Okay, I guess I better send a telegram to Jerzy about the reinforcing. In the meantime, I'd better start refining the rooms and then move onto designing the common area spaces."

"Got a lobby idea in mind?"

"Not yet. But I'll think of something. It will help me take my mind off of other stuff."

"Later, my son. Tell me when Caudy comes in. I want to see what he's coming up with on the master plan.'

"You got it."

The team of six architects toiled late every night. Lenny was still working on Roy Rogers site plans, though Lazarus had decided to tell the roast beef sandwich company to kiss his ass. With Paradi sou Latè, he would be busy for several years and make millions. There was one significant change to the contract, however, sent back and signed by St. Jacques. The first three hotel designs had to be ready in three months. There would indeed be a lot of late nights.

The Wednesday morning Pan-Am flight to Port-au-Prince was like nothing Connor and Dan had ever experienced. Pretty stewardesses catered to their every need. White linens covered their tray tables; mimosas were served with omelets, a fresh fruit cup, and croissants. There were Bloody Mary's afterward. Being in the employ of a banana republic dictator did have its perks.

Connor told Caudy all about Armand Jolicoeur and his unhappy past in Haiti and that his best friend, Rat, had gone missing. Caudy expressed sympathy and ordered another Bloody Mary.

CHAPTER FIFTY-THREE

The Boeing 707 landed smoothly at Duvalier International Airport. The aircraft was less than half full, comprised mostly a few solemn passengers and businessmen. Inside the ten-year-old arrivals terminal, the two architects were met by a contingent of six men in suits. At the head was an imposing black man wearing aviator sunglasses. Another man held a sign that read: 'Lazarus Architects.' St. Jacques removed his sunglasses and moved toward Connor and Dan.

"Mr. West, Mr. Caudy, welcome to our island nation!"

As Caudy shook hands, Connor said, "Thank you. Nice to be here in...paradise." The Bloody Mary's were still having a salutary effect.

"I am Dominique St. Jacques, interior minister. Please follow me. The car is waiting, and we have a big day planned for you. One of my men will collect your luggage and we will have it delivered directly to the Hotel Oloffson where we have secured suites for you. It is the most famous hotel in Haiti. Mr. Graham Greene wrote about it."

"Sounds terrific."

St. Jacques looked at his two guests. *These boys are designing Paradi sou Latè? I will need to speak with Lazarus about this.*

The stretch Lincoln Continental with the American and Haitian flags flying above the headlights had the same effect on West and Caudy as it did on Manny Lazarus. Flanking the car were two uniformed Tonton Macoute with shiny black riding boots perched on Harley Davidson's. Connor looked at Dan and raised his eyebrows with a slight smile. He wanted to say "Holy Shit" but kept his mouth shut. Inside the rear of the limousine, St. Jacques offered them a glass of Haitian rum, and as he poured, elaborated on the day's itinerary.

"The president is looking forward to meeting you, trusted associates of Mr. Lazarus, who he personally commissioned with this most important project. He would like to discuss the development with you over lunch. Then we will return to the airport where the state jet will be waiting to take us to Les Cayes. The drive to the town would be about four hours, but once we construct the four-lane highway, it will be cut down to two. Then the presidential yacht will take us on a short boat trip to Île-à-Vache, about thirty minutes. We will spend the afternoon there and have a banquet in the town of Madame Bernard."

Connor was paying attention, but barely. He was more interested in the sights out his window. The city looked nice enough. There were substantial buildings, parks, and plazas, monuments to heroes and soldiers. The driver knew to avoid the predominantly narrow roads, staying on the boulevards, away from the many decrepit buildings and the vast slums.

When they arrived at the Presidential Palace, the façade reminded Connor of something akin to a French White House: a large center dome with cupola, and two smaller, flanking domes. As the motorcade approached, a pair of wrought-iron gates opened and uniformed men standing by small guard kiosks snapped to attention.

"Mr. St. Jacques, we're just a couple of architects working with Mr. Lazarus."

"As designers of Paradi-sou-Latè, you are very important to this nation, I assure you. Pardon me, however, but you are very young."

"Which is why we are very good."

"Touché. Look, we have arrived."

❖

"May I present his Excellency, President Jean-Claude Duvalier. Excellency, this is Mr. Connor West and Mr. Daniel Caudy. They are working closely with Mr. Lazarus."

Baby Doc, dressed in a shiny grey suit and mundane tie extended his chubby hand for a weak handshake. "It is good to see young people in this work. I am 25 years old myself."

Connor was not sure how to respond. He had never been in the presence of a head of state or one the same age as he was. "Mr. President, it is nice to meet you. I'm just 26. Dan here is 28. We are, ah, happy to be working on your special project."

"Good. You must tell me all about it over lunch. Follow me to the next room, please"

The state dining room was something out of an interior designer's bad dream of gold leaf, flocked wallpaper, and too much ornamentation. Connor was in awe, and not in a good way. Yet it was regal, and he appreciated that the government rolled out the red carpet for him and his friend. The table was set for twelve and looked like a scaled-down state dinner at Buckingham Palace. Off to the side was a large-scale model of Île-à-Vache.

After a lunch of griot with rice and beans, fritay, banan-peze, and Haitian beef patties, complemented with French wines, Duvalier stood to speak.

"My young and talented American friends, welcome to our small but happy nation. I place our future, our dreams in your hands. With your help, Haiti will become a vacationer's paradise on Île-à-Vache. But that will be just the beginning. Our long-term plan is to create resorts at many of our beaches, in the mountains, and close to our great historical monuments like La Citadelle. Our future and yours are intertwined."

Connor, somewhat drunk, leaned over to Caudy and whispered, "Oh fucking great!"

The president did not hear the remark and continued. "Here you see a large model of the island. Later today you will see it in person. Tell me, what are your initial thoughts?"

Connor hesitated. "Mr. President, after we see the island, and receive more information from our support team of engineers and material suppliers, Mr. Lazarus, Dan and I will return to make a full presentation of our concepts.

However, our initial thoughts and ideas are exciting I can promise you that." Connor felt pleased with his response.

"Wonderful. Then let us not delay. You are in good hands with Minister St. Jacques. Tomorrow, I should like a full report. Then we will show you the rest of the island including La Citadelle."

"He doesn't seem like such a bad guy, Connor," Caudy said to his partner as they walked down the long gallery of the palace, out of earshot from St. Jacques and the retinue of assistants and guards.

"No, but he didn't hang your mother either." West shook his head.

"Let's just see what the island is like, okay. You have to admit, it was a pretty nice lunch."

"Yeah, and now we get to fly in the company jet," Connor said sarcastically.

On the Pan Am flight back to Miami, Connor gazed out at the cumulus clouds swirling in the blue sky. The island was everything St. Jacques had said it would be—beautiful, pristine, and bucolic. The wide beaches were soft, white sand stretching for miles. Set back from the shoreline were graceful palm trees—royals, palmettos, Columbian wax, and pygmy. Colorful birds like parrots and macaws flew from branch to branch. Cows grazed in deep green pastures interrupted by interesting rock formations and crystal-clear streams. There was a large blue/green lake surrounded by a lush forest. The islanders, the few allowed to interact with the Americans, were welcoming, with bright white smiles contrasting against their deep black skin. He turned to Caudy.

"Doesn't it bother you a little?"

"Does what bother me?"

"The island."

"The island is perfect. I've already started the master plan in my head. I can't wait to get back to Miami to put it down on paper. St. Jacques said he'd send detailed topographic maps to Manny."

"I mean what we're going to do to it."

"Yeah, we're going to create the greatest resort in the Caribbean. And we have an open checkbook from the government. You heard Duvalier today: "Spare no expense.""

"When we were in the town of Madame Bernard having dinner..."

"Yeah, wasn't that grilled fish incredible?"

"No, not that. I went outside the covered pavilion to use the outhouse. An old man stopped me. In broken English, he told me he was the mayor. His descendants had come from America after the Civil War. He asked me not to ruin his island with development and outsiders. He said: 'Leave us in peace, Blanc.'"

"Connor, the area for the resort will be a fraction of the island. It's eight miles long."

"Yeah, but you saw it. They're already moving people from their homes to make way for the new airport. Our resort will cover several square miles, but its effects will be felt all over the island."

"If it helps, I'm planning on designing a whole new town with housing just for the locals. St. Jacques thought it was a great idea. I mean, they're living in huts now. They'll have houses with running water and indoor bathrooms. It's called progress, West."

"I guess you're right. And I am excited about my design for the resort hotel right on Abaka Beach. I think it must be the most beautiful beach in the world."

"So, there you go! Oh, stewardess, can we get a couple more drinks?"

"Certainly, sir."

CHAPTER FIFTY-FOUR

"Perrault, inform me about any new prisoners." Dominique St. Jacques was abrupt, a mannerism he now found most useful as it got quick results.

"Monsieur, the usual. Thieves, political dissidents, troublemakers."

"What about drug smugglers?"

"Ah, yes, Excellency, now that you mention it. Two weeks ago, a fishing boat was boarded. It was suspected of bringing in drugs. And the Tonton Macoute found a considerable amount."

"You believe them?" St. Jacques knew that was bullshit.

"Yes, why shouldn't I?"

"Tell me what happened."

"The boat was sunk. One of the smugglers was killed trying to escape. Two others were brought before the court. They are awaiting trial, but one had a fever and has been in the infirmary."

"I want to know about them."

"One was either Haitian or from some Caribbean island, perhaps the Bahamas from his accent. He understood Creole. The other was a Blanc. He looked American and seemed quite scared."

"I'm not surprised. What are their names?"

"I do not know. Shall I find out?"

"Yes, you fool. If we have an American in custody, we must inform the embassy."

"Right away, monsieur."

St. Jacques studied the folder on his desk sent over by Judge Perrault. He had been double-crossed by General Raymond; he hadn't seen that coming, but it was not surprising. The man was a schemer, but wasn't everyone in the government? He would deal with his new ambassador later.

Now he had two men in prison, one a Bahamian national and the other an American citizen. This was an unfortunate development. Both countries were extending aid to Haiti. Detaining their citizens would not be well received by their respective governments.

But right now, he needed to resurrect his deal with the Black Tuna Gang. Haiti needed the drug money for Paradi-sou-Latè. That would be easy enough: simply find out where the 4,000 kilos of cocaine, heroin, and marijuana were being kept and take it to Flatshorn on the country's private jet. Fly it to some remote island in Bimini and put the American kid, Tomlinson and the Bahamian, Rollet, on it. They worked for him anyway.

❖

"Monsieur Flatshorn, I have good news." St. Jacques was trying to be as upbeat as possible.

"You found my boat?"

"No, unfortunately, it is lost. But I am prepared to deliver on the 4,000 kilos of product that was our end of the deal and send back Mr. Rollet and Mr. Tomlinson along with it. I can arrange delivery in two days to your selected island in the Bahamas."

"What happened to Delgado?"

"He is, unfortunately, dead."

"So, your little government lost my boat and killed one of my men. Tell me again, why do I want to do business with you?"

"My apologies. Certainly, a rough beginning. But I assure you..."

"No, St. Jacques, let me assure you. Our business is done. I couldn't care less about Rollet and Tomlinson; it's the boat I needed. And Delgado. He was one of my best men. I've cut a new deal with Ballesteros in Honduras. They've got planes. And my guys are your problem now. Let them rot in your prison."

St. Jacques put the phone down. Rot indeed.

PART IV
THE PIRATES OF PENZANCE
1976

CHAPTER FIFTY-FIVE
MARCH 15, 1976

Key West, Florida

Connor drove down the Keys in the weeks after Rat's disappearance, always stopping in Key Largo, Tavernier, Islamorada, Marathon, and even Key West looking for Rat and *Daddy's Money*. No one had seen the young captain or his boat. His friend had vanished into thin air. The last report had been from the Tavernier Marina to the Coast Guard when the boat docked there in December and took on fuel.

The loss was another deep wound. His best friend was probably lost at sea in the vast expanse between Tavernier and Haiti. A 550-mile trip on a little fishing boat crossing an edge of the unpredictable Atlantic in December. An insane idea.

The visits stretched into months, and frequently continued to Key West. He met Armand on his boat and they sat on the back deck drinking Red Stripes, eating cold shrimp, and talking about life, love, Haiti, and Paradi sou Latè.

"How is the re-making of Île-à-Vache coming along? It's been a few weeks since I've seen you."

"I've been busy with the project and worked the last couple of weekends. I needed a break, and this fit the bill. I enjoy seeing you."

"As do I, as do I. And the project?"

"We've busted our asses at the office to get the resort hotel drawings done. Now construction is about to begin. We have to complete the big hotel next, Manny's crown jewel, next to the casino. Then we tackle the singles- only resort. Dan has done a great job on the master plan for the development, but I still have misgivings."

"Why is that?"

"All your stories about Haiti and the Duvalier family. It doesn't square with what I see."

"I am certain that they do not want you to see the 'real' Haiti."

"I feel as if I'm being watched every minute. I can't even go to certain parts of Île-à-Vache. God knows what they're doing to the place." Connor finished his Red Stripe in a gulp. "How bad was it under Papa Doc? I mean you lived there during those 14 years."

"At first, we had high hopes. He was a decent country doctor. But then he re-wrote the constitution declaring himself president-for-life, and in 1959 established the Militia of National Security Volunteers, the Tonton Macoute. From there, things went from bad to worse. Everyone lived in fear of the little man and his thugs, and then economic conditions worsened. We used to joke about it. We said that Duvalier had accomplished an economic miracle. He taught us to live without money, and eat without food. Then finally, he taught us to live without life."

"I think I need a drink. You certainly know how to dampen a nice evening."

Armand noticed Connor's morose demeanor, and it wasn't work related, or because of the economic conditions in Haiti. He sensed his loneliness. For three months he had avoided the Green Parrot and Annie.

"Isn't it time for you to get off this boat and venture onto the island, my friend?" Armand stared at West.

"What are you talking about? I enjoy our evenings together. Mostly, until you go off on my client."

"Annie is still working at the Green Parrot. I see her there during the week when you are up in Miami remaking the island of Île-à-Vache. She has asked about you. Often."

"I'd think she considers me a one-night stand."

"It may have been, but it doesn't have to be. She knows you need time, but she won't wait forever. It's been over four months. Life is for the living, my friend."

"I think you're right; maybe it is time. I think about Annie a lot. And I suppose all the late nights and the talk about the Duvalier's have me both worn down and conflicted."

"You cannot change what you cannot change. Keep your head down and it will all work out."

"I wonder if Annie is there tonight?"

"I have it on good authority that she is. I told her you were coming down to visit today."

"You're as bad a matchmaker as Bob Marlow."

"Ah, your boss in Chicago. It is fair to say that you are like a son to both of us. Go see Annie. Marilyn is not coming back."

❖

"Miss, oh miss, can I get a drink here."

"Well, look who came walking through my door. How are you doing, Cowboy?"

"I'm a little thirsty, and a lot lonely. Say, how come you're not bruised or hurt?"

"Why would I be hurt?"

"Because you're so fine you must have fallen from heaven."

"Connor, you've got to get rid of that self-help book.

"Why?"

Because it isn't helping," Annie smirked. She poured him a stiff Jim Beam. She put it in front of him and smiled, but to his disappointment, didn't stroke his hand.

"Just for you. The 12-year-old stuff."

"Nice. What time do you get off work?"

"For you, 10:00 P.M. Where are we going?"

"How about the beach? There's a full moon tonight. Maybe we can talk."

"Talk would be good. Maybe I rushed things a little last time."

"Don't apologize."

"I didn't."

"Right. Last time was very nice. It was all me."

"I took away your oxygen. You needed to breathe." Annie touched Connor's hand and went to the end of the bar to serve another patron.

Connor took a deep breath. *You're taking it away again, Miss Gallagher, but that's a good thing,* he thought to himself, taking a pull on the fine bourbon Annie had poured.

❖

They drove to Smather's Beach after stopping by Annie's coach house for a beach blanket and a Styrofoam cooler, and then went to a small liquor store for a six-pack of Corona Beer and some ice. Connor parked alongside the beach, which ran parallel to Atlantic Avenue. The night was cool and perfect, and the stars put up a good show against the brilliant moon.

"I think the last time we were together, I monopolized the whole evening talking about me," Connor said apologetically.

"That was fine. I knew all about my life and nothing of yours. And you had a lot to tell."

"So, it's your turn."

"We're the same age."

"That's it?" Connor chuckled.

"I was born in Miami, grew up in Fort Lauderdale. I graduated from the University of Miami with a degree in communications, whatever that is. So I guess bartending is a perfect job. I communicate with the customers. For a while, I worked on a dinner cruise boat out of Miami. Not very exciting. I guess I still haven't figured out what my passion in life is, like you."

"It can be a double-edged sword. Tell me about your family."

"My parents divorced when I was ten. It was pretty traumatic for me, especially because my mom left my dad, me, and Florida for another guy. So, I stayed with my dad. He pretty much raised me. Taught me to be my own person and never settle for second best."

"My mom told me the same thing. Another beer."

"Sure."

Connor reached into the cooler, took out two beers, opened them, and handed one to Annie who was quiet. Finally, she spoke.

"Are you over her now?"

"I don't think I'll ever be over her. Marilyn is a distant, sad, and wonderful memory. But, yes, I think I'm ready."

"Don't expect an invitation back to mi casa tonight."

"I'm not. Let's take it slow, okay."

"Good, but let's make sure we take it." Annie leaned over and kissed Connor. First a peck, then a deep, long kiss.

CHAPTER FIFTY-SIX
MARCH 15, 1976

Fort Dimanche
Port-au-Prince, Haiti

There was a commotion outside the cell. Rat got up and banged on the steel wall. "Trevor, something's going on." He rubbed the scar on his forehead. There was no pain, but he knew his face was disfigured.

Three days in the infirmary had turned into two weeks. Even though his wish for a long stay had materialized, it was because the infection grew worse. The Dominican doctor had to operate on his forehead to thoroughly clean the gash and remove pus and dirt. Then he had sewn it up, and given Rat steady doses of morphine, to which he was quickly addicted. The doses stopped and after three days of chills and sweats, he was clean. But the ugly scar remained. Trevor told him it was a souvenir to be proud of.

To Rat, it was just another memory of the hell his life had become. A life that was now a five-year sentence at hard labor, handed down by the minister of the interior. He and Trevor had been brought before him in chains. Tomlinson thought for a moment that they might be released when the minister acknowledged their nationalities and that he had been put into a difficult situation. St. Jacques said nothing as he pondered his predicament and then issued the sentence. Dragged from the man's office, Rat cried. That night was the worst night of all, pondering his life for the next five years. Trevor spat on the floor of the interior minister's office. Back in his cell, Trevor was whipped for the insolent act.

The cell door opened. "Vini nom, Blanc." Rat now understood a few words of the Haitian Creole dialect. It was a tortured form of French. And because he was a white man, he was called "Blanc" as were all white people in Haiti. He got in line and was joined by Trevor. But today they were not led to the courtyard for hosing down but in the opposite direction.

"What's the deal, Trevor? They letting us go?"

"One can only wish."

In moments they were outside on a dirt street and the prisoners of Fort Dimanche lined up in a single file. A fleet of army trucks was queued on the street and rifle butts and shouts of "Monte nan kamyon an!" gave the two prisoners all the information they needed. Rat and Trevor climbed into the nearest truck, benches on either side with a continuous rail along the floor. A guard got in and chained their ankles to the rail. The truck lurched forward.

"Looks like we're going on a field trip, my friend."

"Always the optimist, aren't you?" Rat responded. However, if it meant leaving the misery that was Fort Dimanche, he was all for the unknown journey.

And it was a journey. Five hours over dusty roads, temperatures in the high eighties. The convoy of over thirty trucks, filled with the occupants of the notorious prison, stopped once for water and so that the convicts could perform their bodily functions. Unchained, some tried to run off into the fields. They were shot or run down by police dogs that tore them to shreds.

The convoy slowed. Rat could smell sea air, though because of heavy tarpaulins covering the back of the truck, he could only see the truck following behind, creating a cloud of dust: the same dust he had inhaled from the truck in front. The trucks came to a stop at a long dock. Tomlinson, Rollet, and the other prisoners were unchained and got out. The afternoon sun ricocheted off the blue water of the Bay of Cayes and blinded them. His eyes finally adjusted to the beautiful sight before him. Blue water, and in the far distance, land. For the last three months, he had seen nothing but hell, the hell of Fort Dimanche. Rat breathed deeply. There was no rot, no dust, and no effluent to smell. It was clean air.

"Deplase! Bato yo." Rat understood 'bato,' it meant boat. By the dock were five or six ferries.

"Trevor, they're taking us to that island out there. Surely they wouldn't take us on a five-hour trip for some sort of temporary stay?"

"We may have a new home, my friend. See, I told you to never lose hope."

The prisoners sat in a large open-air pavilion at tables for eight. People with kind faces served them bowls of pork and rice, slices of thick bread and fruit, and fresh water. Tears ran down Tomlinson's cheek as he ate. He looked at Trevor, who was too busy eating ravenously to cry.

"Trevor, is this a trick? Why are we here?"

"There's probably a huge stone quarry nearby. Don't forget we have been sentenced to five years hard labor."

"I thought you were the optimist."

"Indeed, it seems too good to be true."

A Tonton Macoute with several stars on his uniform and colored ribbons of service on his left breast stood up at the front of the pavilion. He wore the ubiquitous sunglasses and sported large pork-chop sideburns. His aide yelled "Atansyon!"

"I wanna hear this, Trevor; translate for me."

"Always."

The general cleared his throat and spoke, and as he did Trevor whispered in Rat's ear.

"Prisoners of Fort Dimanche, welcome to your new home. Welcome to Île-à-Vache, the island of cows. Your country has given you a special task, an honorable task. You will be the laborers for a great project. A project greater than Duvalierville. Consider this your welcome meal. For those that work hard, you will be fed like this often. For those that shirk their duty to build, you will feel the sting of the lash. The work will be hard, six days a week, twelve hours a day. But it will give you the opportunity to help your great nation and serve our president, Jean-Claude Duvalier."

"So much for a better life..." Rat whispered in Trevor's ear.

"Sushhhh, I'm listening."

"There will be no chains to bind you here. There is no escape. You are surrounded by water and that water is home to sharks. We have no guard towers around the grounds, because where you find forests, they are impenetrable. The swamps are home to alligators. Escape is futile. You will work under the direction of engineers and construction professionals. Obey them and you will be fed like today. Ignore them, and there are special cells for you, open to the sun. We call them the devil's boxes."

"First prize, Fort Dimanche. Second prize, this island." Rat drank the last of his water. He couldn't remember the last time he had a beer.

"I'll take this place over the Fort. At least we can breathe and do something to take our mind off the days."

"There's that optimist I know and love," Rat said with a nudge to Trevor's ribs.

"Quiet, the general is finishing."

"New occupants of this island, you will now proceed to barracks we have built for you. It is a great improvement over your previous home. But remember, we do not care whether you live or die. It is all up to you."

261

CHAPTER FIFTY-SEVEN

Danny Nolan was pleased with himself. So far, the firm had collected the retainer of one million dollars from their new Caribbean client, plus another million over the last three months. Bob Marlow had been silenced by the payments, though he had given Danny a royal ass chewing for forging his signature on the contract with Manny Lazarus.

The lecture from Marlow had reminded Danny of his father's Irish temper. It was the primary reason Francis Nolan, Jr. had deferred to his middle name, Daniel. It was one way to distance himself from Francis Nolan, Sr., a man in whose eyes he never measured up. Being gay in a devout Irish Catholic family didn't help either.

Now Nolan & Marlow needed just one more million-dollar payment from Lazarus to right the financial ship of state. Nolan had even placed the Voodou doll of Connor back on the shelf, and the silver pin in his drawer.

The last check, however, had not been forthcoming. He had sent in the invoice a month ago. He decided to make a rare visit to the drafting hall and Bob Marlow's office. He wanted to check on the progress of the first in what was planned to be a long list of lucrative projects for Paradi sou Latè, the luxury resort designed by Connor West.

"Bob, haven't we completed the construction documents for the resort hotel in Haiti? I haven't received any more money from Lazarus."

"I shipped them last Friday by UPS. A full set of stamped, reproducible, sepia drawings. Exactly 237 sheets. And we haven't been paid?"

"It's no big deal. The invoice is only at 35 days. I'll call Lazarus, make sure he received the drawings. Do you have a paper set? I'd like to see what Connor has conjured up."

"He's conjured up a fabulous design. I know you're in charge of the business side of this enterprise, but it would be nice if you'd take an interest in what we produce as a firm." Marlow looked hard at Nolan and took a drink of his ever-present coffee.

"I've been busy paying our past bills, juggling finances, extending our lines of credit." Nolan was calm, but didn't appreciate the rebuke.

"That's a scary thought."

"Marlow, I don't deserve that. One more check from Manny and the house will be in order." Nolan's Irish temper was on the verge. "Now, I've got some free time. I'd like to see the drawings."

Marlow went over to his reference desk. "Here's the last check set. It's got a few redlines, but you'll get the idea. It's a four-story building that undulates along what I'm told is the most beautiful beach in the Caribbean. The bearing walls mimic the waves at the shoreline and they're forty-five feet high. Jerzy did a great job designing the structure for them. Construction should start any day now. I guess Duvalier is serious about this super-resort."

"Thanks. I can't wait to look at it. Good move on getting Connor back."

"You're welcome."

Phone calls, a proposal for a new educational building at Northwestern, and assembling a marketing package, occupied Danny's time for the rest of the day. At 5:00 P.M. he cleared off his granite desk and rolled out the drawings.   He reached into the credenza, pulled out a bottle of Russian vodka, and poured three fingers in a crystal glass. Nolan loosened his tie and went over to the large windows that looked down on Michigan Avenue. There was still snow on the ground in Grant Park, but it was melting rapidly on the unusually warm March day. Lake Michigan was peaceful, and the sidewalks were full of people finished with their day's labors, heading home. He smiled, returning to his desk. In a week, with one more check, the firm would be out of debt, a bullet dodged thanks to Baby Doc Duvalier. Ruthless dictator or not, he paid better than most of their clients.

Nolan flipped through the opening pages that contained an extensive code analysis, an effort he thought unnecessary for a remote island. It wasn't like they had a code official or even a fire department. The firm could have skipped that and pocketed the money.

After ten or so sheets he came to the first interesting drawing, the site plan. The scale and scope of the project was breathtaking. On the landside was a porte cochère before a great lobby created by four of the round walls covered with a thatched roof. From the lobby, the wings of the hotel went in each direction gently curving back and forth like waves. The entire resort looked out to a pool with fountains, waterfalls, grottos, and swim-up bars. It was enormous, stretching practically from one end of the hotel to the other. In front of it was a row of palm trees set in lush landscaping and the beach. Nolan whistled and took a drink of his vodka.

The next interesting drawings were the floor plans. Nolan stared at them. The logic was there, but so was elegance. Everything fit, and in a seamless way. No wasted space, but there was still the luxury of space. He took another drink and flipped through more sheets. Finally, he came to the elevations. It was as if he were staring at a modern-day version of the hanging gardens of Babylon. Great round walls every thirty-six feet, the edges, cantilevered concrete reaching to the ocean beyond. Between them, floor to ceiling glass, four stories high with planters for lush greenery and flowers.

Nolan flipped over to the sheets full of details. He had seen enough. He went to the bottle, poured himself another glass of vodka and reached for the doll above the credenza, then pulled out the silver pin in his top drawer.

"West, you miserable, talented fuck! I hate your guts!" He took the pin and jabbed it into the doll's head.

At his desk in Miami, reviewing the drawings sent by Marlow, Connor put his hands to his head. The headaches were back.

❖

"St. Jacques, this is Manny." The connection crackled and hissed, but he could hear background voices in his client's office.

"Mr. Lazarus, so good to hear from you."

"You won't think that in a minute. I've sent three invoices to you, over three and half mill. I got payroll to make. I need some oil to grease the wheels of architecture."

"My apologies, my friend. A minor snafu at the treasury. It should be cleared in the morning and the funds will be wired to you. We were concerned about the checks getting lost in transit."

"Good to hear. I don't wanna be a prick, but I'll have to slow down if I don't see some cash soon."

"Please, do not do that. We are just now ramping up construction. The foundations for the resort hotel are being poured as we speak."

"Really? You know, I've been meaning to ask you. Who's building this paradise on earth?'

"Oh, yes, well it's a... an international construction consortium. A French and a Brazilian company, in a joint venture."

"Terrific. Just send the money. Have a great day, monsieur."

"Goodbye, Mr. Lazarus."

❖

St. Jacques put down the phone and returned to the accountants in his office. The project even with prison labor and the local conscripts, forced to work against their will, was hemorrhaging money. The infrastructure cost of electricity, water, sewer, and telecommunications was running at fifty million plus. The new airport, twenty-two million. Dredging the harbor, another fifteen million. And he hadn't started the resort hotel, estimated at thirty million. There was no drug money. Rawlings and the other foreign corporations were balking at further contributions and the tobacco administration coffers were almost dry. Bad, very bad.

To add to that, an audit had revealed that Simone Duvalier, living the good life in Paris, had absconded with over thirty-five million of the country's money, and Claude Raymond another twenty-seven million. The $475,000 he had stolen from the soured drug deal was in retrospect, chump change.

He lifted the receiver. "Get me Marius, at the State Bank."

The call went through quickly.

"Monsieur Directeur, tell me about any proprietary accounts."

"What do mean, your Excellency?"

"There must be other funds in the national treasury. Personal funds."

"Only those of the president, monsieur."

"How much?"

"It is proprietary, sir."

"How much!"

"Le President's account has seventy-seven million."

St. Jacques slammed down the receiver and lifted it up again. "Get me Duvalier."

CHAPTER FIFTY-EIGHT

"Hey Connor, get over here."

West looked up toward Manny's office, grabbed his half-full mug of Columbian coffee, and ambled over.

"What's up, Mr. L?"

"St. Jacques told me they're pouring foundations for your hotel. Better go down there soon and see what they're doing. Make sure they are using re-bar in the walls and that sort of thing."

"It's becoming a waste of time. Every time I go there, I'm treated like royalty, but they won't let me out of their sight. I can't do my job. I'm met at the airport by six guys that look like Joe Frasier in dark suits, put in a limousine with curtains drawn, have a meeting with St. Jacques and then take a two-hour cruise from Jacmel to Île-à-Vache where they do their best to get me drunk."

"Is that a complaint? Caudy said it was the presidential yacht."

"Whatever, but something's not right. That's all I'm saying. They won't let me go anywhere on the island except the hotel site. I want to see how the master plan is developing, the new port, the roads, and the new airport. And I'm concerned about the islanders. They were promised new housing when they were moved for all the shit that's being built."

"You should just worry about the hotel. The rest is out of our hands." Manny shook his head. *Idealistic kids!* "So, tell me, what did you see the last time? How were they excavating the foundations?"

"That's the thing. There were like five guys standing around with shovels, and another guy on a backhoe. They were all clean, had hart hats. Hadn't broken a sweat because they weren't doing anything. At that rate, the project will never get finished."

"I'm sure they're just ramping up. St. Jacques tells me the contractor is a big JV from France and Brazil. Maybe you can inquire some more. Insist they show you everything."

"I've got a better idea. Maybe I'll just go down there unannounced. Have my own little reconnaissance mission."

"Connor, I wouldn't do that. It ain't safe. Those big guys are there to protect you."

"I thought you said things had improved under Baby Doc?"

"Improved, but it's still dicey. Look, I get one of these weekly from the State Department. It's a travel advisory." Manny handed a piece of paper to Connor. As he read it his face turned pale, looking concerned.

"What? The State Department is warning against travel to Haiti. Kidnappings, ransom demands, robberies on the street, false arrests, even random killings! Why haven't I seen this before?"

"Why? Because you go down there first-class protected by those Joe Frasiers."

"Our client is doing all this!"

"You don't know that. He's trying to turn things around. The project gets built, those people on the island are gonna have a better way of life. They'll have jobs."

"Yeah, cleaning the hotel rooms of wealthy Americanos."

"Geesus, kid, they're illiterate. It beats plowing the fields for a few lousy potatoes. You gotta quit being so idealistic. There's islands throughout the Caribbean where the sorry lot of the common people has been greatly improved by tourism."

"I just want to see that this project, my project, gets done right. Otherwise, I'm going back to Chicago."

After another week of grinding out designs for Paradi sou Latè, this one the terminal for the new 'International' airport, Connor headed down to Key West on Friday afternoon. As the summer approached, the traffic on A1A increased. By the time he arrived at the marina, it was six o'clock. He was ready for more than a beer.

Connor and Armand sat on the rear deck in comfortable captain's chairs, feasting on peel and eat shrimp with saltines and two dozen oysters Armand had bought at the Half Shell Raw Bar. Connor had brought a bottle of Haitian rum, Clairin, which Armand served with ice and soda. The young architect recounted his concerns, voiced earlier in the week to Manny, about being stonewalled on his inspection trips to Île-à-Vache.

"Armand, I want you to go with me on my next trip. I'm going there unannounced. I want to see what's going on."

"I dare not return. I would be arrested at Customs."

"Why? You're a citizen of the Dominican Republic."

"The name Jolicoeur is very well known in Haiti, and the government knows all about my family, including our immigration to Santo Domingo."

"So, you left. You had no choice."

"It's not the leaving that is the issue. It's the returning. They would take my return as a possible start of an insurrection. They keep large files and have deep memories, particularly in my case. My mother was an outspoken opponent of the current administration."

"You gotta go back with me. Something's not Jake down there. I just know it. Plus, we can look for Rat."

"Rat, who I fear has drowned at sea?"

"I believe he made it to Port-au-Prince. I just know it. He's probably rotting in that prison Fort..."

"Dimanche."

"Yeah, there."

"It has been over three months. If he is there, he has probably already died of abuse, malnutrition or disease."

"Don't say that. I know he's alive."

"I fear his soul has been taken by Baron Samedi, the spirit of the dead."

"You've got to come there with me. Even if I went by myself, I don't speak Creole."

Jolicoeur poured himself some more rum and added ice. He looked out to the marina. "This is very good rum. I

269

remember it from my days in Kenscoff. If I went back, I'd need a new passport with a different name."

Connor's ears perked up. "Can you get one on the island?"

"In Key West, you can get anything for a price. Our mutual friend, Mr. Jackson may know someone. Give me a week."

"So you'll go back with me?"

"Papa Legba came to me again in a dream last night. He told me I was now at a crossroads."

"Man, you have weird dreams..." Connor smiled and took another pull on his glass of rum.

"Do not mock my dreams, my friend. The spirit world is real. The trouble is, most mortals do not listen to their dreams. I do. And because of that, I will go with you to Haiti. I will probably die there, and Baron Samedi will dig my grave and lead my soul to the underworld."

Connor shook his head. All he cared about was that he would have a friend to travel back to this strange and unholy land.

CHAPTER FIFTY-NINE

Rat and Trevor toiled in the hot sun, the temperature now in the low 90's. Both wore broad-brimmed straw hats to shield them from the sun. Under the hat, Rat's hair had been crudely cut by Trevor and he now sported a short beard. Rat had performed the same ritual on Trevor, both wanting to avoid head lice. On the island, they were able to shower daily, and they lived in relative comfort in a new two- bed jail cell that had a small table and a desk. At seven-feet by nine-feet, it was a palace compared to Fort Dimanche's lodgings. And they were not locked up at night. There was no need—there was no way to escape from the island.

They hammered away, building the formwork for the first of the great round walls, nailing 2 x 6's to plywood, creating a modest reinforced panel, which they stood up vertically. They had built ten during the morning, and had to build another eight before their twelve-hour day was through. It was hot, tedious work.

Tomorrow they would brace the wall and fasten long 2 x 4's against the formwork at forty-five-degree angles for diagonal bracing, known as shoring. Then the first concrete pour would take place.

Rat bent his back up and moaned. "I'm beginning to think rotting in Fort Dimanche was preferable to this. I'm exhausted."

"Lunch will be soon. And the food is, well, its real food. Better than that slop-shit we got in prison." Trevor continued to hammer.

"At least the guards leave us alone."

"They see that we do twice the work of the others. And what the others do is shit."

"I don't know about you, but I don't think this wall is going to hold up against one hundred cubic yards of concrete." Rat climbed down from the scaffolding and walked back to get an overall look. Trevor followed. The bell rang, indicating lunch.

"What do you expect? The so-called professional engineer who designed it is a concrete contractor from Port-au-Prince. He's never poured anything taller than an eight-foot wall, and it was maybe a foot thick. This bad boy is fifteen feet high and three-and-a-half feet thick!"

The two comrades, who had developed an inseparable bond during the last four months, walked toward the thatched hut pavilion. A guard, who had been watching the performance of the hundreds of workers, checked each one as they got into the line for food. The Tonton, an old rifle slung over his shoulder, nodded at the two workers and smiled. He handed them green tickets. It meant extra food and a beer. Others were given a red ticket and would get less food. Some were turned away entirely. Those unfortunate few made an effort to get to the water trough. If they stumbled and fell, unconscious, they were left to the mercy of others to get them out of the hot sun and give them water. Worse yet, the guards would drag them to the devil's boxes to certain death.

Rat and Trevor sat at a table to themselves. They stayed away from the other convicts. The feeling was mutual. Trevor had stabbed one with a handmade shiv earlier in the week. The thug had come up from behind Trevor, wanting to take the money he hid in his pants.

"We've got to build two more extra forms today before we quit. Leave them by the wall. Tonight, we'll come back and take them into the woods. With the two we have, that's an 8 x 16-foot raft."

"We'll need to get an axe. On Sunday we can chop the fallen tree you found into two fifteen-foot lengths."

"I'll steal some rope from the storeroom. Tie the logs to the panels and presto, we're ready to leave this paradise on earth."

"Then the sharks can eat us." Rat wasn't too enthusiastic about his friend's plan.

"Keep your voice down."

"No one understands English."

"You hope."

❖

The next morning, apathetic workers inside the formwork tied the vertical and horizontal rebar in a slipshod fashion. Every third bar was tied to another one. No one checked. Rat and Trevor continued to try to brace the formwork with 2 x 4 shores and had secured a handful of 4 x 4's as well. They braced the wall as best as their resources would allow.

"What's with the platform being built, mon?"

"I think we're going to have some dignitaries attending to watch the first pour of the new hotel."

The sound of a small band interrupted the sounds of hammers and saws. It came into sight, followed by some men in embroidered tropical shirts, and then by Dominique St. Jacques, dressed in a white linen sport coat and open-collared shirt. He wore his signature aviator sunglasses. The entourage was protected by a platoon of Tonton Macoute armed with Uzis and machetes. Any convict would love to kill the minister of the interior and head of the Tonton Macoute. Behind the parade were townspeople who had been trucked in to watch the great event. They'd rather have been fishing.

From the other direction a concrete pump truck appeared followed by several new Redi-Mix concrete trucks painted blue and green with the words *Paradi sou Latè* stenciled on the drum in several places.

"The fun's about to start. Let's watch it from the shade of the pavilion."

"I'll get us a beer. I'll bribe someone in the kitchen."

Rat and Trevor made their way in the direction of the dignitaries, keeping a respectful distance. As they passed St. Jacques, Rat stared at the man who had dictated his life for the next five years. St. Jacques seemed to look at Rat for a moment, his covered eyes hiding any recognition. But he missed a step. Trevor spit on the ground but did not look at the entourage.

The group of swells climbed the viewing stand, and St. Jacques took out a piece of paper.

273

"Workers of Paradi sou Latè, welcome."

Rat laughed. "Like we had a choice."

St. Jacques continued. "Today is a momentous day. Today we see the beginning of the great hotel that will stand here for years to come. All in honor and tribute to our president, Jean-Claude Duvalier. It would not be possible without your devotion and hard work. Continue to work hard and you will repay your debt to your country."

"What a fucking crock." Rat took a swig of his beer.

"I will drink to his sweet words, my dear Richard."

"Stop it."

The wall was now overrun by a different crew, a ragtag assembly of convicts and locals, who climbed the formwork in bare feet and yelled directions at one another. No one person seemed in charge. It was a chaotic scene. The heavy six-inch hose of the pump truck swung into place above the forms and grabbed by two of the stronger men. Rat and Trevor heard the trucks rev up as their drums turned. The first concrete truck moved into place beside the hopper of the pump truck, and the chute opened. Wet concrete began to flow down the chute in great quantities. The hopper took it as fast as it came, and before long a stream of concrete was coming out of the hose.

One of the men who controlled the heavy tube lost his balance and fell into the form, screaming. The work stopped until his bloody body could be fished out. He had impaled himself on the reinforcing.

"That's a great start." Rat shook his head and looked away.

"Let's drink to him, whoever the mon is. He be the first of many casualties on this project."

"I'm sure."

With another barefoot worker taking the dead man's place, the pour resumed without incident. One truck after another poured out its nine yards of mud into the hopper and the hose moved back and forth across the wall. The formwork groaned but held.

The last truck pulled up to the concrete pump. It revved its engine, the drum turned and concrete, wetter than allowed, poured forth.

"Almost finished."

"I don't like that creaking sound."

"They're at the top and I'm pretty sure it's the last truck. This is number twelve."

The groaning increased. The formwork began to bulge. The shoring of 2x4's bowed and then splintered in two like so many snapped toothpicks. Wet concrete started to seep through the openings in the overly stressed formwork. A worker on top of the wall screamed, "Desann kounya!" It was too late. In a mighty roar, the entire assembly began to collapse as the sturdiest bracing, the 4x4s, failed.

Rat and Trevor stared in amazement. It was like watching Hoover Dam collapse, but instead of water, there was wet, gray concrete. Workers who had been using vibrators to reduce voids fell into the wall, screams coming up from the wooden assembly as it collapsed. A river of concrete made its way toward the viewing platform. St. Jacques and the others stumbled over one another to get away from the lava of mud. In a second, they were engulfed. St. Jacques climbed over several people and ran for the pavilion. Though his shoes and trousers were ruined, he was unharmed. He stood there looking at the disaster. Without his sunglasses on, Rat could see the fear and misery in his eyes, not for the sake of those dying in the collapsed formwork, but for the consequences of his own failure.

Rat got up and headed toward St. Jacques.

"Where you going, mon?"

"We're about to get promoted."

"Or decapitated."

Rat quickly made his way toward St. Jacques. A phalanx of Tonton Macoute quickly surrounded him.

"Hey, St. Jacques!" Connor tried to get through the guards with their machetes and guns. He seemed to have no fear. He yelled louder.

"St. Jacques, I'm talking to you!"

A bodyguard hit Rat in the stomach with the butt of his rifle. Others punched and kicked him as he fell to the dirt floor. Rat doubled over, moaning. "Assholes!"

St. Jacques barked an order. "Let him be. Who are you? You look familiar."

"I'm the American you sentenced to five years hard labor for visiting this little slice of paradise."

"Yes, now I remember. The drug smuggler. What do you want?"

"Mr. Minister, if you want what just happened to happen again, just keep the moron-in-charge of this disaster on the job."

"An unfortunate beginning. Now, I remember. You graduated from Yale and Harvard. What? You think you are smarter than my engineers?"

St. Jacques eyed the young man. His appearance had changed. Besides the different hair and new beard, he seemed older, more mature, resigned to his fate.

"I also worked in heavy construction. Bridges, retaining walls. And my friend, he's built big hotels in the Bahamas. We know how to build formwork, and it won't be anything like that pile of crap." Rat nodded toward the wet mound of mud and wood.

"Ah yes, your Bahamian friend. Did you build this formwork?"

"Yes. But it was a shit design."

"How do I know you didn't sabotage it? Why didn't you say something?"

"I'm a goddamn convict. I keep my head down and follow orders. And I'm telling you now. Look, they've already dragged five people out of that pile of shit. I'm pretty sure they're dead."

St. Jacques leaned over to a Tonton Macoute and whispered in his ear. The man walked over to the head jailer, had a short conversation and returned, another whispered conversation with St. Jacques. He nodded.

"They tell me you and your friend are hard workers. What do you propose?"

"Put Rollet and me in charge. I promise the wall won't collapse. But we'll need a lot of heavy timbers and bolts, not nails."

"Very well. And what do you want in return?"

"A palapa on the beach. Two good meals a day. Some new clothes, boots. And beer and rum. And when this project is done, we're free men."

St. Jacques looked over to the carnage of the wall. Hands and heads stuck out of the setting concrete; pools of blood formed on the surface. He turned to the viewing platform. Covered in concrete were several dignitaries. They would surely report this fiasco back to the president.

"Very well, you two are now superintendents of the works. But if the walls fail again, you will rot in Fort Dimanche."

"We have a deal. And don't worry, the walls won't fail. I'll send a list of materials we'll need."

❖

St. Jacques stared out the window of the private jet as it circled over Île-à-Vache. He saw an island in a turmoil of construction, all of it well behind schedule. Duvalier had agreed to relinquish fifty million dollars of his private funds. The interior minister didn't know what he would do after the money was gone. But he knew he would need the American and Bahamian convicts, though their offer could be a clever scheme to escape. He turned to the aide across the aisle from him.

"We must be sure the new superintendents do not leave us."

"How do we lock them up? You just gave them a beach house."

"Start injecting them with heroin. In two weeks, they'll never want to leave. One fix a day. I need them sharp, but hungry. And initiate them."

"Into Voodou?"

"Yes, we must tie their souls to the land."

"The Kanzo rite?"

"Yes, they must partake of the powders. Then they will belong to me."

"As you wish, Excellency. As you wish."

CHAPTER SIXTY

"I owe you a beer, Richard." Trevor looked around their new living quarters. It was a hut on the beach. A bungalow with front room, two separate sleeping quarters, a kitchen counter and an outdoor shower. There was even a small deck facing out to a white sand beach and crystal-clear, light blue water beyond. It included two Adirondack chairs.

"What you owe me is a case of beer, Trevor. And some rum!" Rat smiled broadly. Life was improving, but his ribcage ached, compliments of the Tonton Macoute.

"Look what I found behind the curtain under the kitchen sink. I think the beers are even a little cold. St. Jacques has kept his word. And what do you think of that pretty girl who brings us our meals? Can you believe we had beef and potatoes tonight?"

"Things are looking up. But I'm worried."

"Why?"

"I embellished our resumés a little. How much do you know about building formwork?"

"Enough. We'll figure it out. Didn't you tell me you studied engineering at Yale?"

"Architectural engineering. It's not the same. It's engineering for lightweights."

"We can't do any worse than the cement finisher."

"True. What do you think that shot they gave us was? I'm not sure it was for malaria. I got a pretty good Jones from it."

"They need us alive. I'll accept it for what it is."

"I think I'll go over to the construction office. I want to look at the drawings. I need to figure out how to construct formwork that won't fall down. We have one week to build a new wall. I don't know about you, but I don't want to go back to Fort Dimanche."

"I'll drink to that. I think I'll sit on the deck and watch the sunset."

"Later."

"Hey mon, one thing..."

"Yeah?"

"What about the raft?"

"Let me think about it. Lots of sharks out there. And we're facing the wrong side. The land is on the other side."

"Who said anything about going back to Haiti?"

"So, we float in the sea until a ship comes along? I kinda like the odds right here."

"Okay. But don't get too comfortable. We do too good a job and St. Jacques won't let us leave."

"Right."

❖

Tomlinson tried several of the keys on the ring of twenty. It signified his new status and his responsibility. He thought about the raft. They could finish it in a week. They had access to all the tools and rope they needed. Hell, they could probably build a boat in broad daylight, and no one would say anything.

But the thought of building something permanent began to intrigue him. He could put his education to use, even if he was still a prisoner in Haiti. He wasn't free, but this was better than a three-by-four cell. And Trevor was right. The work took his mind off his five-year sentence.

He thought about the hut on the beach. A lot of pale, overworked New Yorkers would kill for a week living like that. And that servant, Mariel, was beautiful. There was no reason not to take her to his bed in time. Still, the resentment simmered over the events of the last four months.

The third key worked, and he entered the mobile trailer, the job site office. He switched on the lights, looked around. To the right was an office he would claim as his own. At the other end, an office for Trevor. In front of it, a bathroom with running water and a toilet. Between the two

279

offices, a large room with a conference table. Against the wall was a plywood table, an extensive set of drawings on top. He walked over to them and started flipping through the pages.

He noticed the title block on the right-hand margin.

Architect: Lazarus and Berger, Miami, Florida
Associated Architects: Nolan & Marlow and Associates
Chicago, Illinois

Well, I'll be damned. Rat looked at the box noting who produced the drawings.

Designed by: CJW. Checked by: CJW.

He smiled. *Fucking Connor! I should have known.*

CHAPTER SIXTY-ONE

Armand puffed on a Dominican cigar and looked at Connor. He knew the young man had other plans for the evening, ones that did not include sitting with an old Haitian fishing captain.

Connor took a drink of sweet tea. He didn't want to be drunk when Annie served him dinner at her coach house.

"Well, I dodged a bullet. Manny said that St. Jacques didn't need me to inspect last month. Something about the batch plant having problems. I'm learning what building is like in a third-world country. But today Lazarus told me to go down there and see what the hell was going on. Are you ready for our little reconnaissance mission?"

Armand got to the point. "I'm not going to Haiti with you."

"What? Couldn't you get a fake passport?"

"No, I did. Mr. Cicero Jackson fixed me right up with a friend of his. It's a perfect forgery."

"Then what the hell..."

Armand smiled at his little deception. He knew Connor was eager to go back.

"I'm going to the Dominican Republic. And you will come with me. Even with my new passport, we don't want to go through Haitian customs. It's not like you're an unknown quantity. They have photos of you with your hosts from your many trips. Arriving with me will arouse suspicions. Calls will be made. We'll be detained."

Connor breathed a sigh of relief. "So how do we get to Haiti? Drive from Santo Domingo on back roads?"

"By boat. Santo Domingo is on the same south coast as Île-à-Vache. We can stay close to the coastline and make the trip in a day. Camp out early the first night in the Dominican Republic just before we cross into Haitian waters."

"Does Haiti have a Coast Guard?"

"A poor one, manned by thugs—yes, the Tonton Macoute. If they board us, we'll end up in Fort Dimanche."

"I'm not sure I like this plan. Are you sure flying there isn't the best bet?"

"No. Don't worry. While the Coast Guard is sleeping, or drunk, we'll leave at 2 A.M. and get to the island by sunrise."

"Okay. When?"

"Day after tomorrow. Sunday. I have tickets from Key West to Miami at 10:00 A.M."

"I'll meet you at the airport. I'd better go. Annie's cooking dinner."

"Tell her I said hello."

The docks of Santo Domingo were quiet. It was Sunday afternoon and many of the fishermen were enjoying the afternoon feasting with their families after Mass.

"I forgot about Sunday. We'll have to wait until tomorrow. Let's get to a hotel; I know a nice one. Then I'll take you sightseeing. It's a beautiful city. Did you know some descendants of Christopher Columbus still live here?"

"Really. I'm up for being a tourist, especially since it hasn't happened in Port-au-Prince."

"What you'll see today is what takes place when you have a stable government where the politicians, for the most part, care about and answer to their people. I do not know what went wrong in Haiti. We seem to be averse to democracy."

❖

Armand and Rat returned to the dock Monday morning, and Jolicoeur quickly assessed the quality of a few boats. He found one he liked for the 220-mile trip, a Grady White Hatteras Overnighter. He bargained with the boat's owner for what seemed like an hour, walked away three times, only to be brought back to negotiate further. Connor couldn't understand any of the loud and rapid back-and-forths in Spanish.

"Did you get a good deal?"

"No, but that boat has a larger outboard motor and a small cabin. There can still be heavy weather in April, and we also might need to make a fast getaway once we're in Haitian waters."

"You seem to know an awful lot about pleasure boating between the Dominican Republic and Haiti." Connor looked at Armand quizzically.

"If you must know, I lied to you about *Joli's Revenge*. It wasn't my father's boat. He detested the water, got seasick every time. I bought it from a down on his luck American with the money I made running drugs between the two countries. It was very profitable, but the authorities were finally on to me, so I bought the big Bertram for a song and headed to Key West."

"Everyone's a pirate or a drug smuggler in these parts."

"My experience will help in our little clandestine mission."

"Why I invited you along."

"It's a good thing. If you had gone by yourself, they'd have robbed you outside the airport terminal in broad daylight."

"Hey, that's a little harsh."

"Perhaps. Consider this. I know nothing about architecture. Come on. We need to visit a hardware store for provisions, and then the gun store."

"Gun store?"

❖

"The stars are beautiful, especially without the moon."

"I planned it that way. The moon, the tides, all important when you run drugs."

"I should have known."

Armand and Connor sat by a small fire on a beach his former drug runner friend visited often. There was plenty of driftwood and small dead pine branches for a fire. Connor filleted two sea bass he caught on a string line, which they ate with corn on the cob bought at an outdoor market in the city.

Connor laid out his new colorful souvenir blanket and tried to get comfortable. "I better get some sleep. Two o'clock is gonna come early."

"Not like traveling on the presidential yacht, is it?" Armand grinned. He laid down on the other side of the fire, a Glock beside him.

❖

The trip to Île-à-Vache was uneventful. Connor directed Armand to a small beach he saw on a previous trip on Duvalier's yacht. It was about a quarter mile from the Paradi sou Latè construction complex.

"I guess this is where I take over as head of this expedition."

"Lead on. Here, take this." Armand handed Connor a Beretta he bought at the gun store. Connor winced but stuck the gun under his belt.

"What I need is a camera. Manny won't believe whatever I tell him. Okay, let's stay in the underbrush. The hotel site is up just a little way."

After a short but difficult walk among scrub palms and thickets, they came to the end of the underbrush, cleared for the site of the great beachfront hotel. Connor couldn't believe what he saw.

Hundreds of workers toiled under the watchful eyes of guards with sub-machine guns and machetes; some carried whips. The workers were poorly clothed and barefoot and many appeared to be in a zombie-like trance. In front of Connor stood a massive hill of dry concrete and wooden forms, rebar protruding out at grotesque angles. Portions of the hill had deep red stains. The workers used pickaxes to break it up. The work was slow and unproductive. He knew the location; this was where the first great round wall would have been.

Beyond it he could see a finished wall, four and a half stories high, perfectly cast with indentations on the surface he had created to give texture and meaning to the edifice. The cantilevered concrete edges, simulating a wave crashing on the shore, built as he designed. The recesses for the precast concrete deck also appeared to be in their proper locations. He smiled and then saw a worker drop from exhaustion. A guard came up and kicked him. When he didn't get up, the guard unfurled the whip and beat the man until he got back on his feet. Connor felt sick.

Past the completed wall he could make out the formwork for the next one.

"Come on, I need to see more. I want to see that wall under construction."

"What are you going to do, just stroll down there?"

"We'll run to the shoreline and then crouch down and make a run for it. No one is paying any attention to the water. See that pile of lumber, we'll hide behind it."

"This is dangerous, but lead on." Armand took out his Glock from his backpack. "Let's go."

The two spies made a run for the shore and then turned right and fell onto the sand. Connor gave the word, and they were up again, running to the pile of heavy timbers. Beyond it was a great system of formwork, enormous wood trusses, four feet wide, standing vertically, anchored into concrete footings. The trusses, spaced every three feet, supported a tapered wall of wood panels that were further secured with horizontal bracing of 4x4's. The trusses were not as deep as they rose to the top, forty-five- feet in height. It was a masterpiece of engineering, and an army of workers on scaffolding was working to bolt and secure every element.

Two figures came out from behind the far side of the virgin wall. One man was white, the other black. The white man had on a Panama hat, high boots, and a short-sleeved shirt; he carried a roll of drawings. He barked orders in English, translated by the Black man into Creole. Connor rubbed his eyes. Could it be?

"Give me the binoculars."

Armand reached in his pack. He had forgotten nothing.

Connor adjusted the lenses. "Goddamn, it's Rat!"

"No, it cannot be. Let me see." Armand grabbed the glasses, adjusted them again, and looked for what seemed like an eternity. "It cannot be him. This man has a great scar on his forehead and a beard."

Connor grabbed the glasses again, looked hard. The figure turned his back to the field glasses. "Turn around you son-of-a-bitch." The man was looking up at the wall. A guard pointed at a section of it and yelled. Quickly, a worker climbed down and kneeled prostrate in front of his keeper. The guard struck him repeatedly with the end of his whip. Tomlinson ignored the incident, turned in Connor's direction, and looked out to the ocean. He opened up the plans and spoke with his Black cohort.

"Armand, it is Rat. I know it! We found him. But what's he doing here?"

"My friend, I think these are all convicts working on your luxury resort. He is probably one of them, but because he went to Harvard, he has gained some position of authority."

"But that person is being beaten and he doesn't seem to care."

"I'm sure he does, but he can only do so much. He is still a prisoner."

"I've got to get to him!"

"And say what? 'Oh, hello, Rich. I was in the neighborhood, and I thought would visit you. Lovely day, isn't it?'"

"I can't just stand here!"

"How would you like to feel that whip on your back?"

"We need to get him out of this place."

"We've overstayed our welcome. Let's get back to the boat. We can return tonight. If they hold Voodou ceremonies, it will be in the evening. I'd like to see what goes on."

"Armand, it's like something out of the movie the *Ten Commandments*. You know, the slaves building the pyramids for the Egyptians."

"In this case, it's the Duvalier's. The zebra doesn't change his stripes, Connor."

CHAPTER SIXTY-TWO

Connor and Armand motored close to the small village of Madame Bernard. It was mid-afternoon; they had plenty of time to explore before they returned to Paradi sou Latè. They walked along a deserted road to the village. On their approach to town, they saw women wash clothes, cook over small fires, and children in rags play in the dirt or with an old baseball. They saw no men nor had they seen any fishing boats.

Madame Bernard's small harbor changed since Connor's first sanctioned visit to the island when the presidential yacht docked there. All the structures—shops, small houses, and even a church had been demolished. Dredging barges scooped up tons of sand and silt with clam shell buckets and deposited the muck on the deck to be deposited in another location. On land, Tonton Macoute supervised the labor of hundreds of men equipped with shovels, pickaxes, and steel rakes. The sun beat down on bare backs, the humidity stifling on this leeward side of the island, not cooled by ocean breezes.

The two witnessed all this from the safety of a small church beyond the town, aided by the pair of binoculars. An old woman entered, and startled the two sleuths, who exhaled once they saw she had come to pray. Connor walked up to her and bowed; Armand followed knowing he would need to translate.

"Where are all of the men?"

"Kote tout mesye yo?" Armand spoke in his somewhat fractured dialect of Haitian Creole.

"La. Yo te fè yo travay sou pò a ak sou otèl yo."

"She says they are over there at the harbor. And at the hotels. They have been forced to work."

"Are they paid?" But Connor knew the answer.

"Èske yo peye?"

"Trè ti kras. Pa gen anyen pou depanse l 'sou. Mwen ta pito gen pwason yo mari m' kenbe ak legim yo li ap grandi. Koulye a, nou grangou."

"Very little, but there is nothing to spend the money on. Meanwhile her family is hungry because her husband cannot fish, and he cannot grow vegetables."

"Ask her about her house. Did the government pay her for it?"

"Mande li sou kay li. Èske gouvènman an te peye pou li?"

The old woman laughed. "Non, yo jis rive yon jou e yo te fè nou deplase. Nouvo kay mwen an sou wout la. Nou bati yon joupa soti nan bilding yo detwi yo."

"She says the government came one day and made them move. They built a shack down the road with materials from the demolished buildings." Armand was shaking his head, and touched the woman's hand.

"Thank you, madame." Connor's blood was rising.

The old woman nodded in understanding. She gave a weak smile.

The men walked out of the church and back down the dirt road. Off to the left, they noticed recently built shacks and tented areas they had not seen on their walk to the village.

"That must be her new home. St. Jacques told me their first priority was building new houses for the locals, with running water. I guess that's what he meant." He pointed to the shantytown.

"These people are just expendable to the regime, a means to an end." Armand shook his head.

"I've gotta do something."

"Well, do it later. We need to motor to Les Cayes and get gasoline. I don't think there will be any Tonton there. They are all here supervising the workers."

"And letting them die.

CHAPTER SIXTY-THREE

Armand ran the boat safely onto the sand of the beach, and Connor jumped out and lodged the anchor into the ground. They made their way back to the construction site. A small flashlight provided illumination on a moonless night.

It was dark except for the thatched-roof eating pavilion. A half-dozen light bulbs lit the space, tables and chairs moved to one side; it had been turned into a ounfò, a Voodou temple. In the center of the tent, a wooden pole took prominence. Various items were hung from it: a whip that signified delivery from slavery; a crucifix and a rosary—a nod to the people's ties to Catholicism; a skull with a red piece of cloth that meant eventual death and the afterlife; and most importantly, a photo of Papa Doc and another smaller one of Baby Doc. At the base, a ring of candles, with images of the Blessed Mother and Black saints, illuminated the column. Shadows danced and undulated on its uneven bark, on the talismans hung from it, and on the thatched roof. The pole and the open area were the peristil, the center of the Voodou ceremony.

To the side, a fire burned, and around it on the dirt floor designs were drawn in ashes. The drawings, vèvè, were crude but their meanings unmistakable. They were symbols representing Iwa's, Voodou spirits, an invitation for them to enter the ounfò.

Connor and Armand heard the soft drumbeats and prayers. They crouched closer to the temple and hid in underbrush.

"This should be interesting." Armand's hushed voice crackled with excitement.

"What is it?"

"You're going to church, my Catholic brother."

Prisoners, conscripts, and village people began to file in, slowly filling the space. The Tonton Macoute guards were present in large numbers, guns, and machetes in hand. Soon the ounfò was full.

"I can't see anymore. Over there, let's climb on top of that cargo box."

"Why are we staying?" Connor was nervous.

"Patience, you will see much."

The two made their way to the metal shipping container and Connor lifted Armand onto it, and then lifted himself with his strong arms. Now, they could view the ceremony through a small opening several feet high between the heads of the assembled crowd and the roof. Prayers began in Haitian Creole, in French, and even a few in Latin: Catholic prayers that the people recited, and Connor remembered from his childhood.

"Pater noster, Papa Doc, qui es in caelis, sanctificetur nomen tuum ...

"That's Latin." Connor grew interested.

"Yes. Our Father, Papa Doc, who art in heaven...you know the rest."

"Seriously, Papa Doc, our Father?"

"What can I say? The man changed the Lord's Prayer."

The prayers continued, grew louder, the drums matched the rising voices. The devotions gave way to hymns and chanting, and lasted more than an hour. Like the symbols on the floor, the chants were an invitation to the Iwa to enter the ounfò. As they continued, some of the worshippers, faces covered in an eerie white powder, danced to the beat of the drums, now louder yet, and their bodies jerked and flailed in a trance as the Iwa possessed their bodies. Some dropped to the floor or into the arms of the bystanders, their souls occupied by different spirits. The drums beat more fiercely, building to a kind of religious orgasm. The assembled swayed and moaned and prayed to their favorite Iwas, Papa Legba, the most important; then Erzulie Freda, Simbi, Kouzin Zaka and the Marasa—twins considered to be the first children of Bondye, the Voodou name for God.

The crowd separated. A Black man walked through the assembly to the front of the open space. His presence inspired awe. Dressed in ceremonial robes and a cap of colorful hemp cloth, he shook an asson in one hand and held a bottle of rum in the other. The worshipers bowed as he walked around in a circle, chanting, "Papa Bookman-oh, nou nan fen lit nou an. Nou pa t goumen nan Bois Caïman pou kontinye sèvi etranje yo."* He poured rum on the symbols in the ground and into the fire, and flames shot up to the thatched roof.

"That man is the houngan, the high priest," Armand whispered.

The houngan put down the asson and bottle and went behind a curtain that served as a backdrop for the peristil. He returned with a rooster in his hand. He walked around the room blessing the worshippers with it, like a thurible with incense. Then he bit off the head of the rooster and let the blood from its neck ooze out and drip into the fire and onto the symbols on the ground.

The crowd dispersed again, chanting louder. A man entered the ounfò, his face painted white, black circles surrounding his eyes, and his mouth made up to appear as if it had been sewn shut. He wore a long black coat and a top hat. His nostrils were stuffed with cotton plugs. Around his neck was a necklace of bones and a small skull. He carried a silver machete in one hand and a bottle of light brown powder in the other. He possessed an evil smile.

Following immediately behind him were Rat and Trevor hands bound in front. They looked stoned.

"Holy crap, that's Rat and that other guy from the construction site. They look out of it."

"They're high on something to make them not care, Connor. I don't like this. It's an initiation ceremony."

"Into Voodou?"

"Exactly. Watch the man in the top hat. He's the bokor, the sorcerer."

"The big, scary guy?"

"Yes. He represents Baron Samedi, the Iwa of the dead. He represents all that is evil in life and the afterlife."

The bokor slashed the air with his machete, its blade passing inches from Rat's face. He reached down to the floor for the houngan's bottle of rum. He took a drink, the liquid flowed from his mouth, and he sprayed its remnants in Rat's and Trevor's face. Then he smashed the neck of the bottle on the peristil and began to bite the broken end of the bottle. He chewed on the glass; there was no blood. He took another swig of rum and continued to chew. He let out an evil laugh and sprayed the fire with the rum. The flames shot up again. Biting into the bottle once more, he threw the remains in the fire, and some of the worshippers added sticks and dried brush. The fire grew.

The houngan appeared again from behind the curtain with a large palm frond and a goat on a rope tether. The animal bleated as it was tied to the peristil. The high priest held the frond in front of the Bokor, who emptied the contents of the brown powder onto the leaf.

The bokor slowly turned to the compliant Rat and Trevor. "Baron Samedi pral antre nan kò ou kounye a posede nanm ou. Ou fè pati Iwa a kounye a epi ou pral sèvi yo."**

He slowly blew the powder into their faces, watching them inhale it, and then blowing more. Their bodies stiffened, their eyes opened wide, they twitched, arms flailing into the air, in spasms arching back and forth. They exhaled the air from their lungs, and their bodies went limp, caught by two waiting Tonton Macoute. The guards laid the bodies on the floor.

Mesmerized, Connor looked at Armand with fear. "What the hell is going on?"

"That powder is a powerful drug. It's like an anesthetic. They are barely breathing. Hopefully, in the morning, the bokor will give them the antidote and they will waken. But for now, they are the living dead. They are zombies."

"Zombies?"

"As close as you can come. Those workers we saw early today. The ones who moved awkwardly in fits and starts, staring into nothingness..."

"That looked like zombies?"

"Yes, they have been through the full initiation. Three times. After being administered the powder and then brought back to the living, their brains no longer function normally. They have been oxygen deprived. They wouldn't escape even if they could. Their minds are not their own. They belong to Duvalier."

"What about Rat and the other guy?"

"I don't think so. This was their first initiation. We saw them at the great wall. Rat seemed in full control of his faculties. But they may repeat tonight's ritual in a week. To assure they won't want to escape.'

"We've got to do something."

"Yes, but what, I do not know."

The guards put the bodies of Rat and Trevor on stretchers and lifted them just above the ground. Their arms dangled off the side and as they were taken out the guards passed by the roaring fire: Rat and Trevor's hands were barely inches above it. They had no reaction to the flame. In a moment they were gone into the darkness.

The bokor flailed his machete once more. Finally, it came down against the throat of the goat. Blood spurted over the symbols on the floor. The Iwa had been fed, their spirits renewed with the life and vigor of the sacrificed animal, their divine energy restored.

"I've seen enough. Let's get back to Santo Domingo."

"Yes, help me down, Connor."

Connor jumped down from the steel storage box and used his clasped hands as a step for his older friend. Both down, they turned to head for the boat. In front of them a Tonton Macoute, wearing sunglasses, and holding a machete, a twisted smile on his face, stood to block their escape.

* "Papa Bookman-oh, we are at the end of our struggle. We did not fight at Bois Caïman to continue serving the foreigners."

** "Baron Samedi will enter your body and possess your soul. You belong to the Iwa now and you will serve them."

CHAPTER SIXTY-FOUR

Charles Tomlinson rode the elevator to the seventy-third floor of the World Trade Center's North Tower. The firm of James, Merrill and Tomlinson occupied the entire floor and half of the seventy-second. The senior partner enjoyed an excellent view of Manhattan from his corner office.

"Good morning, Marjorie."

"Good morning, sir. Coffee? How was your weekend?"

"Uneventful. Yes, please."

"One of our clients delivered a couple of dozen donuts. Would you care for one?"

"No, thank you, just the coffee."

Tomlinson removed his coat and proceeded to his ritual of perusing the *Wall Street Journal*. An article on page two caught his attention.

Tourism Booming in Florida

As he began to read, Marjorie returned with his coffee. "Mr. Tomlinson I've been meaning to ask you about Richard. How's he doing in Florida?"

Tomlinson thought, *That's a coincidence.*

"I must confess, I don't know. We haven't talked since December when he asked for money. We're not close, as you know."

"Sir, it's none of my business but he's your only child and he lost his mother last year. Perhaps you should make the first move. You're the only relation he has left.'

"He has his Aunt Polly in St. Pete."

"I meant the only parent. I'll be happy to place the call for you."

"Fine. After the morning staff meeting."

"Sir, there's no answer at his boat. I've tried several times. It makes a noise as if the number isn't working."

"Strange, maybe he's out on a charter. It is April after all. Surely his business has improved; at least he hasn't called me for money. Let me give you the number for the marina. They should know if the boat left the dock today."

He thumbed through his Rolodex to the letter "K" and flipped a few cards. "Here it is, *Key West City Marina.*" As he scribbled the number down, he said, "This boat captain foolishness has to stop. It's time for the boy to get serious about his life, about his future." He handed the note to his secretary.

She ignored the remark. "I'll try it right away, Mr. Tomlinson." She returned in a few minutes, her face pale.

"Sir?"

"Yes, what now?"

"Mr. Tomlinson, the harbor master, Tom's his name, says that your son's boat left the marina back in late December. He hasn't been back since. It was headed for a town in the Keys called Tavernier."

"Really? That is a concern. There must be a marina there. Can you look up the number? And I want to talk to whoever you get on the phone."

In a moment Marjorie was on the intercom. "I have the Tavernier marina on the line, sir."

"Hello, my name is Charles Tomlinson. My son owns a boat named *Daddy's Money.* It was reported headed for your marina back in December. Do you remember it?"

"Shit man, the boat was here, and a young guy has stopped by here a bunch of times asking if the boat's come back. It hasn't."

"What was the man's name, did he say?"

"Let me think. Yeah, his name is Connor. He seemed real concerned. I asked him why. He said the boat was headed for Haiti. That's a long-ass trip. Rough water. You from the bank? A lot of people have quit making their payments."

"No, I'm the captain's father.'

"Father? It's been four months since that boat was here. Even a bank would have more interest than that."

❖

"State Department, Office of Caribbean Affairs."

"Carter Madison, please."

"One moment. May I tell him who's calling?"

"Charles Tomlinson.'

"What is this regarding?"

Tomlinson's temper rose. He felt bad that he hadn't called his son for four months. Where had the time gone? And he was missing somewhere between Florida and Haiti.

"Yes, about a missing fishing boat."

"Sir, I believe that would be under the Coast Guard's purview. I can transfer you, but it will take a moment. They're in the Pentagon."

"Let me fucking speak to Carter Madison! We're old friends from college."

"There's no need to use that sort of language, sir. I'll connect you."

Tomlinson took a drink of his Fresca. The wait seemed forever.

"Charlie, how are you? It's been a long time."

"I'm fine, Carter. Yes, we're all busy these days, aren't we? How's the president?"

"Gerry? I get a Christmas card. I'm in Caribbean Affairs; it's not exactly the "A" team. So what can I do for my old Dartmouth roommate? I'm sure this isn't a social call."

"Sorry, I've been covered up, and with Candee's passing..."

"I heard. Sorry."

"My son owns a fishing boat, appropriately named *Daddy's Money*. He left Key West in December and docked in Tavernier. A friend of his believes it was headed to Haiti."

"It's April."

"I know. I lost track of time."

Madison recalled his old roommate. Aloof, cool... no cold. They only kept in contact because his wife Annette had introduced Tomlinson to Candee in college.

"Haiti's a tough spot. Slightly better with Baby Doc, but I think he's just sucking up to us to get more aid. Why would your son be taking a fishing boat to Haiti? That's over 500 nautical miles."

"I have no idea."

"I hate to ask this, Charlie, but is he running drugs?"

Tomlinson was quiet. That hadn't occurred to him. *Why would he do that? He's got a trust fund.* "I take offense to that, Carter. He wasn't brought up that way."

"No offense intended, my friend, but nobody goes to Haiti on a pleasure cruise. It's not a tourist trap these days."

"I understand. My apologies. Can you make inquiries with your ambassador in what, Port-au-Prince?"

"Jeremiah Clark? Sure. He's a big donor to the Republican Party. Started an insurance company in Atlanta and is worth millions. I think his grandparents were from Haiti. I'll get back to you."

❖

"Charlie, Carter Madison."

"Good morning, Carter. What did you find out?" Tomlinson did not care for useless chit-chat.

"Yes, and good morning to you too, Charles." Madison had plenty of time on his hands as Assistant Undersecretary to the Director of Caribbean Affairs, Western Sector. He hoped the call to his old roommate might result in a weekend invitation to the Hamptons. He realized immediately that was wishful thinking.

"I'm sorry. Ambassador Clark told me that no American has been impounded at Fort Dimanche, that's their despicable prison. So, in a way, that's good news."

"I see. But how would he know?"

"Diplomatic protocol requires a foreign government to inform the local embassy of any foreigner detained. So the embassy can arrange for their release, or give aid and comfort."

"My son has disappeared, Carter, and he was headed for Haiti for some godforsaken reason."

297

"I sympathize with you, Charles. As I said, that's a long and dangerous trip. Have you tried contacting your son's friend? The one who found out he was sailing to Haiti."

"No, I haven't. But that's a good next step. Thank you for your efforts, Carter. We should get together soon. Goodbye."

When hell freezes over, Madison thought. He decided to head to the commissary; today was French Pastry Day.

Tomlinson looked out the slim windows of his office and stared at the top of the gleaming Chrysler Building in the distance. *Connor, Connor.* He remembered the boy, his son's best friend at Harvard.

"Marjorie, get me the registrar's office at Harvard."

"Class of 1973, Graduate School of Design. Let's see. Okay, here's a Connor Jones West. Graduated magna cum laude a week late. Death in the family."

"Thank you; do you have an address, a phone number?"

"Sure. 4211 West 26th Street, New York. The number is Murray Hill-7-4853. Lists his mother, Margaret as the contact."

"You've been most helpful."

By the end of the day, Charles Tomlinson had talked to Margaret West, Bob Marlow, and finally, Manny Lazarus.

"Yeah, Mr. Tomlinson, Connor's on a site visit to a big project we got. He'll be back on Monday." A pause. "Where's the project? It's in Haiti, if you must know."

CHAPTER SIXTY-FIVE

Connor froze. He saw the machete in the man's hands. An offensive weapon, of not much use in defense unless you're in a sword fight. Armand glanced at Connor, wide-eyed. Connor looked at the sunglasses, pulled out his Beretta from his belt, flipped it so he held the barrel, and smashed the butt of the gun into the Tonton's sunglasses. The aviator lenses broke into shards, piercing his eyes and face. The policeman let out a scream, dropped the machete, and covered his face, blood seeping through his fingers.

Armand had noticed a Bowie knife secured by a belt to the man's waist. He grabbed it and rammed the blade into the side of the intruder. Armand pulled it out quickly and as the Tonton Macoute fell forward, he stabbed him again, this time in the back.

"Holy shit!"

"Quick thinking on your part. Let's get him inside this box."

Connor, shaking, went to the rear doors and lifted the latch, swung the handle, and opened it. Shovels and other tools lined the walls, but the floor was clear. He went back to Armand, picked up the man's arms while Armand grabbed the feet. In a half-minute, the body was locked inside the box. Connor kicked sand to cover the blood and then spread some underbrush and palm fronds over the ground.

"Let's get the hell out of here."

"I'm right behind you."

They ran parallel to the beach along the edge of the underbrush and tree line. When they got to where they had left the boat, it was gone. The tide had come in during the five-hour Voodou ceremony.

"Damn. We're fucked!" Connor began to shake with fear.

"This way. The wind is blowing south. The tide took the boat with it." Armand switched on his flashlight, and they proceeded down the beach about fifty yards.

"There it is, Armand, in the bushes by those palm trees!" His shaking stopped and he let out a cry of deliverance.

They were quickly at the boat, undamaged, but the anchor and its rope were intertwined in the bushes and trees. After several precious minutes, it was free, and they pushed the small vessel across the sand to the water.

"We need to get out of Haitian waters before sunup. There will be morning patrol boats." Armand pulled the cord on the Johnson 75, and it came to life on the second pull. They quickly motored out to deep water and then west, when Armand opened the throttle. They made good headway.

"How long until we're in Dominican waters."

"Three hours if we go full out."

"Shit. That's not good."

"We're in luck. The seas are calm. I'm heading west and also south to get us outside of the reach of the patrols. Say a prayer."

"Which one, a Catholic one or a Voodou one?" Connor smiled.

"Both."

The engine hummed and Connor stood next to Armand at the wheel in the small cockpit. The first glints of light appeared on the horizon.

"Explain the Catholic paraphernalia at that Voodou ceremony."

"There is an old saying. Haiti is 70% Catholic, 30% Protestant, and 100% Voodou. We worship your God and Bondye, both considered the same deity."

"Which one do you belong to?"

"I'm Catholic, but I subscribe to much of what Voodou teaches."

"Why?"

"I consider it my spiritual insurance policy. This way I have all the bases covered." Jolicoeur smiled.

"Got it. Look, the sun's coming up."

"Well, good morning then. Think you can make a pot of coffee? I brought some along and I noticed an old coffee pot in the galley below."

"I was a first mate, remember? Just try to avoid the waves."

In fifteen minutes, Connor returned with two steaming mugs of black Dominican java. He handed one to Armand, wanted to speak, but decided to keep quiet.

Armand sensed it. "What's on your mind, Connor?"

"You killed that man."

"Did I have a choice? Do you see any patrol boats now? They won't discover his body for a day or two when the smell of the body will alert them. He was Tonton Macoute. They killed my mother and others in my family. I would have liked to kill more of them, but we had better odds with just one. And that was very clever on your part, smashing his sunglasses. We will make a good team to rescue Richard."

"Any ideas on how we're gonna do that?"

"We can't fly into Santo Domingo again. We'll need to have many weapons and ammunition. So it will have to be by boat."

"Excuse me, but I think we're gonna need a bigger boat."

"I think *Joli's Revenge* will serve our purposes, with a little retrofitting."

"Retrofitting?"

"Leave that to me. Do you have any friends that might like to join us on this mission?"

"Not really. What about that guy Cicero? He's a badass."

"Yes, I think we should visit him. And he might know of others who played poker with Rat. What about Annie?"

"Annie? Are you kidding me?"

"She told me she knows her way around a boat. I think she would be handy, not with a gun, but waiting onboard the boat while we retrieve Rat and his other friend, the Black man."

"You've got this all figured out don't you?"

"I had time to think while you made the coffee. It's excellent, by the way. Yes, Cicero—we'll pay him a visit."

CHAPTER SIXTY-SIX

The figure made his way quietly to the bungalow in the early morning, before the first light. He entered, lit a candle, and went into each bedchamber. The bodies were there as if in lying in state, hands folded over their chests. There was no discernable life. He took out a small bottle containing white powder, shook a small quantity onto his hand and gently blew the dust on the face of Rat. The man got up, repeated the same ritual with Trevor, and quietly left the hut, blowing out the candle as he exited. Soon he was lost in the trees and undergrowth.

"Damn, I got some kind of headache. How about you?" Rat sat on the front porch of the palapa and stared out to the sea."

"Yes, mon, the head be hurting. Did we drink rum last night?"

"I don't remember. I don't remember anything about last night. We got our malaria shot, and then, and then? Shit, I can't remember. I'm starving though. Where's Mariel?"

"It's only seven. She'll be here shortly."

"What are we doing here?"

"What do you mean? We're building a hotel. You and I are in charge. We're building big walls, lots of them. Ten more to go."

"That's right. I'm a fucking prisoner in paradise."

"So when are we going to finish the raft, mon, and get off this paradise."

"Trevor, you really want to take your chances out there in the ocean? We've got it made here. They don't beat us."

"A small consolation. No, they drug us."

"So we don't get malaria or yellow fever."

Mon, you live under a rock. They addicting us to the big H."

"Heroin?"

"Yes, mon, heroin."

"Shit. No wonder I'm wanting it so bad. I can't wait for that shot every day."

"We don't get off this island now, we'll never be wanting to leave. And last night, I'm remembering something about being taken somewhere in the jungle."

"I don't know what you're talking about. Trevor, I don't think I want to leave. For once in my life, I'm creating something. I'm not a just a fishing boat captain. I'm building my friend's design. And this hotel and whatever else that St. Jacques is going to build will lift this island out of poverty."

"Rat, you are a prisoner. I think the drugs are going to your head. Why do you care?"

"We can't do anything about being incarcerated. It's our fate. I mean, we were running drugs."

"Drugs the government was selling to us."

"Right. But I'd rather do this than sit on a raft in the hot sun hoping we don't get eaten by sharks. At least here, like I say, I'm leaving my imprint."

"The imprint of a corrupt regime that uses slave labor!"

"I'm going to the office. I need to plan this week's work. I want to pour two walls and train another crew to erect the precast planks. Next week, we'll start masonry."

"The raft, mon, the raft?"

"Have Mariel bring my breakfast to the job trailer." Rat left, ignoring his friend's remarks.

CHAPTER SIXTY-SEVEN

Connor looked at the sketches he made for the new terminal building at Île-à-Vache's airport. He wanted to pick up the bumwad and throw it into the trash. On the flight back to Miami from Santo Domingo, his anger increased. He was through with Paradi sou Latè, and he entertained much darker thoughts. He put them out of his mind.

He and Armand planned to head back to Île-à-Vache on Thursday. If all went well, they'd be motoring toward Key West with Rat and his friend by Sunday morning. He looked up. Manny had just arrived, his voice booming to Esther, "It's a beautiful day in the neighborhood!"

Connor, coffee mug in hand, walked over to Manny's empire, a mess of drawings, sketches, small models, and stacks of construction documents and specifications, barely reviewed. Construction documents were boring; the fun was in the designing.

"Hey, boss."

"Boss, my ass. You work for Danny Nolan. You're just on permanent loan, like a piece of artwork to a museum."

"Don't remind me." Connor sipped on his Guatemalan coffee. It was better than Columbian coffee, despite TV ads by Juan Valdez to the contrary.

"So, how was your visit?"

"Enlightening. They've finally poured the great walls correctly. They look good and the precast decking is being installed."

"Terrific, and I got a big check Friday from St. Jacques. Say what you will about our client, he pays on time."

"That's a plus, I guess."

"I think I'll start working on the design for my new house in Boca. What are you gonna do? The airport?"

"It's designed. Manny, we're way ahead of schedule on everything else. I think I'll take the rest of the week off, go to Key West."

"I knew it. You got a girlfriend down there. What's her name?"

"Annie." Connor went along with Manny's incorrect assumption. No need to tell him he was going on a search and rescue operation.

"Damn, I wish I was young again. You must get pussy every night!"

Connor's face blushed. "I'll see you in a week, okay."

"No problem. Hey, give her a big, fat kiss for me."

"I will." Connor smiled.

He went back to his desk and started to tidy up the workspace. Esther came on the intercom. "Connor, honey, line one is for you."

"Thanks, Mom." 'Honey' and 'Mom' were their private monikers, developed over the last few months.

"Hello, Connor West."

"Connor, this is Charles Tomlinson. Perhaps you remember me."

Connor sat up straight. It was Rat's father. "Mr. Tomlinson, how are you?"

"In a word, concerned. I was hoping you might have some information about Richard's whereabouts. I appreciate that you have been trying to locate him for the last...several months."

"How did you know to call this number?"

"It wasn't easy. I started with the registrar's office at Harvard. I'm quite worried about Rich. I understand he took his boat to Haiti. But there is no record of him there. I checked with the State Department."

"Mr. Tomlinson, he went to Haiti, all right."

"How do you know?"

"I saw him the day before yesterday."

"Is he alive?"

"Very much so. He's a prisoner on an island, building a hotel I designed.

305

CHAPTER SIXTY-EIGHT

Connor arrived in Key West by 8 o'clock and headed for the Green Parrot. The bar was open seven days a week. He hoped Annie was behind the bar. She was.

"Hey, what does a sailor have to do to get a drink in this joint?"

"Just say, miss, may I have a Jim Beam on the rocks?"

"Consider it said."

Annie fixed the drink, a double, and placed it in front of Connor. Leaning over the bar, she kissed him on the lips.

"How was Haiti?"

"Worse than ever, but guess what?"

"I'm all ears."

"We found Rat."

"Connor, that's fantastic. What's he doing there?"

"Breaking rocks on a chain gang."

"You're not serious?"

"No, but it's almost as bad. He's a prisoner on that island where they're building the resort I designed. He's building it."

"Well, F me!"

"Wanna go rescue him?"

"I get off at ten."

Connor, Armand, and Annie waited on the small dock alongside Roosevelt Avenue. It was a moonless night, and only the lights of a few houseboats were visible in the water beyond. The sound of an outboard motor could be faintly heard, growing louder. In a minute a skiff came into view and pulled up alongside the jetty. A large Black man closed the throttle to idle. He smiled and his gold tooth shined in the illumination of a nearby streetlight.

"Launch for the *Pirate of Penzance* now be leaving." Cicero Jackson stood up and he helped the three passengers onto the boat.

The trip took five minutes. The four entered the main room of the houseboat with its unique, tacky nautical theme and two poker tables. Behind the bar, a muscular man with impressive biceps and an eye patch over his right eye was ready to fix drinks.

"Ladies and gentlemen, and you too, Cicero, welcome to the *Pirate*."

"You got that right, Seadog, I'm no gentleman!" Cicero went up to the bar and shook Mike Fineran's hand.

"Folks, meet Councilman Pat and Captain Jack over on the couch. They wanted to be here, insisted actually. What can I pour for all of you?"

Beverages in hand, Connor, and Armand outlined their plan. Glances were exchanged; there were nods of approval and some shaking of heads.

Captain Jack spoke up. "That's a long trip. You go by the shortest route, north of Cuba, you're in the Atlantic. Then you got to head due west between Cuba and Haiti, the Windward Passage, and back around the south coast of that sorry excuse of a country."

"That's why I think the long way is better, around the northern tip of Cuba and parallel to it on the south side in the Caribbean Sea. Calmer waters and after the turn, a direct route to Île-à-Vache."

"You'll need more fuel. And by the way, who's paying for this little pleasure cruise?

West spoke up. "Charles Tomlinson, Rat's father. He said he would pay for everything, whatever the cost. I spoke to him this morning."

Connor had been surprised to hear Tomlinson's offer. Maybe Rat's dad did have a heart despite of the many tales Rat related about his obtuse father.

"Fine, the gas is paid for. What's the tank capacity of *Joli's Revenge*, Armand?"

"Thirteen hundred gallons, but the distance is over 750 nautical miles. We'll need more fuel for the round trip. There's no stopping in Port-au-Prince to re-fuel. We might have enough to make it west to Port Antonio in Jamaica and gas up there."

Seadog took a drink of his Bacardi Rum and did some calculations on a notepad. "Bring the boat over to the naval yard at Stock Island. We'll add a tank on the rear deck and connect a fuel line to the engines below. An additional 500 gallons should do it by my figures. And while we're at it, we'll mount an MK Tripod on the foredeck with twin 50 caliber machine guns. That should handle any Tonton Macoute gunboats."

Connor stared at Annie; his eyes saying it all. "Holy shit..."

Annie looked at him. "Thanks for inviting me to go yachting, Cowboy."

Seadog continued. "We're gonna need guns, semi-automatics if possible."

"Leave that to me. I've got a source at the military base, no questions asked," Cicero replied, all-in on righting the wrong that got Rat in trouble.

Seadog made a note on the guns. "Do we need to blow anything up? That's my specialty, compliments of the Navy Seals." He pointed to his eye patch.

Connor sat up, and stared at Fineran, but said nothing.

Armand looked at Captain Jack. "Jack, since you're the only other boat owner, can you get me this list of additional equipment for *Joli's Revenge?* My radar doesn't work, I need a new Lowrance depth finder, and I think a new wind gauge would be in order. And maybe some new life jackets."

"Not a problem. I'll pick them up tomorrow and bring them to the naval yard."

"Annie looked at Connor. "And what do I do? Cook for the boys?"

Armand smiled. "No, Annie, I'll cook, so will Seadog. You'll be in command of the boat while we're onshore. I'll tell you more later, once we get close to Haiti. Okay then, I think that covers everything. Connor will be in charge of buying food and provisions. Councilman Pat, how about making a run to the liquor store?"

"My pleasure. I can also get a council resolution passed endorsing this trip to save one of our own from the clutches of the evil Duvalier's."

"Much appreciated, but not necessary. We'll leave Thursday mid-morning from the naval yard at Stock Island. Too many questions will be asked if anyone sees our gunboat. The trip should take two-days. We'll arrive mid-afternoon Saturday weather permitting. Early reports show nice weather."

"Saturday afternoon. What do we do until darkness falls?" Connor worried the arrival might be premature.

"Drop anchor seven miles off the coast. If we encounter weather on down, the extra time is our insurance. We don't want to be late for the Voodou ceremony."

"Got it."

Captain Jack stood up. "If that's everything, boys and girls, I want to propose a name for our group."

"What, the 'Dirty Half Dozen plus a Pretty Girl'?" Cicero joked.

"How about the 'Pirates of Penzance'?" the old sailor lifted his glass.

The group lifted their glasses: "To the Pirates of Penzance!"

"Bar is open folks. Step right up." Seadog walked toward the bar and Connor took him aside.

"Seadog, can we talk later."

"Sure, boyo, sure."

CHAPTER SIXTY-NINE

"I hope you don't mind. I had the boat painted gray. Not as easy to spot." Seadog looked at Armand hoping he wasn't displeased.

"No, not at all. Will you re-paint it for free when we return?"

"Sure, any color. I'll charge it to Rat's father. Son-of-a-bitch didn't even inquire about the kid for four months."

"Better late than never. Let's look at the new equipment."

A quick walk around the boat and up to the bridge impressed Armand. "I think we're ready to go to Haiti. I am a little concerned about the exposed gas tank. If we're shot at and it gets hit, were up in flames."

"Relax, Jolicoeur. It's double-walled and the inside wall is twelve-gauge steel."

"It must weigh a ton."

"In fact, it almost does, 1,900 pounds, but I increased the capacity by 100 gallons to compensate for the extra weight."

"You thought of everything. Weapons?"

"Down below, under the main cabin's bed."

"I told Connor and Annie they could sleep there."

"You romantic cuss."

"I am, that's because I'm Haitian. Let's take a look."

They slid several crates out from under the bed. There were M249 machine guns and Browning A-5 shotguns in one crate, and Beretta 92's, Glock 17's, and Smith & Wesson .40 cal. M&P's in the other.

"My friend, we're trying to free two prisoners. We're not invading Haiti."

"It's Cicero, what can I say? Better to have more firepower than less."

"I already killed a Tonton Macoute. I don't feel badly, but I hope we won't have to fire these weapons. Did he get any flash bombs? That would be the best."

"I thought of that. They're in the other cabin."

Seadog and Armand went into the next berth with two twin beds.

"In that box." Fineran pointed to one of two small fiberglass crates.

"What's in the other one?"

"Don't worry about it."

"Hmmm? Okay. Well, I'll go check the galley, see if Connor got everything."

"He did. I think he wants to impress Annie. We even have frozen lobster."

"This could turn out to be quite the trip."

The clear night and a million stars provided all the entertainment necessary.

"You know how to show a girl a good time."

"I told you this would be fun."

Connor kissed Annie deeply, pulled away, and looked at her smiling.

"What?"

"You're so beautiful."

"You're so full of shit."

"You are. Take a compliment."

"Cute maybe, but beautiful? It's the bourbon talking."

"No. I mean it. And I'm not drunk. Tomorrow's a big day. I have to be on my game."

"Are you going to use that sub-machine gun?"

"No, I don't think so. Seadog and I have other plans."

"What? Are you going to host a luau on the beach?"

"No, but it may remind you of the 4th of July from the boat. Let's go to bed."

"And make our own fireworks? Good idea."

311

❖

Joli's Revenge reached its destination by five o'clock. The boat was just six miles from Île-à-Vache. It would take less than an hour to get near the shore. The Pirates of Penzance assembled in the main cabin, the lounge of the boat. Armand stood in front of the galley counter, a clipboard in his hand.

"I've discussed this plan with Seadog. Being ex-military, and a Navy Seal, he has a lot of good ideas. First, *Joli's Revenge* will remain well off-shore, lights out, not even running lights. Annie's in command. She'll station herself at the twin 50 caliber machine guns in case there's trouble. Annie, you did wonderful at practice yesterday. I would not want to be in your line of fire. The rest of us will take the Zodiac to the beach. Councilman, you'll stay with it, with the flares to signal Annie to get closer to the shore when we have Rat and friend."

"I'll miss out on all the fun."

"You can only hope. One of the M249's is for you in case you have to lay down suppressing fire. You know what that is, don't you?"

"I was in Korea. It means pull the trigger and don't let up."

"Right. Shoot at everything except us. Cicero, Captain Jack, and I will make our way to the ounfò, the pavilion where they have the Voodou ceremony. It's our job to get our two prisoners."

"What if they don't want to come?"

"We'll make them. It's likely they're high on something, so that may be the case. Cicero and Jack are pretty stout guys. I think they'll prevail in any argument."

Annie looked confused. "What about Connor and Seadog?"

Seadog answered quickly. "We have a special assignment."

Annie and the others said nothing.

Armand continued. "We go in at twenty-three-hundred hours. We need to rendezvous back at the zodiac at zero-one-hundred hours at the latest. That's two hours. Pat,

312

when you see us, set off the flares and be ready to shoot at anybody pursuing us. Questions?"

"What if Rat and his friend skip church?" Annie asked making a solid point.

"Well, there's always the unexpected in any operation, isn't there? If they aren't at the ceremony, the three of us will head for the prison. The good news is that there aren't a lot of honky-tonks on the island."

Annie looked at Connor. "Cowboy, what are you up to?"

Connor put his finger to his lips and said, "Shhhhhhh..."

"Good. Now let's have some dinner. I understand we're having lobster with corn on the cob and Seadog baked some cookies for dessert."

"Seadog made cookies?" Cicero almost spit out his cigar.

"You got a problem with that, Jackson?'

"No, but I hope they be chocolate chip."

The ersatz band of commandos motored into shore, faces covered in black grease paint. Cicero and Seadog had on their military fatigues. The rest were dressed in black as instructed by Seadog back in Key West.

The team climbed out of the Zodiac and dragged it to the edge of the underbrush by a stand of royal palms. They moved about ten yards away from it to a spot where they had a good view of the pavilion. Pat held the anchor rope, nailed a steel stake in the ground and tied it securely. This time, the tide would not carry the boat away.

Connor and Seadog had carried a large box from the boat. "We'll see you guys later. We'll be back here in two hours."

"Roger that."

Armand took out his binoculars and surveyed the area. Additional lights had been added. The metal storage container was gone, and the perimeter was being patrolled by a Tonton Macoute.

"Damn, they discovered the body and now we have a patrol."

Cicero reached for his knife. "What did you say about the unexpected? I'll take care of him. Let's move in closer, there, over by the cooking shed."

Armand, Cicero, and Captain Jack crouched and then ran to the backside of the lean-to building, which shielded them from the light emanating from the ounfò. The patrolling Tonton would walk within ten feet. They heard the soft footsteps in the sand.

"Now!"

Cicero jumped up and sprinted to the sentry. His huge arm around the man's throat, the knife went into the heart, and then the neck was slashed. He dragged the body to the back of the shed.

"Good job. Now lift me on the roof so I can see. When I give the signal, move in and toss the flash bombs. Then get inside and grab Rat and his friend. I'll throw more flash bombs outside the crowd if necessary and take care of any Tonton who follow you."

The ceremony proceeded as it had the previous week. Women dressed in long white gowns began to sway and move to the loud drums and the songs that called for the Iwa to descend upon the Voodou temple. More women danced this night, and the pavilion filled with more worshippers. Armand shook his head. He wanted to keep any collateral damage to a minimum.

Before long, the women dropped to the ground or were caught by others and taken to an area away from the peristil. The houngan entered, sacrificed another rooster, and poured rum on the symbols drawn on the floor. Finally, the bokor, the sorcerer, entered holding his machete and the bottle of light brown powder. Two prisoners followed, but they weren't Rat and Trevor.

Armand froze. "Damn!"

CHAPTER SEVENTY

Connor and Seadog carried the heavy box up the beach, about a hundred yards from the pavilion. The area in front of them was lit with only a few bulbs, strung irregularly. But it was enough to see the great round walls, ten completed and three others in various stages of progress. Precast floors had been erected between the first three walls. Between the first and second walls the floors were complete, four floors in height. Connor, impressed by the size of his monumental structures, shook his head. *I can't believe I'm going to do this thing*, he thought.

"Let's get going, Connor. This will take a while."

"Same plan as we discussed?"

"No. We don't have enough plastic explosives. But if we place a significant amount of material in the right place on the fourth wall, it will fall onto the next one, setting off a domino effect. The wall is 45 feet high, right?"

"Yes, and the distance between the walls is 36 feet. I get it. One wall falls on the other. Do you think it will work?"

"We need to avoid the first and second walls; they're braced by the floors. If we have time and explosives, we'll come back and do them too, but we'll need to climb up to each floor on those ladders."

"Sounds good."

"Okay, follow me. Lay the wire behind me and bury it in the sand. I'll put the explosives where they'll do the most damage and you wrap the cable around the bags. At each wall, you'll need twenty to thirty feet of extra cable. Then keep going until I'm finished and head back. Let's bury the detonator in the underbrush over there."

"Roger that."

The demolition team proceeded but it was slow going. Connor looked at his watch. Midnight. Seadog placed four sacks of explosives against wall four, a foot deep into the sand. Connor wrapped each sack with one turn of wire and then packed sand above all of it. They back-tracked to wall three.

"I think I can get the precast planks to fall if we place a couple of bags here at the base."

Connor wasn't listening. He looked toward the last walls. "We have company."

Connor and Seadog lay flat against the wall. A Tonton, a semi-automatic rifle over his shoulder, was coming right toward them, but they were well hidden in the darkness. As the patrol passed, Seadog leaped up and was behind the man in an instant. Connor heard the crunch of breaking bones as Seadog wrenched the man's neck at ninety degrees with his mighty biceps. He dropped into the Navy Seal's arms. Seadog dragged him back to the wall and laid him on top of the explosives.

"His body will be a better cover than sand."

"Right." Connor felt sick.

"Let's get to the ladders. I have four bags left. We can put one on each floor. If I do it right, the floors will pancake one on top of the other."

"Sure, whatever. But I think we should head back to the detonator."

"We have time. Stay here at the bottom. I'll do the rest. Watch for more patrols. If someone comes, get deep into the sand and let him pass."

"I'm planning on it."

Connor held the rickety wooden ladder for Seadog who climbed up with the explosives and the spool of demolition wire. The minutes seemed like hours. In a loud whisper, he called up to Seadog. "Hurry up, for God's sake."

Seadog finally appeared with only the spool. He climbed down the ladder and jumped off at the fifth step. "All done. Let's go hook up this fireworks show."

They ran to the underbrush, and Seadog pulled the detonator out of the woods, licked his fingers, and touched a terminal. The spark shocked him. He hooked up the wire to the terminals. "We're good."

CHAPTER SEVENTY-ONE

Armand waved his hands trying to get Cicero's and Jack's attention. Their backs were to him, as they focused on the chants, drums, and the crowd of worshippers. The ceremony continued but without Rat and Trevor. Jack turned and saw Armand flailing his arms, and then shaking his head. Jack nudged Cicero and they returned to the cook shed. Lying flat on it, Armand shimmied to the edge.

"I don't see Rat and his friend! They're initiating some other prisoners."

"We better go and check the prison."

"We've only got forty-five minutes left and it's ten minutes over there." Armand began to think the mission would fail. He turned on his stomach to let himself down and drop into the hands of his two partners. He took one last glance at the Voodou ceremony. The two prisoners were gone. There was a commotion in the crowd, which began to part. Led by a menacing Tonton, Rat, and Trevor were led into the peristil, tied to each other. The bokor smiled, took a drink of rum, and spit in their faces.

Armand turned around to the front edge of the roof. He gave Cicero and Jack a thumbs up, mouthing "They're here."

The houngan joined the sorcerer and held out the palm frond. The bokor emptied the rest of the bottle of brown powder onto it.

"Now!" Armand yelled, not caring if he was heard. The flash bombs would divert any attention.

Cicero and Jack hurled the bombs into the peristil and there were two brilliant flashes and a great bang. The worshippers screamed and ran. Chaos ensued.

The explosion knocked back the houngan and the bokor and the brown powder fell over their faces. Terrified, they tried to wipe it off, but they had already inhaled great amounts of the deadly anesthetic. Their bodies began to twitch, arms akimbo, their eyes dilated, and then they stiffened and fell to the ground.

Cicero and Captain Jack charged into the crowd, pushing terrified people out of the way. A dazed Tonton guard bumped into Cicero, who quickly dispatched him with his knife. Jack faced another, recovering from the blast. His Beretta drawn, a single shot to the groin took care of the man. They reached Rat and Trevor, roused from their heroin-induced state, adrenalin pumping.

"What the fuck?" Rat stared at Trevor. Before they could move, Cicero grabbed Rat, and Jack, Trevor. They pushed them toward the cook shed, holding tightly to their arms.

Armand jumped off the roof with his shotgun and a Smith and Wesson in his hands. He landed on a rock and his ankle twisted over on its side. He let out a moan, and tried to walk, but could only limp. The other four were already at the shed.

"Let's get the hell out of here," Armand cried.

Rat looked at Cicero. "Cicero, what are you doing here?"

"Granting you parole, man. Let's go, there's a boat waiting."

"Go where?"

"Home, man, to Key West."

Trevor turned to Jack and smiled. "Key West sounds great. I'm Trevor by the way, Trevor Rollet."

"A pleasure. I'll buy you a drink on the boat."

Rat looked at Cicero. "But the hotel. I was building it." He began to resist, digging in his boots.

"No more. Come on, don't make me drag you. You're free. Fuck the hotel. Anyway, in a minute it will be history."

"History?"

The pain in Armand's ankle was fierce; he fought through it and walked as quickly as possible using his shotgun as a crutch. The other four followed behind.

Jack yelled. "The cavalry is coming!"

Armand turned. Four Tonton Macoute were running toward them, machetes in the air. He turned, raised the shotgun to his other arm and fired. The blast of the shells quickly dropped two of the pursuers. Cicero pulled out his Beretta and shot another thug at the same time as he wrestled with a reluctant Rat.

Running fast, the last Tonton was on Armand, machete flailing. Armand stopped the attack with his shotgun, but the blow was so strong the gun splintered in two. Jolicoeur fell onto the beach, and the Macoute raised his evil sword for a final blow.

Trevor broke free of Jack's light grasp and dove for the man, pushing him away from Armand just as the machete went down. The soldier fell on top of the blade and screamed. His body went limp.

Rat continued to struggle. "Jack, Cicero? Who else is here?"

"Seadog, Councilman Pat, and your best friend, Connor. He planned this whole rescue mission. So come along like a good boy or I'll have to knock the shit out of you, man."

"I wanna see Connor. I'm not leaving this island until I see Connor."

Armand looked at Cicero and Jack. "It's the heroin, and I think the powder has had a stronger effect than I thought it would. Take him to Connor. He will change his mind."

The group got back to the rendezvous point, Pat waiting anxiously for them.

"Damn, you guys did it! Should I set off the flares?"

"Not yet. Wait until the explosions."

Rat looked at everyone, confused. "Explosions? What explosions? Where's Connor."

Armand looked at Cicero and an unwilling Rat. "Get going; they're up the beach near the construction site. Tell them to do it and get back here without delay. This place will be swarming with Tonton Macoute in minutes."

Cicero and Rat headed toward the construction site with the help of Cicero's flashlight. In the distance from the ounfò they heard shouts and commands, screaming and drums.

❖

"Look, it's Rat and Cicero!" Connor his hand on the detonator, jumped up to greet his best friend. He ran up to Tomlinson and hugged him. "Rat, we did it. We got you."

"Connor, finish this. We need to get to the Zodiac," there was urgency in Seadog's voice.

Rat looked at the detonator. "What are you doing?"

"I'm destroying the hotel, Rat."

"Why? You designed it and I built it."

Connor moved away from his friend and dropped to the ground by the detonator. He lifted the plunger.

"It's unholy, Rat. This whole island is unholy. We're destroying it. The people who live here were fine until Duvalier and his corrupt bunch decided that they needed a resort for rich Americans. They took the local's land and their homes. They're ruining this beautiful, unspoiled place and I helped. They won't have my design, and I'm not giving them their fucking hotel."

"It's my hotel, Connor. I built it. I finally did something worthwhile in my life. And this resort will improve the lives of the people here. They'll have jobs, money, new houses."

"It's a lie, Rat, they'll have nothing. The government doesn't care about them. Look whose building Paradi sou Latè—convicts, slave labor, conscripted townspeople. This building is just Voodou, a Voodou hotel."

"Connor, don't do it. It's a genius design, your design. How can you destroy what you created?'

"Because I created it. It's mine to destroy. It was my gift to Haiti, but Haiti has defiled it. They've tainted it with their corruption, their empty promises and their lies."

"Connor, why did you come to save me? I'm fine. Here, I know what I'm supposed to do. I'm a builder. And I'm going to build Paradi sou Latè."

"You've gone mad, Rat. You're drugged. And if we hadn't come, they would eventually own your mind. You'd become a zombie like most of the prisoners here." Connor looked at the plunger. One movement of his hand and it would be done. He hesitated.

Rat jumped on top of Connor, pulling him away from the detonator. Connor pushed his friend back and scrambled back to the plunger. Rat jumped back on top of Connor. Seadog and Cicero looked at the two combatants, fists now flying.

"Seadog, do it!" Connor screamed as Rat rolled over on top of him.

"It's not mine to destroy, friend."

"Do it! Do it now."

Rat pinned Connor down on the sand, unable to move. "You won't blow up anything today, Connor."

Connor looked at his best friend. The eyes were glassy, disconnected from reality. The face bore a terrible scar and a mottled mess of beard, his body thin, weak from months in a cell. Connor used all his strength, strength imparted to him by Rat at the cold-turkey boot camp on *Daddy's Money*. He lurched up, grabbed Rat's thin arms and threw him off into the sand, and free, clawed his way back to the detonator, reaching the plunger. He looked in the distance at the great round walls, the ocean waves that he had created on the land. His hand trembled.

"Let's get the fuck out of here, Connor. Do it and let's go. The Tonton are coming," Seadog pleaded.

Connor stared at the structure and did nothing.

Rat looked at his friend. "I knew you couldn't do it!" It was a taunt and a challenge.

"Shut up, Rat. I'm gonna blow it to kingdom come!" Connor gripped the handle. He began to push it down. Then he stopped.

The tremor was small, was almost imperceptible. A slight stirring, a deep movement within the ground, deeper than the sand, deeper than the silt below it.

The rumbling in the earth grew. It was a vibration where none should exist. A disorientation of the earth as the waves slapped hard against the shore and the palm trees swayed unnaturally. Connor let go of the plunger and reached for solid ground, but it was not solid. It was moving, shaking, ever more violently.

"What the hell's happening?" Cicero looked at Seadog.

"I think it's an earthquake."

"Holy shit!"

The tremor grew in force and strength. The four dropped to the sand prostrate. The ground moved below, shaking them like rag dolls. They tried to stand up. Connor looked in the distance. The walls were still intact.

There was a great creaking sound, an unworldly groan. Connor looked at the ground; it was sinking under him. A crack appeared, widening under his body. He quickly rolled over, trying to grab a hold of the detonator as the fissure grew larger. He reached for the device, just as it fell into the crevasse. Cicero, up now, stood next to Connor and watched; Seadog and Rat were on the other side of the gaping fissure in the earth, terrified.

The explosion was immense. The great walls lifted from their earthly foundations into the air. Great cracks appeared in the walls, and one began to topple upon the other. Like dominoes, one wall crashed into the next, felling them. The sound was deafening, and the ground continued its violent spasms.

Flares went off in the sky.

"Get to the boat!"

The opening grew wider. Connor and Cicero had to jump across it to get to the other side, the waterside, where Seadog and Rat were ready to grab them.

Connor took a few steps back and ran, even as the earth opened more, wanting to swallow him. He landed on the other side, a foot to spare. Seadog snatched his hand and pulled him to solid ground.

"Come on, Cicero, hurry!"

Cicero looked at the hole in the ground now ten feet wide, fear creasing his face. He took a half-dozen steps back shaking his head. "I can't do it. I can't!"

"You can man, we'll catch you!" Connor shouted above the crashing walls.

Cicero ran. The gap was bigger still. His huge body lunged into the air, and he screamed.

His hands reached out for Connor but missed and hit the sand and slowly slid back across the fine powder, his body's weight pulling him into the void. In a second, Cicero Jackson disappeared into the earth.

CHAPTER SEVENTY-TWO

Connor, Seadog and Rat watched in horror as the crevice increased in size. They heard Cicero's screams, then nothing.

"Run!"

Connor looked one last time at the first two great walls and the floors as the trench in the earth devoured them. He ran back to grab Rat, who was in shock.

"Come on, buddy, let's get to the dingy." He took his arm. There was no resistance.

They reached the water's edge, the surf violent as enormous waves crashed on the beach. In the distance, they saw the running lights of *Joli's Revenge* move up and down. Where was the Zodiac?

"They left without us." Connor looked back toward the pavilion. It had fallen but several Tonton Macoute were gathering.

"Pat will be back. I know it." Seadog looked out to the darkness of the angry sea, as the tremors subsided. He saw a single light move away from the other running lights, and then he heard a faint motor. "He's coming now."

The waves tossed the small rubber boat around like a toy, but Pat navigated the boat well and it caught a wave and came to rest easily on the sand. The three men climbed in, Connor pulling Rat with him. Seadog looked back at the beach.

"The bon voyage party is coming. Get out of here!"

Pat picked up the M249. "Take the helm, Seadog."

Seadog quickly slid to the back of the boat and throttled up the Mercury outboard and headed toward the mothership taking the waves head-on.

Pat started firing his weapon, hitting nothing as the boat lurched up and down. But the Tonton Macoute scattered and dropped to the sand for cover. One fell hard.

"I think I got one of the bastards!" Pat smiled.

Momentarily they were past the rough surf and in the open water, making fast time toward *Joli's Revenge.*

Captain Jack was at the transom as the rubber launch came alongside. He opened the fish hatch and placed the ladder against the stern of the boat. Rat came first, Annie took him into her arms and the young convict dropped onto the deck. Connor followed, a long kiss from Annie his welcome aboard, and then Seadog, who first revved up the engine of the Zodiac, turned it, and let it run out into the ocean.

"Jolicoeur, we're good. Let's go home!" Captain Jack heard the engines come to life and soon they were making fifteen knots.

Connor went over to Rat, got down on the deck, and hugged him. "I bet you could use a drink."

"You destroyed my building, you piece of shit."

"No, the earthquake did. You were right. I couldn't go through with it."

Annie was about to kiss Connor again when Armand yelled from the bridge. "Annie, gunboat dead ahead, and closing in fast. Get to the guns!"

Annie jumped up on the gunwale and quickly made her way to the mounted machine guns. She pulled back the bolt action of the gun and waited as Armand headed right for the enemy vessel. In a second, it was in range, and she began to fire. The enfilade of armor-piercing incendiary bullets did their job. As *Joli's Revenge* swerved to avoid the boat, barely missing it, the gunboat exploded in flames. She thought she heard screams as they sped by.

"Damn, I'm good!" she shouted.

From the rear deck, Connor laughed. "I think I need a drink too. Rat, let's go home."

CHAPTER SEVENTY-THREE

Annie switched on the small overhead spotlight in the main cabin that provided just enough illumination to see Connor's face.

"You sure know how to show a girl a good time."

"You mean this sea cruise?"

"No, silly, just now. You're a very good lover."

"Am I now?"

"Don't let it go to your head."

"The movement of the boat helped."

"I love making love on a boat. It's very romantic."

"You sound like you're pretty experienced."

"No, just you and one other. Back in Lauderdale."

"When you said you knew your way around a boat, I had no idea it meant firing a pair of bad-ass machine guns. You lit up that Haitian gunboat."

"I'm not sure they were coming for us. I think they just wanted to get the hell out of Dodge. They never fired a shot."

"It was a gunboat. I'm happy you didn't blow kisses."

"And I'm glad you didn't blow up the hotel. I've got to hand it to you, you've got some brass ones."

"I was this close. I think if I had, I'd regret it the rest of my life. I might have done it if Rat hadn't protested. I know I was ready. Everything beautiful about Haiti has been desecrated by the Duvalier's. That island doesn't need a resort for wealthy people to play. It needs to remain pure, unspoiled, and pristine."

"Even if Paradi sou Latè would improve the lot of the people on the island?"

"That's a big if. All the able-bodied men were conscripted by St. Jacques to work on the project."

"Well, the earthquake took care of your decision. It certainly won't help the local economy."

The lovers lay in bed, quiet, feeling the movement of the boat through a light chop. Finally, Connor spoke.

"I'm sick about Cicero. He was a good person. He got Rat into trouble but wanted to atone for that mistake. He had a conscience."

"Cowboy, it was a pretty risky operation. And we're not back in Key West yet. Seven hundred nautical miles to go. And we've used over half the fuel."

Captain Jack looked out into the black, moonless night, piloting *Joli's Revenge* toward the USA. Armand slept on the couch in the lounge. Rat and Trevor were asleep in the twin bed cabin and Seadog had taken the bottom bunk; little Pat slept soundly on the top. Everyone was exhausted and slightly drunk from the celebration that followed Annie's demolition of the last hurdle, the gunboat. It included a toast to Cicero Jackson, their lost comrade in arms.

On the radar screen, the modulation line swept round and round, showing nothing. Jack checked his bearings. To use less fuel, he and Armand decided that the best route was the one along the east side of Cuba. They rounded the tip of Haiti as close to Cuba and Guantanamo Bay Naval Base as possible. They were going through the narrow Windward Passage directly south of the American naval base, a thorn in Castro's side. The lease for 45 square miles of land and water had no expiration date.

Shortly, Jack would turn to port and head northwest to home. He looked at the radar again. Nothing. He stared at the screen, the movement of the sweeping line mesmerizing and more interesting than looking out into the blackness. As the top edge as the line swept round, an orange spot appeared. It grew larger as the modulator circled round and round. The orange line was wider now, a full inch across the top of the screen. Jack turned the dial to focus and enlarge the area. Now the orange line was two inches and growing.

"Armand."

No answer.

"Armand, wake up. Get over here!"

Jolicoeur stirred, then sat upright, his mind processing the urgency in the words.

"What is it, Jack?"

"Get over here, look at the radar."

Armand stood up, set his foot down, and pain shot through his leg. He had forgotten about the twisted and swollen ankle. He hobbled over to the bridge and looked down at the screen and the widening band of orange.

"Sweet Jesus, what in God's name? I've never seen anything like that."

"I have when I was in the Far East on a freighter. It's a tsunami."

"Can we turn hard to port and head for Guantanamo?"

"No time. It's moving fast. It's the earthquake! I should have thought of that."

"What do we do?"

"Increase speed. Head right into it. If we turn hard to port or starboard, we'll capsize. Wake everyone and tell them to hold on to their beds. I don't want them up here."

Armand did as ordered, telling everyone rough seas were ahead and to hold on tight. He didn't say the word tsunami. Holding the areaway rails he climbed back up to the bridge and looked at the radar screen.

"It's closing in. What ten minutes?"

"No, five. Get on the floor and hold on to the rail right here. If I lose my balance, be ready to take over."

Jack turned on the overhead searchlights high on the flying bridge. He could make out a white churn in the distance.

"Come on, you son-of-a-bitch, show me what you got!"

"Perhaps a little more humility in the face of Mother Nature would be prudent." Armand realized he was sweating.

Jack pushed the dual throttles to the top. The engines roared and the boat flew across the sea, the glassy calm before the huge wave. He looked out.

"Damn, it's a motherfucking monster! Hold on."

Armand braced his body between the galley woodwork and the control console, crouched at the top of the stairs. He thought he would crush the stainless rail his grip was so tight.

Joli's Revenge began to rise as it hit the outer edge of the great wave.

"Here we go!"

The boat rose to a thirty-degree angle, then forty-five. It kept rising. Jack and Armand heard the yells and screams from the lower deck. He held the wheel tight, pushing the throttles forward to get any more speed possible. He looked out the window. The night sky and a million stars were directly in front of him, the boat now at an ungodly sixty degrees.

From the rear deck, there was a cracking sound, an ominous groan, followed by a loud bang. Armand looked out the rear windows of the lounge. The heavy fuel tank's anchor bolts had ripped off the wood deck. The fuel tank smashed into the transom, demolishing it, and it fell off into the sea.

"Sweet Jesus!"

Jack quickly looked to the rear, the boat's angle easing. "Good thing it was mounted on the back!"

As the boat reached its apex, the top of the wave crashed into the bow, and over it. Another indiscernible, awful noise. Jack saw nothing but water covering the windshield.

The twin 50-caliber machine gun smashed through the windshield like a projectile. It flew above Armand and grazed Jack's head throwing him backward. One hand lost its grip on the wheel, but he managed to right himself and held on with the other. Water surged in through the gaping hole in the windshield as the gun landed hard, coming to rest against the rear door.

The boat leveled, but water still entered the interior of the boat. Suddenly the bow of the boat arched downward, the angle increasing again. Jack cut the engines to cruising speed. Gravity was providing more than enough thrust.

"We're almost through. A couple more seconds."

The boat was angled down at forty-five terrifying degrees. Water continued entering the open wound in the window, and all Jack could see was black water.

Joli's Revenge hit the smooth sea hard, righted itself, and finally leveled off parallel to the ocean, the tsunami behind them.

Armand pulled himself up and smiled at Captain Jack.

"Now what?"

"We just lost 600 gallons of fuel. Ever been to the Bahamas?"

"Not in a while, but I hear it's lovely this time of year."

"We'll go to Matthew Town on Great Inagua Island. It's the closet island. They have an airport. Everyone can fly to Nassau, then home. You and I can stay and supervise repairs. She's a stout boat."

"That she is. I better start the pumps."

Annie, Connor, Rat, Trevor, Seadog, and Pat came up from below bewildered and shaken. Connor looked at Armand.

"Rough seas? What the hell just happened?"

"Nothing much. But the good news is, we're going to the Bahamas for a holiday."

CHAPTER SEVENTY-FOUR

Armand Jolicoeur and Connor West faced each other.

"It's been quite an adventure. I hope you can get the boat fixed here; it's not much of a town." Connor heaved a backpack to his shoulder. The twin engine Bahamas Air revved its engines. "I need to run."

"Captain Jack is at the yard now. He'll have a report when I get back. And yes, that was an adventure. The Pirates of Penzance were a great commando team. But now, I cry for Haiti. So much devastation from the news stories."

"The country can't seem to catch a break."

A ground crew attendant waved to Connor.

"I gotta go, my friend. Annie's waiting too. I'm not letting this one fly by herself." Connor spread his arms and gave Jolicoeur a bear hug. "Thank you for going to Haiti and to help me rescue Rich."

"My pleasure, Connor. Come see me from time to time. I'll be expecting you and Annie."

"Oh, I forgot to tell you. Rat's dad said to send the bills for repairing *Joli's Revenge* to him. Here's his address. I guess he's not such a bad guy, after all. Goodbye, Armand."

Connor shook his hand, turned, and jogged for the waiting plane. He climbed aboard and the attendant lifted the steps and closed the door. The plane turned toward the short airstrip.

❖

"What's the good word, Jack?"

"There isn't one. The damage is beyond this island's ability to repair it. See the windshield."

"Is that Saran Wrap? And duct tape?"

"Duct tape fixes everything, right? And Saran Wrap is transparent. I told them to cover the opening twice."

"I'm not sure it will hold up against the constant winds here."

"The duct tape will hold fast."

"We can't reach Key West like that. And look at the rear transom. Plywood?" Armand frowned.

"Yes, with a wood frame and a lot of caulk."

The two sailors looked at Joli's Revenge and shook their heads.

Captain Jack spoke up. "Here's what I propose. Let's go down to the Cozy Corner and have a few cocktails and a nice, leisurely dinner. In the morning, we'll head for Abraham's Bay, then the next day to Colonel Hill. Work our way up to Nassau, six days tops. Do a little fishing and drinking. And we can bring a few extra rolls of plastic wrap, duct tape and a lot of caulk. In Nassau, I know a yard that will fix this boat up right nice."

"I guess we don't have a choice. Connor told me that Mr. Tomlinson will pay for the repairs. I hope that means the fuel too."

"You know, I've been thinking. If we hadn't had that spare fuel tank and the guns on the bow giving us added ballast, plus everyone below decks, the boat might have flipped backward and we'd be dead. So, maybe this is a blessin' in disguise."

"And I've been thinking... how about you and I go into partnership for charters in Key West? *Joli's Revenge* is a great pleasure cruiser, and your boat's meant for serious deep-sea fishing. What do you say?"

"The Cozy Corner awaits us for further discussion, Mr. Jolicoeur."

The two captains ambled down the white stone lane, the sun setting behind them.

CHAPTER SEVENTY-FIVE

Nassau, Bahamas

Charles Tomlinson stepped out of the cab and paid the driver, leaving a good tip. The facility in front of him was impressive, everything his friend in New York, the head of internal medicine at Sloane Kettering Hospital, said it was. The pale-yellow building with generous bay windows, surrounded by lush landscaping, looked more like a five-star resort than a rehabilitation clinic. It should be. Who would think a tropical island would have such a first-rate drug detoxification facility?

Tomlinson walked up to the doors of the Avante Ibogaine Center. He walked into the generous lobby, painted a stronger yellow with turquoise accent walls, comfortable rattan furniture, and potted Arica palms. Yes, it looked every bit the $500-a-day facility it was touted to be.

It didn't matter. His only son was alive. Addicted to heroin, but alive.

"Good morning, where can I find Richard Tomlinson's room?"

"Good morning, sir. He will be in Suite 1016. Down the hall, left, then down to 1016. It will be on the right."

"Thank you."

The senior Tomlinson knocked gently on the door, opened it, and saw a lovely view of the outdoor pool and the ocean beyond. Then he noticed the hospital bed. His son slept, a tube in one arm, a thin cable monitoring his heartbeat, and vitals. He walked up to the bed, noticed the ugly three-inch scar on his forehead. He winced, then leaned over and kissed his son on the scar. Rat stirred, opening his eyes.

"Father, what are you doing here?"

"I'm paying for this vacation. I want to make sure I get my money's worth."

"I wondered how I got here."

"Your friend Connor called me from Mathew's Town. He said you needed help. Thank God, you're safe. How did you get the gash?"

"Long story. I'll tell you later."

"I imagine you have a lot of interesting stories. Why don't you come to the house in the Hamptons when you're better and tell me all of them? I think we have a lot of catching up to do."

"Is this a ploy to get me to come back to New York?"

"Only if you want to. I want you to be happy."

"I'm broke."

"I heard. Heroin isn't your only addiction."

"I wasn't responsible for becoming an addict. The Duvalier's..."

"I know. I'm not blaming you. But the gambling, you own that."

"I do. I got caught up."

"I have a proposition for you. I'll restore your trust fund, if you promise to get help for the gambling. It almost cost you your life."

"I know. If it weren't for Connor and the Pirates, I'd be a zombie."

"He's a good friend. A very good friend."

There was another tap on the door. A tall Black man entered, black as night, with a short-cropped Afro.

"Trevor, get in here."

Charles Tomlinson stared, and then smiled. "Ah, the other guest I'm paying for."

"Dad, meet my other true friend, Trevor Rollet. If it hadn't been for him, I'd have gone mad in Fort Dimanche."

"Then I'm happy to pay for his vacation as well." The two shook hands and the older man liked Rollet's strong grip.

"How's the detox?

"They said another week and we'll be discharged. Too bad, I kind of like this place."

"I imagine."

"Father, Trevor and I want to start a construction company in Key West. There's going to be a lot of development there. Care to be a money partner?"

"We'll discuss it over dinner tonight. Rest for now." Charles Tomlinson put out his arms, and he and Rich hugged, neither wanting to let go. Finally, Charles pulled away.

"See you two later, around six." He kissed the scar again. "War wound," he said and smiled.

CHAPTER SEVENTY-SIX

"Read the fine print, St. Jacques. It says I'm not responsible for acts of God so I'm not returning any money. You paid for services already rendered." Manny Lazarus puffed on his Cuban and smiled. He knew that was a lie. He had been paid seven million dollars for work that cost him four after he had paid Danny Nolan plus his staff. Three million dollars profit, all his.

"Do you not have a conscience Mr. Lazarus? Our country is devastated, people are without homes, the utilities are in shambles, and the Presidential Palace has been destroyed."

"What about the project, Paradi sou Latè?"

"I'm afraid it will have to wait. The president has put it on indefinite hold. There are other priorities. The earthquake destroyed the hotel construction. Completely. You didn't design it to be resistant to earthquakes."

"Yes, we did, but it was not finished. The walls were not all properly braced. Again, it was an Act of God. Look, if it helps, I'll send back a hundred grand for earthquake relief. Don't spend it on a yacht, Mister St. Somewhere."

"Goodbye, Mr. Lazarus. Remember we know where you live."

No, you don't. I've moved into a nice high-rise condo in Fort Lauderdale and in a year my mansion in Boca will be finished.

❖

St. Jacques put down the phone and looked up at his rotund boss, complete with pork-chop sideburns and a too-shiny leisure suit.

"Excellency, he won't return any of the money. Says it was an Act of God."

"Yes, or an act of Baron Samedi. No matter. The United States, the U.N., and countries all over the world have pledged almost a hundred million dollars to our relief and re-construction. In just four days. I want you to go over to the State Bank and talk to Marius."

"Talk to him about what?"

"Tell him that when the funds come in, to place twenty million of it into my Swiss Bank account."

"But excellency... the people."

"What about them?

"Sir..."

"Very well. Tell Marius to put five million into your account."

❖

Manny looked over to Connor's work area. "Connor, got a minute?"

Connor looked up as he finished packing. He didn't know how Manny would take it, his leaving for Chicago. He was done with the Haitian resort project.

"What's up, Manny?"

"Connor, I got bad news. President Duvalier has stopped work on Paradi sou Latè. Indefinitely."

Connor tried not to smile. "Can't say I'm surprised. The earthquake was a 7.0 on the Richter scale. The center was only twenty miles from Port-au-Prince. Even with Île-à-Vache a hundred miles away, it had to have done a lot of damage."

"Kid, I'm sorry to tell you this but the earthquake destroyed the resort hotel. It's a ruin."

"Oh shit, that's too bad. So, I guess its time to head back to Chicago. I do miss it, and now its summer, the best time to live along the lake."

"Connor, I like you. And Caudy. You're a breath of fresh air in this old firm. Sid's no architect. He writes specs and he's ready to retire. Lenny, well, he's a good draftsman, that's all. And after the Duvalier's, I'm ready to retire. Truth is, I can hardly see anymore, and I got arthritis in my hands. So I got a proposition for you."

Connor's interest piqued. "Oh, what's that?"

"I know Caudy's going back to Chicago, he's got family there. But you're single and have Annie in Key West. I got enough money to retire, so how about you take over the firm. We'll rename it Lazarus and West."

"But you're retiring."

"I gotta have top billing, you know that. Anyway, I got a name, a reputation. I want you to cash in on that. Even if the big shots in the profession think I'm nothing but glitz and outrageous architecture."

"Somehow, I think that's going to change eventually. What are you proposing?"

"A fifty-fifty partnership."

"Seventy, thirty."

"Damn, are you Jewish?"

"No, Irish Catholic."

"Okay, sixty-five, thirty-five."

Connor pondered. "Manny, I appreciate the offer. I really do. It's impressive. But I told Bob Marlow six months ago, that I'd come back as head of design at Nolan & Marlow. I made a commitment."

"I understand, kid. Thought I'd try."

"Manny, I also know nothing about running a firm. I'm a designer. And I'm only twenty-six."

"So I noticed. Well then, let's go have a drink over at the Versailles."

"But it's only eleven o'clock."

"So what?"

"Well, mazal tov." Connor smiled at his friend, Manny Lazarus, and they shook hands.

THE END

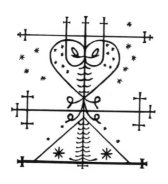

EPILOGUE
AUGUST 5, 1976

St. Paul, Minnesota

Hand in hand, Annie and Connor walked up to the house at 271 Elm Street, colorful balloons attached to the mailbox.

"Nervous?"

"A little. Thanks for coming along." Connor kissed Annie on the cheek.

"I wouldn't miss it. I want to see what kind of children you create."

"Why?"

"You never can tell, Cowboy." Annie kissed Connor back, this time on the lips.

The house was a long ranch painted white with black shutters. The front yard was deep green fescue grass, and neatly trimmed hedges surrounded the house. The front door was painted a dark blue. Connor rang the bell, hearing voices inside.

James Patterson opened the door, looked at Connor and Annie, and smiled.

"You must be Connor?"

"Yes, sir. This is Annie."

"Come in, come in. I'll introduce you. Norah, Connor West is here."

They entered a handsome foyer. To the left, in the living room, a few well-wishers had gathered, sipping on punch. To the right, the dining room table was a smorgasbord of lunch meats, bread, potato salad, tomato salad, other delights, and a crystal punchbowl filled with a red liquid. At the end of the table, a highchair was in front of a layer cake with a big number one on top of it.

"Welcome! I'm Norah Patterson. I'm glad you could come. And you must be Annie Gallagher. So good to meet you."

"Thank you for inviting us, given the situation." Connor felt slightly embarrassed.

"What situation? You're Kevin's birth father. Nothing could be more natural. Everyone's in the family room, including the guest of honor. Some punch?"

"Thank you, that would be very nice."

Connor and Annie made their way into a wood-paneled room with comfortable leather furniture and color television in one corner. Guests were standing and talking, and in front of the fireplace, several toddlers were playing. A brown-haired boy sat in the center, dressed in a navy blue jumper, and played with blocks. The blocks were stacked four high and the little boy was ready to position the fifth one on top.

"He's quite the builder. He loves those blocks. He takes after you; he'll be a great architect someday."

Annie looked down at the small boy, who stood up and placed the last block on the tower, all of it falling in a pile. He started to cry. She reached down and picked Kevin up.

"There, there, fella, it's okay." He stopped crying and reached out for her face, a smile developing. "He's a beautiful boy, Connor, just beautiful."

'You mean handsome. He's handsome," Connor said, rebutting the feminine adjective.

"Here, take him." Before Connor could protest, Kevin Robert Patterson was in his arms. He looked at the toddler.

"Well, hello there, young man. You look just like your mother." Tears welled in his eyes.

"Everyone, meet Connor Jones West and his friend Annie Gallagher. They're from Chicago and Connor is a distant relation to, ah, to Jim."

❖

"That was nice. He is cute, isn't he?" Connor was happy. Things had gone better than planned. And he had met his son.

"Good gene pool, Connor."

"We better head for the airport. You don't want to miss the flight to Miami. Coast Guard basic training starts early at zero six hundred hours tomorrow."

"Right. I think I've finally found my passion."

"Yeah, Gunners Mate First Class Gallagher." Connor laughed.

"After I graduate, it'll be Ensign Gallagher."

"I'm missing you already. Me in Chicago, you in Miami."

"They promised me I'd be assigned to the Great Lakes sector. Pretty boring."

"You prefer drug runners, don't you?"

No, I prefer living with you in your swanky apartment."

"Before I know it, I'll be married to an admiral."

"Your words, not mine."

"I mean it. Marry me."

Annie ignored the remark. "Tell your friend Marlow I said 'Hi'. I feel like I know him already."

"I will. And next weekend, I'm going to bring you back a souvenir."

"What?"

"How would you like a Voodou doll and a silver pin? It's almost better than a pair of 50-caliber machine guns."

"You spoil me."

I am an architect.
I know what is to come by the principle on which it is built.
...I designed Cortlandt. I gave it to you.
I destroyed it.
I destroyed it because I did not choose to let it exist.
It was a double monster.
In form and implication.
I had to blast both.

Howard Roark
The Fountainhead
Ayn Rand

FOOTNOTES

❖ The word "Voodou" in the title is a compromise between "Voodoo" referring to the New Orleans term for the religion, and "Vodou" the Haitian Creole spelling of the word. I did not feel that using the spelling "Voodoo" was appropriate, as the book takes place in Haiti. Additionally, I felt readers would be confused with the unfamiliar spelling "Vodou." Hence: Voodou Hotel.

❖ Francois Duvalier (Papa Doc) was the 32nd President of Haiti, in office from October 22, 1957, until his death on April 21, 1971. Prior to his rule, Duvalier was a physician by profession. During his 14-year rule, he became the most repressive dictator in the Western Hemisphere. It is estimated that he was responsible for the deaths of as many as 60,000 Haitians, most at the hands of the notorious Tonton Macoute, who struck fear into the populace with their methods, dress, and weapons, principally, the machete. Duvalier's regime and tactics were also responsible for the flight of the upper, educated classes (the brain drain) to foreign countries.

❖ Jean-Claude Duvalier (Baby Doc) ascended to the presidency of Haiti on the death of his father. He ruled the country from April 22, 1971, until his ouster on February 7, 1986, spurred on by pressure from the U.S. He returned to the country in 2011 and was arrested by Haitian police. He pleaded not guilty to corruption charges brought against him and died at the age of 63 in 2013.

While Baby Doc brought about cosmetic changes in the country and tried to rein in the Tonton Macoute, thousands still were arrested and put to death. It is also estimated that he stole millions from the treasury (estimates are as high as $800 million).

His wedding to Michèle Bennett in 1980 cost over two million dollars, while Haiti remained the poorest nation in the Western Hemisphere.

❖ Luckner Cambronne was born the son of a poor preacher. He started as a messenger for Francois Duvalier and rose to become the second most powerful man in the government as Interior Minister and head of the Tonton Macoute. In this role he led a campaign of state terrorism, murdering from 30,000 to 60,000 Haitians. He was half-owner of the Hemo-Caribbean. In 1972, the New York Times reported that the company exported 1,600 gallons of plasma to the United States per month, and hundreds of medical cadavers, earning him the nickname "Vampire of the Caribbean." Luckner was not executed by Jean-Claude Duvalier but was exiled by Simone Duvalier in 1971. He moved to Florida where he lived until his death in 2006. He received a Catholic funeral and burial.

❖ General Claude Raymond oversaw the installation of the befuddled 19-year-old Jean-Claude Duvalier as president of Haiti. He was a distant relative and godson of Francois Duvalier. After the fall of the Duvalier's, he did his best to snuff out attempts to establish democracy. In 1973, he was exiled to Spain as ambassador. In 1979, he was summoned back to serve only five months as interior and defense minister. In 1986, after the Duvalier's fled to France he attempted to rally the regime's thugs and enforcers, again without success. He was known as the "Dinosaur." He died in 2000.

❖ Simone Duvalier: During the nearly 30 years that her husband, Papa Doc Duvalier, and son, Jean-Claude Duvalier, dominated the poorest nation in the Western Hemisphere, Simone Duvalier was often regarded as the power behind the throne. Because of her acquired status, her reputation for vanity, and her imperious bearing, ordinary Haitians often referred to her sarcastically as "Mama Doc." Mrs. Duvalier's influence probably reached its peak after the death of her husband in 1971, when her son, still a teenager, succeeded his father as Haiti's "President for Life." She relished the title of First Lady and the power it conferred and was said by associates to deeply resent having to relinquish that role after Jean-Claude Duvalier married Michele Bennett in a lavish wedding ceremony in 1981.

She also cultivated the image of a benefactor, dispensing charity to inhabitants of "Cite Simone," a "planned settlement" named for her that is known today as "Cite Soleil" and is perhaps the most miserable slum in Central America. She died in exile in France, in relative poverty in 1997.

❖ Île-à-Vache (Cow Island) is a small island off the southwestern coast of Haiti. The island is approximately 8 miles long and 2 miles wide. Currently, there are about 15,000 inhabitants on the island. Its history is as described in the novel. In 2013, the government announced plans to make the island an international tourist destination by building 1,000 hotel rooms, an archaeology museum, nightclubs, and retail. This was done by claiming the entire 17.3 square miles of the island as a public utility, stripping the island's residents of their land. The islanders only learned of the plan when it appeared on the website for the Department of Tourism. The resort project was to be complete by 2015. Today, the development remains in limbo given the country's financial and political problems.

❖ The Black Tuna Gang was the name given to the Miami-based organization led by Robert Platshorn (actual spelling) and Robert Meinster that imported over 500 tons of marijuana into the United States in the course of just 16 months. The gang, its name adopted by the Drug Enforcement Administration from the medallion members wore around their neck, was alleged by the DEA to be one of the most sophisticated drug smuggling operations ever encountered. The gang was eventually brought down by a joint FBI-DEA operation. At the trial, the leaders were accused of attempting to murder the presiding judge and bribe jurors. Its headquarters was, for a time, the Fontainebleau Hotel (the inspiration for the Versailles-sur-Mer) in Miami.

❖ Earthquake. On January 12, 2010, at approximately 9:00 P.M. a 7.0 magnitude quake struck Haiti. The epicenter was about 16 miles west of the capital, Port-au-Prince. The earthquake caused extensive damage, including the destruction of the presidential palace, which has never been re-built. Countries throughout the world responded to appeals for humanitarian aid, pledging funds and dispatching rescue and medical teams, engineers, and support personnel. The most-watched telethon in history aired on January 22, called "Hope for Haiti Now," raised $58 US million in one day. Communication systems, air, land, and sea transport facilities, hospitals, and electrical networks had been damaged by the earthquake, which hampered rescue and aid efforts; confusion over who was in charge, air traffic congestion, and problems with prioritizing flights further complicated early relief work. Port-au-Prince's morgues were overwhelmed with tens of thousands of bodies, which were buried in mass graves. As rescues tailed off, supplies, medical care, and sanitation became priorities. Delays in aid distribution led to angry appeals from aid workers and survivors, and looting and sporadic violence was commonplace. On January 22, the United Nations noted that the emergency phase of the relief operation was drawing to a close, and on the following day, the Haitian government officially called off the search for survivors.

❖ Manny: The character of Menachem Lazarus is drawn from New York architect Morris Lapidus (November 25, 1902 – January 18, 2001). Lapidus was known for a unique style of design that came to be called "Miami Modern," after the many hotels he designed in that city during the 1950s and 1960s. This included the Fontainebleau Miami Beach, the inspiration for the Versailles-sur-Mer in the novel.

During a career spanning 50 years, Lapidus designed over 1,000 buildings. Much of his career was spent as an outsider to the American architectural establishment, who dismissed his work as gaudy and tasteless. In addition to the Fontainebleau, he designed the Eden Roc, the Americana, and the Shelburne Hotel. He also designed condominiums, houses of worship including Temple Menorah in Miami Beach, and the Ponce de Leon Shopping Center in St. Augustine, Florida.

In 2007, the Fontainebleau Hotel was ranked ninety-third in the American Institute of Architects list of "America's Favorite Architecture," and in 2012 was ranked Number One on the AIA's Florida Chapter list of "100 Years, 100 Places." In 2008, the hotel was listed on the National Register of Historic Places.

United States – Department of State

Travel Advisory: June 16, 2021

Haiti - Level 4: Do Not Travel

Country Summary: Kidnapping is widespread and victims regularly include U.S. citizens. Kidnappers may use sophisticated planning or take advantage of unplanned opportunities, and even convoys have been attacked. Kidnapping cases often involve ransom negotiations and U.S. citizen victims have been physically harmed during kidnappings. Victim's families have paid thousands of dollars to rescue their family members.

Violent crime, such as armed robbery and carjacking, is common. Travelers are sometimes followed and violently attacked and robbed shortly after leaving the Port-au-Prince International Airport. Robbers and carjackers also attack private vehicles stuck in heavy traffic congestion and often target lone drivers, particularly women. As a result, the U.S. Embassy requires its personnel to use official transportation to and from the airport.

Protests, demonstrations, tire burning, and roadblocks are frequent, unpredictable, and can turn violent. The U.S. government is extremely limited in its ability to provide emergency services to U.S. citizens in Haiti – assistance on site is available only from local authorities (Haitian National Police and ambulance services). Local police generally lack the resources to respond effectively to serious criminal incidents.

The World at a Glance...

Port-au-Prince Haiti

Gang violence racks city: A weeks' long wave of gang violence in the Haitian capital has forced more than 14,000 people from poor neighborhoods to flee their homes and shelter in churches and sports stadiums. The mayhem began in mid-June, when Jimmy "Barbecue" Chérizier—an ex-cop who now heads the heavily armed G9 gang federation—said he was launching a revolution to free Haiti from all elites: the government, the opposition, and the wealthy. Armed gangs looted major food warehouses and set up blockades, making access to parts of the city impossible, and they attacked a Doctors Without Borders clinic, the only source of free medical care in the area. Meanwhile, the corona virus is spreading rapidly, and hospitals are reporting oxygen shortages.

The Week Magazine. July 9 / July 16, 2021

Haitian President Jovenel Moïse was Assassinated at Home, According to the Acting PM

Joe Hernandez, NPR News
July 7, 2021

Haiti's embattled president, Jovenel Moïse, was assassinated overnight at his private residence, according to the country's acting prime minister. Prime Minister Claude Joseph said a group of people attacked the president's private residence and killed him, calling it an "odious, barbaric" act. Joseph said without explanation that some of the unknown attackers were speaking Spanish.

The first lady was wounded by a bullet and is receiving care, he added." Every measure is being taken to guarantee the continuity of the state to protect the nation," Joseph said in the statement.

The streets of the capital Port-au-Prince were largely empty early Wednesday morning, though some people ransacked businesses in one area, The Associated Press reported.

Moïse, a wealthy businessman who made his fortune exporting fruit, became president in 2017 after a lengthy election process. He had never held political office before. He had been batting away calls for him to resign in February of this year at what opponents considered the end of his five-year term. Moïse had insisted he still had another year as president because he took office late. He has been ruling by decree for more than a year because the country has not held legislative elections. The political turmoil in the poorest country in the Western Hemisphere has sparked political protests and an uncontrolled crime wave fueled by gangs.

ACKNOWLEDGEMENTS

Thanks to my fellow Inklings,
Brian Kagan, Ann Roecker, and Kay Olsen
for their wonderful input and support.

A big thank you to Delta Airlines
Captain Jeff Jaeger for assistance with
aeronautical terms and giving veracity
to Chapter 12.

Thanks to Taylor Freeman, who continues
to be my biggest fan.

This novel could not have been as detailed
without the thorough and comprehensive
articles from Wikipedia. Their article
on Haitian Vodou, as an example, is 34 pages in length.

I also would like to thank my wife, Sharon,
for her continued support of my writing.

Finally, to all my readers who have responded with
compliments, support and encouragement—
because of you, I keep writing.

REFERENCE MATERIAL

Adams, David. *Neglected islanders resist plan for Haiti tourism revival.* Reuters International, April 6, 2014.

Belleau, Jean-Philippe. *Massacres Perpetrated In the 20th Century in Haiti.* Sciences Po, April 2, 2008.

Brackman, Henrietta. *Haiti's Hospitality.* New York Times, November 4, 1956.

Camilen, Patricia. *The Law of My Mouth*, BLOG. Various Articles on Haiti and the Duvalier's.

Chamberlain, Greg. *Claude Raymond.* The Guardian, March 7, 2000.

Delices, Patrick. *When Baron Samedi Comes: The Death of Jean-Claude Duvalier.* The New York Amsterdam News, October 9, 2014.

Gold, Herbert. *Best Nightmare on Earth: A Life in Haiti.* Prentiss Hall Press. Copyright 1991, first edition.

Greene, Graham. *The Comedians.* Penquin Books, New Edition, 2005. Copyright by Graham Greene, 1965, 1966.

Kujawinski, Peter. *In Haiti, Tracing a Paradise Lost.* Photos by Christopher Miller, New York Times. December 4, 2017.

Magness, Phillip W. *The Île-à-Vache: From Hope to Disaster.* New York Times. April 12, 2013.

National Geographic Magazine, Special Edition. *Pirates: Shipwrecks, Conquests and Their Lasting Legacy.* June 2021.

Learn Religions.com. *Are Voodoo Dolls Real?*

Rand, Ayn. *The Fountainhead*. Plume Books, Centennial Edition, 2005. Copyright Ayn Rand, 1971.

Rother, Larry. *Simone Duvalier, the 'Mama Doc' of Haiti.* New York Times. December 31, 1997.

Republic of Haiti Submission to the United Nations Universal Periodic Review 12th Session of the Working Group on the UPR Human Rights Council [October 3 - 14, 2011] Criminal Justice. Submitted By: Alternative Chance Center for Constitutional Rights.

Sutton, Horace. *The Pleasures of Haiti.* New York Times, June 8, 1947.

Wall, Kim, Clerici, Caterina. *Vodou is elusive and endangered but it remains the soul of the Haitian people.* The Guardian, November 7, 2015.

Eastern Steamship Caribbean Cruise Brochure, 1954, sailing from Miami. Also, Cunard and French Line Caribbean brochures.

Films:

The Bridge on The River Kwai, Directed by David Lean, 1957.

The Comedians, Directed by Peter Glenville, 1967

The Serpent and the Rainbow, Directed by Wes Craven, 1988

Voodoo, Lost Worlds, New Atlantis Documentaries, 2000.

Wikipedia Articles:

Baron Samedi
Beaches of Haiti
Black Tuna Gang
Luckner Cambronne
Deep Sea Fishing Boats
Dominican Republic
Drug Running in Haiti
Dolphins
François Duvalier
Jean-Claude Duvalier
Marie Denise Duvalier
Simone Duvalier
Fontainebleau Miami Beach Hotel
Fort Dimanche
Guantanamo Bay Naval Base
Inagua Islands, Bahamas
Haiti
Haitian Islands
Île-à-Vache
Haitian Vodou (06-2021)
Hotel Oloffson
Morris Lapidus
Louisiana Voodoo
Presidential Palace of Haiti
Claude Raymond
Santo Domingo, DR
Tonton Macoute
Voodoo Dolls
Vodou Iwa Symbols
Zombies

R. J. Linteau is the author of two previous novels, *The Architect* and *The Black Orchestra*, as well as two screenplays. *Voodou Hotel* is the much- anticipated sequel to his successful inaugural novel, *The Architect*. He is currently writing his fourth novel, *Motor City*, about the auto industry and Detroit.

Originally from New York, he lives in Marietta, Georgia and enjoys Key West, Florida with his wife of 38 years.

Please send your comments to:

RJLinteau.author@gmail.com

THANK YOU!